shadow hand

Tales of Goldstone Wood

Heartless

Veiled Rose

Moonblood

Starflower

Dragonwitch

Shadow Hand

shadow hand

TALES OF GOLDSTONE WOOD

ANNE ELISABETH STENGL

BETHANYHOUSEPUBLISHERS

a division of Baker Publishing Group
Minneapolis, Minnesota

© 2014 by Anne Elisabeth Stengl

Published by Bethany House Publishers
11400 Hampshire Avenue South
Bloomington, Minnesota 55438
www.bethanyhouse.com

Bethany House Publishers is a division of
Baker Publishing Group, Grand Rapids, Michigan

Printed in the United States of America

Library of Congress Cataloging-in-Publication Data
Stengl, Anne Elisabeth.
    Shadow hand / Anne Elisabeth Stengl.
        pages cm. — (Tales of Goldstone Wood)
    ISBN 978-0-7642-1028-0 (pbk.)
    1. Magic—Fiction. I. Title.
PS3619.T47647675S53   2014
813'.6—dc23   2013034266

Book design by Paul Higdon
Cover illustration by William Graf

Author is represented by Books & Such Literary Agency

14   15   16   17   18   19   7   6   5   4   3   2   1

This one is for Tom, Jimmy, and Peter.

PROLOGUE

THEY SAY ALL THE OLD STORIES—all the *true* stories—are about blood. This simply is not so.

All the true stories are about love. And blood. The two so often go hand in hand, they're difficult to separate, but it is important not to divide the one from the other, or the story becomes unbalanced and is no longer true. That is why this is a story about blood and love, and the many things that lie between.

For Foxbrush, this story began on the worst day of his life to date.

Foxbrush's father had insisted that his mother allow their son to travel with him to the court of Foxbrush's uncle, the king, to be properly presented. Foxbrush, a shy, unprepossessing child, considered this visit (and the coinciding obligation to Talk to People) a terror of nightmarish proportions and trembled in the seat of his father's carriage all the way to the Eldest's House.

Upon arrival, he was separated from his father and shuffled into step behind an elegant footman, who led him down strange halls and passages.

His young mind, bewildered by the grandeur around him that far out-matched anything he'd known in his mother's remote mountain home, retreated further into itself. Many of the halls they passed through were not closed in by walls but open to the elements, tall pillars supporting the roof overhead after the fashion of Southlander architecture. The sounds and smells of the Eldest's House assailed Foxbrush from every side. Rather than see too much, he watched the footman's feet treading across the white marble floor.

Those feet stopped. Foxbrush stopped.

"Here you are, young sir," said the footman, opening a door.

A blast of children's laughter assaulted Foxbrush's ears. His eyes grew owlishly large. "Please," he said, "I'd rather not."

But the footman placed a hand on Foxbrush's shoulder and pushed him inside. The door shut. Foxbrush was trapped.

The room was spacious, with a great many tall, open windows all around through which breezes blew, wafting colorful curtains like circus flags. And wafting more colorfully still was an army of children, all in gorgeous clothes, laughing so that their teeth flashed.

Foxbrush, who had little experience with anyone his own age, backed up against the door and held on to his hat as a final defense against the oncoming hordes.

No one paid him any heed; they were busy about their games. After several minutes of terrified observation, Foxbrush thought he began to discern some sort of pattern in the antics before him. One boy stood in the center of the room with, of all things, a curtain pulled down from one of the windows wrapped around his shoulders. Through his terror, Foxbrush recognized his cousin Leo, whom he had known since infancy. Leo held the fallen curtain rod in both hands and shouted:

"Warriors, to me! To me! Twelve warriors!"

Four children, boys and girls, separated from the group and flocked around him, a number that seemed to satisfy the curtain wearer. They were all younger than Leo. *Little ones,* Foxbrush thought from the superior vantage of eight years. They looked up to their leader with awe-filled eyes, ready to do his bidding.

"Shadow Hand!" Leo called across the room. "Are you ready to fight?"

On the other side of the room, another cluster of children crouched in noisy council. One of them stood, and she was the most unusual person Foxbrush could ever remember seeing. Her hair was bright red. And curly! She might as well have been some otherworldly being here among the dark-skinned Southlanders.

She was armed with an unclothed rag doll, which she brandished menacingly. "I am King Shadow Hand of Here and There! And I will slay you, fiend of darkness! Slay you and save my fickle fleeting Fair from your evil mound!"

The curtain-clad Leo frowned. "Hold on," he said, and all his miniature warriors caught their breath. "What's a fickle fleeting Fair?"

"You know," said the red-haired girl. "The maiden King Shadow Hand saves. The one he holds on to."

"I don't remember that," said her foe.

"It's true," the girl-king replied.

"I remember him losing his hands. I remember him bargaining with the Faerie queen. I remember him fighting the twelve warriors. I don't remember a maiden."

The red-haired girl dropped her rag doll weapon and crossed the room to a pile of books left strewn and open upon the ground. It was enough to make Foxbrush recoil in horror: The spines would be all bent and broken, the pages torn by these uncivilized ruffians! But the girl shoved several aside with her foot until she pulled from the wreckage a once fine illustrated copy of *Eanrin's Rhymes for Children* and opened it to a dog-eared page.

"See?" she said, turning to Leo and pointing to a certain woodcut, which may or may not have been intended for young eyes. It depicted a king with a fierce black beard and a noble face clinging to a rather buxom young woman who was—as far as Foxbrush could discern—melting.

Foxbrush shuddered, but the girl strode across the room to her opponent.

"See? There's the fickle fleeting Fiery Fair that Shadow Hand is trying to rescue."

"I don't remember that bit," Leo said, frowning with the determination of one who never could remember anything he did not wish to.

The girl, undaunted, read for all the listeners in the room.

> *"Oh, Shadow Hand of Here and There*
> *The stone of ancients kills*
> *To free his fiery, fickle Fair*
> *From death beneath the hills!"*

She finished and shut the book with a bang that made Foxbrush startle. "We need a fickle Fair for me to rescue from you."

Leo rolled his eyes, then turned to those gathered round. "So who wants to be the damsel in distress?" he asked.

The children exchanged glances. A demotion from warrior to damsel was none too keenly desired. Even the little girls, their braided hair coming all undone, shook their heads.

"There you have it," said Leo, smugly lifting his curtain rod. "No one wants to be her, so we'll play without her."

"No we won't," said the girl-king, her voice so final that even the intrepid Leo blinked and lost some of his smug. She turned and surveyed the room like a hawk selecting which hopping young rabbit she might wish to snatch. Her gaze fell at last upon Foxbrush by the door.

"Who are you?" she said.

"Um," said Foxbrush. That strange stare of hers pinned him to the wall. He'd never seen blue eyes before. He was not naturally a superstitious child. Nevertheless, as the girl-king descended upon him, her eyes full of ruling intensity . . . well, even Foxbrush wondered if, in that moment, he had fallen under a bewitchment.

"Do you want to be the fickle Fair?" she said, drawing near to him.

Foxbrush shook his head. "I . . . I'd rather not," he said.

She looked him up and down, appraising his worth. "Why not?" she demanded. "You'd be good at it."

Foxbrush couldn't break her fearful gaze. Shrinking into himself, he said, "I might tear my shirt."

The flame-headed girl narrowed her eyes. Then she reached out, grabbed hold of the button at his collar, and yanked. It took a couple of hard pulls, but it came away in her hand at last with a satisfying rip.

Foxbrush gasped.

"There," said the girl-king. "It's torn already. Come play with us."

In that moment, realization washed over young Foxbrush; realization that this girl could make him do whatever she wanted him to. And, more horribly still, he wouldn't entirely mind doing it.

He loved her at once for reasons he could not then understand.

So you see? Blood and love—the ingredients of every true story.

"All right," you say, "I see the love. But where's the blood? Give us blood!"

Don't worry, dear reader. We'll come to the blood soon enough.

PART ONE

HERE AND THERE

1

Once more, failure.

Once more, new life did not spring from blood, no matter how much blood flowed. New growth did not flourish from desolation, new breath did not stir the still air. When the dying stopped dying, there was an end of it. No more dying. No new living.

Once more, rootless, drifting, searching.

But it could not make mistakes. How could it? It did not think; it merely acted, instinct driving every deed. Therefore, it could not learn. Therefore, it would try again. And again. And again.

Once more, searching, searching, searching . . .

. . . for one as lost as itself.

The Eldest's groundskeepers were not folks to judge. The rest of the kingdom could turn up its collective nose or raise condemnatory eyebrows as it willed. As far as the groundskeepers were concerned, a week of relaxed duties and a full day off with free cake and mango cider sent from the Big House itself was reason to celebrate.

Let princes marry whom they will. Let councils depose whom they will. Let the worlds gossip and the courtiers go about their intrigues; only let there be cider, and the sun may still shine!

So the groundskeepers gathered, on the day of the crown prince's wedding, beneath the shade of a mango grove. It wasn't much shade, for these were young mangoes, newly planted the year before. The old, stately grove that had once stood on this site had been destroyed during the Occupation. . . .

But there. They would not think of that. Not on such a fine, lazy morning. The new trees cast shade enough, the cider slid nice and cool down the throat, and the crown prince would wed his lady in the Great Hall of the Eldest.

"Lord Lumé, I hope he'll pull it off this year!" said Graybeak, Stoneblossom's husband, around a mouthful of crumb cake.

"Pull what off?" asked Tippertail, who was Graybeak's best mate in the fields.

"This marriage, of course," Graybeak replied. "I hope the crown prince manages to get it done. The last one didn't, did he, now? And they made as much fuss or more over his wedding week."

"Only we didn't get crumb cake," said Flitmouse solemnly. And this was acknowledged with grave nods. No crumb cake; how could that marriage possibly have gone over well?

"Good thing, if you ask me," said Stoneblossom, who never needed to be asked before stating an opinion, "that they went and got rid o' that one, that Prince Lionheart. And lucky for Lady Daylily that she didn't marry him first!"

"Hear, hear!" the groundskeepers agreed, clunking their mugs together as a toast.

"But surely Prince Lionheart couldn't have been *all* bad."

This was spoken by a newcomer, another groundskeeper from a different quarter of the Eldest's estate, judging by the color of his hood. What he was doing here in South Stretch was something of a conundrum to the gathered crew, and they glanced at him sideways, not exactly unfriendly, nor exactly welcoming. Stoneblossom had given him a smaller slice of crumb cake than the rest.

When he spoke up now—fulfilling the role of uninitiated newcomers everywhere by putting his foot in his mouth—the others fixed him with stares of contempt.

"Not *all* bad?" said Graybeak. "Where were you those five years when he left us, run away to safety while we remained imprisoned? And where were you when, on the very week of his nuptials, he brought a dragon into the Eldest's City—"

"Don't be speaking of that!" said Stoneblossom with sudden severity. For when Graybeak spoke, all eyes had filled with haunted memories: memories of a cold winter's day. Of smoke. And fire.

"Don't be speaking of that," Stoneblossom repeated. "Don't go calling bad luck down upon this day by mentioning such things. The devil-girl was banished, the prince sent packing without his crown. It's a new day for Southlands."

"Aye," said her husband, taking a deep draught of his cider. "Aye, a new day, a new crown prince, and very soon a new princess."

"Here's to the princess!" cried Tippertail with determined jollity, and the others took up his cry and clashed their mugs with such enthusiasm that hands and faces were soon sticky with cider. "Here's to the princess!"

They raised their mugs again. But one little boy, a second cousin of Stoneblossom's recently come to South Stretch, missed connecting his mug to Tippertail's when something else attracted his eye, nearly causing Tippertail to lose the whole foamy contents of his mug down the front of the boy's shirt. But the boy scarcely noticed, for he was busy pointing and saying, "Ain't *that* the princess?"

Stoneblossom turned a stern eye upon the lad, prepared to scold him for a fool. But she took a moment to glance the way he pointed. "Iubdan's beard!" she gasped and nearly dropped the plate of crumb cake she'd been passing round. "Look you over there!"

The groundskeepers turned to look beyond their little world of celebration out to the broader grounds in which they earned their bread each day. The Eldest's parklands were not what they'd been before the Occupation. Elegant hedgerows and shaded avenues, long rolling swards of green—all now had given way to scorched craters and ruin. Trees stood like great, burnt matches, and the ground reeked of poison.

Dragon poison.

Once a dragon set upon a kingdom, its poisons remained in the soil for generations to come. It mattered not if the dragon flew away again, never more to be seen.

There was only so much the groundskeepers could do to restore order, much less splendor. But they were true if unsung heroes, doing battle every day to reclaim their king's domain, far out of sight of the lords and ladies they served, lords and ladies they never saw.

So it was that, one by one, the groundskeepers muttered and swore as they watched none other than the prince's bride, running alone down a broken path not far from their grove.

"It cain't be her," said Graybeak with dubious authority. "She's gettin' married."

"Who else is it, then?" his wife demanded, and he had no answer. For who else could it be? Who else in the Eldest's court boasted such a crown of curly ginger hair piled and pinned with fantastic elegance atop her head? Who else could wear a silken gown of silver and white, with billowing skirts and billowing sleeves; indeed, with so much billowing one half expected her to take flight? Who else could wear a coronet set with pearls and opals, a coronet that she even now—as the groundskeepers watched aghast—tore from her head and cast aside?

It was she, the prince's bride-to-be. It was the Lady Daylily.

And she was running, skirts gathered, as though for her life.

"Should we go after her?" whispered Tippertail.

"And what?" Stoneblossom replied. "Drag her back, kicking and screaming? She's a lady, she is, far beyond the likes of us. Let her run where she wills."

No one spoke the thought that nevertheless flitted within their staring eyes: There would be no wedding today.

"More crumb cake?" Stoneblossom suggested.

There are few things more useless than a bridegroom on his wedding day. He goes where he is told, wears what he is told, sits where he is told, stands where he is told; and between these events he waits in stasis, praying to anyone who might be listening that he won't faint or stutter or otherwise make a clown of himself on this Day of Days. However necessary he is to the due process of things, at least temporarily, he is otherwise merely another warm body to be hustled around.

But he might at least look smashing while he is about it.

Prince Foxbrush, his mouth compressed into a tight knot, straightened the already straight fibula on his shoulder and admired himself. He was not a man to make the ladies sigh, certainly not by classical princely standards, being of rather narrow frame with a tendency both to squint and to stoop. He flattered himself, however, on having a decent turnout in red velvet and blue silk, the official colors of the crown prince, everything cut to the latest trends in Continental fashion, complete with a bejeweled collar and a crisp white cravat.

His man stood behind him at the mirror, brushing invisible nothings from his shoulders. "What do you think, Tortoiseshell?" the prince asked, turning his head to inspect his reflection from a new angle.

"A dashing figure, Your Highness," said Tortoiseshell, who knew how his bread was buttered. "Quite striking. And may I congratulate Your Highness on the bold choice of wearing the princely colors rather than the traditional ceremonial white?"

"You may, Tortoiseshell," the prince conceded. "I felt it best to reaffirm in the eyes of all the barons my new role as their future sovereign." Neither he nor his man bothered to comment on the fact that the barons, who had so recently deposed Foxbrush's cousin and set Foxbrush in his place, could just as easily depose Foxbrush should they feel the need, princely colors notwithstanding. Best not to entertain such gloomy thoughts on a wedding day.

Besides, in just a few short hours, Prince Foxbrush was to ally himself via marriage to Middlecrescent, the most powerful barony in the kingdom. So long as Baron Middlecrescent was on his side, the new prince had nothing to fear. Nothing besides Middlecrescent himself anyway.

If he could only get through the ceremony today without mishap . . .

"Something troubling Your Highness?" asked Tortoiseshell, pausing in his work and studying his master's face in the glass.

"Oh no, certainly not." Foxbrush's complexion, which was always rather sallow for lack of sun or exercise, had gone a pasty gray since the Occupation. He, being one of the few trapped inside the Eldest's House for the entire ordeal, had breathed rather more poison than most. It still festered in his lungs.

Now, to make matters worse, at the very thought of his upcoming nuptials and the subsequent marriage and his soon-to-be bride, his skin broke out in a sweaty sheen. Dark patches appeared under his sleeves.

Fumbling to undo the fibula, Foxbrush slid out of his fine jacket, putting up a hand to ward off Tortoiseshell's protests. "No, no! It's hours yet till the ceremony, and I should hate to, uh, to rumple your hard work. Do lay it aside, my good man, and we'll array me once more closer to. In the meanwhile, I'll . . . I'll . . ."

Foxbrush had not had sufficient time in the months since his elevation to adjust to his new role as prince and supportive figurehead of a nation. Having grown up the only child of a reclusive mother, far off in the mountains, away from courtly life, he found the ways of the Eldest's House a trifle unsettling. Much safer was the world of books and ledgers. A man always knew where he stood with those.

"I'll just be in my study," he said and, quick to avoid Tortoiseshell's disapproval, stepped from his dressing room into said study. He drew a great breath.

His work lay on his desk by the window; work to which he had devoted himself since the Council's decision; work that he would have to let lie for some weeks now due to the wedding trip. *A pity.*

No, not a pity! He was marrying of his own volition, and marrying very well at that. Lady Daylily was rich, well connected, and beautiful too, which didn't hurt anything, though he wouldn't have minded much if she were a little less beautiful, all things considered. But still, who was he to complain? How many men in the Eldest's court had desired Daylily as their bride? Lionheart, for one; dozens more besides. Any one of them would give his right hand to marry Middlecrescent's daughter.

"Well, I would give *both* my hands," Foxbrush growled, though there was no one in the room to be impressed by such avowals. He sat at the desk (he scarcely thought of it as *his* desk; it had been Lionheart's for so long) and surveyed his work. Stacks of agricultural reports from every barony and many of the most respected merchants, each more doom-filled than the last. Another orchard failed, another plantation fallen to ruin; export prices rising, reliable sales falling through, competitors out-pricing even the once rich tea trade . . .

Dragons eat those Aja merchants and their insipid green teas! How *could* they compete with the dark and hearty Southlander brews?

For the right price they could.

No matter which way he looked at it, Prince Foxbrush saw only ruin, ruin, and more ruin. Southlands was approaching collapse. That collapse might yet be a few years away, a decade even. But from where he sat with these reports swimming before his eyes, the final crash even now swept toward them.

"Dragons blast that . . ." Foxbrush stopped. There was no curse quite appropriate to curse the Dragon himself.

This marriage was the last-ditch effort to perform the miracles expected of a prince. With Daylily's fortune safely sequestered away in the royal treasury, he would have funding enough for his Great Experiment. Foxbrush's severe mouth softened at one corner with what might have been a smile. His gaze traveled from the reports to a large basket of figs sitting to one side of his desk. The Great Experiment, with which he would prove to the world the rightness of his rule, the justice of his reign, the majesty of his—

"Great hopping Lights Above!"

Foxbrush leapt to his feet, knocking his chair over backward with a thunk. He scrabbled through the papers, his hands shaking with sudden terror. Where was it? Hadn't he tucked it under the fig basket, out of sight? He couldn't have left it in the open! Could he? Oh, cruel, cruel fate! Oh, agony! Oh—

"Tortoiseshell!"

His man appeared at the study door. "Your Highness?"

"Did you see a letter among my things when you tidied up this morning?"

"The one addressed to Lady Daylily, Your Highness?"

Foxbrush's stomach landed somewhere near his ankles. "Yes. Yes, that's the one." His gaze as desperate as a condemned man's, he whimpered, "Where is it?"

"I thought it best to deliver it with all due haste, Your Highness."

"You thought . . ."

"Yes, Your Highness. This being your wedding day, I wished no delay in any correspondence between you and the lady in question."

Foxbrush tried to speak. "Uuuah . . ."

"Did I do right, Your Highness?"

With gargantuan effort, Foxbrush swallowed. A continental shift could not have been more agonized. "When did you deliver it, Tortoiseshell?"

"I put it in the lady's hand not a quarter of an hour ago. I happened upon it while— Pray, Your Highness, where are you going?"

Good Tortoiseshell's words, spoken with such concern, fell upon deaf ears. Prince Foxbrush, mumbling inarticulate curses or prayers (it would be difficult to say which), was already out of the study and into the hall, where he realized he was in his shirt-sleeves, a state of undress not to be borne even under direst circumstances. So he dashed back into his dressing room, crying, "No time! No time!" to a baffled Tortoiseshell, whom he pushed from his way as he snatched the nearest available jacket. This turned out to be Tortoiseshell's. As the household livery was not intended to go over a blousy affair such as Prince Foxbrush's shirt, it was a mercy to everyone concerned that Tortoiseshell was twice Foxbrush's size. The jacket bagged across the prince's thin shoulders and flapped out from his sides like wings as he, thus attired, flew through the corridors of the Eldest's House.

An army of invading guests from across the nation, from as far as Beauclair and the northern kingdoms of the Continent, had fallen upon the House in the last few days. Few recognized the prince, new as he was to the title and half clothed as a valet. Those who did spot him each had some congratulation to make, some remark upon the occasion, the newly rebuilt Great Hall . . . something to stop Foxbrush in his tracks. He, squirming with embarrassment (for he had been brought up to be polite), squeezed and sidled and dodged like a mosquito skimming the surface of a pond.

At last he came to Middlecrescent's series of apartments. And here he faced another, more dreadful obstacle.

"Great Iubdan's beard and mustache!" Foxbrush gasped.

The hall was flooded with women.

Although a bridegroom is a useless enough specimen on his wedding day, the women jointly make up for his lack. Every one, be she friend, relative, nodding acquaintance, or total stranger, seems to have some vital role, which she pursues with as much chatter and flutter and perfume and feminine grace as possible. And each and every one is on the lookout for one particular person.

Foxbrush's jaw sagged in dismay. Ducking his head and muttering "Pardon" as he went, he took the plunge, scraping along the wall, hoping against all reasonable hope.

"Just *what* do you think you are doing?"

It was all over now.

Upon that signal, every woman, matron or maid, turned her predatory gaze upon him and pounced.

"It's bad luck for the groom to see the bride on their wedding day!"

"Trying to sneak a peek before your time, you naughty boy!"

Foxbrush, pinned to the wall, put up his hands, hidden beneath Tortoiseshell's too-long sleeves, to ward off the hosts of femininity attacking from all fronts. "Please," he protested, his voice hoarse in his thickened throat. "Please, I need to talk to her, just one moment, I beg you!"

"That's what they *all* say." A severe personage, possibly a maiden aunt, with stubble on her chin, made gorgeous in silks and embroidered veils after the old Southlander style, stepped forward from the throng. Someone had gilded her fingernails so that they looked like the talons of some otherworldly eagle as she jabbed a finger into Foxbrush's breastbone. "Nefarious!" she declared, and the surrounding women either laughed or growled their agreement.

Foxbrush was on the brink of muttering whatever feeble excuse sprang first to his lips and making good his escape when mercy fell in the form of a most unexpected angel.

"Lumé's light, if it isn't you, dear boy!"

At the voice of the mother of the bride, even the most avenging aunt must give way.

The crowd parted with a rustle of petticoats and creak of supportive wires to admit the passage of Baroness Middlecrescent. She was a creature made impressive by connection and influence rather than by any personal attribute, but this was hardly her fault. Her once renowned beauty long since turned to plumpness and good humor, she wielded the power of her husband's title with all the cunning of a monkey playing the organ grinder's instrument. Which is to say, none at all.

"What a delight!" cried the baroness, for it was her way to see joy and sunshine even where storm clouds gathered. She reached out and took Foxbrush's hands in her bejeweled fingers, pressing them as though he were a long-lost son she had not seen in years rather than the scarcely known, soon-to-be son-in-law with whom she'd dined the night before.

"Have you come to see my dear ducky?" she asked, and it took the following statement before Foxbrush realized she meant Daylily. "Ducky" was not a diminutive one would naturally apply to the Baron of Middlecrescent's daughter. "She looks glorious, simply *glorious* in her gown. You won't even believe it! But then, you'll see her in another few hours, so you'll have to believe it then."

The other women drew back, casting Foxbrush dire looks but not daring to interject as the baroness prattled on. "We had it made for her for the last wedding, you know, to your dear cousin. It was such a shame when they called that wedding off, but then, you're probably not so disappointed, are you, lucky boy that you are! And now she gets to wear her beautiful gown all over again, and could the day *be* happier?"

Any moment could be the crucial one. Any moment could be too late.

"Please, baroness," Foxbrush gasped, scarcely able to speak under the heavy scrutiny surrounding him. "Please, I've got to see Daylily, just for a moment."

"Certainly not, young man!" the maiden aunt interrupted sternly. But the baroness silenced her with a wave. Then, turning another smile upon Foxbrush, she said, "I do hope you'll call me 'Mum.'"

"Please . . . Mum?" Foxbrush whispered, and his ears burned.

"Why, of course you may!" the baroness said with the most brilliant of smiles. She took Foxbrush by the elbow and led him through the protesting gathering.

"Niece of mine, you cannot!" cried the maiden aunt, appalled.

"I don't see why not," the baroness replied, reveling in her power. "It's their wedding after all. I don't see why they shouldn't see one another."

"Think of tradition!" someone pleaded. But the baroness said only, "Bother tradition!" and flung open the door to Daylily's dressing room.

It was as empty as an unused tomb, and equally as quiet, save for the gentle breeze murmuring in the curtains.

"That's odd," said the baroness, tapping her chin with a fingertip. "I could have sworn she was just here with her goodwoman, getting fastened up . . ."

"If you please, my lady."

Foxbrush and the baroness turned to the bobbing women in white servants' linen who appeared at the baroness's elbow. "Lady Daylily sent me and all her waiting women from the room when the letter arrived for her. Told us not to come back till she called, if it please you."

"Well, it doesn't please me," said the baroness with a sniff. "What letter? When did it arrive?"

"Nearly half an hour ago, my lady. I thought you knew. I couldn't say whom 'twas from."

Foxbrush, who had gone a deathly shade of gray, moved as one dream-wandering into the room and across to the window. The open window lead onto a veranda supported by tall pillars hung with stout starflower vines.

A girl would need a great deal of strength to climb down one of those pillars into the garden below. A great deal of strength or motivation.

"Flown the coop," said the maiden aunt, *tsk*-ing like a cicada in summer. "And small wonder. That's what comes of breaking tradition. A groom should *never* try to see his bride before the ceremony!"

2

If it could know sorrow, it would weep.

If it could know frustration, it would gnash its teeth. Had it possessed teeth, that is.

If it could know anger, it would tear apart the trembling Wood through which it rushed, uprooting trees, laying waste to all that was green and growing.

But it was a being of instinct, not thought, not emotion. And its instinct said only:

Try again. Try again.

So Daylily ran away from her wedding.

This was her second attempt at a wedding, but her first wedding gown, for though she was the only daughter of the most powerful baron in all the land, not even he had the finances to waste on a second round of matrimonial finery. Not since the Dragon's coming.

She had never liked the gown to begin with. It was her mother's taste. Regarding weddings, it was usually best to let mothers have their way, and Daylily had made no protest when her ladies had piled on the silver (she'd have preferred gold) and trimmed her out in pearls (she'd have preferred topaz), and pinched her cheeks to make them glow (she was always too pale these days). The result was gaudy enough to impress even the most critical dignitary from the farthest nation of the Continent.

She didn't mind in the least when she heard the hem rip, leaving pearls and lace trimming in the clutching arms of an old, thorn-rich rosebush as she passed.

The world existed in a state of balance, or so the wise said. Up, by necessity, needed down. Hot, without question, required cold. Spring thaw reached out to winter frost; midnight darkness longed for noonday sun. And, if one wanted to get a bit *spiritual* about it, the melodies of the sun must be countered by the harmonies of the moon.

Many would think the balance between Lady Daylily—beautiful, strong, fiery Lady Daylily—and the rather less impressive young man who was contracted to become her husband sometime within the next three hours should please even the wisest theorists. But tip the balance too far in any one direction, and all chaos ensues. Lady Daylily's equilibrium had reached its tipping point. In fact, she was pretty certain it had flipped right on its head.

The elegant lawns of the Eldest's grounds, a once fine setting for the gem that was the Eldest's House, had given way to spurs and thistles, which tore at the bride's feet as she made her escape. At any moment, she would hear hoofbeats behind. At any moment, she would hear the shouts of her father's men.

She tore delicate white gloves from her hands and sent them flying like freed doves fluttering to the ground behind her. Still running, she put her hands to her throat and, unwilling to work the clasp, ripped away the necklace of silver filigree set with enough pearls to fill an oyster bed. It shattered, and pearls fell like rain in her wake. Let the ants gather them and take them to their queen. May she have much pleasure from them!

And still, no pursuit. Such luck was too good to hold. Daylily pulled at the laces of an outer corset, leaving it in a heap behind her, and suddenly she could breathe and run with redoubled speed. For the first time since her flight began, she believed she might reach her goal in time.

The Eldest's grounds ended abruptly at a cavernous gorge. Far below, the Wilderlands' thick treetops veiled what else might lurk down there. Once, it was said, great rivers had flowed through the land, carving these myriad gorges. But the rivers were long gone, the Wilderlands had spread to fill their dry beds, and no one ever ventured down the ancient paths into the shadow of those trees.

Indeed, Southlands would not be the united kingdom it was today were it not for the mighty bridges—unparalleled architectural marvels—that spanned the gorges, arching above the treetops and linking barony to barony.

Daylily drew near to Swan Bridge. Evenwell Barony lay beyond; she could see the bridge keeper's house on the far side, small as a doll's from this distance. The bridge keeper would hail her if he saw her crossing. He would not let her pass into Evenwell but would hold her until her father's men came. And then they would drag her back.

She stopped at the stump of a once mighty fig tree. Like most of the patriarchal trees of the Eldest's grounds, it had been torn apart by the Dragon, its ragged stump now the only remaining testament to its existence. Here, the lady fumbled with the clasps of her shimmery overskirt embroidered in silver leaves, edged in still more pearls. With a certain amount of ripping, she freed herself at last and stepped from the collapsed billow of silk and wire structuring, wearing only her underdress . . . which was still far too sumptuous and heavy for what she had in mind. For now, however, it would have to do.

She reached into her bodice and pulled out the prince's fool letter.

There, on the edge of the gorge, feeling the wild exhilaration of dangerous heights, she drew a long breath and read the scrawled lines again. Not a man alive could have deciphered the expression on her stone-quiet face. But when she came to the end, she crumpled the letter with both hands and tossed it over her shoulder.

When she spoke, it was without malice but with a deep resignation. "That's what I give for your fine sentiments, Prince Foxbrush."

A spasm shot through her body. Hands clasped to her temples, she doubled over. Then, neck craning, she turned her head as though trying to catch a glimpse of something that stood upon her back.

The moment passed.

The lady straightened, her shoulders squared. "It'll drive me mad if I stay," she whispered.

Perhaps it had driven her mad already. Why else would she, on her wedding day, stripped of her glory down to her underdress, her dainty shoes worn to shreds, hike up her skirts and, taking a narrow dirt path that was all but invisible, ancient and worn as it was, descend to the waiting darkness of the Wilderlands below?

She only knew she had no choice.

"I'll disappear," she told herself. "I'll disappear even as Rose Red did. And like her, I'll never come back."

In the quiet by the old fig tree stump, a bird with a speckled breast alighted on the ground and pecked gently at the discarded letter lying there. *Tut, tut, tut. O-lay, o-leeeeee!* he sang.

But Daylily was too far away to hear.

There was no wedding.

Yet there was still a wedding feast. Far too much of Baron Middlecrescent's coin had been spent on fine foreign and expensive delicacies meant to impress dignitaries from far and wide. And the baron declared he would be dragon-blasted before he let any of those sniveling foreigners trundle back to their colder climes without at least one fabulous Southlander meal with which to season their recounting of the day's extraordinary events.

The Eldest was not consulted on proceedings. He, dribbling slightly at the mouth, was hastily bundled off to his royal chambers and tucked away out of sight, the crown removed from his head, the silken cloak removed from his shoulders. Stripped of this finery, he looked little better than the drooling beggar at the city gates. He smiled wanly at his servants and asked after his wife, who had died long ago.

The prince was not consulted either, nor was he offered any of the wedding feast, however hungry he might be. His pride shredded to utter rags, he still managed to clothe himself in just enough dignity *not* to beg, "Might I have a bite of the, you know, the fish, maybe?"

No, he sat quietly, if hungrily, in a corner of the baron's study, doing everything in his power not to let his stomach growl and draw the furious eye of his prospective father-in-law.

The baron was not a man to storm or rage. That reaction might have been more bearable. Good shouting never hurt anyone, and often the shouter vented all that pent-up emotion in the shouting itself, leaving little energy for any real action. But the baron did not shout.

From the moment Foxbrush, flanked by the baroness and the maiden aunt, found the baron and informed him of his daughter's disappearance, Middlecrescent went . . . quiet. His eyes, rather too large for his face to be handsome, may have narrowed a little; his nostrils may have flared; his mouth compressed. But when he spoke, it was in a voice of such calm that his wife went into hysterics on the spot.

"I see," he said. Then after another long breath, in an equally mild tone, he said, "Summon my guard."

When the baron spoke in that way, no one hesitated to obey. He went on to give a series of commands, including an order for the baroness to shut herself up in the North Tower so as not to make a scene. He also sent for barons Blackrock and Idlewild, both trusted men in his entourage, though officially his peers.

To Foxbrush he said only, "Stay by me and, for Lumé's sake, don't speak. I can't stand the sound of your voice just now."

Foxbrush hadn't made a peep since.

Now he sat in that same corner of the baron's study, still clad in Tortoiseshell's jacket, and the light outside was waning so that maids were summoned to light the lamps and, alas, the fire, though it was far too hot and Foxbrush's chair far too near the blaze. He contemplated the merits of either removing the jacket or relocating his seat. Both ran the risk of calling attention to his corner, however, so he remained where he was, sweating, his hands pressed over his rumbling stomach.

A series of people, both common and courtly, progressed under the baron's scrutiny. First Daylily's goodwoman, who could only repeat what she had told the baroness already: A certain letter had arrived for her lady and, upon receiving it, her lady had sent everyone from the room.

"And you did not find this strange?" the baron asked.

"Oh no, your grace," the goodwoman replied. "My lady has often done as much. She likes her privacy."

The baron chewed on that information, asked a few more curt questions, and dismissed the goodwoman. Foxbrush heard him muttering to himself, "Who could have sent the letter? What might it have contained?"

Foxbrush, no matter how deeply he searched, could not find the courage to provide that information. He sat and sweltered and starved, wishing with a general sort of vagueness that he had never been born.

Late in the day, the baron's captain of the guard entered, ushering a group of ragged characters, both men and women, before him. Who could they be? Rebels? Outlaws? Brigands? And what could they possibly add to the sorry story unfolding?

"Groundskeepers, my lord," the captain said, which was a bit of a letdown. Like captives, the six or seven individuals arranged themselves before the baron, heads down, hands clasped. They were of all ages, from just past childhood to quite elderly, but each shared a certain rough-cut freshness indicative of those who work soil and tend green growth for a living. They also looked surprisingly guilty.

"Why have you brought these to my attention?" the baron asked in the same tone a schoolmarm might ask a student about a wormy apple.

"These people, my lord, are the last to have seen your daughter today. At least, so they claim."

"Groundskeepers?" The baron raised his eyebrows, which made his eyes look bigger still. Then, as though performing a task distastefully beneath his dignity, he addressed those gathered. "All right, speak up. Where did you see the Lady Daylily?"

A woman who appeared to be the leader of the group stepped forward, touching her forehead and scraping respectfully. "My lord," she said, "we're keepers of the South Stretch grounds down near Swan Bridge, and we were taking our ease on this day of happiness—"

"Get to the point."

Stoneblossom, for it was she, cleared her throat and spoke as clearly as she could through her nerves. "We saw her ladyship, dressed in her wedding clothes, making her way rather quick-like on the path to Swan Bridge."

"Alone?"

"As far as we could see, my lord. Which was pretty far, I might add."

"And how did you know it was the Lady Daylily?"

"Oh, it's hard to mistake her ladyship! There's not another maid in Southlands boasts a head of ginger hair like hers! Not as would be dressed in pearls and silks."

There was no denying this. Among the dark and dusky Southlander complexions, Daylily's pale skin and fiery hair stood out like a lighthouse beacon.

"And you did not see where she went?" the baron asked.

"I did, sir!" a boy of thirteen or so spoke. "I followed her!"

"Cheek," said Stoneblossom and would have cuffed him had not the baron interceded.

"Let him speak."

"I followed her, and I saw her leave the path to Swan Bridge and cut across a field to the old Grandfather Fig what used to stand on the gorge edge, but which is now a stump, your grace-ship," said the boy.

"Your *lord*, you dolt," Stoneblossom growled, but again the baron ordered peace. "Go on, boy," he said.

"Well, she stood there a moment; then she started to take off her skirt."

If someone had breathed in the silence that followed, the room might have exploded. Foxbrush did not even move to wipe away the sweat that dripped into his eyes.

The baron at last said, "And what did you do?"

"Oh, I turned me back, your grace-lord," said the boy. "Me mum may be a washer, but she brought me up right. And when I did look again, the lady was gone. Leaving her skirts behind her."

"Gone, you say?"

"That's right. It's my thinkin' that she went over the edge, down to the Wilderlands."

"You're daft, Tuftwhistle!" Stoneblossom snapped and snatched at his ear, though he eluded her hand. A look from the baron stilled them both. Then he turned to his captain.

"Have you any corroboration?"

"Indeed, my lord, we were able to follow a clear trail left by the lady all the way to the very place the boy indicated." The captain snapped his fingers, and his men entered, each bearing some token: a pair of lace gloves, a coronet, a necklace in pieces, a jeweled belt, an outer corset, and the ruins of a heavy overskirt in shimmery silver and silk. The remains of Daylily's wedding gown. Foxbrush paled at the sight, then blushed at the shocking mental image of Daylily in her underdress, however sumptuous it might be. That would be at least as bad as a gentleman appearing publicly in his shirt-sleeves!

Then a final guard stepped forward, and all other thoughts fell from Foxbrush's head as he gazed upon what this man held.

"We found this by the tree stump."

The baron stepped forward to take it. "Yes. The catalyst of this mystery," he said. With careful fingers, he unfolded the letter, which had been crumpled into a tiny wad.

Foxbrush earnestly hoped to die and be swallowed up by the Realm Unseen.

The baron scanned the letter. "Ah," he said and nothing more for several moments. "Perhaps this explains a little," he said then. "It appears to be a love letter, unsigned, poorly spelled. Perhaps my wayward daughter had a rendezvous in mind when she made her flight." He ground his teeth, the first sign of anger he had displayed since the whole business began. "A rendezvous with whom, though?"

No one spoke. But the same thought passed through almost every head: Lionheart, the disinherited prince who had vanished a year ago, after his deposition. Everyone knew that he had been intended to marry Lady Daylily. Everyone knew how she had loved him.

"It all comes together now," the baron said.

Only it didn't.

"Um," said Foxbrush.

Every gaze, which had mercifully overlooked him for the entirety of the exchange thus far, turned suddenly and fixed upon the prince. His stomach chose that moment to roar its ire, and he leapt to his feet, trying to hide the noise with another. "Um, I, uh. I feel I must . . . well . . ."

"Have you something to contribute, crown prince?" The baron could order executions in that voice.

Foxbrush tried to meet the baron's gaze and, failing that, tried to meet Stoneblossom's. Failing that as well, he fixed his eyes upon a mark in the wall over the head of young Tuftwhistle.

"That's mine," he said.

The baron looked from the prince to the letter and back again. "This? Addressed to my daughter?"

"Um. Yes."

"You misspelled 'devotion.'"

"It was, um, an early draft. I, uh, I didn't mean to send it."

"No," said the baron, and his fist clenched, recrumpling the letter. "No, I'm sure you did not."

With that, he tossed the sorry little ball of paper at Foxbrush's feet.

Every eye in the room fixed upon the crown prince as he bent to retrieve it; everyone in the room knew now why Daylily had fled. Foxbrush sank back into his seat, hanging his head, and felt he would never have the strength to rise again.

The baron, however, chose once more to dismiss the prince's existence, addressing himself instead to his captain. "She cannot, as this boy says, have descended to the Wilderlands—"

"Oi!" Tuftwhistle protested, but Stoneblossom silenced him with a smack and a "Hush up, you!"

"—so it remains that she must have crossed Swan Bridge and is even now making her way across Evenwell. Put together a company and ride out. Take some of Evenwell's men with you; they know those roads."

The captain saluted and, summoning three of his men, marched from the room. The other guards, at the baron's indication, shuffled the grounds-keepers out. Foxbrush watched them depart as a man watches the last of his allies departing from the field of battle, leaving him alone with the enemy.

But one of the groundskeepers, who had stood silently by with the others, a low green hood pulled over his face, paused in the doorway, his brown hand clutching the frame so that even when the guard hustling him out pushed his shoulder he remained in place. He said in a thick voice, "I wouldn't put it past her."

The baron, who had turned to contemplate the fire, looked up. The firelight playing in his eyes gave him the appearance of some devil trying to recall his victim's sin. "What did you say?" he demanded of the lone groundsman.

"I said, I wouldn't put it past her. Climbing down to the Wilderlands, that is." Suddenly the groundskeeper's voice altered and became almost, but not quite, familiar. He said, "I wouldn't put anything past Lady Daylily. Best not to underestimate her."

Before the baron could reply, the hooded man was gone. The baron took two steps in pursuit before halting and deciding against such a chase. He returned to his study of the fire, and Foxbrush, in his hungry, sweating corner, could only hope the baron would not turn those devil eyes upon him.

At length the baron said, very quietly, "Get out."

Foxbrush mustered himself and fled.

The figs in the basket had all turned to putrid mush in the heat of the day. Foxbrush, hungry as he was, was not quite as disappointed as he might have been. There were times when, no matter how urgently a man's body might cry out, a man's spirit cannot comply.

He felt sick to his stomach.

Foxbrush, like most young men of limited experience misled by centuries of poets, had always believed that heartbreak would lodge itself in . . . well, in the heart. Yet his heart beat on at a healthy if rapid rate.

His gut, however, felt as though someone had scooped it out and filled it with gnawing worms.

He sat gingerly at his desk, perched on the edge of his seat. No one had thought to light so much as a candle in his study, and little of the sky's dusky glow found its way through the window into his room. It was very like—and he shuddered at this—the gloom of the Occupation.

He should light a lamp. One sat at the ready by his elbow. But somehow he could not bear the notion of being alone with himself that night, and the dark kept his thoughts momentarily at bay.

He bowed his head and the worms in his belly writhed. "Why in Lumé's name did I write that dragon-eaten letter?"

What was it Daylily had said to him those few short months ago when he, down on one knee, had asked the crucial question?

"I'll marry you, Prince Foxbrush," she'd said, *"but only with the understanding that you will never love me."*

But she knew. Dragons blast it, the whole kingdom knew that he adored her! Had he not made a fool of himself during her previous wedding week last winter, when her then groom, Lionheart, had left her alone in the middle of the dance floor before the eyes of the whole court? And Foxbrush had stepped forward and taken her in his arms. Gallant Foxbrush, ready to save the day! Noble Foxbrush, eager to salvage his fair one's honor!

Clumsy Foxbrush, who danced like a clockwork soldier, and within three turns had trod upon her dress once and her feet twice.

"Let me go, you dolt," Daylily had hissed so that none but he would hear above the music. And she'd wrenched herself from his arms, and it was his turn to be left alone in the middle of the dance floor, while she made her way after Lionheart.

From that day on, he'd heard the young gallants of the court whisper behind his back: "Foxbrush Left Feet!" But really, Hymlumé love him, was it *his* fault that in all his academic pursuits, he'd never encountered a course on courtly dancing?

There was no one to blame but himself, however, for writing those letters.

In the dark, Foxbrush flipped a switch to open a "secret" compartment in his desk—which wasn't so much "secret" anymore as "understood to be private." A stack of letters emerged as the compartment slid open, letters tied up with a limp silk ribbon. Anyone coming upon them could see in a glance that they were love letters. Not everyone, however, would guess they'd all been written by Foxbrush himself. Written and never delivered.

Foxbrush pulled them out, several years' worth of the most tender and romantic feelings he'd ever put to paper. Such as this one: *And a union of our two houses would prove as profitable to the improvement of our estates as would the union of our hearts to the improvement of our lives.*

Or this: *When weighed upon the joint scales of reason and regard, the balance of my affections proves a sound measure upon which to make your judgment.*

The idiotic yearnings of youthful fancy, perhaps, but truly, if rather haltingly, expressed. Only, thank the Lights Above, he'd never let one of these fall into the adored object's hands!

Until today.

With a biting curse, Foxbrush fumbled for his matches, some notion of warming the room with a blaze of burned hopes and dreams brewing in his mind. He struck a light, held it up.

And he screamed, "Iubdan's beard!"

Across his desk stood the hooded groundskeeper.

"Good evening, Foxbrush," said he. "It's been some time." Then he put back his hood.

"Iubdan's *beard*!" Foxbrush cried with redoubled vehemence.

It was Lionheart.

3

THE WOOD WAITED, as it always did.

It had no need to go hunting. In all the long existence of the Between, before and after the advent of Time, it had proven itself the most effective of predators, not by any great cunning or guile but simply by its patience. If it waited long enough, prey inevitably walked into its enfolding arms as into a lover's embrace. And those whom the Wood embraced, it rarely let go.

For the Wood was full of things that kill: some that meant to, some that didn't, though the latter were no less deadly.

Daylily, her underdress torn, her hair in disarray, her eyes wild in an otherwise calm face, slid the last few feet down the gorge trail and stood upon the edge of the Wilderlands. She knew what she did, or believed she knew. After all, had she not shut her mouth when Lionheart asked if anyone would defend Rose Red? Had she not shut her mouth and thereby pronounced the poor girl's sentence as clearly as though she'd spoken it aloud?

And Rose Red had been banished to the Wilderlands. She had disappeared into its shadows even as Daylily, her skirts clutched in both fists, disappeared now, stepping out of the world she knew into a world of half-light remembered from poison-filled dreams.

The ground was soft beneath her feet. Leaves rustled against the hem of her gown. Silence closed in around her, reaching out to touch her face even as the tree limbs stretched down and caught gnarled fingers in her hair. She passed into the Wood Between, ready for any fate to greet her.

Any fate, that is, except the one that did.

Had Crown Prince Foxbrush been asked how his day might conceivably be made worse than it already was, he would not have been able to give an answer. How could it possibly be worse?

But this was only because he wouldn't have considered the possibility of Lionheart returning.

The match he'd struck burned his fingertips, and he dropped it with a cry, plunging the room back into darkness. For the space it took him to light another and apply it to the nearest lamp, he could pretend that it was all an illusion brought on by fatigue, worry, and hunger. Surely, *surely* Lionheart could not—

Oh yes, he could.

Foxbrush, holding up the newly lit lamp, leapt to his feet, jostling his desk with violence enough to knock the basket of figs over the edge. Figs landed with thuds and scattered across the tiles like so many rodents escaping a trap.

"You . . . you're real," Foxbrush gasped.

"Last I checked," Lionheart agreed with a grin that looked more wicked than usual in the lamplight.

Foxbrush felt the blood draining from his face. He kept blinking, then squinting, as though to somehow drive away that image before him. But no, there stood Lionheart, large as life, ragged as a beggar in his groundsman's clothes, his eyebrow raised in just that expression of incredulity Foxbrush had found unbearable from the time they were small boys and forced to "play nicely" together.

But something was different about his face as well. Something . . . Foxbrush couldn't quite put his finger on it. A sense of depth and height struck him as he looked at this man he despised.

He didn't like it at all.

"I thought you ran away for good the moment the barons declared their decision."

"Try to contain your joy at my fortuitous return, cousin of mine," said Lionheart, bending to retrieve a squashy black fig that had made it as far as his boot. "You know," he said, resting the fig in his palm as though gauging its weight, "these really are only good for goat food. Perhaps your tastes have developed since I've been away?"

A thousand and one thoughts crammed into Prince Foxbrush's tired brain at once, none of them charitable; it was enough to make him burst, yet too much to make him articulate. So he watched his cousin pick up two more figs and begin to juggle all three.

"I mean," Lionheart continued, "goats are amazing animals, reputedly able to digest anything. Even black figs, which is pretty impressive when all's said and done. But you're looking a little peaked around the edges tonight. Perhaps an invigorating diet is just what you need? A goat I used to know once said—"

"Lumé, Leo!" Foxbrush set the lamp down with such force that the oil in its base swirled in a miniature maelstrom. He reached across the desk to snatch back the figs as though retrieving rare gems from a thief. Not knowing what to do with them once he'd got them, he squeezed them into pulp and seeds, which stuck to his fingers. This in itself was testimony to Foxbrush's interesting mental state; the prince's hands were typically clean, each nail well filed and buffed to a high polish.

Lionheart always did have a way of bringing out the worst in him.

"Easy now, Foxy," said Lionheart, watching the fate of those three figs. "No need to get violent."

"Violent? I'm not violent. I'm never violent." Pulling a handkerchief from Tortoiseshell's jacket, Foxbrush began to wipe at the fig juice, snarling as he did so, "I'm working on a solution to our agricultural crisis. One without violence. Ideally, without squabbling among the barons."

And there went that wretched eyebrow of Lionheart's, sliding up his forehead again. "With goat food?" he asked. "What have the barons to say to that?"

"The barons offer no ideas, just arguments," Foxbrush said. "And since I'm not Eldest," he continued, "they don't include me in their various plottings. Not yet anyway. Other than bribes, of course."

"Of course." Lionheart nodded. "So, is this something to do with your response to their bribes, then? Inedible, semi-rotten fruit is highly effective when thrown from upper windows."

Foxbrush opened his mouth to growl an answer but paused a moment. He hadn't actually considered that possible use for his samples. It wasn't all that bad an idea, if rather beneath his princely dignity.

He shook his head savagely, however, and rammed the sticky handkerchief back into his pocket. "Always the clown, Lionheart. Always the jester. Meanwhile, Southlands is on the brink of collapse, in case you hadn't noticed."

"I'd picked up a hint or two," Lionheart replied dryly, taking a seat in a well-cushioned rattan chair, far more comfortable in this room that had once been his than Foxbrush was or ever could be. Foxbrush hated him for it. He hated him for many things just then.

Growling, Foxbrush knelt, righted the spilled basket, and hastily began shoveling the scattered fruit back into it. "Our orchards are in trouble," he said. "Reports come in every day from every barony, telling us of crops and harvests failing. The oldest, richest mango groves have all withered from poison or been pulled up by the roots! There's scarcely a healthy plantation left in the entire kingdom. Do you understand how this affects Southlands, from the richest baron down to the poorest tenant? How can we trade with the Continent without our primary exports? There are the tea plantations still, of course, but we'll have to up our prices if we hope to make ends meet, and how can we compete with Aja or Dong Min at increased costs? *They* didn't suffer under a dragon's thumb for five years! *They* can undersell us with every merchant from here to Noorhitam!

We can't depend on our teas, and we can't hope for anything from our mangoes."

"I know." Lionheart's voice was very low when he replied, though his mocking smile remained in place. He put out a foot and nudged one of the figs out of Foxbrush's reach. "Remember, it was my problem before it was yours."

But Foxbrush didn't hear. This was his way when he got caught up in his theories. For the moment, even the horror of his ruined wedding day was forgotten, and his eyes shone as he eagerly clutched the basket of figs, looking down at them as though he gazed upon the jewels of Hymlumé's garden. "There is a solution," he said in a low, almost desperate voice. "Figs!"

He plunked the basket back down on the desk and grabbed *A History of Southlander Agriculture*, fumbling through the pages. "I've read all about it. Back hundreds of years ago, the elder fig was the primary export for Southlands. It was like gold grown on trees, so high was the demand!"

Once more Lionheart replied softly, "I know, Foxbrush."

"Don't you see? We have elder fig trees all over the country, growing like weeds! The tough old things survived the Dragon's poison with scarcely a mark on them. They're thick with fruit, and if we can simply start tending them as we used to and harvest them, we might be able to establish a new trade!" The heat of excitement carried Foxbrush on so that he almost forgot it was his cousin to whom he spoke. "I've written to several of the baronies, and at least eight have responded, telling me that their estates are full of old elder figs. Enough, perhaps, to get a good harvest!"

Lionheart crossed his arms, his face solemn as he regarded his cousin. When Foxbrush at last ran out of steam, he said only, "Too bad, then, that elder fig trees don't produce edible fruit anymore."

And there was the rub.

Foxbrush's cheek twitched. He put the book back on the table and eyed the spoiling fruit in the basket. "They weren't always. Inedible, that is. We used to know how to cultivate them."

"The brown fig and long hall fig are edible," Lionheart said, "but—"

"But not in demand," Foxbrush finished for him. "Not so succulent or sweet."

Their eyes met over the lamplight. A brief exchange of sympathy, of understanding, such as these two had never before known. In that moment, the weight of all Southlands rested on the shoulders of both cousins, all the impossibilities that would crush a king to death with hopelessness.

But Foxbrush could not bear sympathy from Leo, nor pity either. He turned away. "I keep thinking—"

"Lumé spare us."

"Shut up, Leo. I keep thinking I'll find something. If I keep reading, if I keep hunting, I'll discover the secret to renewing the elder figs. Everything I come up with has been tried before. I'm at a loss, and I don't mind admitting it."

"Well, that's the first step, isn't it?" Lionheart said, his voice surprisingly heavy. "Admitting your shortcomings?"

Foxbrush's eyes flashed. "I've not given up. I'm not going to run away. Not like—"

"Not like I did."

"Yes! Exactly!" Foxbrush clenched his fists. "That's always been your nature, hasn't it, Leo? Even when we were children, you slipped out to play in the woods all summer while I labored over whatever task was given me. You shirk. You run. And when you can't do either, you laugh! You were *never* going to be a good Eldest. You never deserved it, despite your birth. You never deserved the throne, you never deserved her, and you won't have either now, and thank the Lights Above for justice yet in this world!"

He stopped for breath, his body tensed, prepared for the verbal abuse bound to fall upon his head. Lionheart was always the lightning tongued, able to rip Foxbrush at the seams until he could scarcely stand.

This time, however, Lionheart said nothing.

He sat quietly in the chair that had once been his, before the desk that had once been his, in the study that had once been his. All smiles had fallen from his face. His eyes were open, but he had flinched now and then during Foxbrush's tirade as though feeling physical blows. When Foxbrush shouted himself into silence, Lionheart remained in this attitude, making no defense, forming no attack. Foxbrush found he could scarcely breathe.

At last Lionheart said, "Well, *that* at least I did deserve."

The world shifted and only Foxbrush's grip on his desk kept him from falling over. "W-what?"

"You're right, Foxbrush," Lionheart said. "I never deserved to be Eldest. It was all a matter of birth, not merit." He raised his gaze to his cousin's face but dropped it again quickly, and Foxbrush could see him battling with himself. Surely the bitter words would fall at any moment.

It was too much for Foxbrush to bear. He sagged where he stood and groaned. "Of all days, Leo. Of all days! What possessed you to return *now?*"

Then a whole host of new, swirling, furious thoughts assaulted his brain. Foxbrush pulled himself upright once more, as masterful as he could be in his man's livery, and pointed a finger at his cousin. "You did this," he said. "You ruined my wedding day. You! You stole Daylily away, and now you think to intimidate me, and—"

"Really, Foxbrush," said Lionheart, his voice once more full of that cheek that always made Foxbrush want to smack him. "For a chap without a fig's worth of imagination, you certainly can spin quite a yarn when motivated. Perhaps if kingdom ruling doesn't suit you, you could take up penning romances for a living?"

The former Prince of Southlands rose, and though he was no taller than Foxbrush, his presence somehow loomed. For the first time, Foxbrush saw the shirt beneath the groundskeeper's hood and jacket. It was not something he should have noticed in that moment of tension and fury, but it caught his eye.

In the place over Lionheart's heart, there was a hole. And around this hole were dried bloodstains.

"I have come," Lionheart said, "to make peace with my father. I returned to Southlands with no other purpose in mind, and I certainly did not intend to arrive on your wedding day. But now that I'm here, you will find I am no longer a running man."

Lionheart leaned across the desk until he was nose to nose with Foxbrush. The intensity of his eyes made Foxbrush stagger. He would have sat down had his chair not been overturned.

"I shall go to my father now, and I shall say to him what I have purposed in my heart. And then, Prince Foxbrush"—he spoke the title with some bitterness—"I myself shall go into the Wilderlands and find your lady Daylily. I shall return her to you, and you will marry her, and you will rule my kingdom, and you will take my place. And then you will never see me again."

Lionheart was at the door before Foxbrush opened his mouth to speak. Even then he could find no words, so he stood there gaping when his cousin paused suddenly and looked back at him. Evening shadows hid Lionheart's face, but his voice was clear enough.

"I almost forgot. I have something for you."

With a faint *whoosh* and *thump,* an article landed by Foxbrush's feet. He looked down and saw a scroll tied with ribbon. A starflower blossom tucked into the ribbon gleamed ghostly white in the gloom.

"That's from Eanrin, Chief Bard of Iubdan Rudiobus," Lionheart said. "The Lady of the Haven bade me give it to you with her compliments."

"Wh-what?" said Foxbrush, his forehead wrinkling with something between ire and confusion. "What are you talking about? What is this, Leo?"

"Read it and find out," his cousin replied. The next moment, he was gone.

4

ONE MIGHT ASSUME, were one to know Lady Daylily personally, that she was a young woman who could handle herself with aplomb in any given situation. She was, after all, a baron's daughter with a strong streak of domineering lineage flowing in her veins. She was one of those people who never turned her hand to anything unless she was certain to excel, the result being nothing short of constant excellence to the public eye. She danced, she sang, she painted landscapes, she rode, she spoke three languages besides her mother tongue, and she was reasonably confident that, were women in these rather restricted modern times permitted to study fencing using real blades rather than the padded wooden poles deemed "appropriate," she could have bruised the hide of any courtly gallant who stopped running from her long enough to take the beating.

Aside from these outward talents, rumor had done a fair job of adding mystery to Middlecrescent's fairest flower. Some said Daylily had journeyed across the country alone with Prince Lionheart's demon servant and yet managed *not* to fall bewitched. Some said that when the Dragon first came to Southlands, Daylily had rescued Lionheart out from under his very nose, dragging him to safety, the prince being poisoned with dragon fumes at the time.

Some even said Daylily had ventured into the very depths of the Dragon's realm, to the seat of his power in the Netherworld, and that it was she who finally, through courage and great cunning, had liberated Southlands from his foul claws, driving him from the kingdom.

A woman like that . . . well! How could she possibly be afraid of anything? Or anyone?

The problem was, even those who knew Lady Daylily personally did not actually *know* her. There wasn't a soul alive who guessed what went on inside her mind.

No one knew about the wolf.

This was probably for the best, Daylily decided as she pushed her way through a thick growth of ferns. What they didn't know couldn't tear their throats out in their sleep, and everyone was better off for that.

So she pressed on into the Wilderlands, surprised (or as surprised as one as self-possessed as Lady Daylily could be) at how cool it was. After her flight across the Eldest's grounds on a hot summer day, coolness ought to have been a relief, of course. But this coolness was beyond mere shade.

It reminded her of one childhood summer when she'd been sent on her own to visit her old maiden aunt. She'd stepped through the front door into the entry hall and had a sudden, overwhelming feeling of . . . frost. The house was empty; the aunt away for the afternoon, the servants had taken the opportunity to slip out on personal errands. Other than her goodwoman waiting outside and the carriage man at the gate, Daylily was quite alone.

Except not *quite* alone. The smell of her aunt lingered everywhere, like a haunting presence of faded lavender perfume and strong drink (faintly disguised by chewed mint leaves) taking on a life of its own, peering around every corner.

Daylily had stepped back outside, slowly so as not to let that smell know how it chilled her. "I'll not be visiting Auntie today after all, my goodwoman," she had said before returning to the carriage without another word.

The Wilderlands was cold like that. Cold and watchful, uninviting and silent.

But Daylily was not inclined to retreat. The more still the air grew, the more frozen the silence, the more determinedly she strode, yanking her skirts with uncaring rips every time they caught on branch or stone. She liked that sound. It was like the sundering from her old life made audible.

And she thought, *I should have done this years ago.*

She didn't expect to survive. No one who entered the Wilderlands ever came back, and it didn't take a great deal of imagination to guess why not. But for the moment, she didn't care. She gloried. Had she been the type to crow in victory, she would have crowed! Instead, she merely smiled grimly and grabbed her skirt in both hands to give a particularly violent tug when it caught in a thornbush. The tear ran almost to her knee that time.

"You ought to let it go."

Daylily had once boasted a rather fixed notion of the world and its workings. Recent history had made fair headway into reorienting those fixed notions; recent history and the all too real Dragon. Indeed, as far as Daylily was concerned, the world could stand on its head and sing love ditties, and she would hardly bat an eye anymore.

Thus, when the songbird fluttered onto a branch near her head and sang a song that became words she understood, she did not startle but merely turned to give him an appraising glance. He turned his head to look at her with one bright eye and chirped innocently. Daylily was not fooled.

"If you are going to give personal recommendations, you need to be rather more specific," she said to that bird. "Otherwise, I shall be obliged to ask obtuse questions. Such as '*What* ought I to let go?' for example."

The bird—which was good-sized for a songbird and sported a speckled breast—ruffled his feathers at her but without malice. Then he sang, "You know of what I speak."

"You assume a great deal for a bird," Daylily replied.

"I never assume. I know."

"Isn't that nice for you, then?"

"More to the point, it is everything for you."

Not a muscle on Daylily's face moved. Her eyes did not narrow; her jaw did not clench. She might have been bored for all her features revealed. When she spoke, her voice was far too calm.

"I remember how this works. It's been some years since I've read *Eanrin's Rhymes for Children*, but I remember well enough. Mortals enter the Faerie Forest, and all sorts of beasts and unsavory characters intercept them along their way, plying them with misguidance, etcetera. And the moral of each story is never to be swayed from your path." She straightened her already perfectly straight shoulders. "I'll not be persuaded; I'll not be turned. I've made my decision, and it's best for everyone involved. And I'll thank you not to pry."

With that, Daylily gathered the remnants of her skirts and continued on her way. There was no path, at least none that she could see, only tall trees and green undergrowth. Something was not quite right about this Wood; something beyond a bird singing to her in a voice she understood. She paused a moment and looked down at her feet.

One can look a long time at a phenomenon without recognizing it for what it is, especially if one is tired after narrowly escaping a wedding. So Daylily stood for some moments, staring at her feet and wondering what it was she saw that struck her odd.

When at last she realized, she gasped.

Though the forest floor was thick with grasses and ferns and low-growing things, nowhere she looked was there any sign of decay. Not a withered leaf, not a dropped pinecone, not a red needle off a pine bough.

"The Wood Between knows little of Time," sang the songbird. He had fluttered from branch to branch and perched on a twig no more than a foot from her face. "There are places, such as this, where leaves don't drop unless disturbed by a strong gale. Even then, they do not lie to rot upon the floor, but vanish even as they fall."

"I don't care," Daylily said, still staring at the ground. "Do you realize I've stood before the Dragon's own throne?"

She sounded like a child making boasts of courage to the monsters lurking in the depths of her wardrobe.

The bird chirruped cheerfully. "You've done a foolish thing, running away. All you need to do is let it go, and you'll not have to run anymore."

"And what would you know about it?" Daylily glared at the bird. Anger made her forget how wildly her heart pounded in her throat. "What are you? Some figment of my imagination come to life?"

"Certainly not," replied the bird with what was probably a laugh. "The figments of your imagination are far more dreadful and much less awful than I."

This made about as much sense to Daylily's tired mind as you'd expect. She smoothed the scowl from her face with masterful care, turning her features into a mask. In her ignorance, she even smiled a little. "I don't care to discuss it. Least of all with you." Once more, she continued into the Wood.

"You know," sang the bird, keeping pace with ease, "that it will destroy you if you try to contain it."

"Of course," Daylily replied, still smiling. "Better me than everyone else."

That was the secret, down at the heart of this mad flight of hers. She knew this already with a bitter certainty: Nothing in the Wilderlands could frighten her as much as that which she brought into it herself.

The bird said no more. When Daylily finally looked around, she did not see him anywhere near. Somehow she knew he had not gone far, but the relief of his current absence was enough that she let the smile fall from her face. Grim lines assumed places on her cheeks, under her eyes, around her mouth; lines that had become all too familiar in the last year. Ever since Lionheart had vanished.

Ever since Rose Red.

The spasm came. It did not surprise her anymore, but it hurt, and Daylily doubled up with the pain. She choked on it, her hands clutching her sides just below her rib cage, her knees bent, though she refused to let herself fall. Slowly her hands moved up from her sides to her heart; then her fingers crept up her neck and clasped her cheeks, pressing.

She whispered, "No. You cannot come out."

Then she twisted her head, wanting to look, afraid to see, so she closed her eyes. And she growled, "I'm not cruel. You *made* me cruel."

As always, the moment passed so gently, so thoroughly, that were it not for the increased frequency of its coming, Daylily could have made herself believe it never happened. But it had. And she was no longer going to sit back and let the world go on around her, knowing all the while that she would, in time, destroy everything she touched. Not even Prince Foxbrush deserved that.

The Wood darkened.

In those places where Daylily's footsteps left the green grass momentarily bent in her wake, something like mist gathered, springing up in sinuous coils. It was only *like* mist because, *unlike* mist, it was invisible to a mortal's eye. But it moved with the same gentle wafting, spreading and contracting and curling as it went. It crawled across the ground, then up the trunks of several trees, gathering in the branches above.

Daylily continued on her way, unaware.

The something-like-mist watched her with invisible eyes. Reaching out tremulous hands, it crawled from treetop to treetop, keeping pace just behind her, high above her head. Like the barest breath or whisper of wind, it rustled the leaves, but she did not notice or turn her head. She did pause once midstep, but only once. Then, with the slightest tensing of a muscle in her cheek, she proceeded.

The invisible eyes watched her go.

Then one invisible being said to another: "I like it!"

"Me too!" said the other. "Let's tickle it and make it run!"

5

U P UNTIL RECENT HISTORY, Foxbrush would have confidently told anyone who asked that Eanrin, Chief Poet of Iubdan Rudiobus, did not exist.

Eanrin was a figure from nursery tales. Indeed, he was the fictional inventor of nursery tales, including the most famous collection, *Eanrin's Rhymes for Children*, a volume on which Foxbrush had been raised and which was solely responsible for the bulk of his childhood nightmares. (Its woodcut illustrations could be rather gruesome, particularly one of the Wolf Lord pursuing the Silent Lady that was not lacking for blood.) This Eanrin character obviously held a higher estimation of children's abilities to stomach frightening stories than Foxbrush's stomach had merited.

But Eanrin himself was a story. He was a Faerie bard, a shape-shifting cat, one of the Merry Folk and, according to some stories, even a Knight of Farthestshore. All completely impossible according to the rules of the logical, orderly reality upon which Foxbrush had founded his life.

That was before the Dragon.

Foxbrush sat at his desk, holding the scroll Lionheart had tossed him. He didn't open it. He didn't really want to. But he turned it over and over, letting the silky ribbon dangle and the starflower gleam. That flower was an anomaly in itself. Starflowers, the national blossom of Southlands, were red in daylight but turned white under moonlight. However, they never . . . glittered. At least none Foxbrush had ever before seen.

But this one shone like a tiny star. And though it must have been plucked from its vine many hours ago, it showed no sign of wilting.

A trick, perhaps. But somehow, Foxbrush could no longer quite believe this.

Of all the scars the Dragon had left upon Southlands in the wake of his flaming passing, this one pained Foxbrush the most: his inability to believe anymore in the logic of things. In the complete fit-inside-the-box rationality upon which he had always depended. That rationality had never allowed for the possibility of dragons. And then the Dragon had come. That rationality had never allowed for the possibility of poisoned nightmares. And then the nightmares had come.

For a little while after the Dragon departed, Foxbrush tried to convince himself that it had all been some misunderstanding, some large-scale hoax or hallucination. But a man can only fool himself for so long before the truth, however inconvenient, will assert itself once more.

So the Dragon existed. Maybe this Poet Eanrin did as well?

"But, dragons eat it," Foxbrush growled, squinting at the scroll and the ribbon and the flower, "why would he write to *me*?"

Then, because no one else was going to answer that question, he slid the ribbon and starflower off, unrolled the scroll, and read what it had to say. His eyes narrowed still more. He fumbled in a drawer, pulled out a pair of spectacles and, shaking himself a little, read it again.

Then he said, "Dragon's teeth" with very little vim and tossed the scroll onto the desk. It rolled up with a smart snap. The starflower blossom gleamed silver beside it. Its pure, gentle light touched the contours of yet another object on that crowded desk, one that, in the hectic storm of recent emotions, Foxbrush had been almost able to forget.

His love letter. Tossed aside into an unhappy ball.

The worms in his stomach woke up and began chewing once more.

"I myself will go into the Wilderlands and find your lady Daylily. I will return her to you. . . ."

"You will, won't you, Leo?" Foxbrush muttered, slowly removing the spectacles from his face and shoving them absently into the front pocket of Tortoiseshell's jacket. "You'll stride off into the unknown. You'll play the hero. You'll save the damsel. And you'll leave me in your dust yet again."

He slammed his palm down hard on the desk top, cursing at the sting that shot up his wrist and arm. The next moment, still cursing, he crossed the study and flung open the door of his dressing room, which was, mercifully, empty of Tortoiseshell and his disapproving nose. For Tortoiseshell, a man of dignity and taste, would never have approved his master's subsequent actions.

Foxbrush did not own much in the way of hero-ing garments. No stout pair of boots, no long and dramatic cloak. His oiled riding boots would only slow him down, and it was much too hot this time of year to consider a cloak, even the fine fur-trimmed thing he'd been intending to pin to his shoulders for the ceremony that day.

But he found things he thought might work—a pair of loose trousers, a shirt made after the draping Southlander style (thus negating the need for a cravat), some older house shoes that he wouldn't mind getting a little scuffed if necessary. And, to finish off the outfit, a fine belt with a buckle engraved with a seated panther, the emblem of the crown prince. He would not venture into the unknown without some sign of his title.

He stood in front of the mirror, taking in his appearance by the dim moonlight glimmering through the window. His reflection was far more informal than he was used to seeing. The draping shirt made him look more stoop shouldered than ever without the padding his man usually sewed into the shoulders of his jackets. But who ever heard of a hero setting out on a quest in shoulder pads?

In his eyes a light shone, a light of determination that could not be repressed, even when his stomach gurgled. "I'll find her myself," he whispered to his image. "I'll climb down to the Wilderlands and find her myself, and I'll tell her that I don't *want* to marry her. She can do as she likes after that, and I won't care!" He strode from his room as only a hero strides.

He scurried back a moment later to his study and the desk, and grabbed the scroll. After all, if it *were* from the Poet Eanrin, it might not do to leave it behind. Shoving the scroll deep into a trouser pocket, he hastened, rather less heroically, from the room once more.

The Eldest sat at his bedroom window and thought he saw his wife in the moonlit gardens below.

He had been hustled out of the way to this place in the commotion of the day. It was better for him to keep his mind untroubled by unsettling events. He wasn't himself, of course. Everyone knew that. Since his son went away, he'd succumbed to the Dragon's lingering poisons, and now he was little more than a shell of the man he had once been.

So he sat at the open window, alone in his kingly chambers, still clad in the wedding garments no one had thought to take off him. And he thought he saw the queen down below. How she must be enjoying the new rosebuds emerging on the remnant bushes, and the young mangoes beginning to put forth fruit! Those years of bondage had been hard on her, strong woman though she was. The Eldest, as he watched her from above, was glad that she no longer lived in dragon poison.

"Starflower?" he whispered, though he believed he shouted the name. "Starflower, my dear, hadn't you better come in now?"

She did not seem to hear him but continued moving on through the gardens, like a low cloud skimming the surface of the pond. It was growing rather dark. The moon was high for the moment; soon it would sink, however, and anyone out in the night would be left blind. Why did the queen not come in?

The Eldest frowned and decided it would be best for him to summon a servant to send a message to his wife. It would be a shame for her to get lost in the gardens.

"Boy?" the Eldest said, turning a little toward the door, though his eyes remained upon the figure below. "Boy, come to me, please."

"Yes, Father" came the response. His servant was most obliging, the Eldest thought, careful of his master's needs and ever ready at his beck and call. He saw movement from the tail of his eye as the lad drew closer and knelt at his side.

"What can I do for you?"

"It's the queen," said the Eldest. "She's down in the gardens, but night is deepening. Can't imagine why she hasn't come in. Send someone to tell her, will you?"

The servant said nothing. Distantly, the Eldest thought he felt two hands take his.

"Father, she's dead," said his son, Lionheart. Except Lionheart was gone, run away, vanished. "Mother died in the Occupation. Don't you remember?"

"There. I can't see her anymore," said the Eldest, and he struggled a little to free his hands from that earnest grip. His eyes, clouded from too many years of breathing sorrows and nightmares, filled suddenly with tears.

He bowed his head.

"You remember now?" asked Lionheart.

"Yes," whispered the Eldest. "Yes, I do. She's dead. She's not in the garden. She's gone. Like Lionheart."

"No," said his son. "I'm here, Father. I went away for a time, but I'm here now. Can't you see me?"

The Eldest could see nothing, for he refused to look. His son knelt at his feet, still clad in the groundskeeper's hood and the bloodstained nightshirt with the hole in the breast where a unicorn's horn had pierced it. Tears filled Lionheart's eyes for, though he knew his father was frail from the years under the Dragon's thrall, he had not expected to find him so far gone. When Lionheart entered into exile when the Dragon first came all those years ago, the Eldest had been a strong man yet in his prime. Now he sat in his chair by the window, huddled with unexpected age, his face withered and gray.

Lionheart rubbed his father's thin, papery fingers, feeling how loose the signet ring with the sign of the rampant panther had become. He struggled to speak, both because his throat clogged with sorrow and because, well, what could he say?

"Father," he whispered thickly, "I'm sorry."

"Sorry?" The Eldest turned to him then, and for a moment his old eyes were bright. "Sorry for what, lad?"

"For leaving you."

"Oh, that's nothing to be sorry for! You have your other duties. I understand. But you always come back to me, don't you? Faithful boy."

Lionheart forced himself to breathe, though it pained him. Tears fell down his face, one from each eye. The last time he wept had been in the gardens of Hymlumé, standing at the crest of Rudiobus Mountain. He'd wept there at the sudden piercing beauty of the Spheres and their Songs and at what they made him realize about himself.

He wept now because he loved his father, and his father was dying. He was a child again, but without the comfort of childhood innocence. So he clutched the Eldest's hands between his own and let the tears come as they must.

Then the Eldest pulled one of his hands free and rested it on Lionheart's head. "Ah. It's you."

The words were simply spoken. But they went to Lionheart's heart. He closed his eyes and pressed his forehead into the signet ring on his father's other hand.

"There was . . . there was some difficulty between us?" the Eldest said, and his voice held a question but also a trace of comprehension. For a moment he was himself, and though he could not remember much, what he did remember was true.

"Yes, Father," Lionheart managed. "There was some difficulty. But I'm here now, and I'm sorry that I left."

"Did I wrong you, my son?" the Eldest asked, a world of tenderness in his words and in his hand upon Lionheart's head. "I'm an old man now, older than I should be. Did I wrong you without understanding?"

Lionheart shook his head. "You did right," he said. "You did right by me, and I failed to see it. But I see now, and I thank you for what you did."

The Eldest nodded solemnly. "I used to hate my father sometimes," he said. "Hard blows are difficult to take with grace. But you know what? I think sometimes his punishments hurt him as much as they hurt me." He frowned, the creases of his tired face wrinkling slowly, with great effort. "I don't remember what I did to you."

"It doesn't matter," said Lionheart, and he lifted his face and met his father's gaze. For a shining moment, each saw the other truly, and in that truth, they each loved. "None of that matters now. I am here. And I am sorry, and . . . and you did right. You are a great Eldest, the ruler of Southlands. And you are a good father."

The Eldest nodded and turned once more to the window. His brow relaxed, then wrinkled again, and he leaned forward, squinting into the dusky garden. "Lights Above, is that the queen?" he said, his voice quavering. "What is she doing out at this hour? Quickly, boy, go tell her of her error before it gets too dark."

6

A NEW PAIR OF EYES. *Young eyes.*
Eyes a hundred years old are still young. Eyes a thousand years old are still young. It's all a matter of comparison.

These young eyes are keen and see many things, even blurred as they are by tears.

Tears . . . such a strange sensation! Not just the feel of water upon flesh or the burning inside the head. Tears fountain up from the soul. They wash or they drown, but they never truly cleanse. Not a soul such as this.

A strange feeling is a soul, especially one so fierce.

Look through these eyes into the Wood and wander, searching, searching, searching.

A gate into the Near World. That is what we—it—they—I! That is what I want! That world would be a good place to start again. And this one loves that world, loves that Land that is the only land to him. But he cannot find it. Looking through these eyes, there is only the Wood forever and ever.

The tears are blinding. Why must this soul sorrow? Only in death can there be new life. Why can they never understand? Why must they always—
Crescent Woman.

Long ago, he had called it the Gray Wood. Now it was simply the Wood to him as to all others, for it was not solely gray. All colors and no colors might be found in its ever-shifting deeps. He had learned this very soon upon entering (so long ago it seemed to him, for he could scarcely remember the day), and in learning, he had been afraid.

The young warrior did not fear the Wood now, however, as he moved through its depths. Blood stained his arms and neck, blood not his own. He would wash it off eventually, but for now he wore it as a badge of honor to the memory of the beloved dead.

And the watching eyes of the Wood drew back, trembling.

Few things might frighten him now, this stern-faced warrior whose features may have seemed youthful, save for those bloodstains. Around his neck he wore two cords of rough-woven fibers. On one was strung a stone that gleamed like gold or bronze. It was this that caught the eyes of the Wood and left the warrior with a clear path through the gloom.

But it was the second cord that drew his searching fingers. On it were strung two beads. One was red, painted with the crude image of a panther. The second—this one the warrior touched even now, unconscious and tender—was blue and painted with a white six-petaled flower.

Not far off, he heard the songs of sylphs. Their voices drew him up sharply, and he stood as still as a wildcat poised at the beginning of a hunt, his nose uplifted to catch scents, his head tilted to receive all possible sounds. The sylphs were near and they were singing, which meant they were on their lonely hunt. From the sound of the song, they had caught someone and even now dragged that luckless victim of their love into the deeper Wood.

The warrior would have gone on his way without a second thought. Sylphs, after all, are strange beings with their own customs, and while many might consider them foes, they were no danger to him or his at present. So he would have passed into the shadows and vanished from this story altogether, save that his nose caught a scent that brought him up short.

"Crescent Woman!"

The warrior turned and pursued the sylphs.

They moved in a swirling nexus, creatures of air and invisible beauty, unable to hold on to physical form for more than mere moments. In those moments, one might catch a glimpse of a face neither male nor female, of hair long and streaming, of eyes dark beyond existence, like a storm's gale. They were huge and they were small, beings of wind and sound.

And they loved mortals with a dangerous love; as the cold moon must love the fiery sun for its heat; as the ever-changing sea must love the stolid shore for its sameness; as a man must love a woman, so the sylphs loved the dirt-bound mortals and called them into their wild games so that they might touch mortal hair, might feel mortal limbs, might hear mortal voices rising in chorus with their own.

To these aerial beings, the most inexplicable and beautiful mystery of all was mortal death. They pulled and pushed their captives in fey patterns only to watch them fall down, exhausted, battered, and, finally, dead.

The warrior had seen it before. He had come upon hosts of sylphs, each one rendered no bigger than a spring morning's whisper, gathered about the corpse of some luckless mortal, touching its still face with their wisps of fingers and asking one another, "Why does it no longer dance? Why does it no longer sing?"

It was their foolish way. The warrior had long since learned to ignore them.

But he could not ignore the scent of the Crescent Land.

"Come, fickle, fleeting, Fiery Fair,
Come and join our dance!
We'll run our fingers through your hair;

> *We'll dance beyond all thought or care!*
> *Come, and in our wildness share*
> *And leave your life to chance!"*

So sang the strange voices of the sylph in their manic but beautiful song. The warrior chased it, following his ears and his nose, and at length he caught glimpses of the sylphs themselves, their faces reminiscent of a man's but more like a bird's, or perhaps both at once. When he could see nothing else of them, he could still discern the signs of their passing: the wind-tossed branches, the trembling of the trees. The air became thick in their wake, filling with mist in the sudden stillness so that the warrior became nearly blind in his pursuit.

Then he picked up the sound of footsteps and knew he must be drawing near to the mortal caught in the center of the swirling air.

A flash of red drew his eye, red like water or like fire. He saw the mortal at last: a tall, straight figure clad in light, flowing garments that lent themselves naturally to the pulling winds. The red he'd glimpsed was her flowing hair.

"Let her go!"

A dozen unseen faces turned upon him; their unseen eyes fixed him with angered stares. The song turned to a snarl, and he felt them massing together into one great body, ready to blow the flesh from his bones in their anger.

The warrior stepped forward, unafraid. He could see little enough other than the young woman—not much beyond girlhood, he realized—who stood with her back to him, her hair and white gown beating the air behind her in the ferocity of the sylphs' breath. He did not think she could hear his voice, but that did not matter. The sylphs could.

"This mortal is of my kin," the warrior declared. "Born of the Crescent People in the mortal Land Behind the Mountains. You will give her back to me."

The sylphs, wordless in their rage, flew at him. As one force they tore at his face, at his clothes. But they did not topple him, and he put his hand to his throat and lifted up the bronze stone.

"By the Mound of my master, I command you to let her go."

He did not have to speak loudly. A whisper was enough. The sylphs saw and knew. And the sylphs, again moving as one, howled their anger. They twisted around the warrior, around his limbs, his neck, his head. They shied away from touching the stone, however, withdrawing as though stung—if anyone can sting the wind.

Then they leapt back from him, crossing once more to the woman, and their long, vaporous fingers touched her face and hair with a caressing sadness.

The next moment, they were gone.

Lady Daylily sank to her knees and collapsed on her side, deep in the heart of the Wilderlands.

7

PART OF THE LIFETIME BATTLE that comprises Growing Up is learning (then relearning, then relearning again) that you can never go Home.

Home, that ephemeral world of warm, comforting, familiar love where a place is always set for you, where the conversation ever turns to topics in which you can enthusiastically participate, where the food tastes better, and where you sleep most restfully at night . . . it doesn't exist.

In the all-too-real world, people change. Places change.

Over and over again Lionheart had swallowed this bitter pill, and yet it never entirely ceased to surprise him. He himself had altered so much in the months—which felt like mere days to him—of wandering in the Wood Between. He'd faced the Monster. He'd died. He'd been raised up again a new, whole man, albeit with a scar on his chest where a unicorn's horn had pierced his heart.

He had altered forever. Somehow, though he knew better, he'd assumed that the place he called Home would not.

A selfish assumption. After all, could he truly resent an entire nation for moving on and changing in his absence? Home was gone. In its place was this strange world, where his cousin stood in Lionheart's shoes, where his father was weak and tottering, where Lionheart might only walk in disguise. Even the tiles beneath his feet felt unfamiliar and unwelcoming. In light of these alterations, those few things that still looked to Lionheart as they once had took on an aura that both repelled and saddened him.

No, there could be no going Home. There could only be going on.

So that's what he would do. Was he not Childe Lionheart now, servant of Farthestshore, knight in training? The journey to knighthood was his home now; a lonely home, perhaps, but a better one than he had yet known.

"Make peace with your father," the Prince of Farthestshore, his new liege lord, had told him. Well, he'd done that. He'd faced the man he'd once looked to as a near-godlike figure, seen him reduced to mere shreds of manhood, and he'd made his peace.

Lionheart felt a dullness where his heart should be and knew, though he wouldn't admit it, that he wept inside. The Eldest was dying. He wouldn't last the year, probably not even the summer. And then who would sit in his place? Not his son. That young man, who consorted with dragons and demons, could never be trusted to rule Southlands.

"Here's an idea. Let's make Foxbrush Eldest instead!" Lionheart muttered under his breath.

By cover of night he crossed the Eldest's grounds, away from the House and the many people who might recognize him there. His face was unpleasant with scowls, and he knew he should not allow himself to indulge in such bitter thinking. After all, did he consider himself a better man for the job? Recent history had done nothing but prove his lack of worth, his cowardice, his foolishness.

But still . . . *Foxbrush.*

"Anyone else," Lionheart told the uncaring landscape as he trotted under a heavy sky. The moon did not shine that night; perhaps she did not care to look upon the disinherited prince fleeing his kingdom yet again. But Lionheart kept to the main road leading to Swan Bridge, and it was clear enough even in darkness. "Anyone else," he growled. "Even the Baron of Middlecrescent! At least he has a head on his shoulders and some idea how to run a kingdom."

No one could say the same for Lionheart's cousin. The lad could scarcely run his own estate, preferring to leave it in the hands of his steward while he spent all his time at court, making cow eyes at Daylily. Or plastering his hair down with oil, or conducting research in the expansive court library on obscure and insanely boring topics. Like figs.

He believes he can save the kingdom.

The thought was not a welcome one, and Lionheart shrugged it away. After all, he had thought as much himself, and where had that led? A five-year exile, wandering across the unfriendly Continent, betrayal of the girl he loved, worse betrayal of his only friend. Not a record of which he could boast.

The idea that Foxbrush couldn't *possibly* do any worse was no comfort.

So it was in this stormy frame of mind that Lionheart made his way across the Eldest's parklands. His face was set and his feet strode with a determination that would brook no argument. He had failed in everything else to which he'd turned his hand. He'd not faced the Dragon. He'd not saved the kingdom. He'd not delivered Rose Red from the bondage to which he'd so heartlessly sent her.

"All that's changed now," he told himself as he went. "That man died, that Lionheart, that failure. I am made new, and I will rise to new challenges!"

He would enter the Wilderlands once more, and he would rescue Lady Daylily, thereby proving to the worlds that he—

"You understand that you can never absolve your own sin?"

The memory of the Prince of Farthestshore's words came back to him in the quiet of that hot, still night. Lionheart faltered, stumbling over nothing. His heart raced as though he'd heard the heavy breathing of a predator at his ear, but there was no danger. There was only memory. And darkness.

"All that is past is past."

Though he knew it was only memory, Lionheart spoke as though making a defense. "I can't just leave her. I wounded her. I used her and left her, and what has she become now? I can't leave her to herself. I must rescue Daylily."

And again he heard in the quiet place deep behind the arguments of his mind: *"From this moment forth, you will serve me with the courage of roaring lions."*

"I will!" Lionheart cried. Any who might have seen him out there alone on that gloomy road would have thought him mad, for he brandished his fists and shouted desperately, though there was no one to be seen. "I will serve you, my Lord! And I will rescue Daylily!"

"Walk with me," the Prince had told him far away, in a place beyond Time, on the shores of a dark and flowing river. For a moment, standing there on the road with only the chorus of chittering night bugs filling the heavy air, Lionheart thought he heard that rush and roar of water again, that sound of Forever, and his face was touched, however briefly, by a cool freshness that breathed of Eternity.

Then it was gone. He stood alone. No voice spoke to him either in memory or in fact.

And yet he felt an overwhelming urge to turn around and march back to the Eldest's House.

"No!" he growled. For though he had learned a great deal about himself when he'd stood by that water, though he'd looked into the face of the moon and the burning eyes of a fallen star, for all that, he was still himself. Lionheart the stubborn. Lionheart the proud. And he had a long road before him.

"No," he muttered and set out at a run, but the air was far too hot and he was very soon drenched in sweat. "I'll save her. It's my duty! I'll find her in the Wilderlands, and I'll bring her safely home."

Then she would forgive him. Then Southlands would forgive him. Then he could vanish and never return but leave behind at least one good deed in the memory of his kingdom.

He saw the broken stump where the Grandfather Fig had once stood. That tree, so ancient, so gnarled, so stately in its ugliness, had become a familiar landmark to all those who dwelled in the Eldest's House. Famous artists of past generations had done their best to capture it in paint and pottery, and more than one prince or princess of Lionheart's line had been depicted on canvas standing in the shade of those twisted, flower-laden branches.

Now it was gone. Ripped up, torn out, roots exposed. Yet another scar left in the Dragon's wake.

Lionheart approached the stump and looked down the gorge into the Wilderlands below. He heard the shushing of branches not moved by wind as the trees whispered to themselves and pointed at him. They mocked him, he knew. But what had he to fear from their mockery? Let the Wood do its worst. A Path would be given him, and he would walk unscathed through that darkness. He would—

"*Aaaaaaaarggh!*"

The bone-rattling scream carried up from the side of the gorge, accompanied by the sound of slipping rocks. Lionheart gasped, "Dragon's teeth!" and stared over the edge, willing his eyes to see in the dark, hoping against hope that his ears had deceived him.

For the first time that night, the moon peered through the film of clouds overhead. And Lionheart saw.

"Foxbrush!" he shouted. "What are you *doing* down there?"

At his feet lay a narrow path down the wall of the gorge, nearly invisible on that dark night. Only a fool or a hero (sometimes synonymous) would dare make such a descent.

And there, his back pressed to the wall, his feet braced, his hands gripping stones and dirt and tufts of hardy grass, was Foxbrush. He turned a face saucer eyed with terror up to Lionheart. His mouth opened and closed a couple of times, but that scream seemed to have knocked the words out of him. When at last he managed to garble something, his voice was too weak for Lionheart to understand.

"You idiot son of a stubborn mule-jenny!" Lionheart cried. "Get your dragon-eaten hide back up here where it belongs! What are you *thinking*, climbing down the gorge at night?"

Foxbrush, from his precarious position, tried a tentative movement. He'd stepped on something that had suddenly scuttled with rather too many legs for comfort, startling the scream out of him. One misstep more and he would plunge into the rocks and trees below and probably never move again. He tried to swallow his beating heart back down to his chest.

A string of curses overhead and a quick scramble of rocks alerted him to Lionheart's swift descent. Foxbrush set his teeth and, still pressed to the rock wall, began sidling down the trail once more, feeling out each step as he went. "Stop!" Lionheart called to him, but Foxbrush wasn't about to obey.

"You're not the prince anymore, Leo!" he growled, grinding the words through his teeth to keep them from chattering. "You don't give the orders!"

Another explosion of angry curses rained down, along with an avalanche of pebbles. Lionheart, in his fury, lost his footing and slid several feet, clinging to stones and tearing his hands and shirt as he went. In this manner, Foxbrush and Lionheart raced each other down the rock wall, and they could not have been in greater danger of their lives when the Dragon first fell in fire from the sky.

The Wood watched. And the Wood laughed. And the Wood put up shadowy arms to receive them.

Foxbrush managed to reach the gorge bed with his limbs intact. He was only a few yards ahead of Lionheart by this time, and he needed every advantage. His legs rubbery with terror and physical exertion far beyond any he'd made in he could not remember how long, he stumbled toward the Wood and all but fell into the fringes of the first trees.

Immediately he wished he'd done practically anything else.

The light changed. This was often the first sign to those who stepped into the Between that they had left their world behind them. Foxbrush stepped from darkness into what might be midafternoon. It was difficult to say for certain. What little light penetrated the canopy of branches overhead fell in bright pools upon lush green growth and splashed against dark trunks and heavy-laden boughs. Where that light (which may or may not have been sunlight, for no sun or sky could be seen) fell, the greens turned to emerald, the browns to gold. The sound of night insects vanished into a perfect, watching stillness.

Foxbrush began to tremble. He opened his mouth, perhaps to pray, perhaps to curse. But he had opportunity for neither, for he was grabbed by collar and shoulder, swung around, and slammed up against the nearest tree trunk.

Lionheart glared down at his cousin. There were so many things to despise about Foxbrush aside from the hair oil plastering his head, though that had collected such a thick layer of dirt and dust that the hair's original color was indeterminable. His features were so soft, so well tended, so freshly scrubbed. His eyes were too squinty. He was babyish and weak and everything most loathsome in a man.

Perhaps the thing Lionheart disliked most, however, was how dreadfully similar Foxbrush's face was to his own.

"You have to go back," Lionheart said.

Foxbrush made a pathetic attempt to wrest his cousin's grip from his shoulder. Lionheart merely pressed him more firmly into the tree. Foxbrush snarled, "You've had plenty of opportunity, Leo! You've had every chance in the world to play the hero, and it's not as though you've done a rip-roaring job of it!"

Lionheart, by some superhuman effort, managed to not punch his cousin in the nose. "Rip-roaring or otherwise, I won't accomplish anything with you along."

"I'm not asking you to take me along," Foxbrush replied, giving up the fight against Lionheart's grip and focusing his attention instead on making the most obnoxiously superior face possible. "I've come on my own, and I intend to continue on my own. Daylily can't have gone far, and I'll find her, and I'll tell her what I want her to hear. And dragons eat the lot of you!"

"*You?*" Lionheart nearly laughed. "*You* are going to find Daylily? Here? In the Wilderlands?"

"You think I'm not man enough?" Foxbrush cried. "You think you can intimidate me? You think I'm scared of you?"

Shaking his head, Lionheart released his cousin and took a step back. "You'll find far worse than me here in the Wood, Foxbrush. Go back. Get out of here while you still can."

For a moment more, they stood quietly facing each other. Then Foxbrush sniffed loudly and started walking. Without an idea in his head, he plunged into the vast Wood Between, arrogant as only a mortal can be. But Foxbrush always was an idiot.

Lionheart hurried after, debating the merits of clunking his cousin upside the head and dragging him back to the Near World. He had just convinced himself of the wisdom of this plan and was searching for some likely clunking weapon when he noticed something he never would have anticipated, not in his wildest dreams.

A Faerie Path opened at Foxbrush's feet.

Faerie Paths are a strange phenomenon to those unacquainted with the ways of the fey. Lionheart, despite his recent journeys into the Wood Between and the Far World beyond, still did not think he quite grasped what they were or how they worked. He knew there were hundreds of them, thousands perhaps, invisibly winding through the Wood, and each one belonged to a different Faerie king or queen. Some were safe for mortals to walk. Most were dangerous, even deadly. And the Wood itself would lay the more dangerous Paths before the feet of the foolish and do everything in its power to lead them astray.

But Lionheart recognized the Path at Foxbrush's feet. He had expected to find it for himself.

"Wait," Lionheart said, catching his cousin by the shoulder. Foxbrush tried to shrug him off, but Lionheart held tight and pointed. "Do you see that?"

"What?" Foxbrush looked where Lionheart indicated and saw nothing but forest floor.

All in a rush, Lionheart considered many things. Where he walked in the Wood, shadows and trees obscured his way. Where was the Path his Lord had promised? Where was the Way that would be made for him in darkness?

He considered—and this with a curse—that serving as a Childe of Farthestshore was not nearly so straightforward as he might have liked.

"I think," he said with utmost hesitancy, "that perhaps you should come with me after all."

Foxbrush narrowed his eyes at Lionheart, and bile rose in his throat. He knew better than to take at face value anything his cousin said. "Is this a trick?"

"Maybe." But it wasn't. Lionheart prodded Foxbrush again. "Go on. Standing there looking stupid won't find Daylily."

Foxbrush rubbed his nose. His eyes stung with the dust of his climb, and his knees were weak with fear he did not like to admit. Nevertheless, he took a single step.

The sylphs were upon them before he could take a second.

8

SHE CAME TO HERSELF UNWILLINGLY, the song of the sylphs still echoing in her brain but distant enough now that she could discern up from down once more and even remember her own name: Daylily, Lady of Middlecrescent. Soon to be queen.

What was she doing in the middle of a forest in . . . Oh! Great Lights Above! Was this her *wedding gown*?

The rest of her memories crashed back down upon her with such force that she groaned and dropped her head to the dirt. Her hair, which had been so carefully crimped and curled and pinned into an impressive tower that morning, lay in mats down her back, every pin plucked away, every curl pulled straight by the curious fingers of the sylphs.

But she had escaped. Slowly her heart resumed its regular beat and she drew a long breath. She had escaped the wedding, escaped Foxbrush, escaped the future they had for her.

She had saved them all.

She sat up and pushed her hair back from her face. And she saw the bloodstained warrior.

Daylily was not one to scream. She did not scream now. Her eyes widened, and her breath drew in sharply and refused to release for some moments. She could feel her heart ramming against her throat, then plummeting down to the pit of her stomach. But she sat still, holding her hair back with both hands, the ruins of her gown spread in a circle about her. She met the warrior's gaze and did not flinch.

His eyes were black as Aja ink, and his equally black hair was so long that he had braided it back from his forehead. Though his face was young, the expression was not. Judging by that expression alone, Daylily could have believed she gazed into the eyes of an old man . . . an old man who had seen and dealt more than his share of death.

He crouched before her like a panther prepared to spring, his eyes intent. His clothing was savage: skins and coarse cloth forming a loose garment with a sheathed knife hung on its leather belt. He was a figure out of primitive legends, cruder by far than any artist might have painted him, for how could an artist imagine such utter dirt and blood and roughhewn living?

But when the young man stood, he moved like the son of a king or lord, more dignified than a dandy such as Foxbrush could ever dream of being. He was no taller than Daylily herself, yet it did not matter. He was master here.

Daylily's legs felt weak, and she feared if she tried to stand she might fall over. So she remained seated where she was but lifted her chin with a calm hauteur that would have struck Prince Foxbrush down in his tracks. "I am Lady Daylily, daughter of the Baron of Middlecrescent," she said, her voice cold as a winter morning. "Who are you?"

"Sun Eagle," said the warrior, and something that might have been a smile flashed briefly across his stern face. His nose wrinkled as he drew a deep breath of her scent. Many scars marked his dark skin in cruel, pale lines, and his cheeks and neck were stained with dried blood.

"Do I owe you thanks?" Daylily asked, willing her voice not to tremble. "Was it you who called off those . . . *things*?"

He said nothing. Daylily wondered if perhaps he did not understand her. He circled her where she sat, studying her intently and sniffing again. She forced herself not to turn and follow his movements, to sit quite still, like a rabbit in the field, hoping the hawk will pass on overhead.

He came around in front of her, and once more she glimpsed a flicker of a smile.

"Crescent Woman," he said.

His accent was almost too strong to understand. But somehow the words shifted around in her mind, becoming comprehensible as by magic.

"Crescent Woman," he repeated. "But your hair is like fire."

By this time Daylily was fairly certain she could control her limbs, so she stood slowly, arranging her skirts. The hem was ripped into ribbons; the sleeves hung in rags from her elbows; and with every move she made, more pearls fell from the trimming.

The warrior looked her over, his gaze curious, as though he saw things that he knew could not be and yet could not deny. He frowned, a fierce expression when coupled with all that dried blood. "You speak with the voice of a man or a boy child," he said. "It is strange to hear in a Crescent Woman's mouth. Yet you have the smell of my people, my land. Were you sent by my father to find me? Are you some diviner or witch?"

"Certainly not," Daylily replied. "I told you, I am Baron Middlecrescent's daughter."

"*Elder* Middlecrescent?" the warrior suggested.

She did not respond. But a suspicion bloomed suddenly in her mind, a suspicion so strong, it was nearly a certainty. She did not want to accept it. Yes, she'd entered the Wilderlands. Yes, she expected the unexpected. Only, not this. This was impossible.

They studied each other, each slowly peeling back layers of unbelief at what this study revealed. Daylily was a private young woman. She was so private, in fact, that she had long since become unused to anyone noticing anything beyond the surface version of herself she permitted to be seen. At times even she began to believe that the surface Daylily was the only Daylily in existence.

So when the warrior suddenly narrowed his eyes and said, "What is that inside you?" she nearly collapsed again upon the spot.

"Stop looking at me!" she gasped, though she could not tear her own gaze away from his.

"Why?" asked the warrior, his voice soft. "What is that? What don't you want me to see?"

"Nothing!" she replied. "Leave me alone."

She wanted to run, to flee deeper into the Wilderlands. Even to be swallowed into the vortex of the sylphs' dance would be preferable to this! But the warrior's eyes held her rooted. And then she glimpsed something else, something moving behind his black pupils.

"What is that inside *you?*" she asked.

Let us show you.

"Let me show you," said the warrior. He took her face between his hands.

————

The passage between minds is not so great as one might expect. Indeed, for incorporeal beings it is but a step once the gate is open.

The gates of Daylily's mind, which she had thought so heavily fortified, opened easily to the one who now sought entrance.

It found itself on a wide, blank plateau. The sky was dark as a moonless midnight, but the ground shone as though illuminated by a pale sun, though there was no sun to be seen. Desolation spread in vast, lonely sweeps, but here and there green places could yet be seen.

Searching, searching, searching for the lost . . . But the search is easier with eyes, with a body, even here in the landscape of a poisoned mind. So assume a body, assume a shape, assume . . .

Sun Eagle stood on the plateau. Or, if not Sun Eagle, then Sun Eagle's form. A fine, strong, stolid form; a worthy host. And the thing inside Sun Eagle turned him to survey the world of Daylily's mind. In the distance, it could still discern some places of growth where her memories remained unsoiled. It saw a field of rolling grass across which two mounted horses raced, their riders laughing in wild joy, urging, *"Faster! Faster!"*

But the green faded away into the desolation. The riders, flying so swiftly on their steeds, vanished the moment they left the lawn and stepped upon the wasteland. When they were gone, the green died and became part of the sorry whole.

The thing that was Sun Eagle continued turning in place. Dragon poison. This mind was full of dragon poison.

Good. That is good. They—we—I can use a mind like this!

A bird sang, and the form of Sun Eagle spun about, teeth bared in warning, hand falling upon the hilt of a stone knife. No bird could be seen, however. Instead, there was yet another place of growing life, closer than the last, near enough that every detail could be seen, clear and sharp as only mortal eyes perceive such things. It was a mountain stream shielded by trees thick-laden with greenery and flowering vines. Smooth stones formed a natural bridge across the stream, and on the far bank sat a lad just verging on manhood, handsome and fresh faced, a little sad.

"She loved him."

The thing that was Sun Eagle did not startle at this voice. Unlike the birdsong, this rough growl, agonized and dripping with fury, was expected.

Ah, it said, using Sun Eagle's mouth, and it turned, using Sun Eagle's body, to look upon the speaker. *So you are what she's hidden inside herself.*

A red she-wolf crouched on the cracked and suffering ground of that barren landscape. Every muscle in her body tensed as though prepared to spring, to tear, to destroy. Such could never be, however, for she was chained. Each paw was secured in rusty manacles that tore into her flesh, and from each manacle stretched a short chain that fastened to a stake driven deeply into the earth. The wolf could no more escape than fly.

But she strained against her bonds, and when she strained, the world of Daylily's mind quaked.

"She bound me," said the wolf. Saliva dripped from her panting jowls.

Why? the thing asked with Sun Eagle's mouth.

"She does not know what I will do should she let me free," said the wolf.

And what will you do?

Here the wolf laughed. It was not a pleasant sound. "Why don't you free me?" she asked. "Free me and find out!"

The thing inside Sun Eagle did not tremble, but the body itself took a step back. It was, after all, only mortal.

Just then, voices drew its attention back to the scene by the mountain stream. A girl was crossing the stream. She wore rich green and a bonnet askew on her bounty of red hair. She carefully lifted her skirts as she stepped from stone to stone and asked, *"What are you doing?"*

"What are you *doing?"* replied the memory of the boy on the bank. The wolf and the thing that was Sun Eagle watched the girl and the boy sit together and talk beside the cheerful water.

"She thinks of him often," said the wolf.

Who is he?

"Lionheart." The wolf sounded sad. "She thought she would marry him. She thought she would live happily ever after. She thought this place"—the wolf cast baleful eyes across the great expanse of loneliness—"would be green and thriving forever."

The thing that was Sun Eagle watched through Sun Eagle's eyes. Though the sky was dark, in this small corner of memory golden sunlight shone through the branches and sparkled on the water, growing brighter as the two young people talked.

Then a name was spoken: *Rose Red.*

As sudden as the snuffing of a candle, the sun went out. The girl with the red hair stood. *"We'd best be on our way,"* she said, and there was no sunlight in her voice anymore either. *"I left Foxbrush in a bramble somewhere, and I doubt that he's extracted himself. I don't suppose you brought a pair of gloves?"*

She recrossed the stream, and the lad followed. The moment they stepped into the desolate ground they, like the two distant riders before them, vanished. The thing watching from Sun Eagle's eyes saw the stream thin until it was nothing but a slow, muddy gurgle.

She hates him now? the thing asked using Sun Eagle's mouth.

"She would rend him to pieces," said the she-wolf. "*I* would rend him to pieces."

Now the stream was dry, the bed cracked with dust. Wasteland crept up and overwhelmed the greenery until all was gone, and that place of scenic serenity could not be told from the rest of the ruin.

"All the once living places of her mind vanish one by one," said the she-wolf. "Soon there will be nothing left but me. And I am as you see me: trapped."

The thing in Sun Eagle looked down at the wolf, considering. *Does she want to free you?* it asked.

"No!" The she-wolf snarled bitterly. "No, she wants to suppress me forever!"

We want her for one of ours. We have use for her.

At that, the wolf struggled to surge to her feet. She strained against the chains so hard that the ground shook, and the thing that was Sun Eagle staggered and nearly lost its balance. But the chains were fast to the ground, the links too short to allow any freedom of motion. The wolf fell back, and her four legs bled where the manacles bit.

Still she growled, spitting blood. "You'll take her over my dead body!"

No.

The hand of Sun Eagle moved to his throat, touching the bronze stone on the cord around his neck. For a moment, one finger brushed the other stone, the blue one painted with a white flower. The body responded to this against the will of that inside it, shivering with a sudden thrill of passion and resistance. But the hand moved on and untied the cord on which the bronze stone was strung.

The creature within Sun Eagle knelt before the wolf and fastened the bronze stone around her neck.

No, it said. *Over your bound body.*

As though weighed down by a chain far stronger than the four upon her limbs, the wolf collapsed flat against the ruined soil. And she did not move, not even to breathe.

Now. You are theirs—its—

Mine!

———

Daylily gasped. She came awake kneeling in the Wood Between, shuddering, her arms wrapped about herself against a cold that pierced her from the inside out.

Sun Eagle crouched before her, a hand on her shoulder. "There," he said. "There, it's over. You're safe now."

Daylily, her chin drawn to her chest, saw something gleaming. Struggling still to breathe, she grasped the gleam and held it steady. It was like a shard of ice in the palm of her hand and she winced. When her vision stopped swimming, she looked at what she held.

It was a charm, a bronze stone of no particular shape strung on a cord of animal gut.

Her breath came easier with each gasp. Soon she was able to sit upright. The spasm passed; the cold, though present, was bearable. And suddenly she felt stronger than she had in . . . in she could not remember how long!

"What has happened?" she asked the warrior, turning to him as a child to an older brother. Though he was a stranger, she felt somehow that she knew him. She felt that she was—in some odd way—part of him. "What did you do to me?"

"I?" said he. His voice was strangely gentle. "I have done nothing. But you have taken the Bronze. You are now one of my brethren."

He stood then and helped her to her feet. He did not release her hand, and she found that she did not want him to.

"Come. Walk with me," said Sun Eagle. "Let us find your world."

9

"ONCE UPON A TIME."

No phrase is more intriguing to those who know nothing of Time.

Immortals understand Time in the same way they understand air. It is there. It always has been and always will be. They live in it, but it isn't something to be concerned about unless it is unduly removed. Otherwise, who's to bother?

Mortals are different. Time *matters* to them, for they experience it in such limited quantity. Like a man plunged into the ocean who gasps for each breath with desperate urgency, so mortals, trapped as they are by their mortality, put out their hands and try to grasp Time even as it slips through their fingers.

And it's all so fascinating to watch!

This was precisely why sylphs—which are neither immortal nor mortal but simply *are* in the same way that the wind simply *is*—find mortals irresistible. Time-bound creatures existing in a world so other to that which sylphs know are beautiful and beguiling and utterly impossible to pass up.

Once upon a Time . . . and here are creatures, oddly ugly, intriguing mortal beasts, that actually *live* upon a Time like it is the most natural thing in the worlds!

But one sylph did not find the prospect so enticing.

This creature of wind and whisper held back from its brethren, though never so far as to be totally alone. It had been alone too long, and it never wanted to suffer that yawning closeness of isolation again. Even now, free and airborne though it was, it still felt the bite of iron around its neck, a neck made solid with imprisonment, and it remembered its wind-wild spirit trapped in a Time-tortured form.

Once it had been too curious and too clever. It had ventured out of the Between, lured by the voice of the Death-in-Life. And there, in that world where everything gave way to the decay of moments, hours, and years, the sylph had been made the slave.

"Aad-o Ilmun!" the sylph breathed through the leaves as it moved, following the merry shouts of its brothers and sisters. "I am saved! I am rescued! I will never deal with mortals again."

They had caught a new one. The lone sylph could tell by the manic laughter, the triumphant songs.

> *"We have the mortals by their hands,*
> *And so we lead them through our lands!*
> *Oh, laughing, fey, and fair are we*
> *Who spring and sing from tree to tree!*
> *Come and join our dance!"*

They were foolish, but they could not help it. Intrigued by the strangeness, they failed to recognize the horror. So the lone sylph hung back. Let them sing and harry the poor mortals. Only let them never learn the terrors of a corporeal body, the horror of a spirit trapped inside a head, the painful beat of a heart! Even now the memory was enough to make the sylph moan.

Then it heard a shout.

"By the Prince of Farthestshore, I—*oof!*—command you—*arrrgh!*—to release—*ugh!*"

Every whisper of the lone sylph's strange and billowing being sang in response to that voice, which it recognized.

"Savior!" it cried.

Then it plunged forward through the trees, hurtling itself after the congregation of its kindred until it found the mortals clutched at the center of the wild hurricane. The sylphs were not gentle with their new toys but tugged them right off their feet, carrying them through the Wood so swiftly that neither captive could protest, and were indeed hard-pressed to protect their faces from the knifelike branches as they were gusted along. One of the mortals hit a tree trunk, only just putting up an arm in time to protect himself from a severe concussion, then was pulled on around so fast that he could not catch his breath.

"Savior!" cried the lone sylph again.

A horrible, wafting face presented itself before Lionheart's terror-struck eyes. Both visible and invisible at once, it put out its great, gale-like arms and caught him close to its breast. All breath knocked from his body, Lionheart could not so much as moan when he, with a jolt that certainly must have left his stomach far behind on the woodland floor, was torn from the throng of wind beings and lifted up, up, up, until he thought he would break through the canopy of the forest itself.

But no. Not even a sylph has the courage to climb above the trees in the Between. High in the upper branches, however, the lone sylph was able to bear its mortal burden more easily away from the throng. Lionheart felt his head pillowed on a bosom made of breezes, soft and gentle as a mother where his cheek lay. But the rest of the sylph's being billowed tumultuously, crashing through the foliage with all the care of a typhoon.

The gates to the Near World from the Wood are not known to all the fey folk. But the sylph had a fair notion where the mortal clasped in its arms might have entered, and it bore him back that way. In this place, a grove of silver-branch trees, the sylph had waited with its brethren, patient as only those who know nothing of Time may be, waiting for mortals to accidentally step over the boundaries separating their world from the Realm Between Worlds.

So the sylph set Lionheart down beneath these ageless trees. Lionheart, numb with roaring and flight, staggered three steps, then fell headlong. The sylph, ever eager to please, reached out and gently righted him on his feet. Once more, Lionheart tried his luck with a pace or two, but his legs failed, and he collapsed again.

All around him stretched the Wilderlands, and he could see no break in the trees' long shadows. He did not know how close the gate to the Near World stood, for his eyes were untrained. He saw only more Wood.

The sylph bowed over him, touching his forehead.

"Savior," it said. "Now I have saved you!"

"Wh-what?" Lionheart pushed himself up onto his elbows, spitting dirt and leaves, and gazed once more into that face that was not quite a face. "Who are you?"

"Don't you remember?" said the sylph. "I am the poor creature you rescued from the Duke of Shippening."

For the moment, at least, this comment could make no headway in Lionheart's rattled mind. He lay as though paralyzed, unspeaking. The sylph put out a hand and gently played with his hair. "My kindred think too much of mortality and the strange ways of your kind," it said. "The Lumil Eliasul favors you so, you and your dirt-bound bodies. They envy you! I once envied you too. And I suffered for my envy when Death-in-Life bound me with iron chains and gave me to the duke."

A shudder like the sadness of a desolate summer breeze glancing across a dry field passed through the sylph. But its hands continued to gently caress Lionheart's face. "But you!" it said. "You were sent by the Lumil Eliasul himself. You were sent to rescue me!"

Vague memories moved like shadows across Lionheart's stunned consciousness. He saw once more an albino jester, a creature never meant to be trapped in mortal form, unhealthy, unhappy, almost unreal, performing for the amusement of a tyrant. He remembered himself stepping forward and loosing an iron ring from the creature's neck. The burst of wind and roaring had been almost too violent to bear! But the sylph had been freed to its true form.

And it had told Lionheart then, *"I will grant you a wish if I may."*

Now it said, its face ever shifting but filled with smiles, "I have saved you, my savior! *Aad-o Ilmun!* How glad I am to have been the instrument of the Song Giver!"

"I . . . I remember you." Lionheart blinked vigorously, as though to drive the apparition away. "I remember you. And the docks of Capaneus City."

"Yes, the docks," said the sylph, its voice full of joy. Then the joy vanished, replaced with a solemn moan, like the creak of a moored ship on a still night. "There I told you where to learn the secret to the Dragon's final end. A dreadful purpose." Another instant and the shudder had passed. Once more the sylph smiled. "But I never granted you a wish! May I do so now to repay in full the debt I owe?"

Lionheart shook his head, then wished he hadn't, for his ears still throbbed with the painful noise of the sylphs in throng. "I . . . I think you have repaid me," he managed.

"No!" cried the sylph. "For you liberated me from slavery, while I merely pulled you from the dance of my kindred. It is not enough, and I do not wish to live in your debt forever. Have you no task for me now?"

"Foxbrush." Lionheart's eyes flew suddenly wide, and he rose swiftly, swayed, and propped himself against a silver-branch tree. The Wood surrounding him was full of silent but no-less potent mockery. "Foxbrush," Lionheart said and gnashed his teeth. "He's in there. Somewhere."

"The other mortal dancing?" inquired the sylph, whirling about like an eager puppy. "He is with my kindred still. And he will die." Its voice was uncaring but not cruel. It brushed Lionheart's face with its long fingertips again. "Your kind cannot dance so long as mine."

"I must save him!" Lionheart cried. "Can you lead me to him?"

"I can," said the sylph. "But I won't."

"What? Why not?"

The airy being made no reply, but it pointed. Lionheart looked where it indicated, down at his own feet.

And there Lionheart saw the Path for which he had searched. The Path of Farthestshore leading, not back into the Wood the way he had come, but into the grove of silver-branch trees, their branches twining delicately together in what might almost have been an accidental arch.

Lionheart, stepping as gingerly as a cat over a puddle, approached the two trees, following the Path. He stood between their trunks and looked out. He saw the gorge. The rock cliff face, and the trail leading up to the tableland above.

The Near World waited; Southlands waited.

He stepped back quickly. Once more, the Wood closed in on all sides, extending forever. Here in the Between there was no gorge, only darkness and forest and those who dwelled therein. Here in the Between, where Foxbrush and Daylily now wandered, lost as children.

"I can't go back," Lionheart said, muttering the words angrily. "I can't leave Daylily and Foxbrush behind! Must I always be the coward and run away?"

He waited, half expecting to hear his Master's voice and the distant silver song of the Lord Beyond the Final Water. But there was nothing. Nothing but the voice in his memory.

"Walk with me," the Prince had told him.

And Lionheart had vowed to do so.

"Dragons eat it," he snarled and pounded the nearest tree trunk. The tree shivered irritably and dropped a twig on his head. Lionheart brushed it aside, casting about as though desperate for someone to whom he might make an argument.

The sylph wafted closer. "Will you go now to the Near World, savior?" it asked. "The Song Giver is leading you that way. Will you follow him to mortal lands?"

"I—" Once more Lionheart cursed. Then he breathed a heavy sigh. "I must. I've doubted and fought and forged my own way too many times." But he hesitated even so, sensing something more he must do, though he couldn't guess what. "Are you coming with me?" he asked the sylph.

"No, no," it replied. "I cannot pass through that gate. The locks prevent the Faerie folk from entering your country."

"What locks?"

"The locks of Nidawi's people."

"I don't know what you're talking about."

The sylph laughed then like a whooshing breeze and tickled Lionheart under the chin. "Foolish!" it cried. "You know nothing, but you think you know everything! How mortal you are, how clever, how sad." Its laughter ended suddenly, and the sylph itself vanished. Lionheart, for a moment, believed himself alone. Then a little voice in his ear said, "Let me fetch the other mortal out of the dance."

"What?"

"Let me fulfill my duty to you, kind savior. Let me fetch back the mortal you lost and bring him to you. Would that please you?"

"Yes!" Lionheart said. "Yes, that would please me! Find Foxbrush and bring him back. At once, if you can!"

"Farewell, then," said the sylph. And it was gone. The leaves of the silver-branch trees fluttered gently, the only sign of the creature's passing. Lionheart stood alone in the Wood Between.

"I should have asked him to find Daylily," he muttered. But it was too late. And was he now to leave her himself? To return to the safety of the Near World and . . . and what? He'd made his peace with his father. Rose Red no longer waited with faithful friendship; she was long since gone. All his ties there were severed.

"Why, then?" he asked the empty air. "Why would you send me back? Why not let me find Daylily and at least do one good turn by her?"

There was no answer. The Path at his feet pointed to the gate, and Lionheart could not deny it forever.

He passed between the two trees, and the Wilderlands watched him go.

The flock of sylphs crashed through the Wood, singing as they went.

> *"We have him, and we'll keep him!*
> *We'll dance and whirl and sweep him*
> *Through the merry In Between*
> *To places he has never been,*
> *And never more will he be seen*
> *By mortal eye again!"*

At first, Foxbrush could not understand the words, so loud was the roaring of the voices singing them. But the deeper they progressed into the forest, the gentler his captors became, as though more certain of their catch. When at last they let him touch the ground once more—pushing and prodding him when he fell to his knees—he could hear their words very well. But his mind could not accept it.

"That . . . that was quite a gale!" he gasped, clutching his shirt, which had been torn to ribbons by snatching branches. A little afraid what he might discover, he felt around, testing his own limbs to make certain they were all still attached.

He found Lionheart's scroll tucked into his trouser pocket. Somehow, feeling it there made him angry, and anger made him brave enough to stand. He coughed to clear his throat and smoothed down his hair with both hands. "An unusual natural phenomenon," he said, lying to himself for what comfort a lie might offer. "A powerful summer gale is what that was. Probably several accounts of it in *Gullfinger's Guide to the Natural Sciences*."

The next few moments were spent in far more desperate self-lies as he struggled to convince himself that the winds in the trees above him were not whispering to one another.

"Look at me! I'm a natural phenomenian!"

"A natural phenemenon!"

"A natural phenomonomonom!"

Lionheart was nowhere to be seen. But surely he must be close, perhaps only a few yards away. The Wood was so thick here, it was possible for all manner of things to lie hidden within inches of each other. Foxbrush shuddered. His imagination was not keen even at its best, but one needed very little to begin picturing wild creatures lying low, shielded beneath the heavy fern fronds, ready to leap; or snakes slithering silent paths and just brushing one's foot.

"Ahhh . . ." Foxbrush grimaced and tried to straighten the rags of his shirt. "There will be a clear trail back the way I came," he told himself. "Broken twigs, bent grass, so forth. It's always so in the books. Gullfinger himself wrote a section on surviving in the wilds, and I'm sure I can remember most of what he said."

Even as he spoke, his eyes lifted unwillingly to the tree branches swaying above him as the wind creatures passed through, shushing leaves and breaking twigs, chattering among themselves. Despite himself, Foxbrush heard and understood each word.

"It's not as fun as the Fiery One."

"It does not billow as that one did."

"And it's not so red."

At first, the horror of talking breezes was too much for Foxbrush, and he cringed and clutched the hair at his temples. Then he realized what they had said.

"Fiery One?" he muttered. "Red . . . Daylily?"

In a rush, his own fear was forgotten, and he addressed himself to the tossing branches (for he could not see the sylphs themselves). "I say, have you seen my lady Daylily?" He felt the fool indeed and blushed. Did he, after all, expect a breeze to answer?

Lionheart would.

The thought niggled at that corner of his mind he disliked admitting existed; the part of him that measured himself against Lionheart and always, *always* found himself wanting. Foxbrush scowled and, firmly pushing his wind-blown hair down onto his scalp, demanded in a voice he hoped was heroic:

"Tell me, beings of air and . . . and . . . windiness! Tell me where the Lady Daylily is! Tell me if you have spied her in this dark forest!"

The sylphs convened upon an oak's stout limb, lined up like so many curious children at a shop window—or so many equally curious vultures at a dry watering hole—and stared down at their new playmate. One of them pointed.

"Is it talking to us?"

"I think it must be."

"Does that mean it loves us?"

"I'm not sure."

"It's a bit boring, don't you think?"

"Shall I pinch it?"

Foxbrush heard each word as it rang through his ears to his still-protesting brain. Then the oak branch groaned as though under enormous stress.

Foxbrush had just time to gasp "No!" before the sylphs descended upon him, pricking, pulling, smacking, plying, and laughing at every squawk he made. Foxbrush fled into the forest, and the sylphs battered him from all sides as he ran. The Wood laughed and pointed, and this pleased the sylphs so that they redoubled their game, squealing like a playful tornado. Foxbrush ran until his feet bled, without any thought for direction, and would have been swallowed up by the Wood entirely.

But where he ran—though he did not see it—a Faerie Path opened up at his feet, always just one step ahead of him. Without his knowledge or will, he pursued this Path in loops and twists, bypassing all manner of terrors he did not know to avoid. And the sylphs whooped and giggled, as unaware as he, fully occupied by the fun of their new toy.

Their laughs turned to screams in an instant, however, when a roar shattered through their midst. Following the roar, a streak of white sent the sylphs tumbling one way and Foxbrush tumbling another. He saw nothing clearly, for the roar had all but blinded him with terror. He fell with a crash, curled up in a ball, chin tucked to his chest and arms over his head. The voices of the sylphs faded swiftly:

"It's the Everblooming!"

"Fly! Fly! Flee!"

The echoes of that roar pursued them until all dissipated into silence.

Silence fell, as dreadful to Foxbrush as the recent cacophony. He remained where he was forever . . . or possibly for a moment, Time being a fickle friend in the Between. When at length he could bear to uncurl and sit upright, his heart pounding a death march in his throat, he was as pale as a northerner, his eyes wide black circles on his face.

The sylphs were gone.

Another with more woodcraft might have seen the enormous, claw-tipped footprints crushed into the ground and tearing the turf in places, but it was just as well Foxbrush did not; otherwise, he would never have managed to get to his trembling feet.

He stood, swaying and dizzy, and stared around. The Wood, no longer amused, stood in solemn disapproval, and he could almost have believed the trees folded their arms.

He took a few futile steps. He still did not see the Path opening at his feet, and even if he had, it probably would not have comforted him.

"Hu-hullo?" he called tentatively. He could not say to whom he called. In that moment, he was simply anxious to hear something, even his own voice.

He certainly did not expect an answer.

"Go away!"

He froze in place. Here, as in most of the Wood he had seen thus far, the ground was overgrown with tall ferns that acted as an effective canopy for whatever might lurk beneath. The voice had come from low to the ground, but everywhere he looked, he saw only green fronds. Still, whoever it was had not sounded especially threatening. Emboldened, Foxbrush tried again. "Um. Who's there, please?"

"I said go away!"

"I . . . I don't mean to hurt you. I'm simply wondering if you might, as it were, tell me where I am?"

The ferns to his left rustled with sudden violence. Foxbrush turned and, of all things, saw a child rise up like a mermaid from the sea, except not so beautiful. The child's face was wet and a little slimy with weeping, weeping that emphasized rather than softened its vicious expression. It had long hair that was either black or green, hard to tell for the moss grown in it. Its eyes were red, probably from its tears.

The child stomped through the ferns with the ferocity of an angry elephant, though that ferocity was tempered somewhat by the loud snorts it made as it rubbed its runny eyes. Its voice rose in petulance as it neared. "When I say go away, I mean *Go! Away!*"

"I-I'm sorry!" Foxbrush cried, putting up his hands and backing away, for even a child can be intimidating in the Between. "I didn't mean to offend, I simply—"

"*Go!* Go, go, go!" the child cried, wiping its nose with a long swipe of its arm, its face wrinkling up into the hideous expression one makes when trying to suppress more tears.

"Please, little boy," Foxbrush begged, "I don't want to—"

"*LITTLE BOY?*"

The child's shriek turned into an explosion that knocked Foxbrush several yards back until he struck a fir tree whose prickly arms cushioned his fall. He sank to the ground, his eyes staring for all they were worth at the place where the child stood. Only there was no child anymore.

In its place stood the most gorgeous young woman Foxbrush had ever seen.

A white lion leapt into the space between her and him, its mouth a red chasm of snarling.

10

Before, the Wood had loomed threateningly. Now it shivered as if threatened.

All because of a little bronze stone? Daylily wondered and once more lifted the stone on the cord around her neck, attempting to look at it. It was difficult to see at the pace she was obliged to keep, dragged along behind Sun Eagle, who held her fast by the hand. And the stone swung like a pendulum, almost as though it did not want to be seen. It made her slightly sick.

It is very beautiful.

Was it? Very well, perhaps it was. Or perhaps it was just a lump of bronze melted down in some unknown furnace so that the original emblazoned image on its face was completely unrecognizable. Was the stone once a flattened disk? If so, that was a long time ago. Was that possibly the etching of a profile still visible through the melting?

She was very beautiful.

Daylily could not have told how she knew. But even as she trotted after her bloodstained guide and dropped the bronze stone so that it landed back on her breastbone, over her heart, she knew that whoever's face had once graced that melted disk had been beautiful indeed. Beautiful and powerful.

And the Wood, looking at it now—at the face or the memory of the face or perhaps simply at the Bronze itself—drew back and gave the warrior and the fire-haired maiden clear passage.

"Tell me, Crescent Woman," said Sun Eagle suddenly as they went, "do they speak of Elder Darkwing's son in your day?" His voice was quick and low, as though he feared both to ask the question and to hear the answer.

"Who?" Daylily asked. And that was answer enough in itself.

The warrior ground his teeth and shook his head, angry at himself for even thinking the next question that sprang to his lips but asking it nonetheless. "And the Starflower. Do you know . . . does she yet live?"

"Starflower?" Daylily frowned. "I couldn't say. I've known many Starflowers. The Eldest's wife, Queen Starflower, she—" For a moment, Daylily could not speak. But somehow the feel of the Bronze above her heart gave her strength. She was safe. She was not at the mercy of that which lived inside her. She was master of herself. "Queen Starflower died when the Dragon came."

"Dragon? *Queen?*" It would be difficult to say which surprised the young warrior more. He drew up sharply, and Daylily ran into him, staggering back a pace or two and treading on her dress. Sun Eagle rounded on her, his eyes narrowed, his face fierce. "Don't lie to me, Crescent Woman. You are of my kin. Your blood and my blood flow from the same source. Do not lie to me."

Daylily might have been afraid once. But she had entered the Wilderlands of her own choosing; she had danced with sylphs. And she wore the Bronze around her neck. What had she to fear?

A distant part of herself observing from some secret corner watched in surprise as she put up a hand to touch the warrior's bloodstained face. He, surprised as well, flinched but did not otherwise move, standing cold as stone under her fingertips. "What are you doing?" he asked.

"Whose blood is that?"

For a moment she thought he would not answer. For a moment she thought she did not want him to answer.

Then he said, "Dinhrod's. Dinhrod the Stone."

"Who was Dinhrod the Stone?"

"My Advocate."

That distant part of Daylily told her to drop her hand. That distant part of Daylily urged her to back away, to run. That distant part of Daylily felt the danger in those strange words.

But that part of Daylily was bound and paralyzed. She had no reason to heed it now.

"Did you kill him?" she asked and her voice did not tremble.

"No," Sun Eagle replied. "But I watched him die."

Glorious death. From which springs life.

Daylily stepped back, her hand still frozen in the air as it left his face. She was cold but did not know it. The Bronze over her heart warmed her. She asked without fear, "Who is my Advocate?"

"I am," said Sun Eagle. "I found you; I chose you; and you will not disappoint. You have taken the Bronze."

He turned then and led on through the Wood, depriving Daylily of the chance to ask her final question.

Will I watch you die?

She picked up her skirts and hurried after her strange guide. A bird sang, and she glanced briefly aside from her path, glimpsing the flash of a pale, speckled breast in the darker shadows.

"I'm here," sang a silver, trilling voice.

Daylily scowled at him. Then she turned her face away and refused to look, no matter what it might say. Soon the outward portions of herself no longer heard it at all, and what the inner portion heard no longer mattered.

They followed the trail left by the sylphs as they had dragged Daylily along, though Daylily herself did not recognize it. Nor did she recognize the five silver-branch trees growing close together, reaching out tender arms to touch one another with the comfort of kindred. They seemed almost to shine in that gloom, and the Wood stretched forever around them on all sides. The trees meant nothing to her now.

But Sun Eagle stopped. He stared at those trees, his black eyes searching for something he could not quite see. When Daylily glanced at him, she saw . . . what was that expression? Hunger? Yearning?

"I have searched long and hard for this gate," said Sun Eagle. "I have wandered the Between with my brethren, and I have looked upon many worlds. But I have never found what I sought till this day."

Daylily shuddered at the sound in his voice. It was too close to tears, and she could not bear tears, not from him. "I see no gate," she said.

"You have not yet learned how," he replied. He guided her with gentle force toward the trees, and they seemed to quiver at his approach. Daylily thought that, if they had not been caught by roots, they would have sprung up and run.

The two trees in the center of the cluster formed a delicate, curling arch with their branches. Sun Eagle led Daylily until they stood between these trees, and Daylily looked out through the thin veil of leaves.

She saw the Near World beyond, and the wall of the gorge.

This woman who had trod the Paths of Death alone and unguided, who had breathed in more poison than a mortal should and still lived, held herself together like the foundations of a crumbling building. Nothing outward betrayed what she felt.

But the bronze stone over her breast seemed suddenly to throb with a pulse more eager than her heart.

The Near World!

"Please," Daylily whispered softly. "Please, don't make me go back. Not to my world."

"You say that now," Sun Eagle replied. "But then you will be lost too long, and you won't be able to return. Even when you wish to." His face was as sharp as his stone knife, and he would not look her way when she turned pleading eyes to him. "We must return, Crescent Woman. We must return while we may!"

They stepped through the silver-branch trees, passing from the Wilderlands and the forever-reaching Between back into the world of Time and decay.

The light was too bright, and the heat of midday crushed down upon them. Daylily shaded her eyes, blinking, and her vision slowly adjusted. She saw that she stood before the gorge path she had descended. She recognized its twists and turns from but a few hours before, though perhaps it was more clearly cut than she recalled.

"The Land," said the warrior. His voice was a breath, a prayer. Daylily turned to him, surprised by the emotion she heard in his tone. It was too savage to be joy. How long had he wandered in the Between?

Then something struck her that she should have noticed right away but that her mind had refused to see. Or rather, refused *not* to see. The mind is a powerful thing, and it will do all it can to organize the world into understandable forms, even deceiving itself if it deems deception necessary.

But Daylily, however skilled she was at self-deception, could not avoid the sudden truth that overwhelmed her. Her gaze lifted up to the edge of the gorge, to the tablelands above. To the empty place in the sky where Swan Bridge should arch in remarkable majesty.

A scream caught and strangled her, and she gasped for air.

"What do you see?"

Sun Eagle watched as fear fought with self-control for mastery of Daylily's face. But she stood silent, gazing up at the lip of the gorge, and if he could discern nothing else about her, he saw disbelief in her eyes.

"The—" Her voice broke, and she swallowed to wet her tongue and throat before continuing. "The bridge is gone."

"Should there be a bridge?"

"Yes." Daylily traced an arch in the sky from gorge edge to gorge edge, over the Wood. "There. Swan Bridge." Then she shook her head, and a little color returned to her deathly face. "No. No, we've come out wrong. You've followed the wrong trail. This is not where I entered. . . ."

But she knew that wasn't true.

Daylily was many shameful things that she hid from herself and the world as best she could. But she was no coward. With a growl in her throat echoing the growl in her mind, she picked up her skirts and hastened from the shelter of the trees across the stones. Her wedding slippers, long since destroyed, offered no protection either from sharpness or from the heat of the sunburnt stones. Each step was agony, but this only made her quicken her speed. The warrior fell in behind her, and she heard him muttering even as they climbed the trail, their hands clutching the rope for support, "This was not here in my time."

Not in her time either.

But no! She would not think of that! She would not think at all until she reached the tableland above. She heard Sun Eagle taking deeper breaths as they went. As they drew near to the end of the trail, she heard him say with sudden, painful eagerness, "It must be. It *must* be!"

Then she stood at the top, exhausted, sweat drenched, her feet bleeding. But she noticed none of this.

"Gone," she whispered. "Everything is gone."

The warrior, come up beside her, turned slowly in place.

All was wild, untamed, vine-draped jungle. A thickness and greenness and dreadfulness that Daylily had never before seen or imagined, full of the buzzing of insects, the not-too-distant screams of monkeys, and the caws of ground-dwelling fowl. Mango trees, untended, bore bounteous burdens of fly-eaten fruit. The air teemed with life and death and moisture.

Through the thick tangle of vines a narrow trail was cut, leading to the gorge, beaten down by many generations of feet. This alone gave sign of human life in this young, feral land.

And Daylily felt . . .

. . . the surge of ravening desire. The taste of blood on the air.
This is good country.

"My world," said the warrior. Suddenly his face broke as something between a laugh and a sob escaped from his heart. "This is the *Land*!"

"This is Southlands," said Daylily.

She knew this landscape, or a ghostly image of it. But the jungle she knew had been cut back, tamed, fit into a mold of elegance and refinement. There might be the chatter of monkeys, but they were pet monkeys who lived fat lives in the queen's garden or perched on the shoulders of their caretakers. There may be ground fowl, but they were stately, spoiled birds, trailing their long plumes of tails behind them across sprawling green lawns.

There should be a path, yes, but not a narrow dirt trail. Where was the paved carriage road from the Eldest's City across the grounds to Evenwell?

And Evenwell, across the gorge, where was it? Lost in that thick, wild growth? Where was the gatehouse where the bridge keeper lived?

Where was Swan Bridge?

Sun Eagle turned when the moan escaped Daylily's lips. He caught her as she sagged, all but fainting. Supporting her, he lowered her to the ground and held her while she relearned to breathe.

"You are out of your time," he told her, his voice oddly gentle from behind those bloodstains. "Sylphs care nothing for Time themselves and do not understand how mortals may value it."

She leaned her head against his shoulder, staring at nothing. Stroking her hair, Sun Eagle looked around again, and his black eyes swam. "This is not my time either," he said. "The Gray Wood had not grown up unchecked in the gorges back in my day but was held in place by rivers. The rivers are gone now. The mighty rivers . . ."

His stern face could not be softened by tears but rather was made to seem sterner still, even as he wept. Then it was done. All mourning or celebration passed from him, and he stood, helping Daylily to her feet once more. She clung to him unconsciously, her eyes darting this way and that, frightened as a doe who smells but does not see the panther near.

"There is no bridge for you," said the warrior, "as there is no river for me. But the Land . . . the Land is ours!"

The Land is **mine.**

"Come, Crescent Woman." Sun Eagle turned to Daylily with a look in his eye that may have been a smile. "Let us see what we may find."

It's **mine.**

He led her by the hand away from the gorge. He did not take the beaten trail but instead plunged into the jungle itself, always finding just room enough to pass even where Daylily thought the vines grew as thick as a wall. The air breathed with wildness and youth and heat, baffling Daylily's senses. Birds she did not recognize flitted after insects and sang their territorial warnings. Snakes twined through the vines, hidden and hood-eyed, watching the strangers pass. Once a monkey swung down to chatter vicious teeth at them, but it fled at one glance from Sun Eagle.

And it was all real. Daylily, who had seen Death's realm, found herself oddly able to accept it, and her racing heart calmed a little. This countryside was known to her, deep in her heart of hearts. It was like when she was a little girl, and her grandmother had shown her a lovely portrait hanging in the long gallery of Baron Middlecrescent's home.

"Do you know who that is, child?"

"No, Grandmother."

"That was me as a young maid. Was I not beautiful then? I was a free-spirited creature, full of life, full of hope, full of passion. But alas!" and the old woman's voice had become heavy as old sin. *"They always break us in the end."*

Remembering, Daylily gazed upon the untamed landscape around her. "They haven't broken us," she whispered. "Not yet!"

Sun Eagle stopped suddenly, poised for either fight or flight. Daylily watched him test the air, and then he turned to her with a terrible smile.

"I knew it," he said. "I knew we must have returned for a reason! After all my searching, the Land has called me home." His eyes flashed with something Daylily could not understand. "It needs us."

It needs **me***!*

Sun Eagle took her hand again and led her on through the jungle. "Come, Crescent Woman. Walk cautiously and take care not to be seen. You will prove yourself."

"Prove myself?" Daylily did not try to free her hand, though part of her wished to. She followed Sun Eagle with the trusting simplicity of a child. "What do you mean?"

"You will fight," said Sun Eagle without loosening his hold or slackening his pace. "You will fight."

The countryside grew steadily more tame. She saw signs of cultivation, of furrowed fields. Sun Eagle continued sniffing the air, and whatever he smelled excited him. Then Daylily caught a scent for herself, a strong odor of smoke.

"There is a village near here," Sun Eagle said. "Greenwell, it was called in my time. It belonged to Eldest Panther Master. But he must be dead long ago."

Daylily saw the warrior reach up and finger a small bead worn on a cord at his throat, painted blue and white with some figure she could not discern. She did not have a moment to wonder about this, however, for they emerged from the fringes of the jungle and looked out upon the village, just as Sun Eagle had expected.

Daylily knew now where the smell of smoke had come from, for she saw dozens of little fires burning in stone circles, one outside the door of nearly every hut. A squalid, stinking, feeble sort of village, she thought, but well peopled. There were villagers moving about daily tasks, children running on many errands, and old mothers grinding meal by their firesides. She saw men making repairs and herders driving flocks of geese and goats and pigs.

Following a path down from the village came a line of strong-armed women, clad in rough cloths and skins, trailing little ones in their wake.

"There," said Sun Eagle, pointing to a rock-lined pool of roiling water, a deep, ever-moving well. "The well of Greenwell." And then he grimaced. "I thought I smelled her. The rivers are gone. Anything may creep from the Wood Between into the Land now. Even *her*."

Daylily's stomach heaved. She could pick out no distinct smell beyond the woodsmoke. Otherwise, all was a noisome blend of unwashed bodies, goat dung, and stinking mud wattle drying in summer heat. "Who?" she asked, her voice a little faint.

"Mama Greenteeth," Sun Eagle replied. "Look."

The women approaching the well stopped within a few yards of it, setting down their waterskins and bowing, facedown. Then, one at a time, they drew near the water, which churned with bubbling freshness. Daylily watched as one woman took a flat wafer from her pouch and crumbled it into the water. The crumbs sank and disappeared. Only then did the woman fill her skin and return the way she had come, two small children in tow, back up the path to the village.

Daylily frowned. "Superstition," she said with the cold superiority of one who is beyond such nonsense.

But Sun Eagle replied, "Not superstition. Ritual. They must pay the tithe."

"Tithe? What tithe? To whom?"

"Watch."

One by one, each of the women performed the same odd trick. Some of the cakes were bigger than others, and it seemed to Daylily that those who offered them only took water in proportion to her gift.

Then Sun Eagle said, "Ah! Look there."

He pointed, and Daylily searched out what he indicated. A tall girl, not yet a woman, came down the path leading a toddling child by the hand. She could not be the child's mother; a sister, perhaps. But she toted a skin for water over one shoulder and tugged the little one, who was fractious and resisting.

Suddenly the little one plunged a hand into the pouch at the girl's side and pulled out a wafer cake such as Daylily had seen given to the well. Even as the sister cried out, the child stuffed half the cake into his mouth. The rest fell in crumbles about their feet.

The girl scolded, wringing her hands at the toddler, who smiled naughtily around his stolen mouthful. Then, with a heavy sigh, the girl looked back up the way they had come, and down again to the well. Daylily could see her calculating the distance, her mouth twisting with the effort of her decision.

Then she swept up the little one and, staggering under the child's bulk, hastened the short distance remaining to the well. Looking over her shoulder and plunking the child back on the ground, she hastily bent and filled her skin without first making an offering.

Nothing happened. But then, Daylily wondered, what did she expect to happen?

"Tithe breaker," Sun Eagle whispered. "Watch."

The weight of the skin was too much for the girl, and she was obliged to hold it in both arms. She barked a command to the child and set out up the path, the little one trotting behind. But they had gone no more than three paces when the surface of the well began to writhe and roil.

A face rose up from the water.

It was a face without distinct feature, fluid as water, old and foul, with hair long and green, and teeth longer and greener. Others coming down the path shrieked and dropped their skins, fleeing. And the tall girl, her dark face gone gray with fear, whirled about just in time to see that horrible face rise up, up, up, then swoop down, mouth open, and swallow the toddling little one whole.

The next moment, face and child disappeared back into the well.

The girl screamed. The women screamed. And Daylily found that she too was screaming. "Do something! Do something!" she cried, her horror so absolute that she forgot herself.

Do something. Do something.

Sun Eagle stood and clutched her arm, turning her to him. His eyes were alight, and she thought his grimace might be a smile.

"Prove yourself, Crescent Woman," he said. "Forge the bond. Rescue the child."

11

THE HEART IS A PECULIAR THING. It sees and interprets important details long before the brain has started to think there might be something worth noticing. The brain resents this skill, however, and will often spitefully do all it can to repress what the heart might be whispering.

So it was that the moment Lionheart climbed up from the gorge and stood looking across the Eldest's grounds, his heart spoke quietly inside him: *Your father is dead.*

And his brain immediately countered: *What? No! Where do you get that crazed notion? You saw him just yesterday, and he was sick, to be sure, but very much alive. Don't be a fool, Leo, and get on your way!*

Thus fortified, Lionheart shook himself and began jogging across the grassy field on to one of the near roads. In his groundsman's garb, he passed unnoticed among other groundskeepers, who nodded his way but otherwise ignored him and went about their work. Morning was swiftly lengthening toward noon, and there was no time to waste in chitchat. Lawns must be cut, hedges must be pruned, mulches must be laid.

So Lionheart progressed unimpeded. He was surprised as he went to see the extent to which the Eldest's gardens had recovered; indeed, he did not remember seeing them so well tended when he had made this same trek from the gorge just the day before.

Or had it been the day before?

The unwelcome thought stirred in the back of his brain, but Lionheart shook it off and quickened his pace. The Prince's Path was not clear to him now, but somehow he knew he still pursued it as he hastened toward the familiar towers and minarets of his father's house, less familiar now since the Dragon's evil work, but the home of his childhood nonetheless.

Flags flew high from every peak and tower, many long, scarf-like tassels on the wind, blue and red and silver. Lionheart frowned when he saw these. Had they not been gold and white flags just yesterday, in honor of the crown prince's coming marriage? Who had replaced them with the Eldest's colors and the standard of the rampant panther?

Lionheart's road joined with the larger road leading from across Swan Bridge and Evenwell Barony. Here he was obliged to walk along the verge, however, for the road itself was crowded with carriages and horsemen hastening on through the Eldest's parklands toward the House itself. This was strange, Lionheart thought. Should not the Baron of Evenwell be leaving in the wake of the crown prince's canceled wedding? Why should he only now arrive, a day late?

Lionheart's heart said, *Your father is dead.*

To this, Lionheart's brain responded, *If that is true, why aren't the flags at half-mast?*

It was a fine rebuttal, and Lionheart refused to follow it up with any further questions. He merely quickened his pace, dodging to keep from being run over by one of the rumbling carts.

The nearer he drew to the Eldest's House, the more details came into view. Every window, every arch, every balustrade and gable was festooned in thick garlands of starflowers. Only, not real starflowers. These, he saw upon closer inspection, were made of paper.

But starflowers were in full bloom that time of year, and the garlands should be real!

It is months later, whispered Lionheart's heart. *The starflowers have ceased to blossom. And your father is dead.*

It's just a few flowers! Maybe they withered early this year. Because of the dragon smoke, his brain replied, angry now.

The roads near the house were more crowded still, and Lionheart was obliged to walk in the dirt and grass, for there was no room for him among the carriages and horses and beautifully dressed men and women. Entourages bearing the standards of every barony in the kingdom glittered past, heralded by trumpets or criers as they drew near the House gates. He saw the flash of a flag from Milden, glimpsed the livery of powerful Shippening lords, and . . . light of Lumé above! Was that coach approaching from the Eldest's City sporting the royal insignia of Parumvir?

They wouldn't come so far, said Lionheart's heart. *Not King Fidel, nor even Prince Felix. They wouldn't come so far for a wedding.*

But they might for a funeral.

No! Lionheart's brain immediately countered. *Not a funeral! Besides, the flags aren't at half-mast.*

In the bustle and to-do, it took very little effort to slip around through the back ways, cross the kitchen gardens, and enter the Eldest's House by way of the scullery door. Here he was assaulted by an army of smells: everything from the fresh blood of slaughtered animals, to heady spices of various chutneys and deviled vegetables, to the sweet tangs of candied fruits, and the warmth of creamy sauces. Kitchen hands glared his way, and one of the minor cooks brandished a skewer so threateningly that Lionheart (who had been stabbed by a unicorn and lived to tell the tale) leapt back in horror and made a hasty retreat.

He escaped the kitchens into the servants' passage and climbed up to the main house. All the while, his heart was saying, *They're preparing a feast. You know what that means.*

A feast, I'll grant you! his brain replied. *But not for a funeral. These are preparations for celebration, not mourning. And the dragon-eaten flags are not at dragon-eaten half-mast!*

Then suddenly, on a narrow stair in the shadowy space between the sundered worlds of the servants and nobles, Lionheart stopped and pressed his back to the wall.

"My father is dead," he said, and both his heart and his brain understood it for truth.

He knew now why the barons, lords, and even kings of distant nations were gathering in the Eldest's House. He knew beyond a shadow of a doubt.

He whispered one word into the dark: "Coronation."

The Baroness of Middlecrescent was a simple woman. This isn't to say she was stupid or even especially foolish, though it might seem so to some unsympathetic observers. She merely held an uncomplicated view of the world and the order of things, held it with a grasp that had only tightened as the years slipped by. She clung to the perspective that people, on the whole, were generally good sorts with good hearts who wanted good things for the good people around them. Not even five years of dragon smoke had been able to shake this perspective. Indeed, in the surrounding darkness, the baroness had found it more vital than ever to cling to what she believed she knew (which isn't at all the same as actually knowing).

But now she sat in a quiet, unfamiliar room, listening to the sounds of bustle downstairs, and she wept into her handkerchief. Her simple perspective on the world was being rather roughly handled these days, and it hurt her heart. So she sat and she sobbed, and she could not bring herself to summon her maid as she knew she ought.

The dear, dear Baron would be angry. Oh, he would be livid! He had ordered her to make herself fine and fancy, and to present herself a good quarter of an hour ago, accompanied by heralds and ladies and sounds of trumpets. But . . . well, how *could* he expect such things of her? It seemed—and she hated to admit it, even down in the very depths of her throbbing heart—it seemed *cruel*!

So she sobbed all by herself, wondering vaguely if she hadn't ought to summon one of her ladies only for the company (for one does hate to sob by oneself at such times). She hadn't quite made up her mind one way or the other, however, when she heard the door opening behind her. "Oh, Dovetree, I was just going to ring for you," said the baroness, turning.

Then she screamed.

Lionheart was across the room in an instant, clamping his hand over the baroness's mouth and, as gently as he could under the circumstances, pushing her back into her chair and pinning her. She was not a strong woman, but she wriggled in such a flurry of lacy dressing gown that he was hard-pressed to keep her in place. But he managed it, holding on and stifling the squeals she made until at last she ran out of air and blinked up helplessly at him.

"I'm going to let you go now," he said, trying to keep his voice pleasant, though his hackles were raised. "Can you keep quiet if I do?"

He would have liked to suppress the thought, but it struck him how like this was to that time not so long ago when he'd startled a pretty girl by jumping on her from the garden wall (an accident that could very easily have cost him his neck if he hadn't managed to stifle her screams). What a bungling, awful mess that had led to!

Lionheart shook this thought away as best he could while he gazed down into the baroness's eyes and tried to make his own expression comforting. Any moment, he expected to hear the sound of footmen or guards pounding their way down the hall. But there was nothing; just the baroness whimpering. "Can you?" he repeated.

The baroness blinked again, then nodded. He took his hand away from her mouth, ready to clamp it back if necessary, but she merely licked her lips and gasped, "What are *you* doing here? We thought you were dead!"

"Dead?" said Lionheart, frowning and stepping back.

"Yes, dead!" said the baroness, and her gray-streaked hair escaped from its pins and bobbed in tight curls about her forehead. "First you, then Prince Foxbrush and my sweet ducky . . . all disappeared! They say you were spotted about the grounds the day of the wedding, and that you and the crown prince murdered each other over Daylily's hand, down in the Wilderlands somewhere." Her eyes widened still more. "Did you not murder each other after all? Or . . . or are you a ghost?"

"I'm no ghost, Baroness, and Foxbrush, last I saw him, was alive." And now the question he dreaded most to ask. "How long since the crown prince disappeared?"

"Six months," said the baroness. She gazed wetly up at Lionheart, and more tears brimmed in her red-rimmed eyes. "Six months to the day, almost! He vanished soon after my own sweet girl did—on their wedding day, more's the pity. Two weddings spoiled! That's got to be bad luck, don't you think? And her lovely dress all ripped to shreds . . ."

As she spoke, the baroness's gaze darted momentarily to the door. Lionheart followed that glance, then strode across the room and shut the door firmly, locking it and pocketing the key. He turned to face the baroness again. The baroness, who sat at his mother's own desk in his mother's own chambers. Granted, Queen Starflower had died years ago. But the queen's rooms remained hers until such a time as a new queen might be crowned.

The desk that had once held documents of state now supported an assortment of perfumes and jewelry and feathered accessories. From that desk, Queen Starflower had given orders and made rulings equal to those of her husband. Now the Baroness of Middlecrescent sat there, looking twice the fool she was by comparison.

It was a crime for such a woman to sit in his mother's place.

Lionheart swallowed back the bile in his throat. The idea that six months might pass in what had seemed only a night did not disturb him as much as it might have once upon a time. But six months was a long time to a kingdom without an heir.

"There," he said to the baroness, patting the pocket where the key now lay. "No one will disturb us, not for a little while at least. Tell me what has transpired since Foxbrush's disappearance. Why, pray tell, are the barons gathering now? Why did I see royal insignias among the arriving carriages? Why is this House done up for a festival?" *And why do you sit in my mother's chair?*

"It's the coronation," the baroness said, mauling her handkerchief in twisting fists. "They're all here for the coronation tomorrow morning."

"The Eldest?" Lionheart asked. "My father?"

The baroness sniffed and dabbed at her face again. "Poor, poor King

Hawkeye!" she said. "He died soon after Prince Foxbrush did. Or, I mean, soon after we thought Prince Foxbrush did. No one told him about the murder . . . if there was a murder. Did you murder him? I don't even know! But we couldn't bear to tell the Eldest; he was already so low after banishing you. He slipped off gently enough in the end, and he's with the dear queen now, interred and safe."

Her sniffs grew louder, and Lionheart feared he might lose her entirely to a storm of sobs. He grasped her by the shoulders, gave her a shake, and demanded, "If my father is dead and Foxbrush supposed so, who are they crowning tomorrow morning? Who has been named successor?"

He did not need her answer. And it was just as well he didn't, for at that moment, the door handle rattled.

"My dear?" came the Baron Middlecrescent's voice from the hall. "My dear, have you locked me out?"

"Oh!" The baroness stared up at Lionheart, and her face, red from crying, went ghastly white. "Oh, he'll *kill* you if he finds you here!"

She was on her feet in a moment, grabbing Lionheart's hand and pulling him across the room. A great, floor-to-ceiling wardrobe stood against the wall, in which Queen Starflower had once stored documents of relative importance. The baroness flung it open now, revealing an array of crinolines and petticoats. "Quick, inside!" she whispered even as the baron rattled once more at the door.

Lionheart obeyed without a thought, climbing in behind a curtain of petticoats scratchy with lace (a style far too heavy for Southlands' heat but all the rage among the courtly ladies nonetheless). "Give me the key, and hurry!" the baroness snapped, and once more Lionheart did as he was told. There was something altogether strange and a little horrifying about hearing such tones of command from the soft mouth of the baroness. He fished the key from his pocket and pressed it into her plump hand. "Now keep quiet as a wee mousy!" she hissed, shutting the wardrobe door in his face.

Lionheart put his eye to the crack between the doors and watched. The baroness bustled across the room, answering her husband's calls in a fluttery voice. "Oh dear! Oh gracious! Oh, Lumé! I've misplaced the key, my love!"

"Do hurry, sweetest one," said the baron from the other side, his voice just verging on the fringes of patience. Lionheart pondered the advantages of having everyone in the world assume one to be a complete fool. After all, he had spent about five years as a jester himself.

But the baroness is not so cunning, he thought. *Or . . . is she?*

The baroness opened the door at last and stood fanning herself with her handkerchief as her husband stormed into the room, scowling but unsuspecting.

"Oh my! What could have come over me?" she gasped. "I thought I'd put it on my little table, but it wasn't—"

"Never mind, darling," the baron growled. He wore gorgeous robes similar to but newer than the robes of office worn by Eldest Hawkeye himself. They were light and flowing but heavily embroidered after the fashion of Southlands, and the fibula pinning his cloak was shaped like a seated panther.

The emblem of the crown prince.

The baron moved to Queen Starflower's desk and began riffling through one of the drawers. He looked over his shoulder, suddenly scowling as he took in his wife's attire, a ruffled dressing gown tossed over several layers of petticoats and a corset. "You're not clothed to come down. Have you rung for your ladies?"

"Oh no," said the baroness with a heavy sigh and sank into a chair. She fanned herself still more and dabbed at her forehead. "I just don't think I could face it tonight, beloved." If a voice could be fluffy, hers was like duckling down. "Not with our dear girl still missing, and that dreadful Baron of Blackrock always makes such eyes at me, and I so dislike those barbarous foreigners from the north, and—"

Although the baron could boast not so much as a trace of beauty, at the moment he turned upon his wife he looked startlingly like Daylily, whose face always concealed such a storm of fury behind the most placid of masks.

"You aren't coming down?" he asked.

"That's what I'm *telling* you, dear," the baroness replied with a twirl of her handkerchief. "I just can't seem to find the will for it. And with tomorrow being what it is, I think it best if I go to bed early and get my beauty sleep—"

"You are my wife," said the baron. "You are to be Queen of Southlands. You *will* attend me on this night of feasting, and every night I desire. You will support me."

The baroness, seemingly oblivious to the daggers in his voice, sighed and put a hand to her forehead. "Oh, sweetest love, I just can't seem to manage it! I do think it cruel that they're putting up such a fuss and feasting when dear Hawkeye is scarcely cold in his grave. If our own Daylily were back already, then maybe . . ."

The baron's cold fish eyes narrowed. "Daylily is not coming back."

"How can you say that?" cried the baroness, sitting upright in her chair. "How can you say that, husband? Really, you are too cruel sometimes! Of course she's coming back. Prince Foxbrush went to rescue her."

"Prince Foxbrush is dead. How often must I tell you this?"

"Nonsense, he can't be dead" was her reply. She settled back in her chair, her face all practical reason. "He's gone to rescue our ducky, and you can't expect heroism to happen overnight. He might even now be facing a dragon for her dear sake! How can you give up on them so easily?"

Middlecrescent ran a hand down his face, which was now more tired and vulnerable than Lionheart remembered ever seeing it. For the first time in his life, Lionheart wondered if even the baron might be human.

"Why must you be so against this rise of ours, my dear?" he said. "Why do you resist my kingship? Don't you realize what this means for your house as well as mine? Don't you see the good of Southlands in our ascension?"

"Oh, don't be silly, dear," said the baroness with a dismissive toss of her curls. "You know I don't know about such things. My mind goes whirling when I try to think about it!"

The baron's mouth worked as though he wanted to speak. Instead, he returned to his search of the desk. After riffling through papers and not finding what he wanted, he slammed a drawer. "You think I'm wrong, don't you," he said, his back still to his wife. "You think what I do is . . . evil."

"What makes you say such a thing?" said she, tilting her head. "You're my husband."

"Then why," said he, turning suddenly and fixing her with the full force of his large eyes, "will you not come down?"

"I've *told* you and I've *told* you!" said she, sounding very like a child. "I think we should wait for Foxbrush to return! With our Daylily. How silly would you feel, husband, if they were to come out of the Wilderlands in another day or two and you had to step down from the throne?"

A muscle in the baron's broad forehead ticked. Lionheart could almost hear his teeth grinding. Then he said: "I have mastered Southlands as no Eldest in a hundred years has mastered it. Even with the Dragon's poisoning of our fields and our people, I have brought it under my rule. Hawkeye never united the people so. Foxbrush never could. Even that fool, Lionheart, had he not betrayed his own with loyalties to demons and monsters, could never have brought the strength to Southlands' throne that I will bring! I am the true Eldest, even if no royal blood flows in my veins. And to this, all the barons have agreed."

The baroness replied with a guileless smile, "Only because you forced them. Only because they're afraid of you."

A long silence crackled the air between them. In that silence, Lionheart could hear a future of screaming and bloodshed and doom. He waited, unable to breathe, for what he knew must follow from the fire burning behind the baron's cold eyes.

At last, however, the baron sighed. He crossed the room and caressed his wife's plump cheek. "But you aren't, are you, my dear?"

"Aren't what?" asked she, blinking.

"Afraid of me."

"Oh no!" said she, getting to her feet and taking him in her arms. "Silly man! Why would you ever ask that?"

And she kissed him. Lionheart moved away from the wardrobe door, embarrassed at glimpsing such a tender moment between the baron and his wife. He felt his face flushing and dared not look out again for some moments, though he could guess a little at what went on by the lack of talk without.

Finally he heard the baron say with a deep sigh, "Very well, my love. Stay here if you must. Rest and make yourself easy while I face the vipers below. But tomorrow, you will wear the robes I ordered, and you will take the crown when I place it on your head, and you will be the queen I make of you."

The baroness giggled. "Have a nice supper, sweetest," she said.

The stamp of feet, the opening and shutting of a door, the click of a lock, and Lionheart dared breathe again. But the baroness's hurrying footsteps across the room made him draw himself upright just as she flung wide the wardrobe door.

"Get out!" she said, beckoning with both flustered hands. "Hurry, hurry!"

He stumbled into the room, tripping on petticoats. When he saw the baroness crossing the room to her bellpull, he gasped. Would she summon the guards? But why would she give him away now when she hadn't to the baron?

"What are you doing?" he demanded sharply, wondering if he should tie her up or gag her or both.

She looked around at him, her mouth a little O of surprise. "Why, I'm ringing for my page boy, of course."

"What for?"

"So you can clunk him on the head and take his livery." At Lionheart's openmouthed stare, the baroness shook her curls, laughing. "You don't think you're going to stop the coronation without a disguise, do you? Don't be a ninny, and get behind that door. You must do your part, or there's no way we can have ourselves a rebellion!"

12

THAT A VOICE COULD BE HEARD above the lion's roaring was testimony both to its wrath and its range.

"Little *BOY* did you call me?"

Foxbrush lay in a pile of helpless horror, his vision one moment full of teeth and mouth and all things ravening . . .

The next moment, full of woman. And such a woman!

She was tall and willowy but simultaneously full and completely feminine, with legs long as a gazelle's and shoulders straight and bare above a dress made entirely from ferns held together by who-knows-what magic. Her skin color shifted from white as snow to dusky shadows, like a forest's ever-changing visage. Her hair fell in thick black coils about her face, but was grown over with moss and leaves and flowers that seemed to blossom from the hair itself. Vines coiled up her bare arms and legs, living bangles, and more flowers bloomed on these.

The only similarity between her and the child of a moment before were those red-rimmed, furious eyes.

"Do you want to call me a *boy* again?" she demanded.

A woman's wrath is a thunderbolt, quick and electrifying, or so the poets say. Foxbrush, as he lay beneath the fir tree and watched this vision of exquisite beauty descending upon him like the bolt of a lightning god's lance, trembled with the terror of her beauty. Her fists were raised as though to strike, and though they were the most perfectly formed fists in the worlds, Foxbrush did not doubt they would slay him.

But she stopped at the last moment, and her enraged face twisted into an expression of surprise. She took a step back. The white lion—a lioness, really, and all the more vicious for it—padded up beside her and snarled, black lips wrinkling back to better display a set of amazingly bright teeth.

"I know, I know," the woman said, as though in response to the lioness. "I see it too. But are you quite sure?"

The lioness shook her massive head. Tall though the beautiful woman was, the animal's ears still reached as high as her shoulder.

Foxbrush stared from one to the other, and it crossed his mind that he'd rather not die. He tried to swallow and couldn't, so it was with a dry throat that he said, "Um, may I—"

"Quiet!" snapped the woman, and the lioness's lip curled again. They circled, the woman one way, the lioness the other, until both had circumnavigated their prey and stood once more before him.

"It's true, then," the woman said, as if something had been decided that Foxbrush could not guess. The expression on her face was of displeasure.

But the lioness settled down into a comfortable position, no longer snarling, and began grooming one of her colossal paws as though she had no further interest in the matter. She spread her toes and chewed them thoughtfully, her eyes half closed with dozing.

The woman, on the other hand, crossed her perfectly rounded arms and narrowed her eyes. Tears still clung to her lashes. She said, "Speak, mortal!"

Foxbrush opened his mouth but found he didn't know what to say. Usually if he started talking, something would happen, but now there simply were no words. Worse still, he felt a sneeze coming on, of all things. That horrid tickle behind his sinuses, that inevitable foretelling. And he hadn't a handkerchief!

"Um . . ."

"Speak!" The woman took a menacing step. "Tell me at once why you are on that Path!"

The tickle was getting worse. Were thistles hidden among the ferns? He'd always been allergic to thistles. "I . . . I do beg your most excellent pardon—"

"Well, you can't have it," she replied. "Tell me now. Why the Path?"

She would have sounded petulant were her tone not that of honey and velvet and vanilla cream all rolled into one. The very smell of her was heady and wonderful. And it did not help the oncoming sneeze. Lights Above, was he allergic to *her*?

He grabbed his nose and caught the sneeze so that it burst angrily in his head and ears. "Um. Pardon me," he gasped, rubbing his eyes.

The woman stared at him. "Did you explode?" she asked.

He shook his head.

Her eyes narrowed. "I think you exploded."

"No," he protested thickly. "No, I'm still quite whole."

"Are you magic?" she demanded.

Again he shook his head. "No. I'm not. I'm just—"

"Then what are you doing on that Path?"

"What path?"

"*That* one, of course!" said she, and pointed at his feet. He looked but saw nothing other than crushed ferns and pine needles. Twisting in place, he sought some other sign of a path nearby. As far as he could discern, there was none.

As the woman watched him, her fury dissipated into curious interest. "Don't tell me you can't see it."

"Your pardon, my . . . my lady," he gasped, then sneezed again, once more startling her so that she stepped back and stamped one of her feet like a nervous filly. Foxbrush wasn't entirely certain that "lady" was the correct form of address for this maiden who *certainly* would not be welcome in the courts of the Eldest attired thusly. But it seemed the safe bet at the moment. "I see no path."

"Ha." The first sound was not a real laugh. But the next "Ha!" she gave, was. Then she tossed her bounty of hair, and her fern dress rustled, and the vines on her arms writhed as she laughed for real. "You walk the Path of the Lumil Eliasul, and you *don't even know it*!"

She shrieked as though it were the finest joke she'd ever heard. The lioness, by contrast, looked up from her grooming, gave a disinterested sniff, and put back her ears.

"If I might inquire," Foxbrush managed with some shred of dignity when at last she seemed to be quieting. "What is this, um, Lumil Elia-something, please?"

He might have been the stupidest thing to ever crawl out from under a rock for the look she gave him. Foxbrush died a little on the inside; a man doesn't like a woman such as she to look at him that way.

"The Lumil Eliasul?" she said, shaking her wild hair and blinking her amazing eyes. Everything about her, every movement, every word, was huge, not in its size but in its power. Even the trimness of her waist was huge in its own way. "The Prince of Farthestshore? The One Who Names Them, the Song Giver, the Eshkhan, the . . . I don't even remember all his names! Don't you know *any* of them?"

"Um. Well, Farthestshore sounds familiar."

"It *should*!" Another shake of her head, and flowers dropped their petals in colorful cascades from her hair. "He's only the Lord of all the Faerie folk, son of the King Across the Final Water. Even *I* am subject to the Lumil Eliasul!"

"And, um, who are you, please?" Foxbrush asked.

"WHO AM I?"

The whole forest around them shook with the enormity of her ire. Foxbrush squawked and hid his face in his hands, and even the sneeze that had been building vanished as he curled up into a fetal ball, expecting imminent smiting.

But the lioness put up her head and gave a loud whuffle, effectively snatching the gorgeous woman's attention.

"Did you hear what he just said?" the woman demanded of the lioness, pointing at Foxbrush with both hands. "Did you *hear* him?"

The lioness grunted and shook her ears again, her face patient and serene.

"Oh, fine. Fine, fine, fine!" said the woman. She rounded on Foxbrush once more, rolling her eyes at his quivering form, but her voice was less piercing when next she spoke.

"I am Nidawi the Everblooming, Queen of Tadew." Her face sagged a little, though it became no less beautiful. And she amended her previous statement with a quieter, "Queen of Tadew-That-Was."

Foxbrush looked up between his fingers just in time to see the woman crumple, sinking into the form of the wild child once again. She buried her face in her hands and burst into another round of stormy tears, more violent than the first.

The lioness got heavily to her feet and padded over to the child. She put out her raspy tongue and began licking the back of the child's head until her mass of hair and moss stood all on end. The child pushed ineffectually at the insistent muzzle and even took an angry swipe at the lioness's nose. But the lioness, ever patient, ignored this and went on with her grooming until Nidawi had quite finished her cry.

Then both turned to Foxbrush, who still lay where he had fallen, watching all with horror. Even an interview across from Baron Middlecrescent's fish-eyed stare would be preferable to the gazes of the lioness and her now-small mistress.

Nidawi the Everblooming said, "Say you're sorry."

"For what?" Foxbrush gasped, but when he saw her face screwing up to a violent degree, he quickly sputtered, "Sorry!"

Oddly enough, this seemed to pacify the child, who got to her feet, all legs and elbows, now standing nowhere near as tall as the lioness's nose. She crossed the short distance to Foxbrush and stood over him, imperial as the queen she claimed to be but rather less majestic with slime on her face and puffy eyes. Up close, however, he saw that these eyes were the shade of demure violets hidden in the deepest shadows of the forest. And her lashes were dark green like pine needles.

She looked him up and down, considering, her head tilted a little to one side, a stance mirrored by the lioness a few paces behind. Then Queen Nidawi said, "You are from *There*."

He snuffled back another sneeze. "Pardon?"

"There. The Other Place. The Near World, the Time-bound land. What are you doing *Here*?"

"I . . . I hardly know," Foxbrush replied. "I'm not even certain where *here* is. I raced my cousin down the gorge, and we're searching for my betrothed, Lady Daylily of Middlecrescent. I thought the . . . the wind, I suppose, said something about her, though I might be mistaken, and I hope . . ."

He stopped talking, for he saw that the child was paying him absolutely no mind. Rather, she was staring at the space over his head, her mouth moving as she muttered to herself in a voice that began out of Foxbrush's range of hearing but which swiftly rose to a near unbearable pitch.

"Here. There. There. Here. Here and There!" She clapped her hands and spun about in place, scattering petals in a rainbow storm all around her. "Here and There! Are you a king?"

With this last, she fixed her gaze with such fire upon poor Foxbrush that he thought he might actually melt. He quickly shook his head, wondering if it was safe for him to get to his feet, scarcely daring with the lioness standing so near. "Um. No," he replied. Then, sniffling, he added, "Not yet anyway."

"Then you will be!" exclaimed Nidawi the Everblooming. "You will be, which means you are, which means you *always have been*! The King of Here and There!"

She whirled again, and when she came full around, she was once more the gorgeous woman, not so tall this time, her face more youthful (though no less dreadful) in its eagerness. "You are the King of Here and There! And you will marry me!"

"What?"

Foxbrush leapt to his feet, though he fell back into the arms of the fir tree, which tickled and pinched him unkindly. One branch prodded into his trouser pocket and pulled out the scroll, which it tossed to roll through the ferns.

Before Foxbrush could reclaim himself from the tree, Nidawi pounced, plucking up the scroll between a long index finger and equally long thumb. Before Foxbrush could think to make a protest, she experimentally stuck the end of the scroll in her mouth. She made a face, pulled it back out, and opened it.

"What's this?" she said, frowning. "I can't read this. Are these evil signs? Witch work?"

"Please, that's mine!" Foxbrush gasped. The lioness growled. "Or rather, take it. It's yours. It's a gift. For you." He shrugged, trying to look anywhere but at the lioness. "I didn't want it anyway."

Nidawi put the paper to her mouth once more and licked it. Another unhappy face, and she tossed it over her shoulder, where it curled up on itself like a frightened hedgehog. Nidawi smiled at Foxbrush.

"I like presents," she said. "And I like you. When shall we wed?"

With that, the Everblooming stepped toward him, her eyes so full of otherworldly feelings that she was quite a terror to behold. She placed her hands on Foxbrush's chest and would have kissed him had he not, in that moment, sneezed. This startled her into stepping back, and he took the opportunity to drop to his knees and crawl rather desperately away. He was just putting out a long arm, trying to reach his scroll, when he felt her hands on his shirt and belt, hauling him back.

"Come here, king!" the Faerie woman demanded, and with amazing strength set him on his feet, spun him around, and looked at him with the most brilliant set of eyes. The colors of them swirled from violet to gold with flecks of green and deeps of blue. They were the eyes of a whole forest, all rolled into tiny points of light. And they were irked.

"Don't you like me?" Nidawi asked.

"Oh no! I mean . . ." Foxbrush's head was light and whirling, for the nearness of her was a bath of summer wine, intoxicating, thrilling, and a little messy. It would be too easy for an ordinary man to forget himself, to forgo his responsibilities and commitments, to become lost in the smell of flowers in her hair and never be heard from again.

"I'm engaged!" he cried in a last desperate defense, grabbing her hands and pushing them away as gently as he could. One might just as easily dislodge mountain roots.

Nidawi's eyes narrowed, and her perfect posy of a mouth bloomed into a full pout. "Engaged?" she said, taking a step back. The lioness muttered behind her. "Engaged to whom, may I ask?"

Her fingers loosened, and Foxbrush took advantage of the moment to back away into the shushing ferns. The lioness and Nidawi watched him, and he knew it would be foolish to try running, so he swallowed, his throat constricting painfully, and tried to straighten his hopelessly bedraggled shirt. "To Daylily, Lady Daylily, the woman I mentioned before."

"You never mentioned a woman," said Nidawi, who was not the sort to remember any woman besides herself. Tears brimmed yet again. "Faithless, heartless, cruel man—" she began.

"No, no!" Foxbrush put out both hands. "Please don't cry! It's . . . it's nothing against you, I assure you. You are by far the loveliest woman I've ever clapped eyes upon—"

"Oh, well, that's settled, then," said Nidawi, and her tears vanished at once behind a satisfied smile. "If I'm lovelier than this Daylily creature, then who cares if you break off with her to marry me as you should?"

Foxbrush rubbed his nose and took another tentative step back. Though not the most insightful man in the worlds, even he could conclude that now was not the time to mention his intention of ending his betrothal to Daylily. The lioness flicked an ear his way, and he froze once more. "It's a, um, a matter of honor. I must honor my promise to her. And I must find her as well. So you see, I don't have time to marry anyone else."

"Find her?" said Nidawi, her pout returning. "Find her, why?"

Foxbrush breathed a heavy sigh and dropped his gaze. He saw the scroll lying near, a little mangled by Nidawi's pearly teeth. "She ran away into the Wilderlands. I'm not sure what became of her, but I must—"

"If she ran away," the Everblooming said, settling down to the ground as elegantly as though she sank into the cushions of a fine couch, "she can't like you very much, so I don't see why you make these protests. Come. Sit by me." She patted the ferns beside her, smiling invitingly and making Foxbrush's stomach drop. "I like you well, and besides, I need you to kill someone for me. She can't say that much, now, can she?"

For a brief, thrilling moment, Foxbrush almost took one step, then another, then sank into those alluring immortal arms. All thoughts of his life and his mission and his world could so swiftly be forgotten.

But a timely sneeze returned enough of his sense that her words sank even to the dullest places of his mind. "I'm not killing anyone," he said, rubbing his nose.

"Not yet." Nidawi ran long fingers through her own hair and shrugged prettily. "But you will. Which means you have, which means . . . Oh! *So much!* Now come here, mortal king, and let me kiss you."

Foxbrush fled.

He did not run, for he knew that it would do no good, but he turned on heel and walked very fast, stopping only long enough to grab up the scroll as he went. His face flushed deeply with something between panic and dread, and his heart thudded madly in his breast. He could easily imagine the tear of the lioness's claws in his back, the fire, the rip, the end. . . .

His hands in fists, he strode as fast as he could, and the trees parted to make way, though he did not notice this. He knew the name of the Everblooming. What child in Southlands did not? She featured in many rhymes and nursery tales, even in the *Ballad of Shadow Hand*, if he remembered correctly.

But that was just it. This nursery story wanted to—he nearly choked at the thought—wanted to *kiss* him! This children's book character, this figment of some strange man's even stranger imagination! Real and voluptuous and terrifying and . . .

It was too horrid. He must escape.

"Where are you going?"

"GAHHHH!"

Her voice in his ear propelled Foxbrush into a faster pace, though he maintained enough control over himself to keep from breaking into a full-out run. "I . . . I . . ." He panted, for she had drawn up beside him, striding on her long legs, the leaves of her gown fluttering. Foxbrush could feel the silent thud of the lioness's feet behind. "I am simply, um, going . . ."

"I haven't told you whom to kill yet," she said, using a patient voice that was more terrible even than her wrath. "You mortals really are odd beasts, aren't you?"

"I'm sorry," he said, trying but failing to outpace her, for she matched her stride exactly to his. And his own wasn't great in any case, what with his shoes falling apart and leaving bits of themselves in his wake. "I really can't kill anyone. And I really can't marry you either!"

"Oh, that's what you say *now*," Nidawi replied with a merry laugh. "But you'll change your mind. Mortals always do. I'll make you a Faerie king, and though I won't give you three lives, I'll give you one nice *long* one. You mortals like that, don't you?"

He caught another sneeze. His head was beginning to throb. Why, oh why had he not thought to grab an extra handkerchief before setting off on this fool's errand? "I think you're very kind, my lady," he said, "but I prefer the life I've always had, humble though it may be."

"A *mortal* life?" she asked, a sneer in her voice.

He nodded and she fell silent beside him. The trees cast their green shadows around them, and Foxbrush noticed for the first time that he heard no other sounds besides his own footsteps and the beat of the lioness's paws. Nidawi moved without even a murmur of her fern-leaf gown, and there were no birds in the trees.

A grove of five thin silver-branch trees grew up nearby. Nidawi saw them and twisted her pretty mouth thoughtfully. "I'll take you back to *There* if you like, my king," she said, and her voice was quieter than it had been hitherto. "I'll take you back to the mortal realm."

"I . . . I can't go before I find Daylily."

"Lumé's crown," she snapped, and her long-fingered hand clamped down upon his arm. "If I never hear another word about this chit of a mortal girl of yours, it'll be too soon!"

She whirled him about to face her. She was suddenly neither a young woman nor even a child, but a much older woman, stern, beautiful, not alluring so much as commanding. There were streaks of silver amid the black and green of her hair, and her large eyes glowed with purple fire.

"I can't make you love me, but I can certainly make you obey me!" she snarled, and her voice was deep and dreadful, and it struck him in the gut. "You're going to the mortal realm, and you'll think about what I've told you. And when I come to you again, I hope you'll have a different song to sing into my ear!"

Foxbrush opened his mouth to speak but did not have a chance. For Nidawi the Everblooming pushed him violently. For a moment, he glimpsed silver branches overhead as he flew and he fell . . .

. . . and he lay stunned.

Several moments passed before he realized that he did not lie upon crushed ferns. Nor did the canopy of the Wood's branches and leaves close above his head but rather, blue sky, open and clear.

No sign anywhere of Nidawi or the lioness.

Foxbrush sat up, frowning, and looked about. He still clutched the scroll in one hand, and it comforted him, though he could not say why. Not many yards away stood the Wilderlands, casting long shadows that could not quite reach him. But he himself lay beyond its borders on rocks like the floor of a long-dry river. The gorge wall rose steeply behind him.

Frowning, Foxbrush got to his feet and brushed himself off. How he had come to be here, he could not guess. Had everything in recent memory been no more than a dream?

"Hullo?" No one answered, neither the specters of his imagination nor even Lionheart, whom he thought might still be near. His head hurt where he'd struck it, and he rubbed it uneasily, groaning.

"I know," he muttered. "I know what happened. You hit your head when you slid down the trail. When Leo chased you. You must have knocked yourself out, and it's all been a crazed dream . . . the sylphs, the woman, the lion . . . all a dream."

But what a dream! Especially for a man who usually dreamed in numbers.

He shook himself out, noticing with dismay the tears in his shirt, the state of his shoes—both buckles missing—and the rents in his trousers.

He should have known better. He should have known better than to think he could find Daylily. Hero-ing was not for the likes of him.

Moving stiffly, too dizzy to make the climb, he started up the path, clutching the wall as he went. His sneezes were fading, so that was a mercy at least. He could draw a complete breath and his eyes were clearer. The sun was high and very hot overhead. He did not seem to have been unconscious very long, which was just as well. Strange that no one had come searching for him yet. They were probably all in a clamor at the Eldest's House, and when he returned and told his tale, they would nod solemnly, then laugh to themselves as soon as his back was turned.

Maybe he could sneak in unnoticed?

He flushed angrily. Oh, how the rumors would fly, and the jokes as well once it became public knowledge that Daylily had fled her own wedding. Was it evil for him to hope that she may have been abducted, not run off on her own?

Shaking his head at his own folly, he scrambled up the last of the path and slipped at the end, nearly vomiting his heart out in a moment of terror on the edge of the gorge. Then he gained the upper country and stood in the Eldest's grounds.

Only, they weren't the Eldest's grounds. They couldn't be.

For where the stump of the old fig should be stood a great, spreading, fruit-laden tree. And beyond, all was wild, dark, teeming jungle.

"Dragon's teeth," Foxbrush whispered, his hands turning cold. "Where am I?"

13

*THE BEATING OF A HEART. The thrilling sickness of a gut. The rush,
rush, rush of adrenaline coursing through veins.*

*How strange are these things called emotions, and how exhilarating.
How could one ever become accustomed to such sensations?*

The utter, ecstatic delight of terror!

She must be mad. Why else did she run from the shelter of the jungle?
Why else did she plunge through the screaming throng of women, pushing
them aside like so many frail dolls?

She must be mad. Why else was her voice upraised in something like
a scream or battle cry?

Daylily's feet beat the ground with painful insistency. She did not know
what she would do when she reached the well. Could a hero be taught to

slay a dragon before the dragon descended? Could a maid outsmart an ogre whom she had never met? As the challenge came, so must it be overcome.

She covered the distance to the well in mere moments. Only when she reached the lip of that churning water did she pause, and the wind caught at her hair and her gown so that to those watching she looked like some fiery angel poised on the brink of the Dark Water.

The well was green and black, a witch's caldron of bubbling evil.

The child can't live, some piece of her mind argued. *Not in that. He's drowned already. You cannot help.*

Dive! Dive!

Or die!

Daylily bared her teeth and plunged feetfirst into the water.

The surging froth and closing darkness was full of malevolence. Daylily felt it immediately, as thoroughly as she felt the cold. Water filled her nose, for she had not thought to take a proper breath, and she struggled upward for air. Her skirts closed around her legs, binding them. But she broke the surface and gasped a half breath.

Something caught her ankle. Something pulled her down.

It was like being caught by waterweeds, slimy and clinging but stronger by far. She was pulled into a blackened world, and even when she opened her eyes, her vision was filled only with stinging murk. She struggled and kicked at whatever held her, but to no avail. Her sumptuous underdress weighed her down, and she sank farther than she would have thought possible into the coldness of the well. She thought her lungs would collapse with the need to breathe.

First, there were bindings upon her wrists. Second, she found that air was given her, though she did not know why or how. She breathed it in desperately, then opened her eyes.

Two white lanterns pierced the darkness of the well. Daylily looked into the face of Mama Greenteeth, who grinned, her fangs gleaming in the light of her own expressionless eyes. Then the apparition swam away, and Daylily followed the trail of light left by her eyes to see where she went. Across from her, not many feet away, was the stone wall of the well, perhaps man-made, perhaps lined with homey care by Mama Greenteeth herself.

The child was bound to the wall. Daylily saw he wore over his mouth a flower gleaming pale green in the light of the monster's eyes. A similar flower covered her own mouth, and she wondered if this provided the source of air. The little one was unconscious, she saw and was grateful for his sake.

Mama Greenteeth made certain of his bindings, then poked him cruelly. With that, she pulled out from some crevice a handful of wafers and began to eat them. But the light in her eye as she studied the child said that she preferred warm meat to wafers.

Horrified, Daylily strained against her bindings. She could not see her hands, tied above her head. Her hair floated across her face, blinding her still more. But as it waved to and fro, she caught a glimpse of something at the very bottom of the well.

A leafy plant grew in the center, its big leaves stirring of their own volition. And from this grew, like a stalk or stem, the sinuous body of Mama Greenteeth herself.

Daylily's eyes stung with the murky water, and she could see nothing else clearly. But this she saw with the clarity of noonday, and she fixed her gaze upon it even as she worked her hands against her bindings.

Dive and die! Dive and die!

Daylily gnashed her teeth, tearing the flower the monster had secured over her nose and mouth to keep her alive and her blood fresh. Mama Greenteeth was still gnawing at her wafers, but one long finger and longer thumb pinched the child's arm, testing.

The time must be now. *Now!*

Daylily pulled. With strength she had never before possessed, she tore her hands through the bindings, shredding her skin and filling the well with the taste and scent of her blood.

Mama Greenteeth's slitted nostrils flared. She dropped the child's arm and turned. She saw her prisoner, struggling against the encumbrance of her wedding rags, swimming for the rooted plant at the well bottom.

Daylily grabbed a stout leaf, and though it waggled against her hold, she pulled herself down and wrapped her hands around the very base of the plant, right down to the roots. She did not look up, even when the roar of Mama Greenteeth reverberated through the water and struck her with a hammer force. She braced herself against the muddy floor and, using her own weight as a lever, pulled.

Mama Greenteeth reached her just as she pulled, and a clammy, claw-tipped hand struck Daylily across the face, tearing streaks down her cheek. But Daylily did not lose her hold, and she pulled a second time. Mama Greenteeth screamed and shuddered as the plant came partially loose. She lashed out again, tearing the flower from Daylily's face.

Immediately all was dark and drowning and the life-ending pressure of deep water. Even the lantern eyes of Mama Greenteeth vanished, and Daylily felt she was alone in the well, and her last moments were upon her.

A wolf in her mind. Bound to four stakes. Paralyzed by a stone of bronze. Only the red rolling of bloodshot eyes.

And then—a snarl!

Daylily snarled. One last time, she hauled on the plant, putting all the strength of her remaining life into her effort.

Roots sprang up from the mud.

The wail of Mama Greenteeth exploded from the well in a geyser rush. The sobbing women around the well clutched their children and pulled them back, and the men running from the village stopped in their tracks, eyes wide at the sight. Sun Eagle stood hidden in the jungle shadows, watching all, and his face was like a rock, but his mouth moved as he whispered: "You'll live. You'll forge the bond."

The great fountain of Mama Greenteeth's shriek fell back in a splash all around the well. And when it flowed away and the people gathered dared look once more, they saw a strange figure lying partially draped over the well stones, clinging to land.

It was Daylily, her red hair flattened across her blood-streaked face like a veil, her undergown clinging to her limbs. She held the child in her arms.

She must be dead. But this was not the Netherworld, where the dead wander, this place of swirling darkness and pain. Or perhaps it was. After all, the last time she stepped through Death's gateway and descended the long road into his world, she had been one of the living. Perhaps the pain and darkness were saved only for the truly dead.

Then her body convulsed.

Daylily coughed up a flood of dark water. Her ears swam with wet and distant sounds, but they were living sounds. And the thud of her heart, painful against her breastbone, told her she was not yet passed to the Realm Unseen.

The women of the village held back from the well even after the burst of water left the two sodden figures lying like drowned corpses upon the edge. Then the skinny young girl gave a cry and sprang forward, reaching for the child and for the strange ghostly maid who was his rescuer.

But Sun Eagle was there first. He took Daylily in his arms and held her upright in time for more water to cascade from her lips in a sickening gush as her stomach heaved and lungs burned. She pushed her heavy hair back from her face and, though she did not yet remember what she sought, instinctively looked for the child. She found him mewling in his sister's clinging arms. He was alive.

"I saved him."

The worlds crashed and danced in Daylily's mind as she clutched Sun Eagle and lay upon the bank. Her body, relearning to breathe, shuddered and shivered even in the heat. But her thudding heart soared to the heavens. "I saved him!"

"You did, Crescent Woman," Sun Eagle replied, and she blinked without recognition up into his triumphant face. "You have proven yourself. You are a warrior."

The men from the village, tools brandished like weapons, swarmed down the incline, joining the women and children. They hesitated at what they saw. Should they attack these strangers, this otherworldly girl with her bright hair, this savage youth with blood on his hands and face? But the skinny girl, her sibling held close as though she would never let go, caught Daylily's hand in her own and kissed it again and again. Then she began to speak, garbled and quick. Daylily wondered if it was the sobs that made her words incomprehensible, or if she spoke another language entirely, an older, wilder language.

Sun Eagle, still crouched with his hands supporting Daylily's shoulders, said, "She wants to know how she may repay you."

"Repay me?" Daylily ineffectually wiped water from her eyes. "No," she said, her voice a whimper. "No, no payment."

A woman and a man reached them now, the parents of the two children. They put their arms around the girl, helping her to her feet. The mother grabbed the little one and held him, weeping, to her shoulder. But the skinny girl would not release her hold on Daylily's hands. She continued speaking earnestly, tears flowing down her cheeks.

"No, please!" Daylily said, frightened somehow by the intensity in those words she could not understand. She turned to Sun Eagle. "Please, tell her I want no payment!"

But Sun Eagle shook his head solemnly. "You cannot deprive her of that right," he said.

Then he addressed the parents, speaking with swift assurance in their language, or a language very like it that they understood but Daylily did not. But Daylily watched the expression on the mother's face change, so full of relief one moment, so full of devastation the next. She reached out and put her arm around the skinny girl, drawing her to her side.

On the girl's face, all expression vanished.

The father stood by, unmoving save to adjust his grip upon the weapon in his hand, a wooden club set with a sharp stone at one end, a crude hammer. Sun Eagle, his voice low, even gentle, said his piece, then stood looking from father to mother.

The man stepped forward, his hammer upraised, and would have brained Daylily on the spot.

It was over before Daylily could react. By then, the man lay in screaming agony, his arm twisted too far behind him, so far it must be broken, and Sun Eagle's foot upon his neck, pressing his head into the ground. The mother screamed and dragged her children back, and the villagers all exploded in shouts and screams as well. Only then did Daylily find her voice.

"What are you doing? Let him go!" she cried. Though weak from her ordeal, she flung herself at Sun Eagle as though to drag him off. But she found the gathered crowd of villagers closing in, and she saw from their faces that she and Sun Eagle both would be torn apart in a moment.

Sun Eagle dropped his hold on the man, stepped away, and then took hold of the bronze stone about his neck and lifted it high. It flashed in reflective fire from the sun, so blinding that even Daylily shielded her eyes.

"In the name of my master!" Sun Eagle spoke in a language unknown but understood by all. "In the name of the Sacred Mound! By the bonds uniting the Far and Near, and the blood that must spill to make all things whole, I say to you: Stand down!"

The villagers drew back. Though they kept tight hold on their tools, their fists clenched in wrath, their eyes were full of terror, and they crowded against one another in their efforts to back away.

Sun Eagle took hold of Daylily, who was near collapsing once more. He supported her, keeping her upright until she found a tentative balance. The crowd parted with frightened murmurs as they made their way through, every man and woman bowing their heads as though to some dread sovereign. Only the children dared look, and they from safe hiding behind their parents.

Sun Eagle half carried Daylily, but he made her take each step, however slow, all the way back up the incline. Only once they had reached the sheltering jungle and were hidden from the villagers' eyes did he allow her to sink against him with a moan.

Gently, he helped her to kneel, then waited until her body stopped heaving up more water and sickness. He stroked the back of her head like he might stroke a dog, even after she had finished and merely sat unmoving in the dirt. Her once white underdress was brown, and leaves and bits of bracken clung to it.

"I'm sorry," she gasped at last.

"No," said Sun Eagle. "It was your first fight. You are brave."

Daylily wiped her mouth, shuddering with sickness, with fear, and even, she realized (and this was most strange), with pleasure. A sickening, sensational pleasure such as she had never before known. She looked up at Sun Eagle. "Why did that man try to kill me?" she asked.

"He did not want to pay the tithe," said Sun Eagle. "But he will. Following the Circle Ceremony, they will all pay their due."

14

FOXBRUSH STOOD ON THE EDGE of the gorge, exhausted, panting, seeing nothing familiar around him and yet—he rubbed his eyes so hard that sparks burst behind his eyelids—and yet he knew where he was. Only it was impossible, so he could *not* know it.

He swayed a dizzying moment as his eyes cleared of sparks. The jungle was still there, thick and moist and full of dreadful sounds. Enormous trees, trunks too broad for him to put his arms around, branches as thick as his waist, draped with starflower vines so dense that he could scarcely see a half dozen paces into the shadows . . . it was all too vivid. But none of it could be true.

"I'm still dreaming," Foxbrush told himself. "I'm lying at the bottom of that gorge and I'm dreaming, and I'll wake up in a minute with a splitting headache and . . . and by all the stars of the heavenly host, I'm going to *pound* that Leo when I see him!"

This last vow, accompanied by a string of curses, sapped Foxbrush of whatever energy remained to him. His knees buckled and he sat down beneath the spreading fig tree growing on the edge of the gorge. With a groan he bent forward until his forehead pressed into the ground, and sat in this broken attitude, unwilling to move ever again.

Something tickled his face. On reflex Foxbrush smacked, hitting himself but missing the tiny wasp, which flew out of his range and disappeared. Dropping his hand and blinking several times, Foxbrush tried to breathe.

Something tickled his neck. Once more he smacked, once more he missed, and another wasp flitted away.

Foxbrush closed his eyes, wondering if he could make himself sleep and perhaps wake up in the gorge where he should be, escaped from this nightmare. He drew three long breaths, hoping to calm his racing heart.

Something fist-sized and spherical landed hard on the back of his head, exploded, and filled the world with the fury of a hundred and more tiny wasps.

With a yelp, Foxbrush was on his feet and running from the tree, covering his ears, closing his eyes as the wasps followed him in a cloud. They stung his neck, his ears, his shielding hands; they stung any exposed skin they could find, and he screamed as pain like fire flowed under his skin.

He ran into a tree, fell in an agonized bundle, and lay at the feet of a tall stranger.

"Great hopping giants, you fool!" a rumbling voice bellowed. "Have you no sense?"

Foxbrush, however, did not understand the words, for they were not in a language he knew. He yelped and rolled, desperate to escape the wasps. The tall stranger, whom he had not yet seen—for the wasps were diving at his eyelids for all they were worth—leapt over Foxbrush's prone form and strode toward the fig tree, shouting as he went:

"Call them off, Twisted Man! Leave the dragon-kissed fool alone!"

A voice (that was in no measure human and spoke without words but that, somehow, Foxbrush understood as he did not understand the stranger) replied:

"He disobeyed! He violated! He lay upon my roots!"

"And it hasn't hurt you, has it?" the stranger replied.

"He violated! He broke treaty!"

"Well, he's sorry enough for it now. Call off your wasps!"

"Then pay his tribute!"

With a sigh, the stranger plunged a hand into a leather pouch at his side and withdrew a fistful of dried petals—water lily petals, had Foxbrush been capable of noticing. These he tossed at the roots of the tree under which Foxbrush had lain, shouting in a tuneless chant:

> *"Oh, Twisted Man, whose bark is thick,*
> *Who plunges rocks for wells to find,*
> *Here is tribute! Here is tribute!*
> *Take it, Twisted Man, and quick!"*

Completing this odd ritual with a clap of hands and a turn in place, the stranger ended with a bow in the tree's direction. The next moment, the branches stirred without a breeze and thick leaves rustled and buzzed as though a million wasps sang at once in reply. The wasps surrounding poor Foxbrush suddenly lifted as a single unit and flowed through the air in a swift stream, past the stranger and back into the shivering leaves of their tree home.

"Thank you," said the stranger with a wry smile. He saluted the tree once more, then turned to Foxbrush, who lay gasping where he had fallen, his eyelids red from the poisonous stings, welts covering his hands, his neck, and his face. The stranger grimaced, though Foxbrush could scarcely see it, so thickly were his lids swollen.

"Don't you know better than to lie beneath a black fig tree?" the stranger said, approaching Foxbrush and crouching beside him. Again, though he heard concern and even kindness in the stranger's voice, Foxbrush understood none of his words. He sat up, touched his stinging face, and groaned.

The stranger clucked, shaking his head, but he frowned as he looked over Foxbrush's clothing. "You're not from these parts, are you?" he said.

"Please, sir," Foxbrush said thickly, for even his tongue seemed to have been stung and now swelled in his mouth. "I don't know what you're saying. But . . . but thank you for . . . for whatever it was you did for me."

The stranger rose from his crouch and stepped back in surprise, his hands up as if in self-defense. He stared down at the young man before him, and his heart began to ram against his throat. Then he spoke in a different language altogether:

"You speak like a Northerner."

The accent was a little thick, a little harsh to Foxbrush's ears, and the cadence was unlike any he had heard before. But the words he knew.

The stranger knelt again, peering eagerly into Foxbrush's face, studying the complexion and the features, which were scarcely recognizable anymore, and frowning the while. "You're not a Northerner," the stranger said, "yet you speak like one. Do you come from the North Country? Did King Florien send you? How did you find the Hidden Land?"

Foxbrush's head swam with fear and poison. He opened his mouth, intending to introduce himself, to make some explanation, some apology, perhaps. But all that emerged was a sad little gurgle as he toppled to one side in a faint.

There was something sticky on his face.

Foxbrush disliked sticky things, particularly anywhere near his face. He raised a hand to wipe it off only to discover that—dragon's teeth!—his hand was sticky as well. In fact, as awareness slowly returned to him, bringing with it a monstrous headache, he discovered that stickiness covered the greater portion of his body, accompanied by a sweet smell that might have been pleasant under other circumstances. Under these, it made him gag.

He wanted to open his eyes, but the stickiness sealed his lashes together, and it took some effort to free them. By the time he succeeded, panic had made good headway into his outlook. After all, one does not like to wake up in unknown circumstances coated like a babe who got into the syrup jar.

He succeeded, however, after a certain amount of rubbing and straining (if you've never strained a resisting eyelid, you don't know what straining is) to free his lashes and crack his eyes open for a look at his surroundings. In that moment, he believed he could be surprised by nothing.

Thus he was all the more surprised to find Daylily's curious face hovering over his.

He did not scream. He might have, had his mouth not been sealed shut with the stickiness, but since it was, he could manage only a pathetic harrumph in the back of his throat. He did sit up rather abruptly and, discovering he wore no clothes, snatched at the skin pelt that had been spread over his nether regions and clutched it like a lifeline.

The face that was Daylily's backed up a little, still curious, her head tilted to one side, and Foxbrush realized this could not be his betrothed after all. For one thing, this was the face of Daylily as he'd first met her. That fateful day when, obliged to take part in a recreation of King Shadow Hand's triumph, he'd been dubbed the Damsel in Distress.

These memories were many years old now. But here sat Daylily's childhood image, complete with the tangle of wild red hair, though this girl's was held back with leather strings rather than ribbons. And she wore a sack-like garment of rough weave that Daylily would never have permitted near her person. Her doppelganger, however, did not seem to mind.

She inspected Foxbrush solemnly, and he noticed, despite his terror, that her eyes, unlike Daylily's, were dark brown.

"You're awake," she said, though at first he did not understand her. But when his horror receded enough for him to make an attempt at rational thought, he realized that he did know her words. Her accent was simply so strong that it might almost have been another language.

Foxbrush worked his jaw back and forth until he could crack his mouth open and speak through the stickiness. "Where am I?" he demanded hoarsely.

She frowned and stood up, backing away a little. "Da!" she called over her shoulder, never taking her eyes off Foxbrush. "The wasp man is awake!"

"Don't bother him!" rumbled a voice from without.

Foxbrush, however, could not understand any of his words and heard only the growl. He began to tremble anew and cried out, "I'm not hurting her, I swear! I'm merely lying here all . . . sticky. And I would like my clothes, if you please!"

"Stop talking," the girl said, making a disapproving face at him. "You chatter like a bird."

"Are you bothering the man, Meadowlark?" the voice rumbled again. There were footsteps, a curtain of woven reeds was pushed rustling aside, and Foxbrush had his first real glimpse of the man who had met him by the black fig tree.

He was a terrible sight.

Like the girl, he was crowned with a mass of red hair, which had crept down over time to give him a full, curly beard as well. But between forehead and mouth there was nothing to disguise the disfigurement of his face. One of his eyes looked as though it had been nearly torn out long ago, and the scarring and puckering of his skin had closed over it so that he was partially blind. The other eye too was surrounded by scars, and a large chunk was gone from his nose. The skin was tight and white in places, as though it had healed without the aid of stitches.

And when he grinned hugely, as he did at the sight of Foxbrush sitting upright on his pallet, clutching the skin pelt and dripping oozy medicine, he was by far the ugliest man Foxbrush had ever seen.

"Ah! You are awake indeed," the stranger said, ducking his head to step into the chamber, which was quite small and lit by only one window and the light that made its way through many chinks in the walls. Stooping so as not to knock his head on the ceiling, he put a hand on the girl's shoulder and looked Foxbrush over. "And much improved already, by the look of you."

He addressed Foxbrush in the same language as the child's, though with an accent nearer to Foxbrush's own. Still, it was an accent far more clipped than Foxbrush was used to hearing, though Foxbrush recognized most of the words.

"Please, sir," Foxbrush said, his head light and throbbing at the temples. "Who are you? Where am I?"

"I am Redman, and you are in the Eldest's House," the stranger replied and crouched, bringing his head nearly level with the girl's. "You had a nasty encounter with the Twisted Man and were all over wasp welts when I found you. My oldest girl here, Meadowlark"—he hugged the child to him—"has tended you with silver-branch sap, which is a great cure for wasp stings, if a little hard to wash off."

The girl did not shift her solemn dark eyes from Foxbrush's face. Her gaze made him more nervous. He tried to blink and found his lashes heavy. "Sap?" he managed to croak.

"Sap." Redman nodded. "And a few herbs and bits and pieces Meadowlark mixed with it. Nothing too foul, I promise you."

As the man spoke, Foxbrush's gaze began slowly to rove about, taking in his strange surroundings. He saw the walls made of stones, sticks, and mud. He saw the thatched roof and heard the birds roosting and the mice scurrying above. He saw the dirt floor covered with fresh rushes, the doorway hung with reeds, the pile of skins on which he lay, the pelt across his lap.

"Where are my clothes?" he asked, his voice a whimper.

"We had to cut them off you," said Redman. "Hymlumé's scepter! So many buckles and buttons! I never saw the like, certainly not around here. You see what's left of them there." He indicated a pile of fabric neatly folded in a corner of the tiny room. Foxbrush, turning sad eyes that way, saw that most of the buttons had, in fact, been removed, leaving gaping holes in his shirt and trousers.

The remains of his shoes, he realized, were adorning Meadowlark's small feet. He could see the toes of her right foot peeking out through a hole in the seam.

Foxbrush looked down at his nakedness and the ooze that covered his torso and arms. "What am I to wear?" he asked, a little desperate.

"Why, those of course, if you want them. They're still quite good enough for wearing, if not so fine as they were," Redman said. "Or we'll provide you with something more comfortable if you like. But look here . . ."

He reached out to the pile and took something from its depths. It was the scroll, a little battered but still in one piece. Redman unrolled it, scanning up and down the page. Surely such a wild beast of a man would not understand the content therein! But Redman's eyes—or at least the good one that Foxbrush could see—were intent, and his mouth moved a little as he struggled with the words.

The stranger turned to Foxbrush, holding up the scroll. "You had this writing on you. I can almost make it out, but it has been such a long time, and I have never been good with my letters. Tell me, is it yours?"

Foxbrush nodded. It was too dark in the room for him to clearly see the verses of the ballad, but he recognized the scroll well enough.

"Is it a message?" Redman persisted. "From the North Country, perhaps?"

"No," Foxbrush said, shaking his head. "No, it's mine. My cousin gave it to me."

"Your cousin?" Redman, shaking his head with some perplexity, allowed the scroll to roll up with a snap. "And you can read this?"

"Of course." Foxbrush wondered if he dared swipe the scroll from Redman's hands. It was a tempting if perhaps futile thought. After all, Redman was many times his height and girth, and he wasn't sticky with medicinal sap.

"You can read North Country writing?" Redman persisted.

"I . . . I'm not certain what you're asking," Foxbrush said, his voice a little petulant. Sap and fear had this effect on him. "When you say North Country, do you mean Parumvir?"

Redman chewed thoughtfully on the end of his mustache. "Parumvir," he said, tasting the strange name. "Parumvir . . . *Smallman*." Then he chuckled, and his good eye twinkled. "Very well, my friend. I have been away for some while, and I'm game for a change. So tell me, do you read the writing of *Parumvir*?"

Foxbrush nodded slowly but couldn't help adding, "It's not Parumvir writing. It's Southlander."

"*Southlander?*" Redman tapped the scroll absently against his own drawn-up knee. "Not a message for me from King Florien, then, eh?"

Foxbrush shook his head.

"And are you from . . . from Parumvir?"

"No. I'm—" He hesitated, and his sticky body suddenly went clammy with sweat. Did he dare, in this strange wherever-he-was, tell anyone his true identity? After all, one didn't like to blurt out in a houseful of savages, "I'm the crown prince! Unhand me at once!" So he licked his lips, tasting sugary sap with a bitter aftertaste of some herb he did not recognize.

"Don't eat it," said the girl, stepping forward and shaking a finger under his nose. Foxbrush recoiled from her as though she were armed, once more seeing Daylily all over that otherwise unknown little face.

"Don't bully him, Lark," Redman said, and she drew back beside her father. "Now," said he, "who did you say you are?"

"Um. Foxbrush," said that unfortunate prince. "I'm Foxbrush. May I have my scroll?"

Redman held it out, but though Foxbrush took the end of it, he did not release his hold. "And you're not from around here, are you, Foxbrush? Despite your name and your face, you aren't a man of the Hidden Land."

"Hidden Land?" Foxbrush whispered. Then a thought that had been nudging at the corner of his brain since Redman first spoke suddenly prodded its way into prominence. His eyes widened and his voice rose. "Lumé have mercy! Did you say the *Eldest's* House?"

"Yes," Redman replied. "Eldest Sight-of-Day is not home to make you welcome. We look for her return this evening, and then she'll decide what's to be done with you."

"She?" Foxbrush's head spun, and he had not the awareness of mind to catch the sharp expression Redman shot his way. "The Eldest is a woman? Where am I?"

"The natives call it the *Land*," Redman replied, his smile a little cold this time. "It is known in more distant realms as the South Land, however, being the southernmost peninsula of the western continent." He watched the play of shadows and lights trickling through the wall cracks move across Foxbrush's face. "But you know that already, don't you?"

Foxbrush felt Redman's stare and the equally compelling stare of his daughter. His mouth went dry with rising panic. "This is Southlands?"

"The South Land, yes."

At this, Foxbrush let go of the end of the scroll he'd been trying and failing to pull from Redman's grasp. He fell back upon the pile of skins, too dizzy to remain upright. Fur stuck to his skin and he groaned.

Redman, unimpressed, stood—or stood as much as he could in that low chamber. "I think," he said, "you need your rest. My daughter's salve will cure those stings soon enough, but you'd best not move too much in the meanwhile. Perhaps this evening you will be well enough to be brought before the Eldest. She will decide then what is to be done with you."

With a last look at it and a shrug, Redman tossed the scroll to land beside Foxbrush on his makeshift bed. He shook his head, puffed behind his mustache, then drew his daughter after him out of the room, saying to her in the language of the girl's mother, which did not come naturally to him:

"It's all right, child. The man is a little mad from the wasps, I think. You've cleaned him up well, though; your mother will be proud. Let him sleep now and we will see about him later."

"I like him, Da," the girl said. "He's funny. Even if he doesn't talk right."

"He's certainly something," Redman agreed, allowing the reed curtain to swing over the doorway as they exited. He looked back over his shoulder, eyeing that curtain as though he could see through it to the occupant of the chamber beyond. It had been many long years since he'd heard his native tongue, the language of the North Country, spoken by anyone beyond his small family. However thick this stranger's accent, the language itself was unmistakable. But how?

He must leave it for now; some mysteries could bear a wait before solving.

Foxbrush, however, lay panting in the near darkness. Birds in the thatching above him screamed noisily, and their voices were echoes of his own crazed mind. He reached out and, trembling, snatched up Leo's scroll.

"I've got to get out of here!"

Then he turned to the wall, grimacing but determined. After all, it was only made of mud.

15

Prince Felix of Parumvir was bored.

The advantage to this was that a bored face could easily be mistaken for an expression of solemn dignity. So he told himself he must look extraordinarily solemn and dignified now as he stood with the Parumvir ambassador to Southlands on one side and the Duke of Gaheris on the other, crammed into a high gallery in the newly rebuilt Great Hall of the Eldest's House.

Felix had been pleased enough when his father sent him as emissary from Parumvir to the coronation of the new Eldest. He'd never been to Southlands before. Indeed, he'd never been farther south on the Continent than Beauclair. And Parumvir, in recent history, had become rather . . . well, he hated to say, but it had somehow become a little small.

A lad cannot travel deep into the Wood Between and the worlds beyond without finding his former world tight about the seams upon his return.

An adventure down south was just what he needed, both he and his father, King Fidel, had agreed.

So here he was now, stuffed into a suit of peacock hues and a stiff collar dripping with jewels, far too hot for this southern clime, slowly melting away into a puddle of former princeliness. All for the sake of crowning some fellow who, rumor had it, was nothing short of a usurper.

"What happened to Lionheart?" Felix had asked Sir Palinurus, the ambassador at whose sumptuous house in the Eldest's City the prince was being hosted. "Was he not Eldest Hawkeye's heir? I heard some rumor about him."

Felix had heard more than rumor; he had actually met Lionheart in strange worlds beyond the borders of the mortal realm. But he'd never quite managed to talk to him or discover more than a few hints of his story. So he listened with interest as Sir Palinurus explained Prince Lionheart's disinheritance and his cousin Foxbrush's subsequent rise to power.

"All right. But then this Foxbrush fellow, he ran away?" Felix persisted. Rumor traveled swiftly across the Continent, yet Felix wasn't much of a gossip hound and found himself woefully lacking in details.

"Oh indeed, my prince!" Sir Palinurus agreed with almost as much vigor as a fishmonger's wife sharing a juicy tidbit. "On his very wedding day, he and the lady in question both vanished! It is rumored the former Prince Lionheart was seen upon the grounds that day, and some say that he abducted and murdered them both out of vengeance."

Felix, standing in the gallery now, mulled over this piece of information. He didn't think he believed it. Lionheart was a scamp and scoundrel who'd caused more than a little trouble in Parumvir, and Felix hadn't a great deal of love in his heart for the former prince, but . . .

But he had seen Lionheart lying dead upon a dark stone, stabbed through the heart by a unicorn's horn. And he had seen him return to life and stand in the presence of the Prince of Farthestshore.

These weren't memories Felix dared to share with any of those around him. No one would believe him, not even after all the recent doings with dragons and myths come to life. But he knew what he had seen.

Lionheart was no murderer. So perhaps Prince Foxbrush was not murdered?

It didn't matter, Felix decided with a shrug as he attempted to loosen his collar. All around him the Eldest's Hall was crowded with a glory of noblemen and women, holy clerics in robes of an old style, barons and dukes and kings of distant nations, all come to see the new Eldest of Southlands crowned. And really, was it any of Felix's business whom these dragon-eaten foreigners chose to make their king? He had only to stand here, representing his nation with dignity (or boredom), as was right and proper.

Some cleric began to chant, and others joined in. A solemn procession of men and women in holy garments marched stolidly up the hall, bearing incense and starflowers according to some old custom with which Felix was unfamiliar. The various barons of Southlands marched in the wake of the holy orders, each carrying the shields of their baronies, and they were also crowned in starflowers.

Somehow, the sight of all those artificial blossoms made Felix think of Dame Imraldera. He couldn't say why, exactly. Most things made him think of Dame Imraldera these days. She had saved his life, after all. And she was so very . . . wonderful.

His young heart sank to his stomach in a manner miserable yet not altogether unpleasant, and he lost himself momentarily in a melancholy dream. One day he would find her again. One day he would . . .

Hang on! Lord Lumé above, what was *that*?

Felix tried not to crane his neck too obviously as he watched the newest spectacle coming down the aisle. It was, he gathered, the soon-to-be queen, a plump, pleasant-faced woman squeezed into sumptuous garments that all but smothered her short figure. She was surrounded by ladies of the court, including the ambassador's wife, all of whom carried great bundles of paper starflowers in their hands.

And holding up her train in the back was the tallest, gawkiest, most shuffle-footed page boy Felix had ever seen in his life.

"Lionheart!" he whispered.

Felix knew him at once. Dressed in servants' livery several times too small for him, his head bowed and only partially hidden beneath a floppy, flower-rimmed hat, he clung to the train of the queen-to-be and did everything in his power to make himself unnoticeable. Surrounded as he was by all the grandeur of the courtly ladies, he very nearly succeeded.

But from where Felix stood, it was as though a beam of brilliant sunlight fell solely upon the head of the disinherited prince, making him impossible to miss.

Felix glanced from side to side, but no one around him seemed to have spotted the suspected murderer in their midst. Should he speak up? Should he shout some warning?

But the horns were blaring now, and the chant of the holy orders had risen to a tempestuous crescendo. The man who would be king—the Baron of Middlecrescent, whom Felix had not yet met—appeared at the end of the hall. All eyes fixed on him, all eyes, that is, except for Felix's. He stared at Lionheart shuffling into hiding behind the baron's wife. Hymlumé and all the starry host, did the woman actually turn and *wink* at her supposed page boy? Did she not know who he was? Or . . . or maybe . . .

Below the noise, skimming beneath the sounds of two hundred singing voices and great shattering horns, came a sound like silver and water flowing over smooth stone. A voice of birdsong that struck Felix's ear and caused him to turn his head. For a moment—a moment so brief, he must have imagined it—he saw the Prince of Farthestshore standing before him. Only he was standing in midair, which was impossible. That smile on his face, his hand pointing down toward the floor below the gallery—it was all a vision brought on by the heat and fancy clothes and odd foreign foods.

The moment passed. The vision was gone.

Felix, gulping, took a step forward and looked down over the gallery railing. He saw a man-at-arms directly below, dressed in red and armed with a tapered southerner's sword. Beyond the guard was a door, cracked open so that Felix could just see a curving stairway spiraling up.

The Baron of Middlecrescent was midway down the aisle now, moving in a stately stride, his head high, his cold, fish-like eyes staring before him as though daring anyone in that company to question his right to kingdom and crown. His wife smiled and clasped her hands at the sight of him, and behind her the disgraced prince crouched and watched and waited.

Felix looked at the armed man below, at the door, and back at Lionheart. He did not know what it meant, but he thought he heard the birdsong again. His muscles tensed, and he grabbed the gallery rail. Sir Palinurus placed a warning hand upon his arm, but Felix ignored him.

The baron drew near the front now and paused to receive a blessing from one of the holy men, to drink from a certain cup, and to offer the wreath of paper flowers on his own head in exchange for the crown to come. Then he strode up the steps of the dais, where the queen-to-be stood to one side. And the holy man in golden robes, flanked by others of his order, approached with the crown of Southlands glittering in his hands.

It was so near. The baron's eyes shone with the desire of it, and one could almost believe he would reach out and snatch it from the holy man's hands. But instead he flung back his gorgeous robes, prepared to kneel and make his vows to people and country.

Before he knelt, however, the page boy sprang out from behind the baron's wife, grabbed the baron by the top of his head, and pulled back sharply, holding a knife at his throat.

The assembly erupted. All music and sound of trumpets vanished in the cries of the people and clash of weapons being drawn. "Stay back! Stay back!" Lionheart shouted as he dragged the baron away from the clerics, moving swiftly across the dais. His voice could scarcely be heard in the din. The baron, his arms flailing, tried and failed to get a hold on his captor. With the blade at his neck, he could scarcely breathe, and his huge eyes rolled.

The queen, her mouth a little O of surprise, sprang forward just as the baron's guardsmen mounted the dais steps. She flung herself at them, perhaps for protection, and dropped in an elaborate faint so that many fell over her in their efforts to reach her husband.

And Felix, watching from above, saw that Lionheart was making for the little door and the spiral stair.

Can you hear me? sang the songbird in his head.

The armed man by the door brandished his weapon and started toward Lionheart from behind.

"He's not a murderer," Felix whispered.

The next moment, Felix leapt over the gallery railing and came down on the guardsman's back, flattening him. He landed harder than he'd expected and rolled to one side, struggling to reclaim his breath. He saw another guardsman coming and, moving on reflex rather than thought, stuck out a leg and tripped him. He righted himself then, just in time to see Lionheart reach the doorway, dragging his prisoner behind.

Lionheart looked at him. Felix saw a flash of desperate thanks in his eyes. Then the door slammed behind him and the baron. Guardsmen hurled themselves at it, their weapons thunking into the heavy wood.

It was bolted from the inside.

16

THERE, IN THE WOOD BETWEEN, a shadowed circle.

Deeper shadows drew near to the rims of the circle, silent as ripples of darkness on the face of a moon-empty lake. Eyes downcast, they stood, arms upraised, reaching out toward one another but never touching. Fingertips stretched, but always the emptiness between.

They were united.

They were alone.

The Bronze gleamed about each of their necks, breaking the shadows into points of light.

One figure, taller than the rest, nine feet at the least and crowned in great, curling horns, opened her eyes. They flashed gold in the light of the Bronze.

She spoke: "Our Advocates are dead."

Her voice sibilated in the hollows of trees, through the close-gathered branches, into the minds of her brethren.

She said: "Whom do we advocate?"

These we have chosen.

"Let the chosen step forward."

Six shadows entered the circle, drawn together by the intensifying light from the Bronze around their necks. So Daylily, pale and ragged, saw for the first time those whose hearts beat in rhythm with her own. She saw a woman with a face partially covered in feathers, weeping through a fixed smile. She saw a man, thin, winged, and fierce, whose hair floated behind him like clouds in an autumn sky. She glimpsed one whose body was twisted like gnarled tree roots, so strange, so unlike anything she had ever before encountered that her mind refused to accept it and blinded itself to the sight so that, for all she knew, nothing but a young tree stood in that one's place.

She could bear no more, so she stared down at the Bronze upon her own breast and thought nothing but allowed herself to be thought through.

These we have chosen.

These he has chosen.

These I have chosen.

Daylily's breath was like ice in her throat, and she continued to stare at the Bronze as though following a lighthouse through a storm.

Then something broke. Some bond, some pact of which she had been unaware vanished with such suddenness that she staggered and her hands reached up to grasp the Bronze, which glowed between her fingers.

The horned one said, "There is a mortal among the offered. Who advocates a mortal?"

"I do," said Sun Eagle from the edge of the circle, behind Daylily's shoulder where she could not see him.

"A mortal advocating a mortal?" said the horned one. "Is this right? Is this fair?"

"She is of my kin," said Sun Eagle. "I smell the Crescent Land on her skin. I feel the pulse of Crescent Land in her blood. She is my sister."

"Give her in tithe, then," said another voice, deeper than that of the horned one. Daylily dared not raise her head, but she turned an ear its way. If bears spoke in the tongues of men, she would have sworn it was a bear. "Let her pass through the door."

"She was chosen," said Sun Eagle. Compared to others speaking, his voice was all warmth and sunlight. Though she did not turn, Daylily's heart reached out to the sound, clinging desperately as the strangeness of the dark circle washed over her, tugging like the tide with unknown fears. "The Bronze chose her," said Sun Eagle. "She is one of us. And she has shown us a new host."

"A new host, you say?" The horned one shifted, and her massive hooves shook the earth so that all the six standing within the circle stumbled and put out their hands to catch their balance. "Where?"

"My own land," said Sun Eagle. "She showed me the way back to my own world. We walked a Path made by sylphs, and we passed through the gate. It is good, green, thriving country!"

"Mortal country," said the horned one. "Are you a fool, Sun Eagle?"

"Do you think so, Kasa?" Sun Eagle's voice remained as calm and warm as ever, but there were knives behind his words. "Then tell our master! For he chose this girl for his own, and he, through her, obligated the people of my country to him. They owe in tithe for the life of one of their own."

"If this is so . . ." said a new voice, a thin whisper that tickled the ear. Daylily, her head still bowed, permitted her eyes to glance up at the speaking shadow opposite her on the edge of the circle. When this person spoke, green fire shimmered in his mouth. "If this is so, then our foot is in the door. We may take root."

We may come home.

"We have never carried the Bronze into a mortal land," said the horned one. "How will it bear us?"

"Better than it bore the coming of wolves and dragons," said Sun Eagle. "For we will deliver the Land from evil. They will gladly pay the tithe."

And we will be home.

"And we will be home," Daylily whispered. She heard the other six with her in the circle whisper the same. A coldness grew from inside her and spilled out over her tongue, washing down the front of her, wrapping about her feet, her waist, her neck—a coldness she could not understand, could not fear, could not resist. So she stood quietly, and she spoke in one voice with the others.

"We will be home."

"I will be home."

"He will be home."

Home. Home.

The horned one stepped then from the edge of the circle. She was a great giantess, thinly proportioned but strong as a sturdy tree. Her legs were those of an elk, and elk's horns grew from her brow. Where she walked, the ground rumbled. She was naked save for the fur that covered her hide, and for the long hair that fell from her head down her back. The Bronze looked very small upon her chest, and it gleamed there like a melting star.

"Very well," she said, and her golden animal eyes fixed upon Daylily. "Very well, we will carry the Bronze into the mortal realms. And we will make them—"

Mine.

The twelve spoke the word as one, and they did not know what they said.

Mine!

In the deepness of night, hours before hope of dawn, the village of Greenwell slept fitfully. Men lay with hands upon weapons, and women clutched their little ones close. Guard dogs lay upon the threshold of every door, dozing between alertness and sleep.

One dog, a shaggy brown lurcher, growled in his dreams.

The boy sat up on his pallet and gazed across the dimness of his family hut. He saw the outline of his massive protector lying in a bundle at the door. And yet the boy did not take the usual comfort at the sight.

"Bullbear," he whispered.

The dog, instantly awake, heaved itself to its feet and hastened to the child's side, careful even with its lumbering bulk not to step upon the other children lying on near pallets. The boy put his arms around the dog's neck, feeling the beat of that great, loyal heart. "Bullbear, sit," he said, and the dog sat.

The boy waited. He did not know for what. But he waited with his hand on Bullbear's back. Outside, the night was full of sounds, birds and monkeys and insects, a cacophony of noise that the boy and the dog scarcely noticed. Instead, they both listened to the silence of the well; the well in which Mama Greenteeth no longer sang her wicked songs.

Bullbear growled. And as he growled, the boy heard the first call.

Send out your firstborn! Send out your firstborn!

The boy stood. His dog growled more savagely than before, then crouched in a whine when the child motioned him to silence. Moving like one in a dream, the boy crossed his father's hut and stood in the doorway.

"Fall-of-Rain," said the boy's father behind him. The boy did not turn but stood silhouetted against the night sky, listening. "Fall-of-Rain, back to bed," said his father.

Bullbear's growl was continuous now. He pressed up against the boy's side, his haunches nearly as high as the young one's shoulder. He rumbled in his throat, then let out a vicious, snarling bark.

The boy smacked the dog's face. That massive head drew back, and the dog yelped at this sudden cruelty from its master.

"Fall-of-Rain!" said his father sharply as he rose from his bed. Then he too heard what the boy had heard.

Send out your firstborn! Send out your firstborn!

"Cursed flame!" the man gasped. His wife was up now, reaching for her little ones, who hastened to her circling arms. She put out a hand to her oldest son, calling his name.

The boy stood with his back to them, his head tilted a little to one side. His heart beat a wild resistance in his breast, and yet his body moved of its own accord. He stepped out of his father's house into the dirt of the village street.

Through the darkness, twelve bright lights approached. Tall figures of shadow loomed like storm clouds, low to the ground and moving swiftly, thundering as they went: *Send out your firstborn!*

Other children appeared in the doorways of all the village houses, some older, some very small, all those old enough to walk but not yet adults. They, like the boy, stepped out into the street and gathered together. Mothers followed and fathers as well, catching at their children, struggling to lift them off their feet, to carry them back. But it was like catching at smoke. Their hands could not grasp what no longer belonged to them.

The tithe is due.

The Bronze Warriors standing beyond the village fringes raised their arms in summoning. And the firstborn children, moving like phantoms, flowed down from the safety of their homes and hearths, their eyes full of the Bronze light. Mothers screamed. Fathers grabbed weapons and charged down the hill.

But one figure outstretched the others. Bullbear, faithful and true, his mouth red with snarling, caught up to his young master and leapt between him and the otherworldly beings. His nose caught the scents of distant worlds and a scent deeper and more dire. His whole body trembled with the terror of what he smelled, but far outweighing terror was devotion.

He flung himself at the nearest of the warriors.

And she, her red hair streaming behind, stepped forward with her shining stone upraised, and plunged it into the neck of the leaping dog.

Bullbear fell broken at her feet. She put out her arms to the boy, who stood so near, unable to see for the light of the Bronze in his eyes. Daylily opened her mouth, and words came forth:

Come to me, firstborn. We will make the worlds new.

The child was in her arms then. She lifted him as though he weighed no more than a feather, and she carried him away from the village, following the footsteps of her brethren. She felt the presence of the other eleven around her, as near to her as her own skin. She was one with them, and they with her. She clutched the boy close to her heart as gently and as firmly as a mother might, and she carried him away into darkness—him, and other children as well, caught up in her wake and that of the Twelve.

What are you doing?

Daylily gasped and dropped the boy, who lay still and dull upon the ground. Daylily bent double, her hands clutching her head as the wolf, ravening and furious, tore at her mind.

What are you doing? Are you a puppet on a string? Will you never let me free?

"Get out!" she screamed. "I don't want you!"

It doesn't matter what you want! I am your deepest, truest self! And I won't let you bow to this new idol as you bowed to the idol of your father!

"You are no longer part of me! I bound you!"

We bound you.

I'll always be part of you, the she-wolf roared as she hauled against her chains, rattling Daylily's body to the core. *You'll never subdue me, not for long!*

"I'll kill you, then," Daylily replied. "It will be as though you've never been."

You can't! You'll only kill yourself!

"It does not matter," said Daylily. And her mouth moved and spoke of its own: *It does not matter. It is mine.*

She knelt then and picked up the child, and once more carried him in the path trod by the other warriors. She followed the gleaming of their bronze stones into the night, into the shadows, moving swiftly across terrible reaches and landscapes that her heart knew. For this was her homeland.

This is my home.

They came at last to a great space bare of trees other than an enclosure of four walls of saplings. These were clad not in their own greenery but in the shining white of starflower blooms, pale little faces turned to the sky, reflecting the stars above. As Daylily drew nearer, she saw that the saplings, though thin, were far taller than she had expected, lifting the starflowers high into the night. Water flowed amid the trees, gentle and life-giving. This was a place of magic far deeper than spells or enchantments.

This was the heart of the land; the center that can neither be found on a mortal map nor seen by mortal eyes. It was the core from which the heart beat the lifeblood of a nation, of a people.

The warriors, holding the children tight, ringed round the starflower-laden trees, and they stood silent and solemn, Daylily in their midst with her Advocate, Sun Eagle, on her right. All faced inward to those trees, to those blossoms, to the water shining in the light of stars.

A wind arose and touched the treetops with cold fingers. Wherever it moved, starflowers fell in rain of gleaming white, like snow.

"How solemn it is," Daylily whispered, to herself rather than to the boy she held. "Surely we wait for the voice of a god or a prophet. Something good is near."

But the wind grew harsher, and it seemed to spiral from the tops of the tree branches down, down, down to the ground, scattering more starflowers as it went. And Daylily saw that wherever it touched, the trees were bare and dark. The valley itself, bereft of their light, fell into ever-deepening gloom.

A silver voice sang behind her ear. Daylily glanced over her shoulder and thought she saw the white breast of the speckled songbird flash in swift flight across her vision. But she shook her head and gazed once more upon the valley of the starflowers.

Suddenly a great light, like a shining crown, burst from the center of the darkened trees, and the trees themselves, stripped of their glory, fell before it in ruin. The Bronze stones around the necks of the warriors gleamed in response to the building light, and Daylily found her voice crying out with theirs in a chant she did not know she knew:

"From blood springs life! From life springs blood!"

Over and over again they spoke. And as the chant rose into the night, a shudder passed through the ground beneath their feet. The soil moved and shifted, bubbling up in the center of the broken grove. Then, like a terrible boil, something burst through the earth and rose up, eclipsing the shining light. Even the stars in the sky gasped and hid their faces behind clouds at what they saw taking place below.

Up from the heart of the land rose the Mound. Like a tumor it swelled, a black mass clutching at the soil with hands like roots. All over its rising head sprouted thorns, and green branches grew up, withered, and dropped their leaves at once.

The warriors ringing it bowed.

"From blood springs life! From life springs blood!"

The wolf in Daylily's mind whimpered. *No . . .*

Then Daylily, along with the other warriors, stepped over the broken saplings, their feet crushing the petals of starflowers, grinding their lingering light beneath their heels. The children not carried followed as well, and they too trampled starflowers. The company descended into the very shadow of the Mound, and there Daylily saw a gaping hole in its side from which rose a black, hungry stench.

No! screamed the wolf.

Daylily turned to her Advocate, searching his face for some explanation. But she saw only solemn reverence building to awe. And his voice chanted along with the others, "From blood springs life! From life springs blood!"

He carried a girl child in his arms, and other children followed in his footsteps. He, like the other warriors ahead of him, approached the hole in the side of the Mound. Daylily advanced behind him.

Mine!

The voice came now from the Mound itself, bringing with it a waft of stink and decay and old, old blood.

Mine!

One at a time the warriors took the children in their arms and threw them into the hole. Daylily, last of all, the boy held tightly, drew up beside her Advocate. She gazed into that darkness and knew it for her own face.

Then she looked down into the face of the boy. But his eyes were full of the Bronze light, and he could not see her.

Mine!

She threw the boy in after the others. And the door of the Mound was shut behind him.

17

THE LITTLE ONE STOOD in the open doorway of his mother's house and solemnly sucked two fingers. He watched mud plaster fall and blinked his large eyes. He watched a hand emerge through what had been a wall and blinked twice more, even paused in his sucking. As the hand groped about blindly, then began peeling mud from the edges of the gap it had created, the child drew a deep breath, then resumed sucking with earnestness.

A head appeared. The evening was growing heavy as fleece in the sky, so few details of this head were discernible. A great deal of plaster stuck to any available portion of skin, creating a ghoulish aspect only made more terrible by the black hair standing up in wild and wooly tufts. Eyes swollen by wasp stings squinted about in a desperate attempt to find bearings. They fixed upon the child in the doorway. They widened.

The child went on sucking. With his free hand, he offered a tiny wave.

The head tried to retreat back through the wall but couldn't quite fit. The child continued watching, fascinated, as the erstwhile prisoner contorted until he got one shoulder and then an arm outside. More plaster rained down from above until his whole head was white with it. The child took his fingers from his mouth and substituted a still more comforting thumb.

"Dragons blast it!"

With this strange cry, the prisoner made a final, crumbling burst. Then, with a last look at the child, he gathered himself up from the wreckage and took to his heels, stumbled, fell, recovered, and ran again down the dark side of the hill upon which the house was built. A curse and a rustle of leaves signaled his disappearance into the jungle.

The child, thumb in place, took a step out the door, craning his neck for a better view.

"Wolfsbane!"

That sharp voice could only belong to an elder sister. The child turned to the girl who was a source of equal parts awe and comfort in his young life. She pounced on him like a rabbit on clover, catching him up in her arms.

"You know better than to go outside on your own!" Lark chided, "oof-ing" to get her brother up on her skinny hip, which was really more bone than hip. She was just ten years of age and slightly built like her mother before her. But her twig-thin arms disguised wiry muscle. After all, she was the successful watchwoman over a brood of siblings, which required strength as well as cunning.

The aforementioned Wolfsbane took his thumb from his mouth and grabbed his sister's ear for stability in his newly elevated position. "Bake," he said, then added appropriate crashing noises with his lips.

"Break?" Lark said, using the gift of translation common in the ranks of big sisters. "What did you break, Wolfie?"

"Nuah!" Wolfsbane protested, the picture of affronted innocence. He pointed.

Lark stepped out the front door of her mother's house for a better look. The main house was built of stone and mortar, strong and sturdy after the practice of her father's people. But many of the attached wings were assembled according to the building standards of her mother's less architecturally inclined tribe, easy enough for a determined man to break through if need pressed.

"Da!" Lark called, clutching young Wolfsbane by a dimpled leg as she swung about to call into the house. "Da, the prisoner's escaped!"

"What prisoner?" her father's voice bellowed from inside.

"The wasp man!"

"I told you"—Redman appeared from down a short stone passage, a knife in one hand, an onion in the other—"he's not a prisoner. He's a guest who isn't allowed to leave, and what do you mean, he's escaped?"

Lark and Wolfsbane pointed as their red-bearded father joined them in the doorway. His good eye, used to the cooking fire over which he had been crouched, took a moment to adjust to the evening's blue gloom. Then he muttered, "Well, Flame at Night . . ." and trotted out for a closer look at the breakage. Lark, with Wolfsbane in her arms, trailed after, and the two children watched their father as he peered inside and inspected the hole. "Flame at Night," he said again, speaking in the tongue of his people when he swore, which always made his children giggle. "He certainly has escaped, and left a trail of plaster a blind man could follow. It'll take me all day to fix this mess."

"What about the wasp man?" Lark asked.

"I suppose we'll let the totems have him," Redman said.

"Da!"

"All right. Since you've taken such a fancy to him, I'll fetch him back to you. Pesty girl."

Lark sniffed with great dignity at this, and Redman addressed himself to his son. "Guard this until I return," he said, placing the onion in Wolfsbane's wet hand. "Should I perish, you'll know what to do with it."

Wolfsbane stuck the onion into his mouth.

"Let me go with you, Da?" Lark asked, catching the onion before her brother violently discarded it as unfit for consumption. "I can help."

"Me! Me!" Wolfsbane added with equal fervor.

"No," Redman replied, sheathing his knife as he started down the hill toward the jungle. "Go wash up young Wolfish there, then you and your sisters finish supper. I'll be back hungry, so be sure you make plenty!"

With these words, Redman vanished into the shadows, following the trail of plaster. Lark set her brother on his feet and stood a moment holding his hand. The lights of the village cooking fires shone like beacons in the deepening night, surrounding her mother's stone house on all sides, save the one leading down to the jungle. Down there, all was dark. Dark and dreadful.

"Poor wasp man," Lark whispered. She hoped her da would find him. Before the totems did.

One never fully appreciates the blessing that is a pair of shoes until one is suddenly without them in a deepening jungle twilight, fleeing, one presumes, for one's life.

The jungle teemed with insects, and with creatures that ate the insects, and with creatures that ate the creatures that ate the insects. Foxbrush could have safely bet there were creatures that ate those as well, but he wouldn't let himself consider that far up the hierarchy.

The insects themselves were bad enough. Everything with wings and far more legs than should be permitted swarmed to the sticky mess smeared over Foxbrush's skin. They weren't wasps at least, but many of them were biters. More welts swelled on his arms, his neck, his hands, and his poor bare feet.

Foxbrush was out of breath before he'd gone far. Lack of exercise and terror made it so that he could scarcely keep himself upright as he plunged through the tangle of vines. By necessity he found the beaten trail. There was no break in the foliage anywhere else, so he ran down the trail with all the speed he could muster. He did not know where he was going or what he hoped to achieve by this foolish dash. Perhaps he had gone a little mad.

This was when he started hearing things.

"Danger! Danger!"

"Stranger!"

The voices relayed this rumor as fast as he could run, faster even. He heard it whispering through the treetops, darting on ahead of him, then looping round and coming back. They did not speak in a language he knew, but he understood the words even so.

"Danger! Stranger!"

It must be the figs. He must have eaten too many bad figs, and this, all this, must be the result of one spoiled-fig-induced nightmare!

Something landed on his shoulders.

Foxbrush screamed as he was knocked flat, and he felt strong fingers grabbing first his ears and then his hair and then his chin, twisting his head as though to wrench it off. He scrambled for balance, and something coiled and serpentine slithered over his bare hand. He screamed, and the thing on his back screamed as well, and the thing that had crawled over his hand screamed louder still, and then something struck his heel.

It was like having a nail driven swiftly into his foot, then yanked out with equal swiftness. Foxbrush's screams intensified, but his voice was drowned out by all the other voices shouting: *"Danger! Stranger! Danger!"*

Monkeys and birds and who knows what else erupted in eerie chorus on all sides. The whole world came alive in screeches and caws and bellows and shrieks and even a sound like a great wooden drum being thumped by enormous fists.

Foxbrush curled up into a ball, his hands over his head, his knees hiding his face, and felt fists and beaks and claws pummeling him from all sides. He waited to die.

It was in this position that Redman found him.

The light was mostly gone from the forest by that time, but Redman's one good eye was comfortable in the dark, and he feared none of those living near the village. So he stood, his arms crossed, and looked down on the crumpled form of the stranger. "Well," said he, "we're not all born to be heroes."

With that he knelt and took hold of Foxbrush's shoulder. Foxbrush only curled tighter, like an overlarge hedgehog. Redman snorted. "Come," he said, valiantly disguising any hint of disgust. "Let's get you back to my wife's house and clean you up again."

Foxbrush, hearing a mortal voice, dared peek between his fingers. "Where . . . where are the monsters?" he gasped.

"No monsters, lad," said Redman.

"They were attacking me!"

"They're all gone now. I paid totem-tribute, and they've backed down."

Though he understood none of this, Foxbrush did not resist as Redman hauled him to his feet, though he winced at the pain in his wounded heel. Redman, noticing, put Foxbrush's arm over his broad shoulders. There was no use in fighting. Foxbrush submitted like a docile sheep to Redman's prodding, and together they hobbled back the way they had just come. Lemurs watched with solemn moon eyes, and night birds laughed from their perches. It was as though the whole of nature was amused at Foxbrush's expense, and he, feeling the shame, hung his head and thought he'd never lift it again.

Then the wind spoke his name.

It howled down from the sky above the trees, touching only the topmost branches, but these with such wild force that all the creatures dwelling above hastened to climb down. As it blew, the wind called in a voice Foxbrush thought he recognized.

Foxbrush! Foxbrush, I have come for you!

It moved on, passing quickly like a shudder. Foxbrush, frozen in Redman's support, heard the echoes calling. *Foxbrush! Foxbrush!*

Redman stood quite still, his eyes upturned. "A sylph," he said.

Foxbrush could not deny it, not even in his head. He'd tried hard enough while wandering the Between. But this was not the Between. This was the mortal world, the world of clay and death and of cold, hard reality. He really was here. He really had just heard a sylph calling his name in this real world where such things should not exist.

He hated his life more in that moment than he ever had before.

"That's no good," Redman said, readjusting his grip on Foxbrush's arm. "They start calling your name in the night, and you begin to think you need to go after them. Don't follow a sylph's voice, lad! You'll never be seen again."

Foxbrush tried to speak, but the pain in his foot with each step cut him off. At last he managed to gasp, "Are there . . . are there many of them? In Southlands?"

"What? Sylphs?"

Foxbrush nodded.

"Enough, that's for sure. They and others of their kind. Faerie beasts, as the Silent Lady called them. The rivers used to hold them back, but now that the rivers are gone many venture up from the Wood."

Foxbrush felt he should understand this. His brain hurt when he tried, however, so he stopped trying. They took several more painful steps.

Redman said, "Why would a sylph be calling for you?"

"I don't know," Foxbrush replied honestly enough. Another two hobbling steps, then, "I think I met sylphs earlier today. In the Wilderlands."

"Today?" Redman made a sound somewhere between a snort and a laugh. "If it was sylphs you met, my boy, it was likely a hundred years ago. Or a hundred years from now, perhaps." He gave Foxbrush a sideways glance. "Or more than that."

"Is that . . . so?"

It was difficult to discern any detail in the evening gloom, and Foxbrush was such a mess by now that his own mother wouldn't have recognized him. But it wasn't his appearance that gave him away. It was his voice. And Redman was no fool.

"You're not from this time," he said.

Foxbrush drew a long breath. "I don't believe so. No."

"But you are a man of the South Land?"

Foxbrush said, "Yes." He hesitated. Then, "I'm soon to be Eldest."

Redman was not a man to be easily surprised. He had seen a number of strange sights in his day, met a number of strange folk. He had walked dark roads in dark lands unknown to other men and faced monsters in that darkness. But the idea of Foxbrush being Eldest of anywhere or any time very nearly undid him. "I think," Redman said, his mouth twitching against a laugh, choosing his words carefully as he spoke, "that you should tell me everything."

So Foxbrush did. In a haphazard, backward, and circular manner, he told Redman all that he could, from Daylily's flight, to Lionheart's disgrace, back to a certain childhood summer holiday when Leo befriended a goat girl and left Foxbrush behind with algebraic equations. He spoke of the Dragon, the poison, the dying Eldest Hawkeye, Nidawi and the Lioness, the Baron of Middlecrescent, the sylphs . . . even the figs! Everything spilled out, and Redman listened and asked no questions, and it was a wonder if he made any sense of it.

They were still in the jungle when Foxbrush ran out of air. Redman paused and leaned Foxbrush up against a tree, giving both of them a much needed reprieve. Foxbrush couldn't remember the last time he'd talked so much in so short a span of minutes, and he was quite gasping from the effort. He wiped sweat from his brow, which wrinkled with a sudden thought.

"What distresses me most," he said, not speaking so much to Redman as to himself in that moment, "is that all it took was my letter. I've never seen Daylily falter. Not when the Dragon came, not when the kingdom was poisoned, not when Leo was banished . . . not once did I see her flinch! I thought she was—" He shook his head ruefully. "I thought she was invincible. But all it took was one letter. One *stupid* letter. And she broke."

He sagged against the tree trunk then, and the pain in his feet disappeared as the worms in his belly once more resumed their wretched gnawing.

Redman watched him. The scars of his ugly face throbbed with a flood of memories all his own. He had listened to Foxbrush's rambling tale with interest and not a little disbelief. But now it was at its end, he regarded the young man who claimed to be prince, and could not decide what he felt. Pity? Disgust?

Hope?

"The funny thing about stories," Redman said after a silence (which wasn't really a silence with the night so alive around them), "is their way of happening again. And again."

"Pardon?" Foxbrush, still leaning against his tree, looked up.

"Stories, a friend of mine once told me, cling to a certain pattern," Redman continued. "Like the seasons, cycling round and round. And they always find ways to fit back into that cycle, and nothing we do can stop them."

Foxbrush made no answer. He squinted and frowned and stood like a lump.

Redman heaved a great sigh, perhaps of sorrow, perhaps of mere tiredness, perhaps of neither at all. Then he grinned at the forest floor, shaking his head. "I too was meant to be a king," he said. "Once upon a time, long ago and far away. I was like your Leo. I too was born to be crowned. I too was pledged to wed the daughter of my most powerful supporter." He sighed again, but his grin remained in place. "I too had a cousin who took both my throne and my bride."

Foxbrush stared at the dark shadow from whence came Redman's voice.

"I suppose this means I was in your cousin's shoes," Redman said, "and I should resent you for his sake. Perhaps I do. A little. That is, of course, if any of the wild tale you've just spun me is true!"

"It is true," Foxbrush whispered.

"I think it must be. Because only true stories cycle with such precision. Only a true story would have led you to me so that I find myself once again coming to the aid of one who would take the throne his cousin will never sit upon. For some, unlikely though they may be, are born to be king. And some, however likely, are not. Such is the truth of stories." He shrugged. "It all comes back to blood and love in the end."

Foxbrush tried to swallow. There was sap in his mouth, and it tasted sickly upon his tongue. This conversation had quite gotten away from him, and he wasn't certain what to do about it. He wasn't certain of anything anymore. Perhaps he never had been certain of anything.

"I've got to find Daylily," he said quietly. "That's all that matters. I've got to find her."

Redman shook himself suddenly, like a dog after a bath, and smiled at Foxbrush, who was just as blessed that he could not see it. On Redman's scarred face, smiles were gruesome.

"Well, Prince Foxbrush, I don't know how to find your lady or how to get you back to your time. But never fear! No doubt the rest of the story will present itself. And in the meanwhile, I *do* know where a warm meal waits and a bed upon which you may rest your head. Will you stop awhile in the Eldest's House?"

"I will," Foxbrush replied. He accepted Redman's proffered shoulder once more, and they continued on their hobbling way back through the jungle.

18

*T*IME AND AGAIN. *Time and again.*

And yet, what is Time? Measured out in the beatings of these hearts.

Disappointment heaped upon disappointment. And yet, what is disappointment without desire?

Desire . . . ah yes. Desire surges in these veins, pounds in these heads. Blood and love, and the fire that flows between.

This land is good. This land is fair. This land is rich. This land is . . . Mine!

"Mine," Daylily whispered. A thrill akin to both sorrow and delight washed over her, leaving a strange prickling in her head, behind her vision. She followed Sun Eagle, her eyes round and wide and intent as a young dog's fixed upon its master. Her Advocate. That's what he called himself and what she knew him to be in a deep, instinctual place of her mind. She would follow him.

She would kill for him.

This is what it means to be free, she thought as the Wood Between shuddered and drew back to make room for their passing. *To be free is to be ruthless, and ruthless will I be. All to the good of the land! The land I have too long watched succumb to poison and invasion. I will fight for my . . .*

. . . for the master.

And it was good, even in her head, for the wolf could not resist her now, could not hurt her or hers.

They came to the gate of silver-branch trees, and Daylily now saw it for what it was. How could she have missed it before? Of course there were gates leading to all worlds, all times! Of course they would look nothing like mortal gates, for they were not made by mortal hands! It was all so simple and so clear now. After the Bronze was taken. After the first blood was spilt. After the first tithe was paid.

Sun Eagle said nothing as he led the quiet girl out of the Between and back into the vibrant, hot air of the Near World. Indeed, he could not speak at first, so keen was the quickening of his pulse, the thickening in his throat. How many far and fantastical countries had he seen since that morning long ago when he, a mere boy on the threshold of manhood, had passed into the Gray Wood to make his rite of passage and bring honor to his father's name? He had passed into the Gray Wood, and the cord that secured him to his own world and time had broken. So he had become lost, never to return to his father's waiting arms, never to return to his lovely chosen bride.

He felt again for the blue bead painted with the white starflower that he wore in the hollow of his throat, above the dangling Bronze. Her name mark. Her final gift. She must have believed that he died long ago.

She must have died herself.

But he had no time to think of this. Not now, with the whole of his native country opening before him, and the drive to protect, to save, to . . . to possess. To possess for the good of all!

So Sun Eagle led, his head full of too many thoughts to put into words, and Daylily followed. She was tired, and she knew it with a distant vagueness, but she would not dream of resting. Who could rest now? There was so much to do!

They came out of the Wood Between, and she saw that they had come to a different gorge than that she had climbed down in her flight from her wedding. This one was narrower and deeper, but as with the other, a path led up to the table country above. Sun Eagle climbed and Daylily hurried after. And when they reached the summit, they found the land clearer here, not thick with jungle but well tilled and wide with rolling green hills.

"Crescent Land!" Sun Eagle exclaimed, his eyes shining.

"Middlecrescent," Daylily whispered. She felt a jolt in the pit of her stomach. Then they reached for each other, hand clutching hand, as linked now by the spirit of their homeland as they were by that which lived inside them.

Then a cloud passed over Sun Eagle's face, and his grip on Daylily's hand tightened. "Do you smell that?"

"What?" asked Daylily.

"Faerie beast." Sun Eagle snarled the words. "A fey power living in our country. An intruder."

And Daylily said in a voice as soft and gentle as that she once used to order tea or a certain gown laid out for dinner, "We must kill it."

Sun Eagle nodded. "We must."

They moved swiftly across this landscape, unhindered by the growth of jungle. And the air was hot, but the wind was fresh, and they both laughed as they ran, though Daylily's limbs trembled with the thrill of fear and delight that was becoming so mixed up in her being that she could scarcely tell the one from the other.

Tocho sensed their approach.

Tocho sat on Skymount Watch, a rocky outcropping that rose above the fields and greens of this pleasant country. He was still relatively new to the Near World, but he liked it well. In the Far World there were too many others of his kind, brutal and greedy, and many much larger than he. Here, he could be master if he liked, for there was little enough the mortals could do.

Amarok the Wolf had had the right idea, all those ages ago, when he came to the Near World and made himself a god over these little people.

But, Tocho thought, *I am not a fool like Amarok. He lost his godhood because he was too fond of the pretty women of this land. A woman with a pretty face will always bring a fellow low in the end. I don't fall for a pretty face, however, for was there ever a face as pretty as mine?*

So he sat contented upon his rocky seat, and his whiskers twitched with sensitive interest at every breeze that passed. Silky black fur clothed his lithe body, even his cheeks and around his eyes, though otherwise he was much like a man, if far bigger. His toes and fingers were extraordinarily long and tipped with lovely, lethal claws. His ears were large and tufted, and his mouth split into a cleft cat's grin. When the sun shone upon him, as it did now, faint jaguar blotches showed in an elegant but subdued pattern across his torso and haunches.

He was Tocho the Panther, Big Cat of Skymount. And the rock on which he sat was carved in his own likeness. Ugly, perhaps, to mortal eyes. But what did mortals know?

When the mortals came up from their village, climbing to this place of his totem stone to pay him tribute, they brought him fresh meats, still alive and bleating, and they bowed down and sang songs: songs to the length of his tail, to the whiteness of his whiskers, to the saucer moons of his copper eyes, and to the gleam of his smile.

What a happy life was his. A fat, happy, sun-bathing life. Let Lumé shine down upon him with disapproval; what did Tocho care, so long as the rays were warm! Thus he sat atop Skymount Watch, and the tip of his tail twitched as he idly sharpened the claws of his right hand upon a stone, making sparks.

His whiskers sensed them first. Then his nose picked up their smell. Last of all, his ears twitched to the beat of their hearts.

Tocho dropped his filing stone and stood upright, staring out across the land that was his own little demesne.

"The Bronze!" he said. And then he threw back his head and sounded the panther's rasping roar, spitting it through his fangs as a challenge. It echoed out from Skymount, rolling down to the land below his rocky fortress. The villagers living near stopped their work, their gazes rising in fear and curiosity to the stone outcropping high above, which could be seen for miles in that part of the country. Was the tribute not paid? Was the offering unsatisfactory?

Must they fight once more for their flocks, fight an immortal power far greater than their stone weapons?

But Tocho stood trembling where he was, invisible to all searching eyes. He had a panther's knack for becoming no more than a shadow. The roar rolled down and round him for some time even as he stood in silence once more, staring into the valleys and on out as far as the distant gorge.

"The Bronze," he whispered again. Then he turned, leapt from the stone, and ran at a loping gait down the side of Skymount.

He must drive them out. Now! Before their power grew too strong. He could smell them—smell *it*—and he knew the bond had been made already and the first tithe delivered. Who had died? Who among his Faerie brethren had succumbed already to one of the Twelve, the spilled blood effectively sealing the country for the Bronze? He could not guess. He kept himself apart from the other Faeries as much as possible, preferring the solitary kingdom he'd made for himself in these parts. But one had died; he knew this for certain, dreadful truth.

There was still time to drive them back out. One dead surely could not form a bond so strong that Tocho could not break it! He would kill as many of them as dared draw near and let the rest flee back to their cursed Mound and say, "Not that country! Let us find a land more gentle!"

Yes. Yes, that's how it would be. Tocho panted as he ran, his great arms sweeping aside branches, his great legs tearing up the ground, his claws shrieking as they raked into stone. He was mighty and he was dreadful. To be sure, he had become a little fat and lazy in this fat and lazy country, and the mortal air was thin in his lungs. But he was Tocho still, a name to be feared! Had not his own queen driven him from her demesne at the terror of his bloodthirsty name? Had not warriors and hunters alike fallen prey to his teeth and jaws, to his strike in the dark, and his stealth and cunning? Did not even the Knights of Farthestshore, so brave and so glittering in their self-righteous glory, fear to cross his path?

So he puffed himself up even as his breathing grew short, telling himself truth and lies with the same fluid ease with which he had once stalked Faerie woods of the Far World.

Sun Eagle, still holding Daylily's hand, came to a halt. They were two miles from the gorge now, standing in a fallow field. Daylily smelled the nearness of a village, though she saw no signs of life.

Sun Eagle could smell the approach of Tocho.

"He is coming," he said, squeezing Daylily's fingers eagerly.

"Who?" Daylily asked, a little breathless and excited, though she knew not why.

"Our new enemy. Are you ready to kill?"

She thought of the dark well, the blackness brightened only by Mama Greenteeth's eyes. She tasted the blood in the water. And she felt a mortal child in her arms.

No . . . whimpered the wolf in her mind.

"I am ready," said Daylily. Then she said, "I have no weapon."

"You have the Bronze," said Sun Eagle. He took his own melted medallion from around his neck as he spoke, and Daylily saw that it was shaped like the head of a spear. How had she not seen it before? Or had the shape changed since last she'd bothered to look?

She let go of Sun Eagle's hand and pulled her own medallion until the cord snapped behind her neck. It was bigger and brighter than ever, brighter even than the sun above. She felt the pulse of blood in her wrist flow into her hand with surging energy. The stone was like a great golden tooth, the tooth of a predator far deadlier than any she knew.

It was her own tooth. She was the predator now.

"There he is," said Sun Eagle, pointing.

Daylily shaded her eyes with her free hand, and she saw the black shadow at a distance, moving swiftly across the clear country. It disappeared into a valley, then reappeared, now near enough that she could make out its form and even, she imagined, its face.

Tocho stopped in his tracks. He saw them: two small, solitary figures standing in the middle of a field of grass and weeds, the one brown and strong, the other white and frail but crowned with hair like fire.

He saw the stones in their hands.

His courage, which he had convinced himself was live and strong and bloodthirsty, proved itself the fleeting ghost it was and fled his body in a rush so painful that he roared again, his voice slashing at the wind. The sound rolled over Daylily like nothing she had ever heard, and it terrified her.

She smiled. Without a command from Sun Eagle, her feet started moving, the thin remnants of her wedding slippers falling away at last so that she ran barefoot.

She chased Tocho.

He saw her coming and he fled. Back the way he had come mere moments before, he ran with the great galloping pace of a panther, silent but pulsing with dread. He knew she followed, and he knew that she could not hope, in her own strength, to outpace him.

But he also knew that she did not move of her own strength. Not anymore.

Though her heart beat with mad terror, Daylily ran, her teeth set in a snarl and her hair flying behind her. Sun Eagle came after, but he could not catch her, for the thrill of the hunt was not so new in him. He shouted warnings that he knew she would not hear, then stopped wasting his breath. They pursued the panther all the way back across the fields of his little demesne, and the villagers, after one glimpse of their oppressor thus pursued by the red girl and her dark companion, hid in their homes and caves, shielding their faces from the sight.

Tocho's eyes fixed only upon the peak of Skymount Watch, his totem, his haven. If he could only reach it, he lied to himself, he would be safe. They'd not touch him there!

Already he could feel the bite of the Bronze in his flesh. No! He was Tocho the Panther! He could *not* die!

Up the incline he raced, on all fours now as he scrabbled up the rocks, sending many larger stones hurtling down at his hunters. Daylily was struck in the cheek by one small stone and narrowly put up her hand to protect herself from another, which bounced off the Bronze and shattered into tiny pieces behind her. She was so close, she could feel the pound of his heart, and she wanted him gone from her country like she had wanted nothing before in her life.

She wanted him dead. By her hand, not Sun Eagle's.

Tocho leapt. He caught the top of the carved likeness, and he pulled himself up, up to that stone watch from which he had ruled and feasted for years he did not count. Whirling to face his enemies at last, he crouched, his hands clutching the stone, his feet braced, all his claws out and gleaming. He snarled, his face splitting with teeth and a great pink tongue.

Daylily saw him and screamed inside, but she could not have said whether it was a scream of fear or of hunger now, so strong was the drive to kill. Her feet slipped on the stones shifting beneath her, but she caught herself, tearing her hands, and crawled the last few paces to the base of the stone.

Tocho looked down at her and snarled again.

But it wasn't Tocho.

I will fight you! roared the red wolf. For it was she whom Daylily saw upon the stone, the heavy bindings about her neck and limbs dangling, for the moment, uselessly.

Daylily went white in a wash of freezing cold. "How did you get free?" she whispered in a breath.

I will fight you! roared the wolf, saliva dripping from her jaws. *You will never be rid of me!*

"No!" Daylily screamed.

Tocho, standing above, forgot his own fear as he stared down at her, this vicious warrior woman screaming and collapsing to her knees below him. She feared him after all! His big cat's leer turned to a smile, and his tail lashed a moment as he caught his balance.

Then he leapt.

He landed atop Daylily, wrapping his mighty limbs about her, and she felt the heat of his breath upon her face, her neck, in her hair. But it was the wolf, not Tocho, who fought her in her addled mind, and she shrieked and dropped the Bronze as they grappled together down the stony hill. She caught the cat by the throat, and for a moment, when they reached a flat place and paused in their tumble, she was on top, her hands at the beast's throat, her knee pressed into his heart.

The wolf in her mind, whom she believed she held in her grasp, gagged: *You are not a killer!*

"You are!" Daylily screamed. "You'll kill us all!"

Tocho, not understanding what was being shouted in his face by this wild creature, tried to smack her off with a swipe of his claws. But she was empowered by a force far stronger than any he had ever known, and somehow he could not land a hit, though his claws tore through her hair and tangled there. He managed to overbalance them, however, and once more they fell down the incline.

Sun Eagle, watching all as he advanced from below, yelled a feral battle cry from the days of his youth long ages ago. Even as the girl and the Faerie beast rolled in brutal embrace toward him, he leapt as swiftly as his own long-dead fighting dog had once leapt into the fray at his command. And his Bronze fang sank home, deadly and accurate.

Tocho screamed. Then he went limp in a heap of silky fur, Daylily's arm pinned beneath him.

Sun Eagle stood, withdrew the Bronze stone, and quietly retied it, stained and dripping, about his neck. Only then did he kneel and push the heavy bulk of the dead Faerie beast off the girl. Daylily lay wide-eyed, struggling to gasp a breath. Sun Eagle felt her for wounds and broken bones but found nothing.

"Get up, Crescent Woman," he said, his voice heavy with disappointment and therefore angry. "Get up. Why do you tremble so?"

Daylily could not move. Her head and neck quivered as she tried to speak, to swallow. Shaking his head, Sun Eagle took her in his arms and hauled her upright. But her limbs would not support her, and she fell again, landing on the dead hulk of her so-recent prey.

Sun Eagle narrowed his eyes.

This land is good. This land is fair. This land is rich.
Gather the tithe! Gather the tithe!

He rubbed his face with one hand, the same hand warmed by the kill-ing stroke. Then he bent and picked up Daylily, cradling her in his strong arms. She clung to him, and he thought she wept.

"I have no time for this," he growled, but his voice was gentler now. Against the instinct pounding in his head, he carried her back down the incline and on across the country, making for the gorge.

Tocho lay at the base of his totem stone, never to move again.

19

Lionheart stood, heart pounding, upon the winding stair, the Baron of Middlecrescent powerless in his grasp with a knife pressed to his throat. He stared at the bolt on the door, heard the pound of weapons and hands without.

But the bolt held, for the moment.

"You fool!" gasped the baron, his voice strangely gurgling against the cold blade. "I'll stretch your neck for—"

Lionheart did not let him finish. With a strength that belied the trembling in his limbs and the sickness in his gut, he hauled the baron around to face the winding stair, shifting the blade to point into the side of his neck. "Move," he said, his voice husky with fear. Recognizing the threat of death when he heard it, the baron started climbing.

The shouts of guardsmen and the uproar of all those gathered in the hall below faded as they wound their way up. The North Tower had once been used as a prison for high-ranking captives. More than one traitorous noble had spent his last weeks in comfort there. Its lofty height offered a fine view for a man awaiting his execution. He might even be able to watch the scaffold being built.

That was a few generations ago now. But while the chains had long since been cleared away, the iron rings remained in testimony to this former practice.

Lionheart propelled the baron up to the very summit of the tower, where a landing made a sort of hallway and three doorways led to three chambers. What had the baroness told him? The one on the right? Did she actually know her right from her left?

There was no time to investigate. A crash below told Lionheart that they had breached the lower door.

He pushed the baron before him to the right-hand door, which proved to be unlocked as the baroness had promised. He slammed the door shut and gasped, "Silent Lady bless us!" in desperate relief.

For although this chamber was a prison and all the locks were meant to be on the outside, just as the baroness had promised, the lock on the right-hand chamber had been reversed.

Lionheart turned the key, withdrew it, and dropped the first of three bolts in place with a finger-crushing thud, only just removing his hand in time. The hairs on the back of his neck rose, and he saw a shadow fall across the door. He dropped to his knees as a knife embedded itself in the wood where his head had been, driven by the powerful fist of the baron.

Lionheart twisted and kicked; his foot connected with the baron's knee and sent him sprawling. He should have known the baron would not go unarmed to his coronation, despite the ancient protocol!

The baron, his eyes bugging from his face with pain, rolled up to a crouch and lunged at Lionheart, both hands reaching for his throat. Lionheart, being younger and spryer, dodged and brought an elbow down hard into the small of the baron's back, knocking him flat. "How many other blades, Middlecrescent?" he growled, grabbing the baron's right arm and twisting it behind him. The baron rasped out a curse and struggled, but Lionheart tightened his grip and twisted harder. "How many other blades on your person?"

"None!" barked the baron. A lie, and Lionheart knew it. He could see the baron's free hand scrambling for his boot.

Lionheart, his knee pressed into the baron's back, kicked with his other foot, knocking that searching hand away. Pressing more of his weight painfully down, he grabbed the baron's arm and twisted it to join its mate. The baron groaned, agonized, and Lionheart felt a dart of guilt. But he daren't back down now.

The door of the chamber thunked with the cleaving weapons of guardsmen beyond. "My lord! My lord!" muffled voices cried. As the baroness had promised, however, this prison door was so thick that those beyond could scarcely be heard.

The baron, his face pressed into the stone floor, grinned suddenly. "You will pay, Lionheart!" he spat. "They'll have you out of here like a rat from its hole, and I won't stop the dogs from worrying you as a rat deserves!"

Lionheart did not answer but dragged the baron to his feet and across the chamber. The chains had been removed, but the baroness, as promised, had seen to it that a stout rope was provided, tucked away secretly under the sumptuous bed.

Indeed, the whole room was the last word in lavish comfort, Lionheart noted as he bound the baron's hands and secured him to an iron ring in the wall. Those awaiting death in this chamber would certainly do so in a state of ease. Lionheart's own chambers as crown prince had hardly been more luxurious.

Somehow, it seemed cruel.

The baron stared up at Lionheart. He did not glare and he did not frown. His face was an icy mask, save for the blood and spittle flecking his mouth. This gave him a rabid appearance even in his kingly garb.

The men-at-arms pounded and shouted at the door.

"They'll be through within moments," said the baron. He winced and spat out a tooth, then grinned bloodily. "This is a prison, not a bastion."

Lionheart stood back, hoping his trembling fingers had secured the knot well enough, at least for now. His breath wasn't coming quite naturally, but he did not think he'd disgrace himself. Not yet anyway. Another thud on the door signaled the breaking of some poor guardsman's shoulder. In the narrow landing without, there was no room for a battering ram of any size such as they must have used on the door below.

Lionheart returned to the door and pulled free the baron's embedded knife. He retrieved his own blade and the key, which he'd dropped in the scuffle, and secured them in his belt. Then, shaking his head at his near forgetfulness, he returned to the baron and pulled off his boots, his cloak, and his outer tunic, discovering quite a number of delicate little instruments in the process. He could only hope he'd found them all.

"You'd better kill me," the baron said as Lionheart tore the fibula of the rampant panther—the Eldest's insignia—from his shoulder. "It's your only option. If you don't want to see me on your father's throne, my death is your one hope. So why not add murder to your other crimes. It'll take the hangman longer to read out your wrongs to the crowd at your execution; buy you a few more breaths."

The door boomed again. But it held. Its hinges were iron and its frame was stone two feet thick. The door itself was many layers of dense mango wood, seasoned with salt and kiln-dried, made fast with iron fixtures. It did not so much as shudder when struck.

Lionheart sank to the floor, his back to the door, and stared dully across at the baron. He forced himself to draw several long breaths, hoping to ease the bubbling sickness in his belly. He watched the baron's gaze rove the room and saw it at last fix upon the lock.

It should have been impossible for those enormous eyes to widen. But they did.

"You forgot," said Lionheart grimly. "You forgot that the Eldest long ago had this chamber transformed into a bolt hole. A supplied man can fend off all assailants from here."

The baron's face drained of color. But then he smiled and spat more blood and foam. "For how long, Lionheart? Until the Council of Barons decides to reinstate you? To crown you Eldest?"

Lionheart shook his head. "I'm not so patient as that, baron," he said wryly. "We have only to wait for Foxbrush's return."

"*Foxbrush?*" The baron laughed mirthlessly. "You'll risk your neck for the sake of that dullard?"

"He is my father's chosen heir."

The baron laughed again, his voice nearly drowning out the shouts of the assailants behind the door. "A poison-addled choice, and well you know it. And a choice that means nothing now. He's dead."

Once more they struck the door without. Lionheart held the baron's gaze for longer than he would ever have believed possible. In the end, however, he broke first and buried his tired face in his hands.

I vowed to follow you, his heart whispered desperately. *Is this right? Is this what you would have of me?*

But he heard no answer beyond the shouts of those who would kill him the moment they broke through.

20

"THIS WILL STING."

Foxbrush did not understand the child's words and was therefore unprepared when she slapped a greasy poultice to the cut on his heel. He yelped loud enough to draw the attention of all the children gathered in the room.

The child, another redheaded girl, younger than Lark, glared at him. Then she called over her shoulder to her sister, "He won't sit still!"

"Grab his ankle," Lark replied from her place over the cooking fire.

Once again Foxbrush did not understand. So when the little girl grabbed hold of his foot in both her hands and pulled, he resisted for a moment. Then, grimacing, he allowed her to straighten his leg and reapply the poultice. Surely a child that small couldn't mean him any real harm, no matter how dirty her face.

He sat in a stone room in the main square of the Eldest's House, his back to the wall. He could not remember the last time he'd sat on the floor. Certainly never a dirt floor like this! But there was little to no furniture in the house, merely skin rugs and a few rickety chairs that looked at least as uncomfortable as the floor, if not more so. Therefore he sat where he was, surrounded by children.

The girl tending him was called Cattail—*Kitten* by her father. She took her meticulous time over her duties with all the gravity to be found in a child of seven or eight. Meanwhile, a baby boy stood behind her, sucking his fingers and grinning wetly every time Foxbrush glanced his way.

Children were not Foxbrush's area of expertise. He hadn't much liked children even when he was counted among their number. And these children were stranger than any he'd known back then, like small adults with round, solemn faces and eyes that had already seen their share of death.

They were, truth be told, a bit frightening.

Redman sat by the central fire, helping his oldest daughter finish preparing a meal. He ground spices beneath a stone while Lark spread slices of onions and gingerroot and tiny smoked fishes over a cooking stone. They sizzled, and the air was soon full of a strange but pleasant mixture of aromas.

Foxbrush's stomach growled. A mournful wave washed over him at the sound, bringing the too-near memories of his wedding day, uncelebrated, and his wedding feast, untasted. How long had it been now since he'd eaten? Hundreds of years? Or, as he seemed to have fallen *back* in time, perhaps he'd never eaten at all?

His brain halted. Until he had some food in his belly and possibly a night's sleep, he wouldn't try to pursue that mental path any further.

A drum beat somewhere out in the night. Deep, rumbling booms carried up from below the hill. And suddenly the room erupted with even more children than Foxbrush had realized lurked in the shadows. Two more little girls, skinny and scrambling and ginger haired, shouting, "Ma! Mama!" ran from the room, and Cattail let go of Foxbrush's heel and nearly knocked her little brother over in her eagerness to follow her sisters. Even Lark left her onions on the fire, grabbed up young Wolfsbane, and bore him out of the room, shouting as loudly as any of her sisters.

"My wife returns," said Redman, using a stone knife to stir the onions and fish before they burned. "She is Eldest here and she is wise. Years ago when the rivers vanished, all the South Land was thrown into turmoil. But

Eldest Sight-of-Day united five of the thirteen tribes, and others since have come under her mark. Suffering invasion as we do, still we have prospered by the Eldest's leading. The Silent Lady herself trained Sight-of-Day for this role. You know of the Silent Lady in your time?"

Foxbrush nodded, awed to his core. The Silent Lady was the most famous heroine in all Southlander history or legend. "I . . . I thought the Silent Lady died when she fought the Wolf Lord," he said. Then he added thoughtfully, "Or . . . or hasn't she met him yet?"

"Oh, she met him," Redman said, his mustache twitching with a possible smile. But he offered no other explanation.

Soon after, heralded by her eager swarm of young ones, the Eldest herself entered the room, and Foxbrush pulled himself awkwardly to his feet and bowed.

Eldest Sight-of-Day was not a woman of great stature or presence. She was scarcely taller than her oldest daughter, who was tucked affectionately under her arm. Unlike her husband and her children, she was dark as a Southlander, darker even than the women of Foxbrush's day, with a rich sheen to her hair despite the silver threading the black. She wore long skin robes, and decorative bangles covered her bare arms up to her elbows. No crown marked her status, but a stone necklace, a crude starflower chipped into its surface and decorated with white, uncut gems, lay heavily across her collarbone. Her face was lovely, if lined.

"My children tell me we have a guest," she said, speaking in her own language so that Foxbrush did not understand. Her eyes swiftly found Foxbrush where he bowed and squinted in his corner. "A guest from foreign parts."

"Foreign indeed," Redman said, stepping forward and saluting his wife with a kiss. "But his story can wait until you have rested." He peered earnestly at her face in the firelight. "You are tired. Was the journey so hard?"

"No, no," she protested. "The road to Greenwell is easy, with few tributes to pay along the way. But . . ." Here she sighed and shook her head. "Let me sit for a moment."

She took a place away from the fire, and one of her daughters fanned her with a wide fig leaf. The Eldest's face was scored with more than fatigue, and she stared without knowing what she saw at the juices of cooking onions running off the heated stone into the sizzling coals.

The children gathered around her, gazing at her with no less adoration than they might have bestowed upon a goddess. Foxbrush listened with care to their talk. He found that he could, upon occasion, pick out a word or two, even an entire phrase. Perhaps their ancient language was not so dissimilar to his own.

Forgotten in his corner, he felt awkward in this setting of family warmth, coupled so strangely as it was to the knowledge of blood and death and dirt etched on every face present, both young and old. Even small Wolfsbane was not untouched by it, and his dark eyes, so odd beneath a mop of curly red hair, were sweet but not as innocent as one might expect in a child of his age.

"I fear I bring evil tidings from Greenwell," Eldest Sight-of-Day said at last. To Foxbrush's amazement, she spoke now in Redman's language, which Foxbrush could understand. At first he was surprised by this. But then he saw that the younger children did not know what she said, and he wondered if she meant to spare them hearing the news she brought. Only Lark, alert and bright-eyed, seemed to follow the conversation.

"I thought as much," Redman said, motioning to Lark, who brought him carved wooden bowls. He served up their meal as he and his wife spoke. "So the Greenteeth of Greenwell is no longer accepting the agreed-upon tribute."

"Mama Greenteeth is dead."

A sudden stillness took the room. Even the fire seemed to shrink into itself. The children, who did not understand, read the gravity in their parents' faces. The two little girls whose names Foxbrush did not know clung to each other and hid in the shadow of their mother, while Lark took hold of both Wolfsbane and Cattail, drawing them close in silent protection.

Redman cleared his throat and continued serving. "Lark, child," he said, his voice a deep growl. "Come, help me as you should."

Lark obeyed, handing out the steaming, aromatic concoction, which the children and the Eldest accepted. Foxbrush, whom Lark seemed to have forgotten, watched hungrily and dared not speak up.

The Eldest selected a small chunk of fish from her bowl and held it between two fingers. "Blow," she said to her son, and Wolfsbane obeyed, his posy mouth spitting with the effort. The Eldest blew on it herself, then fed him like a baby bird.

Redman banked the coals and settled back along the wall near his wife. He did not look at her. "Dead, you say?"

"Dead." Eldest Sight-of-Day continued to feed her son from her bowl. "When I arrived late this morning, I found the village in uproar."

"Another Faerie?" Redman asked. "Worse than the Greenteeth?"

But the Eldest shook her head. "So I thought and feared. But they tell me otherwise. They say a maid came out of the jungle, a maid wearing a bronze stone about her neck. She dived into the well after a child who was lost. No one saw what happened, but she disappeared and more than an hour passed before suddenly the well frothed and churned and spat her up again, with the living child in her arms. Later they found Mama Greenteeth's body, withered and shrunken like dried waterweeds."

"And this maid," Redman persisted. "Not Faerie?"

"They claim not. They insist she was mortal. A fiery mortal, they say, with hair as red as yours."

At this, Foxbrush felt his empty stomach heave and drop. Redman turned to him sharply, as though he'd heard. "A fiery maid?" he said. "Could it be your lost one?"

All eyes in the room turned to Foxbrush, and he writhed under their stare. The Eldest regarded him with interest now, a knot forming on her brow. "Do you know something of this, stranger?"

"I . . . I'm not sure," Foxbrush admitted, finding it difficult to speak with the dryness of his mouth. Lark, suddenly reminded of his existence, hopped to her feet and filled a bowl for him, which he accepted from her even as he spoke. "I am come seeking my betrothed, Lady Daylily of Middlecrescent, who is not of your . . . of your . . ."

"What our good Foxbrush wishes to say," Redman interrupted, smiling at his wife, "is that neither he nor the maid he seeks are of our time."

The Eldest accepted this with far more ease than Foxbrush might have expected. "Sylphs?" she asked.

"Aye. Sylphs," said her husband. "Though he is a man of our own Land, he wandered into the Wilderlands in search of his missing lady and, as far as I can gather, was caught in a sylph storm. They dragged him far from his own Time. I would be willing to bet my beard his lady was caught by sylphs as well, for it would appear she is the fiery maid of whom the people of Greenwell speak."

"But sylphs care nothing for mortal time," the Eldest said. "I'm not surprised if, caught in their dance, this man was dragged away from his time. But I find it hard to believe that he and his lady would both end up in or near the same small slice of their history. The sylphs may have left her anywhere in the Wood, at any time, both past and future."

Redman acknowledged this with a nod. "You're right, my love. But perhaps our Foxbrush here is guided by another hand. A hand that could direct even the wild dance of the sylphs."

In silence, the Eldest and her husband shared an understanding glance, the significance of which entirely escaped poor Foxbrush. Then the Eldest turned to him, and there was sympathy in her eyes. "I pity you, poor man. A sylph dance is a dreadful thing, or so the Silent Lady tells us. But answer me this, if the Fiery One of Greenwell is indeed your lady, do you know if she makes a practice of slaying Faerie beasts?"

"Um. Not . . . not so far as I'm aware," Foxbrush said hesitantly. After all, if he was honest with himself, there was a great deal about Daylily he did not know, and a great deal more he did not understand. Oddly enough (perhaps it was the presence of young Lark and her sharp resemblance), he found himself remembering the first time he'd met Daylily—Daylily the warrior-king Shadow Hand, fighting monsters and leading armies, even if only in imagination.

He frowned suddenly and put his hand to the pocket of his torn trousers, where he had secreted Leo's scroll before making his escape. The scroll was gone. He must have lost it during his flight through the jungle.

A dullness settled in his heart at this. One more loss. One more failure. But at this point, what difference did it make?

"Not so far as I am aware," he repeated softly, looking down at the bowl of onions and fish. "But . . ." He recalled Leo, hooded and shadowy in the Baron of Middlecrescent's chamber. What was it he had said? "I wouldn't put anything past Lady Daylily."

"Was this red lady at Greenwell when you arrived?" Redman asked his wife.

"I'm afraid not," said the Eldest, accepting a piece of flatbread from Lark and using it to spoon her meal. "They said a strange young man also came from the jungle and took her away again. Another mortal, they insisted, but wild and bloodstained. And he too wore a bronze stone."

Redman studied his wife. She would not meet his gaze. "What are you not telling me?"

She took a bite, chewed, and swallowed slowly. Then she said, "The night following Mama Greenteeth's death, all the firstborn children of the village vanished."

The silence that followed was like darkness. It fell upon the room with sudden, obscuring terror, made more dreadful by the lack of understanding it brought.

"All of them?" Redman repeated at last, his voice scarcely making a dent in the weight of that silence.

The Eldest nodded.

"Light of Lumé," Redman breathed. It was a prayer for protection. But somehow Foxbrush felt that the shadows drew closer to that small cooking fire and the red-lit faces gathered round it.

The Eldest said, "The strangers, the red lady and her companion, demanded tithe for Mama Greenteeth's death. They said the bargain was struck in Greenteeth's blood."

"And did the men and women of Greenwell put up no fight?"

"There was no one to fight. Voices called in the night, and they tell me there were lights like shining candles. The children stepped from their parents' homes and vanished without a trace. That was three days ago now."

Redman put both hands to his scarred face, hiding for a moment from all that was dreadful and crushing upon his soul. Only slowly did he lower them again, looking around at his children. His gaze lingered longest on Lark. Then he turned to his wife with a snarl in his voice.

"We must find them. We must find these two warriors and recover the lost children."

The Eldest shook her head. She held her breath for fear of a sob escaping. But she set aside her bowl and put out a hand to her husband. "There is more to this than we yet know, my love," she said, her voice thick in her throat. "More to these Bronze Warriors. We must learn before we can fight."

"And meanwhile, what if they strike again? What if they kill more totem beasts and demand yet another tithe?"

The Eldest simply shook her head, for she had no answers to give.

Foxbrush sat with his meal cooling in his hands. Hungry though he was, he had no will to eat, not with the strange, sad scene playing out before him. Everything they said was incomprehensible to him.

Quietly he set aside his bowl and got to his feet. Still no one looked his way.

"Your pardon," he said with as much dignity as he could muster while clad only in his trousers, his feet bare, his torso still smeared with Lark's healing medicines. The Eldest and Redman looked up at him as though surprised by his continued existence. "Your pardon," he repeated, "but I must be on my way now. If you would have someone point out the road to this Greenwell, I would be obliged. . . ."

Redman frowned at him, his ugly face far uglier in the firelight. "You're going to set out now, in the dark, on a road you've never traveled?" He made a scoffing noise and did not bother to go on, so ludicrous did this idea strike him.

"Please," said the Eldest, more kindly, "stay a little. You'll not find your red lady, even if she is the one you seek. My men, expert trackers all, searched the whole of that area for any sign of her or her companion. They found nothing save this on the lip of the well." She put a hand into a pouch at her side and withdrew a slip of dirtied silk, once white. This she handed to Foxbrush, who took it with a shudder. A scrap of Daylily's wedding gown.

"I must find her," he said, clenching the sorry remnant into his fist.

"As must we," said Eldest Sight-of-Day. "We must find them all and the children they stole. Stay with us, stranger. You may be able to help. Not tonight. Not in the dark. The dark is full of too many hungers."

Foxbrush felt his legs giving way at those words and hastily sat before he disgraced himself further. He curled his knees to his chest and studied the fire even as Redman and the Eldest conferred together in low tones. Their words trailed with the smoke up through the hole in the roof, for Foxbrush could no longer listen or even try to comprehend.

He saw Daylily in the flames. Daylily, his resentful bride.

Daylily, the monster slayer.

For the first time since all these dreadful events began, his heart beat with terror for someone other than himself.

Lark, sitting beside her mother, watched Foxbrush. Then she crossed to him, picked up his bowl, and placed it in his hands. She took a seat beside him. "Eat," she said and grinned, which was an odd but welcome sight in that room of solemn fears.

Foxbrush, who never ate without silver, grimaced down at his bowl. Worms—that's what the cold onions resembled, coiled round the chunks of fish and spices. Grimacing but feeling the pressure of Lark's gaze, he selected a sliver of onion and popped it into his mouth.

The explosion of heat on his tongue was enough to make him choke. Sweat broke out on his nose, and his eyes watered.

Lark giggled. "Hot," she warned rather late. Then she scrambled to her feet, all elbows and knees, and scampered to a dark corner of the room. She returned with a bowl of goat's milk, which Foxbrush drank gratefully despite the taste of grass and mud and lingering goat. It cooled the burn, and he could then taste the variety of flavors so rich upon his tongue. Cinnamon and sugar, peppers and ginger, along with spices he did not recognize combined in ways he had never before imagined. Yes, there was also a taste of dirt—one to which he must become adjusted in this era of dirt—but if anything, it enhanced the whole. He had never, in all the royal banquets and feasts at which he had dined, tasted anything like this.

"Good?" Lark asked.

He managed a smile, braced himself, and took another bite. "Good," he said, gulping down more milk.

Far beyond the village borders, a wind stirred the tops of the jungle trees. In that wind a voice called eagerly, *Foxbrush! Foxbrush! Where are you? I'm coming for you, Foxbrush!*

21

BY THE TIME THEY REACHED THE WOOD, Daylily was breathing properly. But with breathing came words, and she moaned and whimpered and made a fool of herself. Sun Eagle told her to be silent, and his command was sharp enough to shut her mouth at least until they'd descended the gorge and regained the shadows of the Between.

There Sun Eagle allowed Daylily to collapse beneath a tree, shuddering and drawing her knees up to her chest, clutching at the sides of her head. He stood back at first and watched her, fighting the various urges that pushed him this way and that. Then he shook these off and was himself for a moment at least. He knelt and put an arm around Daylily's shoulder.

"You have nothing to fear," he said quietly as she buried her face in his neck. "You have taken the Bronze. Nothing can hurt you."

But she shook her head and moaned again.

"Was it that thing inside you?" Sun Eagle asked.

She nodded. In a voice like a child's she said, "She will always hunt me. She will always plague me. I will never be free. And then she will devour me."

Sun Eagle sat holding her, silent and uncertain what to say. Something fluttered into the branches of the tree above them, and he looked up to see a songbird there, brown with a speckled breast and bright eye. The bird sang, and the song fell over the two below. Sun Eagle shivered at that sound, and his stomach turned.

Form the bond. Do what you must.

He stood, leaving Daylily where she was, and his voice was no longer comforting. "Stay here," he said. "I must go to the Land and establish the tithe for the beast's death. Don't go anywhere." He bent and pulled the bronze stone from beneath her tangle of hair, arranging it so that any who might happen by this way would see it at once. Daylily made no move but to press against the tree, shuddering. He scowled at her. "I'll return shortly," he said.

Then he was gone and she was alone in the Wood. Or not quite alone.

"You know what I told you," sang the bird in the tree above.

Daylily, startled, looked up and glared at the bird. "You again? Why don't you leave me in peace?"

"If I leave you," replied the bird, hopping from branch to branch, "you'll have no peace. Do you remember what I told you?"

"No," she said, which was a lie. But the bird knew it was a lie, so it didn't much matter.

He ruffled his wings, then cocked his head to one side. "You'll have to let it go," he sang. "If you don't, it will eat you, just as you fear."

"If I do, it will eat me; if I don't, it will eat me. The end is the same either way," said Daylily. Her voice was dull now with a quiet acceptance. "But I have done my duty. I have taken it away into the Wood, and I have found one who can bind it better than I could. It will eat me, but it will eat no one else!"

"There's where you're wrong," said the bird. "The longer you cling to it, Daylily, the stronger it will—"

She snarled, interrupting the song of the brown bird, drowning out the words so that she could not hear them. Then she groaned, bowed her head, and sank into a deep, troubled sleep.

————

In the broad, barren landscape that was both dream and memory, the being which assumed Daylily's form walked, searching and sniffing and watching warily. The being knew it would find the she-wolf if it looked hard enough. There wasn't much else to find in this place. Not anymore. Not in this new, strange, wonderful, awful mind.

What a find it was! What a catch! A mind like this, properly tempered, could do so many things, and the face of Daylily smiled a smile that was not Daylily's.

"So you're wearing *her* now, are you?"

The figure of Daylily turned in a flurry of torn wedding clothes, and the smile that was not hers grew at the sight of the red she-wolf. The rusted manacles tore more deeply than ever into the wolf's flesh so that the ruddy red of her coat disappeared under the scarlet red of blood. But the wolf's eyes flashed ice-blue. "I don't think that aspect becomes you at all. You look a fright!"

The face that was Daylily's frowned. *Oh, you think so? How sad. Perhaps we should . . . oh, wait! We almost forgot!* The smile that wasn't hers returned, quick as a knife. *Nothing you say can matter anymore. You're practically dead.*

"Not dead yet!" said the wolf.

Better than dead, said the figure of Daylily. She knelt and touched the chains. The wolf tried to lunge at her, and she flinched, then relaxed. The manacles were far too strong.

But she saw that the bronze stone she had tied about the wolf's neck had slipped off. She picked it up.

How did this happen?

The wolf panted in agony, but there was a grin in her voice. "Don't you wish you knew?"

The figure of Daylily sat and looked upon the wolf. Then, with a strength beyond any she knew outside of dreams, she took hold of the chain securing the wolf's right forepaw and twisted it, twisted the wolf's leg, farther and farther, up unto the breaking point and then—*Snap!*

The wolf screamed in Daylily's voice. The whole of that barren world, the gray plain and the dark sky, rocked in agony. And when she stopped and the wolf lay gasping in agony, the figure that was Daylily tied the bronze stone on its cord about the wolf's neck to dangle beneath the huge iron collar.

You're much stronger than we thought.

The wolf could not answer through the pain.

We know how to break you. We know all your secrets. You see, we are Daylily now. And she is us. And we are strong together.

The wolf's voice was a puppy's whimper. But already her leg was beginning to heal, though it was warped and painful still, for the bone was unset. Her lips curled back from her teeth, revealing pale white gums. "You'll never be strong enough," she gasped.

Won't we?

The figure that was Daylily sat upright.

Behold our strength.

She put out an arm. It reached for miles, for leagues, for years. It reached beyond worlds and beyond minds. And it found a place where a young man hid in the topmost reaches of a tower, the door bolted and blocked, his captive bound to an iron link in the wall. He sat with his back to the door, listening to the whispers of those outside planning how to get in, fighting exhaustion and terror in his struggle to keep awake and alive.

The thing that was Daylily grabbed him by the collar and lifted him out of himself, hurtling him back across distances so vast they could not be fathomed, for such is the distance between each mind. And he, as dreamers do, thought nothing of this strange flight. If he felt anything at all, it was relief to be, however briefly, freed from the *knock, knock, knock*ing on the far side of the tower door.

He stood upon the barren plain, his eyes closed, feeling nothing save the ground beneath his feet.

Then the she-wolf said, "Lionheart?"

He turned. What he saw startled him so much that he staggered back three paces and flung out his hands to catch his balance. Then he whispered, "Daylily?"

For it was she whom he saw bound by the manacles to the dirt-driven stakes, facedown with a chain about her neck. Her red hair fell freely over her shoulders and face, her only covering in that desolate place. For here she could have no protection.

"Daylily!" he cried and leapt forward, unaware of anything else that might watch them. He did not know if he dreamed or if, by some strange magic (many strange magics had been happening to him lately) he had been transported here. He fell to his knees beside her, searching for some lock or catch he might undo. "What happened to you? How did you come to be so bound?"

"Go away, Lionheart," said she, her voice husky and low. "Don't touch those chains."

But he tried anyway, for such was his nature, always contrary, always disobeying. He could find no means to free her, however, and at last he had to sit back, his fingers bruised and bleeding, staring at her aghast.

She struggled up to her knees. The length of the chain allowed her that much freedom at least. Her hair, longer here than it had ever been in life, fell across her front and covered her knees like robes.

"Did you return to Southlands?" she asked.

"Yes," he said.

"After I was gone?"

"After you were gone."

"But that didn't matter, did it? You did not come for me."

Lionheart tried to swallow. The air was very dry, cold, and still in this place. "I came to make peace with my father."

"That is good," said Daylily, bowing her head so as not to look at him. "He is dying."

"He is dead," said Lionheart. "But I saw him. Before the end."

She nodded. Then she said, "What did you do? When you left me, what did you do?"

"I died."

Her icy eyes flashed up at him from under her shielding hair. "A ghost, then? Is that why you're here?"

But he shook his head. "Not a ghost. I'm not dead anymore."

He wasn't. In the darkness of this place under that midnight sky, Lionheart's face glowed. A glow of change, of growth, of life beyond anything Daylily had ever known or experienced. The closest thing to it she remembered seeing was in the face of a newly opened lotus flower just as the first breath of morning touched its petals. It had seemed to respond with a song of color and vibrancy that Daylily herself could not hear but could just barely see.

It was a sight she hated, for she could not share it. And she hated it now in Lionheart's eyes.

She tried to raise her hands as some sort of shield, but the chains on her arms restrained her. She could only turn her head and stare out across the blight of her mind toward a horizon of darkness.

"Did you find Rose Red?" she asked at last. "Did you save her?"

Lionheart studied that profile, the crisp lines of her jaw and brow, harder and more stern, yet simultaneously more vulnerable in this barren land. Beautiful Daylily, not so beautiful now. He found it difficult to speak.

"No," he managed. "That is, I did find her, but it was not I who saved her. She is safe now though. She is . . ." He stopped, uncertain how to continue, and Daylily heard many things in that silence, things he might not have intended to reveal. "She is safe," he said. "And she is whole."

"By whole, I assume you mean no longer hideous," Daylily said, still gazing out to the emptiness. "Did you come upon some beauty spell and, just like magic, solve all your problems?"

"Rose Red was always beautiful," said Lionheart. "I was simply too blind to see it."

How she wished to laugh! How she wished to throw his words back in his face, to ridicule, to . . . to bite.

To tear.

To rip.

The red wolf turned suddenly and lunged at Lionheart. But he did not move, for he had seen already what she was, and he knew that she could not reach him. As he looked at her, tears welled in his eyes, spilled over, and fell to the dust, where they disappeared, unable to touch the dryness.

"I wish—" He stopped, waiting for his breath to allow more words. "I wish I could save you, Daylily," he said.

The she-wolf growled and lunged again, and fresh blood flowed from the bite of the chains. "I don't *want* you to save me!" she roared. "I want to *kill* you!"

"I see now," Lionheart said, quiet before that ravening fury. "You bound yourself. Your true self. Deep inside."

"But I'll get free!" the wolf raged. "I'll get free, and I'll see you dead! I'll see them all dead!"

"You're killing yourself. From the inside out."

"At least I'll be free from all of you." Again and again the wolf struggled and tore at the earth and howled and shook her shaggy head. But the stakes held, and the chains, though they groaned, were strong. At last the wolf collapsed again. The bronze stone about her neck weighed her down.

Lionheart stood looking upon her, and more tears coursed down his cheeks. "I wish I could save you," he said. "But I understand that I can't. This is why I wasn't sent after you. This is why I must remain."

"You'll *never* come after me! Coward!" The wolf panted, scarcely able to get the words out, so thick were her mouth and throat with foam.

Lionheart turned even as she hurled curses and abuse at his back. He walked away into the empty plain, each pace taking him farther from her sight. He disappeared at last into the gray and the dark.

The wolf collapsed and did not breathe, strangled under the weight of the Bronze on her cord.

The being that wore Daylily's shape stepped outside, back into the Between, where Daylily sat pressed up against a tree, her head bowed to her chest. Her eyes flickered softly open, and consciousness flowed back in, however unwillingly.

There. We are safe now. The wolf is dead.

"No," Daylily whispered. "No, she isn't. She always revives."

She said no more but waited quietly until Sun Eagle returned. She looked to him as one might look to a stern but adored father from whom one expects protection. Her face was, very briefly, beautiful again in this expression, and Sun Eagle stopped in his tracks, surprised by it. Then he advanced and knelt before her, reaching out to take her hand.

"It is done," he said. "The bond is made. The tithe is paid."

"Is it well, then?" Daylily asked, her voice simple as a child's.

"It is well. Come, Crescent Woman. Our brethren have taken the tithe for Tocho's death, but that does not mean you may continue to sit here. There is yet much to do."

He lifted her to her feet and led her back through the Wood. The little brown bird watched them go, then took to his wings and followed.

22

OVER YOUR SHOULDER, like this," said Redman.

Foxbrush winced as rough grasses scratched the back of his neck. He shrugged into the shoulder straps of an enormous wicker basket tall enough to extend above his head. It was empty for the moment and therefore light. How heavy it would be by the end of the day was anyone's guess.

Lark stood beside him, her own smaller basket slung, her face frowning but not unfriendly. She took the measure of the young man her father assisted, watching as Redman secured the leather straps across Foxbrush's chest.

"There," Redman grunted. "You're as ready as you'll ever be." He stepped back, looking from Foxbrush to his daughter and back again. He spoke in the North Country dialect, addressing Foxbrush. "I'll not ask you to look after my girl. She's a smart little thing, and she'll look after you, more like! But this is her first time without her da, and, well . . ." He stopped and shrugged, leaving Foxbrush to wonder how he might have finished that sentence.

Redman turned to Lark and spoke to her in the language of her mother's people. "You have the tributes?"

Lark put her hand to a pouch at her waist. "Yes, Da. I'm ready. There are only three totems."

"True enough, and you know them all." Redman crossed his arms and indicated Foxbrush with a slight nod of his head. "Are you sure you're willing to bring him along?"

"I can't fetch the lot on my own," Lark replied demurely.

"True. But I can find one of the village boys if you like."

Lark made a face at this. One of the village boys would domineer and stick out his chest and do everything to take charge. Where would the fun be in that? She shook her head and smiled up at Foxbrush, who understood none of the conversation taking place between her and her father and offered only a weak half smile in return. *He* certainly wouldn't try to take the lead! But to her father Lark said only, "He knows nothing. He needs to learn."

"Don't think unkindly of him, Larkish," said Redman. She rolled her eyes at his use of her pet name, but he continued, "If there's one thing I've learned in all my years, it's that heroes come in many shapes, sizes, and forms. Might be we have a hero here in our midst."

Lark glanced again at Foxbrush, who was picking at his nails. She'd never seen a man who worried so about his hands. Or his washing. Or his hair! Foxbrush had spent a good portion of the morning plastering down his hair (which was unusually short) with water and combing it with his fingers. All to no avail; the humid air quickly caught all that thick hair of his up into a curly dark halo.

A hero? Lark covered her mouth to force back a laugh, then readjusted the basket on her back, saying solemnly, "I'll take him, Da. I'll show him the totems."

"And back before sunset?" Redman said.

She nodded. Then she reached out and took Foxbrush's hand. "Come!"

With a hesitant look back over his shoulder (which the tall basket made difficult), Foxbrush followed the ginger-haired girl down the hill from the Eldest's House to the jungle.

Three days had passed since Foxbrush had made his wild escape attempt. Three days during which he had learned how to tie on a pair of trousers made from animal hide, how to wrap his feet in hide to protect his tender soles, how to eat by pulling meat from the bone with his teeth, and how to sleep with nameless creatures eating, breeding, birthing, and dying in the thatched ceiling above his head.

Three days of nightmare. Then this morning dawned, and Redman (who'd spent the previous two days repairing the wall Foxbrush damaged) announced that the time had come for Foxbrush to earn his keep.

Lark led him by the hand as the green of the jungle canopy closed over their heads. Daylight rendered the shadows no less ominous than they had seemed three nights ago. The path was narrow and roots trailed over it in treacherous twists, ready to trip up the unwary. Great fronds reached out to caress Foxbrush's cheek, and these dripped with wetness from the rain fallen the night before.

Eyes watched their every move.

Foxbrush fixed his gaze on the little girl before him, the least threatening sight in his field of vision. Her red hair was shiny with grease, but he had already ceased to smell the body odor of her or any other member of the village. The senses can only stand so much, after all. Besides, he knew he would very soon smell as ripe as any of them.

Light of Lumé! He needed to get out of this place!

He closed his eyes for a few paces and let the coos and caws and shrieks of life surrounding him swallow up that thought. He couldn't leave. Not without Daylily.

When he opened his eyes, Lark was looking up at him with an oddly solemn expression.

"We are nearing the first totem," she said.

Foxbrush blinked with surprise. Her accent was strong, the cadence a little strange. Nevertheless, it was unmistakably a variation on the South-lander Foxbrush knew. He frowned at her. "Did I just . . . I understood you just now, didn't I."

Lark grinned back, pleased by his reaction. "I speak Northerner as well as my da, better than my ma. My sisters are still learning, so Da and Ma speak in Da's tongue when they do not want the little ones to know what they say. But I am the oldest. I know." The gleam in her eye vanished suddenly, and she dropped her gaze, softly repeating, "I know." She put a finger to her lips then. "We approach the first totem. You must be quiet."

"But how do you—"

"Hush!"

Her reprimand was enough to freeze Foxbrush's tongue in his mouth. At a sign from her, he stayed put, watching as she continued up the path, pushing overhanging branches from her way. Soon he could see only the top of her bright head.

Then he heard her small voice calling (though he did not understand the words): "Crookjaw, restless one, little nimble fingers!"

Foxbrush ran to catch up with Lark, nearly stumbling over her in his haste. She turned a furious glare up at him and again put a finger to her lips. Then she took a hard, flat cake from the pouch at her side and stepped toward a low stone Foxbrush had not seen before. It was black and nearly hidden in foliage, but Lark uncovered it to reveal the image of an ugly old man's face, rendered crudely with deep crevices around its mouth and almost no nose. Someone had painted it long ago in garish pigments now mostly flaked away by the elements. Red and blue circles still ringed the closed, heavy-lidded eyes, however, and the cruel lips were orange stained. The top of its head formed a flat surface covered in bits of dead leaves and bird droppings that gave the appearance of hair.

Lark set the flat cake on the stone. Then she clapped her hands and called again, "Crookjaw! Crookjaw, I bring you tribute! Does it please you?"

Lark spoke in a singsong, her childish voice sweet. An odd little superstition, Foxbrush supposed. He'd read about such things in his studies, the crude beliefs and practices of older times. Funny, he'd never thought to see—

A screech erupted overhead.

The trees began to shake as though blown by a tremendous storm. Had it not been strapped to his back, Foxbrush would have dropped the basket as he hunched and craned his neck. Some dark shadow hidden by thick greenery swung through the branches above, then dropped onto the stone head.

It was a monkey. A large, smelly, evil-eyed monkey, brown and bearded, picking bugs from its ears with long, many-jointed fingers. It inspected each bug with the eye of a connoisseur. Some it tossed aside. Others it popped into its mouth and ate with great smacking and apparent enjoyment. It did not look at Foxbrush, Lark, or the cake but seemed absorbed in this nasty pursuit.

Foxbrush hated monkeys, even the little tame things that noble ladies sometimes wore on their shoulders at festivals in his day. But this creature was more hateful still. Its jaw, which looked as though it may have been broken at some point, hung crooked and sagging when it wasn't munching.

"Crookjaw, I bring tribute," said Lark, repeating her singsong chant. She pointed at the cake, demanding, "Does it please you, Crookjaw? Does it please you?"

The monkey flared its nostrils at her. Then it yawned hugely, displaying a terrible set of yellow fangs incongruously large for its small, wizened face. It extended a hand, fingers wriggling. Lark stepped forward fearlessly, picked the cake off the stone, and dropped it into the monkey's grasp.

With a shriek that could shatter glass, the monkey stuffed the cake whole into its mouth and vanished up into the treetops. Birds screamed and fluttered out of its way; the world rained broken branches and falling leaves. Foxbrush covered his head against this storm and felt more than a few unseen items land in his open basket.

"What was that?" he asked a little breathlessly.

"The first totem," Lark replied with a smile. "There are two more on our way to the Twisted Man. Come!"

She set off without further explanation, leaving Foxbrush to page through his mind for some memory of that strange word. He knew he'd read it before somewhere. And . . . yes! He'd even seen one in the Eldest's gallery. A totem, a statue from old Southlander history, usually carved in stone, though some decayed wooden totems had been found. The one on display at the Eldest's House was a hook-beaked bird with furious human eyes, outspread wings, and a flat-topped head such as Foxbrush had just seen. The old Southlanders had purportedly left ritual offerings on these stones to appease godlike beings.

A ritual he had now witnessed firsthand.

He adjusted his basket and drew a deep breath of muggy, buggy air. "Tell me, Meadowlark," he said to the back of the girl's head, "was that—"

"Lark. Not Meadowlark."

"Very well," said Foxbrush. "Tell me, Lark, was that one of your gods?"

The look she turned upon him stopped him in his tracks. "We don't have gods," she said.

"Oh now, don't be angry," Foxbrush persisted, falling back into step with her. "I know you people are very religious. You worshipped the Wolf Lord once, and the Dragonwitch—"

The girl whirled upon Foxbrush with such ferocity that he braced for attack. And, small child though she was, he was not convinced he could fend her off.

"I *never* worshiped the Wolf Lord!" she snarled, her dark eyes blazing. In her fury, she kept slipping out of Northerner into her native tongue and back again. But Foxbrush had no trouble understanding her meaning. "Or the Dragonwitch! The Silent Lady bested the Wolf Lord, calling down his death, and he will never plague my people again! My father, mother, and the Smallman King of the North Country battled the Dragonwitch, and the rivers rose to fight her with them! They brought down her Citadel and buried her beneath it, and all this land"—she swept her scrawny arms as though to encompass the entire jungle—"grew up green and thriving in gratitude so that her ruins will never be found again! We have no monster gods in this country, and we will nevermore be bound in slavery! And one day—" her voice broke with the intensity of her passion. She was obliged to draw breath before continuing, and then she finished in a quieter voice. "One day we'll drive out the Faerie beasts as well."

With that, she turned and continued down the winding trail. Foxbrush, cowed, followed quietly behind. He decided not to tell her that it was impossible for a jungle this thick and tall and old to have grown up since her father's youth. He also decided not to mention that it was impossible for a Silent Lady to *call* anything.

But one piece of Lark's strange speech did linger in his mind. *The Smallman King.* He knew that story. He'd learned on his nursemaid's knee long ago how the Smallman King came down to Southlands and battled the Dragonwitch. Accompanied by . . .

"His scar-faced cousin," Foxbrush whispered.

At the next totem, Lark performed a ritual similar to the first, leaving a flat cake on an ugly, painted stone. This time no animal emerged, but after a minute or two, Lark declared, "She is satisfied," and continued on her way. Her fury seemingly forgotten or forgone, she said, "Eanrin will someday put it in song. The story of my father. He promised."

"Eanrin?" Foxbrush said. "You know of Bard Eanrin? Here?"

"I've met him," said Lark.

"You've *met* the Faerie Bard, Chief Poet of Iubdan Rudiobus?"

Lark's shrug was almost hidden beneath her wicker basket. "Well, I don't remember it. When I was born he came to honor my da and my ma. Back when the Silent Lady was still with us."

"The Silent Lady? *With* you?"

"Yes." Lark graced Foxbrush with possibly the smuggest expression he had ever seen. "She is my great-great aunt. She lived with us until I was five years old. Then she left. But she taught us how to appease the Faerie beasts so that they don't harm us."

These claims fit nowhere in Foxbrush's view of reality—dragons, sylphs, totems, and Faerie queens aside. He smiled. "If you say so."

Once more, Lark rounded on him. "You don't believe me."

"I didn't say—"

"You don't believe me!" She brandished her fists at him. "Do not speak to me like I'm a child! I know what I know, and I know more than you do! You don't even know about the totems! If my father hadn't found you in the jungle, the Faerie beasts would have eaten you alive, and then where would you be?"

"Easy, easy." Foxbrush, quite alarmed by now, raised both his hands. The jungle, interested by the goings-on below, gathered in many feathery, furry, winged forms in the branches above and called down encouragement in all manner of animal voices, urging a fight. Its hopes were disappointed, for Foxbrush, in a tone far humbler than he had perhaps ever used in his life, said, "Forgive me, Eldest's daughter. I am out of my time and equally out of my depth. I do not know your land or your laws, and the things you say to me seem like nursery tales. It is difficult for me to understand, and I beg your patience."

Lark was quick to wrath but quick also to forgiveness. Her scowls vanished in smiles, and she reached out to take Foxbrush's hand, smiling even more when he flinched at her touch. She led him on in peaceful silence, leaving him to wonder how much he believed of her strange stories and how much he dared not believe.

They passed another totem like the first two. Here a tall white egret stepped out of the greenery, its head moving in pulsing rhythm with each step. It took the cake Lark offered and walked on without a word; and as far as Foxbrush could guess, it may have just been a bird tamed to expect food from this devoted source.

But Lark said, "He is pleased," and they continued on their way.

Sooner than Foxbrush expected—though it was difficult to gauge time on this green-grown trail—the jungle thinned and he saw the gorge opening up before them. He also saw the destination of their day trek: the gnarled, rock-grasping black fig tree.

Foxbrush's footsteps faltered even as Lark continued on her way. His memories of those first moments after he'd climbed from the gorge were convoluted at best. He remembered the wasps well enough, and he remembered the burn of their stings. He also remembered the inhuman voice that had responded to Redman, but he did not want to remember this, so he nearly convinced himself it had been a dream brought on by his terror.

This lie comforted him briefly. Even as he stood on the fringes of the jungle, Lark approached the tree and called out:

> *"Oh, Twisted Man, whose bark is thick,*
> *Who plunges rocks for wells to find,*
> *Here is tribute! Here is tribute!*
> *Take it, Twisted Man, and quick!"*

This time she withdrew from her pouch a handful of dried lily petals, which she threw at the tree just as her father had done days before. Even as she clapped her hands and spun about in place, a wind seemed to rush through the fig tree's leaves. Its branches spread like grasping fingers, caught the fluttering petals, and drew them up inside.

Then the Twisted Man stepped out.

He was exactly what his name implied, every limb twisted and gnarled like a branch, the skin—if such it could be called—deeply creviced like old bark. From each limb sprouted many branches as twisted as the arms themselves, and at the end of each branch was a twiggy hand. His face, on a trunk-like torso with no sign of a neck, was that of an old, craggy man, and his hair was green leaves.

"I like the tribute well," he said in an inhuman language that, horribly, Foxbrush understood. Black eyes shot with green looked down on Lark contemplatively. "You are smaller than the mortal who usually pays me."

"He is my father," Lark replied without even the slightest tremble in her voice. "I am his sapling, sprung from his seed, grown at his roots. I have come for your benevolent bounty."

The Twisted Man tilted his whole body as a dog might curiously tilt its head. The many little grasping hands joyfully shook their fists full of petals.

"I like the tribute well," he said. "You may take of my bounty."

"Call off your wasps, then, Twisted Man," Lark said. "Send them sleeping to their nests until it's time for them to wake."

"Very well," said the Twisted Man. Then he stepped back and vanished into his tree. Its great boughs wavered a moment, the big leaves rustling before going still.

Only then did Foxbrush realize he'd stopped breathing.

He collapsed to his knees, gasping for breath, his mind desperately running for any reasonable explanation it might find and coming only to dead ends. If he fainted, he told himself, who could blame him? Would it truly unman him to succumb to the white whirling in his head, the bright lights bursting on the edge of his vision?

Lark turned to him, shaking her head. "Get up," she said. "Take off your basket and help me. We must gather fruit while he still remembers the tribute is paid. You don't want to get stung again, do you?"

In a numb wave of determined disbelief swiftly ebbing into an ocean of overwhelming—and completely unwelcome—belief, Foxbrush did as he was told. Both he and Lark took off their baskets; then he lifted the girl into the black fig tree's branches, where she scrambled about, nimble as a ginger-haired monkey, gathering fruit.

Foxbrush harvested his share as well, filling the baskets quickly. Every fig he plucked buzzed as though it were alive, which startled him so much the first few times that he nearly dropped them. He swiftly realized that the buzzing was caused by the wasps living inside: tiny, delicate, shimmer-green wasps, with lacy wings and enormous stingers for their size. A few crawled out and even perched upon his hand. He broke out in a sweat at this but continued moving methodically.

"They won't sting you," Lark told him. "The Twisted Man called them off."

"Right," Foxbrush replied breathlessly. He picked until his own basket was nearly half full before he managed to ask, "Is . . . is the Twisted Man, then, as it were, the *spirit* of the fig tree?"

"What? Oh no!" Lark, perched in the branches above, laughed merrily. "What makes you think such a thing?"

Foxbrush scowled. "I'm trying to make sense of the situation according to the rules of nature that seem to prevail in this world of yours. It struck me as a logical assumption."

Lark laughed again, probably because she did not understand half of what he said. "The Twisted Man is a Faerie beast. He came up from the Wilderlands, like all the Faerie beasts. The rivers in the gorges kept them out for ages, but when the rivers rose up to drown the Dragon-witch, they left the gorges behind and the Wilderlands grew. Now Faerie beasts of all kinds cross from their world into ours. They like it here," she said this with a certain pride in her nation. "We have lush forests and rivers and—"

"You said the rivers dried up."

"No, no, the Faerie rivers that were gate guards are gone. We have plenty of normal rivers flowing down from the mountains. The Faerie beasts like those. And the Twisted Man liked this tree, though he had to battle Crookjaw for it when first he came. What a fight that was . . ."

The child rattled on for some time after Foxbrush had given up trying to listen. They finished filling their baskets with the wasp-infested fruit, then shouldered them to make the return journey. The weight of figs in such bulk surprised Foxbrush; he was puffing and panting within a few paces. Lark, by contrast, proved the strength of her scrawny limbs and seemed no more burdened than when they had first set out.

" . . . so we pay the tribute at the totems as the Silent Lady taught us," she was saying when next Foxbrush bothered to listen. "This keeps them from pestering us, though most of them are harmless enough, not like Mama Greenteeth." She stopped here, and her brown little face took on serious lines unusual in one her age.

"Mama Greenteeth?" Foxbrush said. "I heard your parents speak of her. She was killed."

"Yes," Lark acknowledged. "By something worse than she. By the red lady who wears the bronze stone."

"What is the bronze stone? Do you know?"

Lark shook her head. "I'd not heard my parents speak of it, even in Northern tongue, until that night. But whatever it means, it is worse than Mama Greenteeth if it demands firstborn children as tribute. Even she was satisfied by wafers."

She fell into a silence made all the more dismal by the variety of noises around them. They neared the totem where they had seen the egret, and Lark made as though to pass without stopping. But Foxbrush glanced at the stone. And he gasped.

"What are you doing?" Lark demanded, for Foxbrush leapt to the side of the trail and pushed the leaves back from the totem, revealing what lay upon its flat top.

"My scroll!" He reached out but paused suddenly before touching it. "It's my scroll, the one my cousin gave me. May I . . . is it . . ."

"If Kolkata put it there for you, you may take it," Lark said, nodding approval.

So Foxbrush picked up the scroll, which looked a little worse for wear but still whole despite the nights it had spent in the elements. His trousers had no pockets, so he tucked it down the front of his shirt. For some reason, he felt better knowing it was there and he hadn't lost it. Along with everything else he'd lost.

They continued on in sweaty silence. After they'd passed the second of the totems, Foxbrush said, "I'm curious about one thing. Why are we going so far out of our way to gather wasp-infested black figs? Are they goat feed?"

"No," said Lark. "They're for the elder figs."

"The what?"

"The elder figs. We need black figs to . . . to . . . I don't know how you say it. To make them fruit. To give them life, to . . ."

"To cross-pollinate?"

Foxbrush stopped in his tracks. His heart froze, then leapt to his throat and thundered there to escape. Not even when he'd fled the sylphs and the wasps had it pounded so vehemently. "You cross-pollinate *black figs* with elder figs?"

Lark shrugged. "Without black figs, elder figs can't be eaten. Hurry up!" She was nearly out of sight within a few paces, so thick was the growth over that trail. Still it was several moments before Foxbrush could find the breath to leap after her.

He could not believe it! Of all the unbelievabilities he'd faced in recent life, this was by far the most outrageous!

"I can save Southlands," he whispered. Then he laughed a choking, gasping, desperate sort of laugh, and tears sprang to his eyes. "I can save Southlands!"

23

LIONHEART WOKE from violent, unruly dreams to discover that the baron had mostly cut through his bindings.

It took him a moment to realize what was happening. After sitting for so many hours, his body felt like a bundle of knotted cord. He'd not intended to drift off, and he shook himself now, desperate to regain consciousness. His brain was full of red wolf and barren landscape, and he sat in a haze, trying to clear these images from his mind.

With a start like a kick in the stomach, he saw what the baron was doing and was on his feet and surging across the room before his legs were quite ready to move. Thus he fell headlong into the baron but succeeded in knocking the little knife from his hands and sending it clattering across the floor.

"Dragons eat you," said the baron in a voice that would freeze bonfires. He said nothing more but sat watching with a calculating gaze as Lionheart retied his bonds, now with a much shorter length from the iron ring.

Exhausted and bleary, Lionheart backed away from the baron, studying him. Where had that knife come from? The man was barefoot and bereft of his outer garments. But his undershirt was billowy and dark and might conceal many things.

Lionheart plucked his own knife from his belt and stepped forward. He saw the baron flinch, but only just; after all, he'd expected murder all along.

"If I were going to kill you, I wouldn't have gone through all this bother," Lionheart said as he cut away the baron's shirt and pulled it off his body in rags. There were two more knives attached to his elbows and one tiny penknife at his wrist. Lionheart appropriated these and, after a moment's hesitation, tossed them out one of the windows to break upon the courtyard stones below. "Even *I'm* not such a fool."

"Fool enough," the baron said. He looked strangely . . . small. Stripped of his majestic trimmings, not to mention the hidden weapons, he was almost a pathetic sight.

Yet his eyes were like knives themselves.

"Do you hear that sound, Eldest's son?" he asked even as Lionheart returned to lean his back against the great, heavy door.

Listening despite himself, Lionheart heard nothing; nothing save a faint murmur far below, the clatter of hooves in the courtyard, and occasional gruff shouts. North Tower stood too high above it all for him to make out any words.

It took him a moment to realize what the baron meant. No one was knocking at the chamber door.

"That is the sound of your doom brewing," said the baron softly. "First they flung themselves against the breakers, useless and weak. Now they mass for a tidal wave that will sweep you away."

"Right." Lionheart offered the baron a grim half smile. "But only if they can get through the door."

"How long do you think you can hide in here?" the baron persisted, twisting in the attempt to find a more comfortable position. With the rope shortened, his wrists bound together at chin level, comfort became an elusive friend at best. "How long do you hope to prevent me from taking my rightful place as master of this kingdom?"

"At least as long as the supplies hold out," Lionheart said with a shrug. "What supplies?"

All along Lionheart had known this was a foolish plan, though, if asked, he would have preferred the word *daring*. Kidnapping the most powerful man in the nation on his coronation day was perhaps not the wisest notion ever to take a young rebel's fancy.

But it might have worked. The baroness, after all, had proven a willing and even reasonably cunning ally. Had she not made certain the door to this chamber was open and ready? Had she not sent servants discreetly bearing rope in readiness for her husband's binding?

Had she not *promised* to supply abundant food and water for the probability of a long siege?

Trying to appear calm, Lionheart got back up to search the room. The cupboards and the great wardrobe were empty; the sumptuous canopied bed hid nothing beneath but a chamber pot.

"Overlook a little detail, Prince Lionheart?" said the baron, watching as Lionheart climbed up to check the top of the wardrobe, just in case. "I noticed while you slept, and I wondered."

Lionheart clenched his teeth to hold back the tirade of furious words bubbling up inside. He could not suppress an angry whisper of: "Dragons take that woman."

The baron's chin lifted a little, and his great eyes narrowed. "What woman?"

Lionheart dropped down from the wardrobe and stood with his back to his prisoner. How long could he hope to keep this up? He was confident—or mostly so—that no one would break through that door short of setting it ablaze. But how long would it take Foxbrush to return?

How much could one count on a sylph's word?

"You are going to die, Prince Lionheart," said the baron. "Either quickly by the hangman's noose or slowly through starvation. One way or the other, you will die."

Lionheart turned and regarded the baron. Oddly enough, he felt peaceful despite the looming truth of his captive's words. "I've already died, Baron. I'm not afraid."

With this, he returned to his place by the door, listening carefully. He knew they were there. They may have given up their pounding assault, but they wouldn't leave their intended king alone. No, they would be waiting just outside the door, swords drawn.

He closed his eyes, this time not in sleep or even exhaustion. He simply sat there, letting his mind clear. And he listened. He listened more intently than ever before, with more earnest, striving energy than he had ever put into anything. He sat, head bowed, and his heart pounded with the need to hear, the need to know.

What would you have me do, my Lord?

And the voice in his memory, which seemed so long ago now, repeated: *"I ask that you return to Southlands and the House of your father."*

He had obeyed, had he not? He had hastened back to King Hawkeye's side, and they had been reconciled. But there was more.

Frowning, Lionheart now recalled his journey home through the Wood Between. Scarcely had he begun his lonely trek down the still-unfamiliar Path when he saw a familiar face beneath a tall oak tree.

The Lady of the Haven had smiled at his approach.

"Childe of Farthestshore," she called in greeting, and he gasped in relief at the sight of her.

"Dame Imraldera!" he said, hurrying to her. "Did you not stay awhile at the coronation feast?"

"I did, Childe Lionheart," she said. "But I left three days ago to ensure that I should meet you here."

"Three . . . three days?" Lionheart frowned at this. "I just . . . I just took leave of Queen Varvare minutes ago."

"To be sure," Dame Imraldera replied. "And soon after you did so, I followed suit, and that is three days gone. And now we are both here." She laughed. "Time is a funny and a dangerous thing here in the Between. Don't be afraid. You'll soon accustom yourself to ways beyond the Near World. Sooner than you think."

He gave her a shrewd look. "Did you?"

She opened her mouth to reply but paused. Then, with another smile, smaller and more enigmatic than the first, she said, "I am not yet so accustomed as I wish to be. Even now, I scarcely understand the flowing to and fro of Time. What we do now, what we do then, and all the ripples throughout history."

She held out a scroll to Lionheart. "I have something for you. Rather, something for you to deliver."

Lionheart took the scroll. "I will deliver it as soon as I may," he said, hesitating. "The Prince of Farthestshore has sent me on a mission, however. I am to return to Southlands, to my father's house, and make my peace with him."

"I know," Imraldera replied. "And while you are there, you will see your cousin Foxbrush. That is a message for him. From Eanrin, but you needn't tell him so if you don't wish to. He'll learn it soon enough."

"From Eanrin?" Lionheart frowned, studying the scroll.

"Indeed. You may read it if you like."

As though afraid of changing his mind, Lionheart swiftly slipped the ribbon from its place, opened the scroll, and read. What he saw deepened his frown.

"For Foxbrush?" he asked.

"Yes."

"But . . . but why?"

"Because if he does not receive it now, he never will. And all that you see written there will never come to pass."

Imraldera laughed at the look on Lionheart's face. "I know none of it makes sense to you! No *common* sense, in any case. But perhaps one day your *uncommon* sense will wake, and the worlds will become more bearable. In the meanwhile, trust me and deliver this message for your cousin."

Lionheart, shrugging, let the scroll roll up. "I'll do as you ask, Dame Imraldera, if it is within my power. I cannot guarantee that Foxbrush will see me, however."

"Make him see you," she replied. "Make him take it. This is all you must do, but you *must* do it."

With those words, she had left him standing alone in the quiet Wood.

And now . . . what? He'd delivered the message, the strange and foolish message. Was any of it right? Was he on the Path he was meant to walk?

Lionheart closed his eyes more tightly still, squeezing away the questions and listening, listening. *Please, my Lord,* he whispered in his heart. *Please tell me what I should do!*

To his surprise, he felt two thin arms wrapping around him, deep in memory.

His mind's eye opened and peered down into Rose Red's face. She, his most faithful friend, his truest companion. She, whom he had betrayed.

He could not decide, here in his memory, which face he saw. Was it the bizarrely ugly face of the goblin girl he had known as a child? Was it the face of the queen who now sat on a throne in a distant Faerie realm? It didn't matter. She was Rose Red; that's all he knew or needed.

"There ain't nothin' you can do that will turn me from you," she said.

But this wasn't true. He'd betrayed her. He'd betrayed her and been unable to save her. And he must not seek atonement.

She stepped away from him now. And he saw that she was clad in royal robes, her head adorned in roses. The newly crowned Queen of Arpiar. He'd kissed her cheek. What a crazed, foolish act! How dare he even look upon her face, much less offer such a salute under any guise?

But then, he might never see her again. And if his last memory of his dearest friend—dearest and best loved—must be of a stolen kiss, so be it. When he died again, whether by starvation, noose, or blade, hers would be the last face before his vision, the last thought within his heart.

He opened his eyes in the deepening gloom of the evening-filled tower. The baron, catching his gaze, smiled like a dragon.

24

THE NIGHT AFTER FOXBRUSH'S TREK to the Twisted Man's tree, Redman and his children sat around a fire outside their front door, using stone awls to enlarge the tiny eyehole at the bottom of each black fig. Through these holes they threaded strings made of stout grasses, gathering figs into clusters of five or six. The wasps buzzed dully as they pursued this work. Most of the adult wasps, Redman explained to Foxbrush, had fled, leaving only their pupae deep in the heart of each fig. "But they'll grow soon enough," he said. "And then you'll see what they do."

Foxbrush offered to help, but after his first few unskilled attempts with the awl—during which he very nearly succeeded in puncturing the fleshy part of his palm—Redman took the tools away from him and told him that he'd done enough for one day.

So Foxbrush took himself to the far side of the fire, sitting with his back to the jungle, watching the family at work. And his heart beat with an almost sickening thrill every time he considered what they did.

But I must watch. I must wait and see how it continues, he told himself. After all, he didn't yet know how the process worked. He didn't want to go running back to his own time with only half an idea in his head; not when a whole idea could save his kingdom!

There was also the difficulty of not knowing how he was supposed to get home again. And of course there was Daylily.

An overwhelming sense of helplessness washed over poor Foxbrush as he sat with the wildness of the jungle behind him and the wildness of the people who lived so near it before him. He did not belong in this world. He never would. He did not belong anywhere save in his own quiet study, with books and ledgers and interesting equations spread before him, his door shut on anything that might disturb or distract him from his work.

He did not belong here. And he did not belong on the throne of Southlands.

His hand went to the front of his shirt, and he drew out the scroll hidden there. Hardly knowing what he did, he unrolled it, then turned himself so that the light of the fire might fall upon the words written so elegantly in, he guessed, a woman's hand. So much for it being a message from Bard Eanrin! Who was blind anyway, if Foxbrush remembered the stories correctly, and, if he existed, probably couldn't write at all.

Yet Lionheart had felt the need to deliver this scroll and the message it contained. Why? Some mad joke of his? Leo always was one for jokes.

"What is that?"

Foxbrush looked up and found Lark standing over him, her awl in one hand, a cluster of figs in the other. Glancing beyond her, he saw that Redman had stepped away from the fire, leaving his three daughters and little son alone for the moment.

"It's a message, I suppose," Foxbrush said, a little unwillingly. Privacy seemed to be an unknown commodity in this village.

"Who from?" Lark persisted, sitting cross-legged beside him. She began work on the figs she'd brought with her, her head cocked to one side, waiting.

"Bard Eanrin," Foxbrush replied with a mocking snort.

But Lark did not find this difficult to believe. She indicated the scroll with her awl. "You can understand those marks? You can read?"

Foxbrush nodded. Lark let out a plaintive sigh. "My da used to read, he says. He once showed me letters in the dirt, and he told me about reading. But he can't remember now, and none of us knows the way. It is a strange and wonderful magic!"

"It's not really . . ." Foxbrush stopped. What was the purpose of protesting magic of any kind in this new world? "Would you like to hear?" he asked, surprising himself. He'd not intended to make the offer. But he felt her pleading, though she'd said nothing.

Lark's eyes fairly shot out of her brown little face. She sprang to her feet and called to her siblings in their mother's tongue. "Come here! Come here! The wasp man is going to *read*!"

The three little sisters—Cattail and the two who were not twins, though they looked very alike and were only a year apart in age—grabbed their work and their brother and hastened over to join Foxbrush and Lark. Without a word they sat, pulling small Wolfsbane down between them and shoving a rag doll into his hands. He paid no attention to this but watched Foxbrush with fascination equal to that of his sisters.

"Um," said Foxbrush, a little nervous at this sudden, eager audience. "They don't understand me."

"I'll tell them what you say," said Lark with a grin. "Read to us, wasp man!"

Foxbrush shrugged and tried a smile at the grave, upturned faces. They did not smile in return. "Well, all right. This is a story told in . . . in my country. A famous story. You might know it yourselves. It is *The Ballad of Shadow Hand*." He raised his eyebrows questioningly at Lark.

She shook her head. "Who's Shadow Hand?"

Foxbrush frowned at this. Shadow Hand was, after all, one of the oldest and best-known heroes in Southlander history; his tale not quite as beloved as the tale of Maid Starflower and the Wolf Lord, but very nearly so.

"Well," said he with a shrug, "I suppose that's what I'm here to tell you. Lumé! Perhaps I'll be remembered as the first man to tell this story! Take that, why don't you, Bard Eanrin?"

The children exchanged puzzled glances at this. But Foxbrush, chuckling to himself, unrolled the scroll to its full length, which was long indeed. And he read as best he could by the firelight (supplying the rest from distant childhood memory). Lark translated as he went.

> *"Oh, Shadow Hand of Here and There,*
> *Follow where you will*
> *Your fickle, fleeing, Fiery Fair,*
> *O'er woodlands, under hill.*
> *She'll not be found, save by the stone,*
> *The stern and shining Bronze . . ."*

Here, his voice faltered. As a child, he'd paid little heed to the story, certainly not to poetic details. Poetry never had been his area of comfort or even interest. But when he came to the word *Bronze*, his voice cracked, and he scowled at the page. He recalled suddenly what the Eldest had said a few nights previous:

"*They say a maid came out of the jungle, a maid wearing a bronze stone about her neck. . . .*"

Foxbrush felt the blood drain from his face with sudden, dreadful foreboding that he could not understand and was quite certain he did not wish to.

"Is that all?" one of the look-alike sisters demanded. Foxbrush, who did not understand the words, understood the meaning and read on.

> *"She'll not be found, save by the stone,*
> *The stern and shining Bronze*
> *Where crooked stands the Mound alone*
> *Thorn clad and sharp with awns.*
>
> *"How pleasant are the Faerie folk*
> *Who dwell beyond your time.*
> *How pleasant are your aged kinfolk*
> *Of olden, swelt'ry clime.*
>
> *"But dark the tithe they pay, my son,*
> *To safely dwell beneath that sun!"*

There was a great deal more written close upon the parchment. Foxbrush read to the end but scarcely heard himself. The story was familiar: the old, comfortable familiarity of nursery tales known since before real memory begins, associated ever in his mind with a certain smell of leather binding and the soap-roughened hands of his nursemaid holding him in her lap and turning pages.

But as he read it out on that darkening night with children gathered round—their laps full of figs, their nimble fingers working awls—the familiar phrases took on new meaning. Darker meaning that comes when childhood fantasy slips into reality and is not quite what one expects it to be.

> *Here and There.*
> *The Bronze.*

These words rang in the forefront of his mind so that he scarcely heard his own reading. Thus he was surprised when Lark interrupted with a noisy, *"What?"*

"What?" Foxbrush echoed, looking at her over the scroll. "Is something amiss?"

Lark, her hands on her hips, the awl still gripped in one fist, wrinkled her nose at him. "Read that verse again."

"Which verse?"

"The one you just read!"

Foxbrush looked down at words that swam before him in the shadows, trying to recall where he'd been. Then he read:

> *"In broken sleep upon the ground*
> *The dear one lost now lies.*
> *Yet a kiss in faithful friendship found,*
> *And love opens wide eyes."*

"He *kissed* her?" Lark said, making a face. Her sisters and little brother, not understanding her, giggled at her expression and hid their faces in their hands.

"Well, yes," said Foxbrush slowly.

"To wake her up?" Lark's laughter redoubled the giggles of her siblings. "That's silly!"

Foxbrush looked at the verse again. He had to admit, it was a bit silly when one stopped to think about it. But then, what Faerie tale wasn't? It was all nonsense in the end, packaged up in frills and pretty verses. "It's a classic theme," he explained to the incredulous Lark. "An enchanted sleep can always be broken by the kiss of a prince or a princess."

"Prince or princess?" Lark repeated, and her laughter subsided into a more thoughtful expression.

"Yes. Like an Eldest's son," Foxbrush said.

"Or daughter."

"Or daughter, yes." Foxbrush eyed the girl, surprised to find her considering this information so intently where but a moment before she'd been a small mountain of scorn. "Would you like me to finish?" he asked.

She nodded, and he read through the last few verses to the end, there declaring along with the original poet, *"Recall you now my ancient story!"*

With that, as Lark finished her translation, he let the scroll close up on itself. When he raised his gaze, he saw Redman standing on the other side of the fire, watching him intently out of his one good eye. What the scar-faced man thought was anyone's guess. And Foxbrush did not care for guessing games.

Suddenly a wind rose up in the distance, moving swiftly among the topmost branches of the jungle trees. With it came a voice calling, *Foxbrush! Where are you, Foxbrush?*

"Quick. Get inside," said Redman. "Stop up your ears so you can't hear it calling."

And Foxbrush, scrambling to his feet, hastened to obey.

Early the next morning, before the heat became too oppressive, Foxbrush was roused from his bed and made to march with the children to the orchard growing just outside the Eldest's village. It was an impressive orchard (considering the work required to keep back the ever encroaching jungle) of stately elder figs just beginning to fruit.

The children carried bunches of black figs slung over their shoulders and held more clumps in each hand. Foxbrush, similarly laden, followed them into the murmuring shade of the trees and watched how they tossed their black figs up into the elder fig branches. Tied by the stout grass strings, the black figs caught and looped around each branch, hanging like holiday decorations in the boughs above.

"When the baby wasps grow," Lark explained to Foxbrush as she showed him a better way to toss his figs, "they crawl out of these figs and climb into the growing elder figs, thinking they are black figs. They lay their eggs in the black figs, you see. But the elder figs, though similar, are different from black figs; there is no place for the wasp to lay her eggs!"

"I see." Foxbrush gazed up into the branches, studying the clumps above. "So the wasp pollinates the elder fig, but she cannot lay her eggs, which would render it inedible like black figs."

It was so beautiful and so strange. Foxbrush moved up and down the orchard after the children as the morning lengthened. Soon the orchard was full of hanging black figs, though Lark told him they would need to make many more trips to the Twisted Man's tree to gather of his bounty. "These black figs will shrivel up in a few days, and we have to make certain there are enough for all the elder figs to grow," she said.

But the elder figs *would* grow. And they would ripen and plump up and be as golden and delectable as those Foxbrush had read about. Not merely lifeless little lumps fit only for birds and monkeys. Real, abundant, marketable explosions of juice and flavor and . . .

Once more he whispered to himself, "I can save Southlands."

As soon as they'd finished the task, Foxbrush hurried to find Redman, who was hard at work repairing one of the goat sheds down the hill from the Eldest's House. "Something tried to get in during the night," he said when Foxbrush inquired. "One of the fey folk; a newcomer, I fear. Broke partway through and caught one of the kids. Couldn't get it out of the pen, thank the Lights Above, but broke its leg."

Foxbrush looked at the poor little kid huddled up among the frightened goats at the other end of the pen. Someone had already splinted and wrapped its leg, but it bleated in pain. Redman cursed at the sound even as he worked.

"We'll have to set up a new totem to appease this one. I can only hope the tribute won't be too high. The Faerie beasts get more violent and more prevalent every day! It's an invasion, my lad. That's what it is. An invasion of the South Land."

Foxbrush nodded sympathetically, but his heart was still soaring at what he had learned that morning.

"I have to go," he said.

"Fine, fine," said Redman, intent upon his task. "No need for you to stand around here, I'm sure. There's always more work to be done, just ask my Meadowlark, and—"

"No, no," Foxbrush interrupted, hurrying on with more confidence than he felt, "I mean, I have to go. To leave your village. I must find Daylily and return to my own time. If I can. I can't waste another moment."

"Waste?" Redman paused and frowned up at Foxbrush. His face was very ugly when he frowned, though scarcely more ugly than when he smiled. "You call your time enjoying the Eldest's hospitality a waste?"

Foxbrush opened his mouth to answer but stopped. After all, he would never have learned the secret of the black fig wasps had he not come here. How many other unknown blessings might he have received these last few days?

"No," said Redman, wiping sweat from his red-burnt brow. Though he wore a makeshift hat of sorts, his skin, unsuited to the sweltering climes of the South Land, was forever peeling and freckled. "No, it's my opinion you should rethink that last thought of yours, crown prince." Foxbrush cringed at the title, which sounded so hollow and pointless in this place. "Your Path led you here, and your Path is not, so far as I can see, leading you away just yet."

"What do you know of my path?" Foxbrush asked, his tone more surly than did him credit. But Redman did not seem to mind.

"I've traveled the Wilderlands down below," he said, returning to his task of repair and handling his tools with expert grace as he spoke. "I've seen sights I could not begin to tell you and wouldn't try if asked. I've walked my share of Faerie Paths; I've followed in the footsteps of a star. I recognize a Path of the Lumil Eliasul when I see one."

Without so much as glancing back over his shoulder, he pointed at Fox-brush's feet. These were clad in tough leather cloths tied across the insteps and ankles with string made of animal gut. Foxbrush stood in a patch of mud and weeds, and as far as he could see, there was no path save the one a few paces behind him leading up to the Eldest's House.

But he remembered suddenly Nidawi and her lioness. Especially Nidawi's screeching yet oddly alluring laugh. *"You walk the Path of the Lumil Eliasul, and you don't even know it!"*

He had very nearly convinced himself that this encounter had been a dream. But it wasn't. No more than the Twisted Man or the sylphs or the leather-tied shoes on his feet.

Still he said quietly, "I don't see any path."

"You walk it even so. Don't try to escape it, and don't try to hurry it." Redman looked thoughtfully up at Foxbrush. "I know you want to find your lady. But you cannot simply wander off into the jungle and expect to happen upon her. I know the play and pattern of stories. I've lived enough of them by now to know! You were brought to me, a balance to my own tale, I should imagine. You need to stay here until it becomes clear that you must move on."

"But how will I know?" Foxbrush asked, his voice a whisper of pent-up frustration.

"You'll know." Redman heaved a great sigh and stood, turning the full intensity of his one-eyed gaze upon Foxbrush. He reached out and clasped the young man's shoulder, opening his mouth as though to say more.

But a nearby cry of "Redman! Redman!" sent them wheeling around. A man ran up through the village between the mud-and-wattle houses, and villagers with anxious faces gathered in his wake. He fell to his knees before Redman, not kneeling but simply giving out at the end of what must have been a long run. Redman silently waited for the man to regain breath enough to speak. Foxbrush, sensing the anxiety in the gathered crowd and feeling more than one unfriendly gaze turn his way, stepped back a little, though he watched all with interest.

The man gasped out a string of words Foxbrush did not understand. Redman drew a sharp breath and barked an answer. The man shook his head and spoke again, then bowed down, exhausted, and did not move until someone brought him a skin of water, which he first poured over his flushed face before drinking.

Redman stood silently, looking neither at the villagers nor at Foxbrush but at the wounded kid in the goat pen. Then he drew a long breath and took the hat from his head as he rubbed a hand down his face.

"Your red lady has been seen again," he said in Northerner.

Foxbrush leapt forward. "Where?" he demanded, looking from Redman to the messenger and back again. "Where is she?"

Redman shook his head. "She's gone. She and others wearing the Bronze were seen in the Crescent Land not three days ago. This man ran all the way to tell us. They killed Tocho, the Big Cat of Skymount Watch. One of the most powerful totems in all the Land."

None of this made sense to Foxbrush. But he grasped the one detail he did understand and held on like a lifeline. "She was seen there? At Skymount Watch? Where is that? Can he take me?"

"No, I told you," said Redman, his voice angry now. "She is no longer there. They came and they went. Warriors wearing bronze stones about their necks. Killers of Faerie beasts."

"But there might be something!" Foxbrush insisted, his eagerness blinding him to the look on Redman's face. "There might be some sign, some token! She might be held against her will by these warriors you speak of! She is no warrior herself, and she couldn't kill anything, I know. I must—"

"You must be quiet," said Redman. And Foxbrush, though he wanted to protest, shut his mouth. "You do not know of what you speak. These warriors wearing the Bronze are moving throughout the Land. The messenger tells me there have been other sightings. And if your Daylily is wearing their stone, she is one of them."

The villagers gathered did not understand a word passing between their Eldest's husband and this stranger. They watched with fearful eyes, for the world had become a darker place since even the night before.

"Do you want to know what they demand in tithe for services rendered? For the killing of Tocho?"

Foxbrush didn't want to know. But he couldn't speak or even shake his head, so Redman continued: "Firstborns. Children. For every beast they kill, for every life they save. They demand the firstborn children of the Land. And they take them, Foxbrush. They come in the night, these warriors wearing the bronze stones. They came to the five villages nearest Skymount Watch, and they took all the firstborn children, leaving no trace behind.

"Your red lady, Prince Foxbrush, is stealing the blood of the South Land."

Foxbrush stared at Redman. The words, foreign and dark, filled his head so that he could not comprehend. All was blackness and pain, and he felt his temples throbbing.

The only words clear in his head were two lines from the ballad he had read to the gathered children just the night before:

> *But dark the tithe they pay, my son,*
> *To safely dwell beneath that sun!*

Foxbrush did not leave the Eldest's village that day. The villagers gathered in the Eldest's House with Sight-of-Day and her husband to discuss what might be done in light of these dire happenings. Foxbrush, to no one's surprise, was not invited but sent out among the children.

"What happened?" Lark demanded when Foxbrush appeared and descended the hill. Wolfsbane, balanced on her hip, added his own experimental, "Wha?"

But Foxbrush shook his head, which was full and aching. He continued on past Lark and her little sisters, who fell into step behind him like goslings behind a mother goose. They trailed him all the way down the hill and on through the village, ignoring the looks of those they passed, who did not like or trust the stranger (though they made respectful signs to the Eldest's children).

"What is it?" Lark persisted as they went. "Is it the Bronze? Have they had more news?"

"Yes. No. I don't know," Foxbrush said, which wasn't entirely untruthful. Lark, however, was unconvinced.

Still carrying her brother, she caught Foxbrush by the sleeve and yanked him to a halt with surprising force for her size. "Don't talk to me like a child," she said, which never ceased to sound strange coming from her childish mouth. "What news did the runner bring from the Crescent Land? I know it's about the Bronze Warriors, and you needn't try to hide it!"

Foxbrush looked at her hand on his sleeve, then at her. She scowled fiercely, and her three sisters, gathered behind, mirrored her face. Wolfsbane chewed on his fingers, but his eyes were no less solemn than those of his sisters, and they were very dark beneath his mop of red hair.

"We are the Eldest's children," Lark said. "We are strong and we are brave. We fear only ignorance. So tell us, wasp man."

Foxbrush squeezed his eyes against the throbbing in his temples. Then he shook off Lark's hand. "The Bronze Warriors are demanding firstborn children in exchange for the monsters they kill. Will you leave me in peace now?"

A variety of expressions flashed through Lark's eyes. Then she bowed her head and took a step back, holding Wolfsbane close and allowing her sisters to close in around her. Foxbrush bit his tongue until it hurt, wishing he'd had the sense to do so before it spoke of what it shouldn't.

With a bitter curse, he turned and walked away from the children, making for the fig orchards where he had spent that morning. Evening was descending, bringing with it the sultry heaviness of an oncoming storm. All was dark, and the black figs hanging in the branches of the elder fig trees looked ominous, like so many little black heads hung up as a warning by some cruel warlord.

Foxbrush shuddered as he passed on through the orchard. Now and then, when he looked up, he thought he saw the flit of wings and the glow of bulbous eyes. Perhaps they were merely evening birds and lemurs. Perhaps they were fey folk, drawn out in the gloaming murk, ready to mock him. *"He can save Southlands?"* they might ask each other. *"What a laugh!"*

"What a laugh," Foxbrush whispered. How hollow and foolish all his grand plans sounded. How hollow and foolish he was! He tried to put his hands in his pockets, found he had no pockets, and stood a moment, awkwardly wondering what to do with his arms.

Suddenly his nose began to tickle. He rubbed it but could not drive back the force of an oncoming sneeze. It burst out of him with an explosive roar, and he wished very much for a clean handkerchief . . . any handkerchief at all, for that matter. Rubbing his nose with the back of his hand, he cast about for a fig leaf as a substitute.

"You were thinking of me."

Foxbrush startled and fell back against a tree trunk, one hand still pressed to his nose, staring about. He knew that voice, or thought he did. "Where are you?" he gasped.

"Right here, darling. Didn't you see me?"

And Nidawi the Everblooming stepped out from behind the very tree against which he'd taken shelter, sweeping around to stand before him. She was mere inches from his face, one hand pressed into the tree on either side of his head, leaning in and smiling the most secret and brilliant and dazzling of smiles.

"You were thinking of me!" she said again. "I heard you. You thought of me and something I said to you, and I heard it, so I came at once. I *knew* you wouldn't be able to get me out of your mind! Are you ready to marry me now?"

25

S UN EAGLE AND DAYLILY passed through the Wood in silence and once more came to the gate. They entered the Near World and stood in the gorge, looking up to the tableland above. Daylily, dulled by now to the comings and goings, still looked unconsciously for the bridge she knew should be there. For this was the gorge near the Eldest's House, or rather, near where it would one day be.

"Come," said Sun Eagle, and they began the long climb. Worn and trembling, more disturbed than rested by her sleep in the Between, Daylily lagged behind Sun Eagle. He reached the top and waited there for her to catch up. A certain gnarled fig tree seemed to watch him, and he eyed it back and made certain it could see the Bronze upon his chest. It did nothing, and though Sun Eagle suspected a Faerie dwelled therein, he chose to ignore it for the moment.

In time, they would deal with them all.

Daylily reached the top of the gorge trail and sat, breathing hard and looking into the jungle. It was unusually quiet. In the deeper reaches, birds and monkeys called, but here not even the buzzing of an insect disturbed the air.

"They know who we are," Sun Eagle said, answering Daylily's unspoken question. "They know the master has come to this realm, and they are afraid. As they should be."

When Daylily was rested enough, he made her get to her feet. This time, when they progressed into the jungle, they took the man-made trail. "Our brethren are spreading throughout the Land," Sun Eagle told her. "Every tribe and every village will see us and thank us and fear us for what we do. It is good work."

"Good work," Daylily echoed. "But what about . . ."

There flashed through her mind an image. She saw herself holding a child, carrying him toward a yawning black door. Who was that child? Where was he now?

Ask if you dare, snarled the wolf.

So the wolf was alive. Just as she'd feared.

Yes, I'm alive. You'll never be rid of me. Ask this Advocate of yours what happened to that child. Ask what happens to all the children!

"I'll do nothing by your order," Daylily whispered fiercely. "I am not your slave."

You are a slave, but not to me, the wolf growled, then subsided for the time being. Silence fell upon Daylily's mind, interrupted only by the shushing of the wind overhead.

For a moment, oddly enough, Daylily thought she heard a voice in that wind. *Foxbrush! Foxbrush!* it called as it wafted overhead. *Where are you, Foxbrush?*

Daylily frowned, an unpleasant taste rising in her throat. Why should she think of that name now? Of all people, Foxbrush was the very last she wanted to remember. Her spurned groom, her unwanted lover. She shuddered and quickened her pace behind Sun Eagle. He glanced back and read things in her face she did not intend to reveal. He could not read all, for he knew so little of her. But he read enough.

"You must let go of your past," he said, "if you hope to survive in this new life."

Her eyes flashed, and she was again, however briefly, the cold Lady Daylily of Middlecrescent, who could freeze a man's blood with a glance. "Who are you," she said, "to tell me what I must or must not let go? What right have you to judge?"

His face remained impassive before her tight-lipped wrath. "I am your Advocate," he said. "I have every right. And if you wish to be an Advocate yourself one day and take on an Initiate, you will do as I say."

Daylily drew herself up, her tiredness forgotten in her ire. "Do as you say? Do as you do?"

"Both."

"Let go of my past? Is that what you have done?"

"This is what all of us must do in order to devote ourselves fully to the master."

Her gaze ran up and down his savage form—his skins, his bloodstains, his weapons, his scars. Then she said, "If that is so, why do you still wear those two beads about your neck?"

Sun Eagle's face did not move. Slowly one hand rose to the necklace on which hung the clay beads, the blue and the red, name marks given him long ago to carry into the Wood as he made his rite of passage. He touched them now as though he didn't quite know what they were.

The Land is all. All we need.

"All we need," mouthed Sun Eagle, but he still caressed the blue stone. Then he smiled grimly. "We have work to do. No more talk."

He passed on into the jungle, and Daylily had no choice but to follow. Thunder rolled overhead, threatening rain, but the air was already so thick with moisture, plastering Daylily's body with sweat, that she felt rain could scarcely make a difference.

Suddenly Sun Eagle stopped. He lifted a hand and Daylily also froze, tilting her head to listen, lifting her nose to sniff. But she sensed nothing. Nothing but jungle and greenness all around.

"What is it?" she whispered.

"A Faerie beast," said he. Then his lips drew back in an animal snarl. "One I know. One I know too well!"

The next moment, he was running, disappearing into the green, and Daylily was hard-pressed not to lose him.

Foxbrush sneezed again.

He couldn't help himself. It's not something a fellow likes to do when a stunningly beautiful woman is leaning toward him with an expression on her face like Nidawi's wore. But sneezes are not prey to the wants or wishes of those inflicted with them. He sneezed so violently that he nearly knocked his forehead against Nidawi's exquisite little chin. She leapt back lightly, frowning at first, then shaking the frown into a rain of laughter.

"True love is such a beautiful thing!" said Nidawi the Everblooming. "It has made me decide to find that odd little quirk of yours charming. I can find anything charming if I love it enough. Even mortals!"

"Pardon," Foxbrush gasped and pulled a fig leaf down to wipe his nose, simultaneously trying to sidle away from the tree and put it between himself and the fey woman. For she was overpoweringly beautiful with a natural, breezy, frolicking sort of beauty, like a flower or a young tree or a fawn on delicate, gamboling limbs. Her hair was loose and tangled, with thick braids of moss and flowers, and her leafy gown fluttered in the wind of an oncoming storm. One could far more easily believe she had sprung up from the ground than ever been born of a mother.

But she was too frightening for words. Trying to escape her, Foxbrush rounded the tree and started to back away when he felt a gust of warm breath on his neck. His mouth opened, his lips drew back from his teeth with the desire to scream, but his throat closed up. He turned his head ever so slightly and found himself gazing into Lioness's black-rimmed eyes.

She started to purr. Foxbrush thought it a growl and nearly died on the spot.

"Lioness has decided she likes you too," Nidawi said. Taking Foxbrush's hand, she turned him to face the beast. "She wasn't certain at first, but after we talked about it, she agreed you would be a fine husband."

Lioness's mouth was open, her pink tongue showing hugely between her teeth. If one strained the imagination, one could believe it was a smile. But one required no imagination whatsoever to think it was a hungry expression. Foxbrush felt his knees giving out.

Nidawi caught him before he collapsed, easing him gently to the ground. Twilight was deepening, bringing with it a heavy summer storm. The first few drops began to fall, and Nidawi, seated with her arms around Foxbrush's rigid body, tilted back her head and caught rain in her mouth. "Delightful! We shall have a drink to toast our betrothal!"

"B-betrothal?" Foxbrush shook his head, trying to find strength to protest. Despite the warmth of the evening, he began to shiver.

"Why, of course! Now that you love me, I see no reason for us not to wed. Just as soon as you've killed my enemy."

Foxbrush's head continued shaking for some moments before he could find words, during which time Nidawi laughed and stuck out her tongue to catch more rain, then suddenly turned and planted a huge kiss on Foxbrush's cheek. This worked like a lightning bolt, shooting him instantly to his feet and out of her arms.

"See here, my good woman, I . . . I . . . I thank you for your kindly, um, thoughts of me, but I—" His hair flattened down across his forehead, and he pushed it back nervously. "I haven't changed my mind. I still can't marry you. Or kill anyone," he added quickly.

Nidawi blinked. Despite the darkness, everything around her shone brightly. Her lashes caught the rain into tiny diamonds rimming her violet eyes, glittering like prisms, casting and creating gleams of light. How magical and beautiful and thoroughly petulant she was in that moment.

She crossed her arms. "If you don't want to marry me, why were you thinking of me?"

"I wasn't thinking of you."

"Yes, you were. I heard you. Ever since I sent you back, I've been listening for you very carefully. You thought of my laugh, and you remembered it as *alluring*." She grinned slyly up at him. "I knew you wouldn't be able to resist the memory of me. Not once you got home to your own world."

"H-Home? My own world?" All temptation to yield (which may or may not have been slowly building in Foxbrush's heart) vanished as he gasped out those words. He opened his mouth and roared like a young lion himself, *"You sent me back into the wrong time!"*

She drew up her legs and sat more primly, her face an entire world of affront. "No, I didn't. I don't deal in Time."

"You pushed me! You pushed me out of the Wood, and I landed *here!*"

"No, actually you landed *There*," said Nidawi. "*Here* is . . . elsewhere. If you ended up anywhere, it's because of the Path you're on. Nothing to do with me."

Foxbrush opened his mouth, but nothing happened, so he shook himself and managed a weak, "I don't know what you're talking about!"

He felt the breath of Lioness again. The great animal pushed her massive head under his hand and rolled it around so that he now stood with his arm up and across her neck. She blinked sweetly at him, her mouth still open as she exhaled a puffing lion's purr.

"Um," said Foxbrush. Then he sneezed again.

Lioness nosed him affectionately in the chest.

"Really, Lioness," said Nidawi crossly as she scrambled to her feet. "You are too forward sometimes." And she hurried over to take Foxbrush's other arm, clutching it tightly. She smiled at him again, and he was nearly blinded by the glitter both of her teeth and of the rain in her eyelashes and hair.

"Please," said Foxbrush, stepping back and trying to free his arms. "Please, I think I'm allergic to your lion."

"My what?"

"Your lion."

"My . . . oh! You mean Lioness?" Nidawi laughed like chiming crystals and refused to release Foxbrush's arm no matter how he tugged. "She's not *mine*! I mean, I suppose she sort of is. Are you *mine*, Lioness?" she asked the white lion, who shook her head briskly and padded away to lie down in a dry patch under a tree. She continued blinking Foxbrush's way, but the tip of her tail swished quietly through the grass and over the roots.

"There now, you've offended her," Nidawi said, shaking a finger under Foxbrush's nose. "She's not *mine* like a slave. I never kept slaves, not even when I had a world of subjects!"

A change came across her unbelievably delicate features. They sagged suddenly with heaviness, bags appearing under the eyes, lines deepening into framing crevices around the mouth, which, in turn, thinned to a narrow line. The black hair tumbling over Foxbrush's shoulder and arm faded to gray, then to white. Nidawi the Everblooming let go her hold on Foxbrush and stepped away, bent and tottering so that she had to put out a hand and support herself against the tree.

It was unnatural and so sudden that Foxbrush took a moment to catch his breath. Then he licked rain from his lips and said, "I say, I'm sorry." He put a hand on Nidawi's bowed shoulder. "Was it something I said? Is it . . ." He grimaced. "Is it about the betrothal?"

But she shook her head. When she spoke, her voice was as heavy as her face but paper-thin and frail. "No, it's just painful to remember." She drew a shuddering breath that Foxbrush feared might shatter her body. When she turned to him, the lights had gone from the rain in her lashes, and instead her eyes brimmed with shining tears. "A mother should never outlive her children."

Then she was sobbing an old woman's sobs, dry and broken. Foxbrush put his arms around her and held her close to his chest, and her tears mingled with the rain. But unlike the rain, which was warm on that summer's evening, Nidawi's tears were cold, and they chilled him. Still he held her and smoothed her thin hair, from which dead leaves fell and littered the ground at their feet.

The moment ended with Foxbrush's sudden yelp of pain. For Nidawi's hands, which had been wrapped around him, dug into his skin with a surprising sharpness. Foxbrush looked down to see the white head sinking into a black mop of tangles, and Nidawi was a child again. A child turning away from him with a vicious snarl, her fingers curled into claws.

"*Cren Cru!*" she shrieked.

Lioness sprang to her feet, her ears pinned back, her growl outmatching even the thunder that rolled across the darkened sky. Foxbrush turned to look where they looked.

His heart stopped beating.

It must be a dream or an illusion brought on by the magic intoxication of Nidawi's presence. It must be, for how else could he see, even through dark and rain, that form in white rags, her hair falling free in red-gold tatters below her shoulders, her icy eyes fixed upon him in unbelief. His bride: his beautiful, broken, terrible bride.

"Daylily!" he cried, taking three strides. But he had not taken a fourth when, with a roar that shook the orchard, Lioness sprang over his head and charged in streaking, snarling fury right at that vision that was no vision, but which breathed and moved and looked right at him.

"No!" Foxbrush shouted, though he did not know he shouted. Like one in a dream, he could not run, could not make his limbs move, straining against the pull of resisting time. Seconds, half seconds, were hours too long, for the white lion bounded with the speed of lightning.

Daylily shook herself free of her shock at seeing Foxbrush in this of all places and focused her gaze fiercely on that which approached. It was not a wolf. It was a Faerie beast, an invader, and her enemy.

Our enemy!

She snatched the Bronze from around her neck and crouched, prepared for battle.

Save our land!

The Lioness leapt, and Daylily, though her arm was none too strong, would have driven her sharp stone up and into her flesh as she descended, had the great cat not turned in the air at the last and landed to one side. Lioness lashed out, claws flashing, but caught Daylily's gown and not Daylily herself. The lion's second swing struck Daylily in the side, sending her crashing to the ground and her Bronze stone spinning through the air.

Daylily bared her teeth and reached for the stone, but Lioness pressed her to the dirt with an enormous, crushing paw. Claws tore into Daylily's shoulder and she screamed. Her voice pierced the rain and the thunder and Foxbrush's heart, and he screamed as well and threw himself at the lion.

But just as he did so, a savage yell rang out, and a wild man in skins, his hair pulled back in a long braid, fell from the branches of the fig tree above and landed square upon Lioness's broad back. With strength greater than his size indicated, he unbalanced her, pulling her off Daylily so that both of them rolled across the ground. Foxbrush narrowly avoided losing his face to Lioness's flailing claws, and found himself standing clear, staring down at Daylily's flattened form.

Nidawi caught Foxbrush's arm and pointed at Daylily, screaming, "Kill it! Kill it, my king!"

Then, without another word, she turned to Lioness and the wild man, who were grappling together. Sun Eagle was on the lion's back, his arm around her shaggy neck, holding on with desperate force even as he struggled to grasp his own Bronze stone. Lioness reared up on her hind legs, twisting her long body and catching Sun Eagle by the leg. He yelled a brutal, angry yell but held on a few moments more before Lioness pulled him free and flung him from her.

Nidawi, still a child but with the face of a demon, flung herself at him, her claw-like hands tearing the skin of his chest into ribbons of blood. He struck with the Bronze, and where it touched the skin of her arm, it burned. The smell of burnt flesh filled the orchard, and steam sizzled in the rain.

Nidawi fell back, clutching her arm. "Kill it!" she cried out to Lioness.

Lioness crouched, her eyes intent. Then she leapt, her powerful body unfolding to its full lethal extent. But she landed on empty ground, for Sun Eagle gathered his limbs beneath him and fled. He hurtled into the deeper dark of the orchard, plunging on into the jungle, Lioness close at his heels. Nidawi, still holding her arm, ran after, screaming wild, incoherent threats. And the three of them disappeared, followed by the echoes of their voices.

Foxbrush stood in the dripping orchard, staring after the vanished figures and telling himself that none of this could be true.

Daylily moaned.

This at least, be it dream or real, he could not ignore. Foxbrush spun about, his skin-clad feet slipping in the wet grass, and all but fell to her side. Her eyes were closed, her face a rictus of pain as she rolled onto her side. Her fingers, muddied and scraped, clutched the Bronze.

She neither saw nor heard Foxbrush as he awkwardly lifted her, apologizing and cursing in turn. Her mind was full of pain. Pain and the driving voice still urging, *Our enemy! Our enemy . . . our enemy . . .*

At last even that faded into the fire in her shoulder.

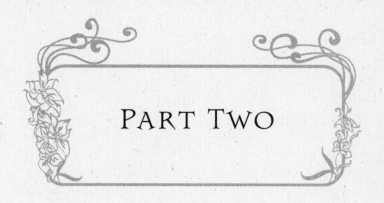

PART TWO

THERE AND HERE

1

F EW FOLKS LIVE in the Wood Between. The Wood is not a place to call one's home, for it is never safe, even at the best of times, and is predictably unpredictable. Nevertheless, Dame Imraldera had come to consider her little corner of the Wood as more of a home than anything else she had known.

The Haven in which she dwelt had been constructed by Faerie hands long ages ago, though it had since fallen into such disrepair that when Dame Imraldera first came to it with her comrade-in-arms, they had spent many days and nights (difficult to count in the timeless Between) repairing it. Thus she took more than a little pride in its stately halls and elegant, nature-rimmed chambers, and justly so. The library was particularly splendid, boasting shelves upon shelves of books, scrolls, parchments, and brass-bound tomes, most of which she had taken down in her own hand after learning to read and write in Faerie, a difficult but rewarding language. Here she kept histories and lineages, prophecies and prose, instructions for heroes on their quests, and obscure rules of etiquette, useful should one find oneself visiting faraway fey courts.

She also recorded poetry, the task at which she worked now. Most of the poetry in need of transcribing and cataloguing had been written by the same poet—the most renowned poet in the history of the worlds, to be sure, but a cheap rhymer, when all was said and done. Worse yet, he knew it!

But awareness of deficiency never stopped him from bringing more and more benighted verses to her, scrawled ingloriously on whatever scraps had been under his hand at the time. This latest had been written in what appeared to be beetle blood on a strip of birch bark that kept rolling back up on itself every time Imraldera opened it.

The poet little cared to make her job easier. And the rhyme itself made her cringe. It went something like this:

> *I wish I were in Rudiobus,*
> *Where the mountain touches the sky,*
> *Where Gorm-Uisce mirrors the stars,*
> *And we're together, Gleamdren and I!*

"Well, you've got your wish now, fool cat," the good dame growled softly even as her pen scratched away. "In Rudiobus with your lady Gleamdren, and far away from any work to be done. I hope you're happy!"

This irritable grumbling was perhaps unworthy of her, but the poem went on in this, she thought, inane vein for ten full verses—enough to try anyone's patience. Besides, she was a little tired and feeling ill used.

Imraldera was not herself a Faerie, though after more than one hundred years of life in the Wood Between and no sign of aging she began to suspect that she might be immortal. Her face was that of a young maiden, her skin smooth and brown, her hair glossy black and pulled rather severely back from her face and tied with a scarf so as not to interrupt her work. Her tunic was long and lavender, its billowy sleeves rolled up past her elbows, and underneath she wore green trousers of a light, loose fabric.

She made a sweet, if earnest, picture, Sir Eanrin thought when he stepped into the library. Her brow set in a stern line of concentration, her lips parted slightly back from her teeth (which were a little crooked—proof that she had been, at one time at least, mortal—no woman of Faerie would suffer such imperfection). It was a shame to disturb her, hard at work as she was, so Eanrin stood a moment, his hand on the doorframe, and watched her, glad at the sight of her and thinking many things that his golden eyes might have revealed had anyone been looking.

Then suddenly he sank down into the form of a bright orange cat, tail high and soft as the plume of Imraldera's pen. "Prrrrrrlt?" he said, honey-sweet, and Imraldera dropped her work and spun on her stool to face him.

"You!" she said. "How dare you show your face after all this time?"

"Time, old girl?" the cat replied with another cheerful trill and a flick of his tail. "What do we care for time?"

"*You* may not, but *I* certainly do!" the good dame said. For a moment she looked as though she might throw her pen at him. "You said you'd be gone for a month, Eanrin. A month. Not *three years.*"

The cat shrugged a cattish sort of shrug and began grooming a paw. "I don't see what you have to complain about," he said between licks. "You were gone for, what was it, fifteen years at least? Gallivanting about your old world, bothering mortals with this, that, and the other. I'm not much on time and its nuances, but as I remember, three years and twenty years are hardly—"

Imraldera threw up her hands in exasperation. "It's not the same thing at all! I was about our Lord's work, tending to the needs of my people. They were—and are, last we knew—under invasion! It's not as though I could simply *leave* them, with the Dragonwitch newly dead, no leader to turn to, and Faerie beasts crawling in at the borders."

"Well," said the cat, primly placing one forepaw beside the other and twitching an ear at her, "I was about my work as well."

"Work? You were playing the fool for Lady Gleamdren!"

"That shows what you know." The cat stood and stretched, forming a fluffy arch with his back, and when he had finished, he unbent into the form of a man. Sir Eanrin, clad in scarlet with a gold-edged cape and a feathered cap, removed said cap and ran a hand through his tawny hair, as much a cat in this form as he was when more blatantly feline. "I am first and foremost a Knight of Farthestshore, even as you are yourself, my girl," he said with an easy grace and confidence that never failed to make Imraldera want to smack him. "Servant of the Lumil Eliasul and all that."

"Eanrin, I—"

"But I am also," he continued, holding up a silencing hand, "the Chief Poet of Rudiobus, and I have a duty to my king Iubdan and his fair queen, a duty I neglected all the while you were away in your old country so that I could—*all by myself*, I hardly need add—guard the gates of our watch. Faerie beasts might crawl thick and fast into your homeland, but by Lumé and Hymlumé's eternal song, they did *not* get through any of the gates under this guard." He crossed his arms and gave her such a stare as only cats can give. "Fifteen years, Imraldera. By myself. I think I earned a bit of a holiday."

She opened her mouth to speak, venom waiting to spit from her tongue. Then she stopped herself and shook her head, momentarily defeated. "All right, you win," she said, turning back to her desk and taking up her quill. "I can't grudge you the reprieve. And I'm certain King Iubdan and Queen Bebo both were grateful to have their bard back for a little while."

The cat-man slid up behind Imraldera and said with a satisfied smirk, "They and—ahem—others too."

She glared round at him. "I can see that you're brimming. Tell me, then: Did Lady Gleamdrené Gormlaith speak to you this time?"

Eanrin smiled a brilliant smile and began to nod his head. But he stopped and shook it at the last. "Well, no," he admitted. The big smile sank into a smaller, more rueful one. "A tad awkward, that."

"I would imagine it is awkward, yes, wooing a woman who has vowed never to speak to you again."

Eanrin shrugged. "I haven't lost heart! Indeed, I do hope very soon now to win her over with my perfumed words and glorious lyrics."

Imraldera gave him a look. "No, you don't."

Again he smiled. "No, I don't. You're right. But what can I say? It adds to the drama, to the romance! There's nothing quite like unrequited passion, is there, old girl?"

She shook her head, rolling her eyes and turning back to her work.

Eanrin, meanwhile, suddenly flushed and backed away. Finding a chair partially buried under a pile of unused parchment, he shoved aside the clutter and made himself comfortable, lounging with one leg over its arm, the picture of feline grace, clad though he was momentarily in manhood. "I've begun composing a new ballad, you'll be interested to know," he said. "An epic."

"Lights Above save us," Imraldera muttered without looking around.

"You'll like this one!" said Eanrin. "It's the tale of how the Dragonwitch snatched my lady Gleamdren from the very bosom of Rudiobus and locked her away in her high tower. It's taken me long enough to get around to it, but I figured I should begin the composing while it's still fresh in my mind. Would you like to hear?"

"Spare me, please," said she.

"Just my favorite bits! Like this one, when the Dragonwitch first carries her off."

"Eanrin, I'm trying to—"

But the poet, still seated, threw out his hands and began to declaim as though he'd not heard her.

> *The witch of fire bound her tight*
> *Before Eanrin's very eye!*
> *She bore his lady far and fast*
> *And locked her in a tower high!*

"Isn't that grand, then?" He looked eagerly her way.

She sighed, put down her pen, and asked rather gloomily, "Is there more?"

"Scads! This part is the Dragonwitch's speech:

> "'*Where flows the gold, sweet Gleamdrené,*
> *The gold for which I thirst?*
> *Where flows the gold, the shining gold?*
> *Tell ere your life be cursed!*'

"And now you hear Gleamdren reply."

"Really, Eanrin, must you—"

"Attend!

> *"'I'll tell you not, foul fiery dame!*
> *I swear upon my hand,*
> *You'll ne'er set eye on the Flowing Gold,*
> *Not while Sir Eanrin stands!'"*

Imraldera narrowed her eyes. "Oh, is that what she said? I seem to remember things differently."

"Poetic license, old girl," said the cat-man. "The joy of my art is in the embellishment."

"And by *embellishment*, I presume you mean *falsehood*?"

At this, Eanrin swung his leg back down over the arm of the chair and rose, adjusting his cloak with great dignity. "The greatest art is that least appreciated but done for art's own sake," said he, looking rather pleased at the line. "I shall take myself and my art from your presence, most unappreciative of dames, and leave you to your mundane tasks."

"I'm recording lyrics of yours, Eanrin."

He sniffed and started for the door but did not reach it before she called after him, "Look to the gates, cat! I've been making the rounds *and* trying to keep pace with the records piling up, and it's high time you did a bit of work around here again."

"Aye, because we wouldn't want goblins breaking through a gate unguarded, now, would we?" said Eanrin, pausing in the doorway. "Not like last time. Oh, wait! Whose fault was that?"

He ducked before her inkwell struck and hastened down the passage beyond, chuckling to himself as he went.

It was always a pleasure and a delight to visit Rudiobus, the country of his origin, and to sing and perform for his king and his queen. But that delight was nothing to the delight of returning to the Haven and his duties; and the pleasure of his sovereigns' smiles could not hold a candle to just one of Imraldera's scowls.

It was good to go but better to be back, he decided as he stepped through the Haven door and into the vast and quiet Wood Between. He and Dame Imraldera, as knights in the service of the Prince of Farthest-shore, kept guard over this part of the Wood, protecting the Near World from the darker forces of the Far that might try to infiltrate. Certain gates fell under their watch, gates that might not look like much to a mortal eye but which Eanrin knew at a glance (or sniff, depending on his form). That moss-covered boulder there, for one; this gnarled old tree with an opening in its bole was certainly another. So many little entrances through which the fantastic might creep to harry, harass, and even harm the poor mortals of the Near World.

Mortals had not been Eanrin's concern for long. He had spent a great deal of his immortal life carefree and a little heartless when it came to mortals and their woes. What did he care if monsters plagued the Near World? He had songs to sing, dances to dance, and festivals of the sun and moon to celebrate!

But that was all before Imraldera. And before his knighthood, of course.

He journeyed now on familiar ways through the Wood, walking always in the Path of the Lumil Eliasul, for it was dangerous to step off the Path even for a moment. The Wood was treacherous and filled with treacherous folk. The cat-man feared few, but he was a cautious fellow nevertheless.

Everything was quiet enough this day, however. Imraldera, for all her complaints, had kept the watch well. An extraordinary woman, no doubt about it!

Eanrin smiled and hummed a tune in time to his stride. She was glad to have him back. To be sure, she put up a scowling front, but that was Imraldera for you! He knew her well enough by now. She missed him; that's what all this disapproval signified. She missed him, which meant . . .

"Many things, I think," Eanrin said to himself. "Many things that bear consideration."

And he did consider as he checked the gates and made certain the locks in place (which might look like nothing more than a leaf or a twig to mortal eyes) were holding. "Has the time come at last?" he asked himself, his expression oddly serious on his golden face. "Has the time come when truths must be declared? You've waited and bided well, old boy. But a fellow can't wait forever and, well, what have you to fear? You're a jolly catch and a handsome devil, and she can't possibly . . ."

His voice trailed off as his heart did something rather sudden and painful, and it startled him. He stopped in his tracks, one hand pressed to his breast, and grimaced. Then he cursed bitterly, cursed himself for the coward he was.

"You'll never do it. You know you won't. If you haven't done it up till now, you'll never do it later. And it's for the best! What would you say anyway? Foolish, foolish Eanrin. Dragon's teeth!"

He kicked at the dirt and went on his way, his face a furious mask. Any who might have watched from the branches drew back into deeper shadows and made not a sound at his passing. But Eanrin was a cat through and through, and could not long contemplate anything too disparaging of himself. Was he not the Chief Poet of Iubdan Rudiobus? Furthermore, was he not a Knight of Farthestshore, chosen by the Lumil Eliasul for this great and glorious work?

"Light of Lumé, don't be a gloomy sort!" he told himself, beginning to smile again. "There will always be some excuse out of it, but that doesn't mean you shouldn't press forward. And press forward you shall, just as soon as—"

A lion's roar, deep and bellowing, rumbled through the Wood.

Immediately Eanrin dropped into cat form, his eyes wide and his pink nose twitching. He smelled the lion and knew it was near. What he could not smell was whether it was friend or foe.

It was definitely on the hunt.

His first instinct was to turn around and leave well enough alone. He was a cat, after all, and survival was chief among his concerns. Indeed, he had even turned and made the first few paces back toward the safety of the Haven when another sound, nearer than the lion's roar, caught his attention.

It was birdsong.

His tufted ear twitched and, though he showed his teeth irritably, he looked back over his shoulder. He did not see the bird, nor did he expect to. But he knew the voice.

"Lumil Eliasul," he whispered. And then he saw what he sought. A new

Path opened up from the one on which he stood. It led into the deeps of the Wood. It led toward the sound of the hunting lion.

"Bother it all," the cat muttered. But he had made vows of service, and he meant them, no matter how inconvenient. Tail bristling and body low to the ground, he skulked swiftly through the underbrush, pursuing this new Path. It opened up before him as he went, like the birdsong itself, flowing swiftly and unpredictably but with a true course. It led him far and fast across the Wood, away from the Haven, which he did not like. But he dared not disobey, even as the scent of lion and the sound of its roaring grew.

Before he found the lion, however, he found its prey.

A young man in savage clothing—a mortal by the smell of him, though so long in the Between that much of his mortality was already lost—lay on the ground where he'd collapsed, blood spilling from a gash in his leg and pooling around him. Eanrin pulled up short, his nose wrinkling at the stench of fear and flight. This was the lion's prey, no doubt about it; the wound smelled of predatory claws.

The lion would soon be upon them. Even now Eanrin felt the thuds of its feet, the pulse of its shortened breath. He must act quickly if he would act at all.

He stood up into man's form and approached the fallen youth. "Are you awake?" he demanded, beginning to lift the stranger without waiting for an answer. The young man, startled by his voice, drew back with a cry and would have fought, however feebly. Eanrin quickly said, "I am a Knight of Farthestshore, and I can help you. Trust me. I'll get you free of your enemy, and my comrade-in-arms will tend your wounds."

Sun Eagle, for it was he, stared wordlessly at the golden stranger before him. Then he nodded and allowed Eanrin to help him to his feet. As they scrambled to get upright, Sun Eagle snatched the Bronze from around his neck and tucked it deep into a pouch at his side, a swift gesture that went unnoticed by the cat-man, for Eanrin was distracted by yet another roar from the oncoming lion and another, higher voice shouting, "Find him! *Kill* him!"

"Referring to you, I presume?" said Eanrin, stepping onto his Path and hastening as best he could while supporting the youth. "You've certainly made some hard and fast enemies. Takes talent, that does!"

"Please," said Sun Eagle, his voice thin with pain, "get me away."

"That's the idea," said Eanrin.

They hurried on in silence. The lion was near enough that had they not been walking the Path of the Lumil Eliasul, it surely would have seen them. But while they were on the Path, it could not find them even if it were to pass within inches of their location. It knew they were near, however. Eanrin could hear its low, frustrated growl. It was following the trail of blood, for Sun Eagle's wound bled freely. His skin was ashy gray, and his eyes rolled in his head.

"It's a wonder you made it this far," Eanrin said, more to himself than to the stranger. "You're from the South Land, by the smell of you, and that's far from this watch! You must have fallen on a Faerie Path by accident, and lucky for you."

Sun Eagle did not answer. His arm was round Eanrin's neck, and his other hand clutched at the wound in his thigh, desperately trying, but failing, to staunch the bleeding.

Before they reached the door of the Haven, Eanrin began bellowing Imraldera's name. He had little hope she would hear, wrapped up as he knew she would be in her work. But lo and behold, no sooner did the Haven come in sight than Imraldera flung wide the door and stood upon the threshold looking out.

"Eanrin?" she called. "What's wrong?"

"Oh, nothing much," he replied. "Just lions and gore and fainted youths. The usual, you know."

"Dragons eat you, cat," she snapped, hastening to them. She reached out to the stranger, whose head was bowed to his chest in groaning agony. "Easy now," she said. "You're among friends. You're safe."

She touched his shoulder. His head came up, and he stared at her with eyes that flashed dark fire.

"Starflower," he gasped.

2

WHAT IS THAT?

On a dark plain under the starless sky, figures began to move. At first they were nothing more than wafting shadows. But they assembled themselves with dignity, climbing stairs that did not exist to a balcony made of nothing. They carried instruments in their hands: dulcians, pipes and tabors, psaltries, viols, and a great set of richly decorated drums. As they took up these instruments, their shapes became at once both more indistinct and more real; they existed purely for the song they produced.

Soft, sweet, mournfully beautiful melody flowed down from the sky.

What is that? asked the mouth of Daylily that was no longer Daylily's.

The she-wolf, flattened to the ground, blood dried in her coat, did not raise her head. But her icy eyes glanced up at the figure beside her. "Music," she said.

We don't like it.

The she-wolf snorted. "Since when did you start having likes or dislikes? Before or after you stole bodies?"

The figure of Daylily made no answer but watched as more shadow figures moved. These assembled below the musicians, and they formed strange figures and patterns as they flowed in and out from one another, always in time to the song.

"Dancing," said the wolf. And she sighed. "I used to love dancing."

Two figures stepped out from among the rest until they may have been the only two. And these, as they danced, became more vivid. A prince in white with a fibula of a seated panther on his shoulder; a lady in a flowing headdress, furs draped across her smooth shoulders. They danced and they smiled into each other's eyes.

The wolf shook her head. "They never looked at each other like that. Only here in her mind. It was never so beautiful."

The figure that was Daylily sneered but watched curiously even so.

The music changed. The tune became lighter, merrier, but despite this alteration, the mood of the scene suddenly darkened. The smiles fell from the faces of both dancers.

"Don't leave me, Lionheart," said the lady. "Don't leave me standing here."

But the prince stepped back, his face a stern mask. He let go her hand, and as he backed away, he disappeared into the surrounding shadows. And the lady stood alone, the merry music falling like sharp glass shards around her.

The she-wolf growled. "I will kill him one day," she said.

Wait, said the figure of Daylily, frowning. ***Does he return?***

For a moment it looked as though he did. A man of much his build and coloring, also dressed in white, stepped out of the shadows, his arms extended to the lady. She turned to him, her smile momentarily flashing again.

But the man changed. His shoulders bowed, and his stance became awkward. His eyes, large and dark, squinted, either with nerves or near-sightedness. Rather than a fibula on his shoulder, he wore a crown upon his head.

"Let me dance with you, Daylily," he said earnestly. "Let me take Lion-heart's place."

And the lady, her face colder than ice, took his hand and allowed him to dance her away, spinning into shadows. The music fell into dissonance and then a silence darker than the blackness of the sky.

"All is lost," said the she-wolf.

All is mine, said the mouth of Daylily.

"My da will kill me."

"I doubt that very much," said Foxbrush with a weak laugh that earned him a scowl from Lark. The little girl knelt on the floor beside Foxbrush's own pile of animals skins (which he still resisted calling a bed). Daylily lay upon them, lost in some fevered dream that left her moaning.

Foxbrush had managed with some difficulty to carry Daylily most of the way up to the Eldest's House before he realized that the people of the village would not take kindly to the presence of the "red lady" of whom they'd been hearing. Did they believe in fair trials in this age? He could not count on it.

So he'd left Daylily in the shadows near the jungle and, praying she would still be there when he returned, went to find the only person he felt he could trust.

Lark asked no questions, but after one look at Foxbrush's face, left her sisters and brother in their small chamber and followed him out into the darkening night. The Eldest, her husband, and most of the villagers were gathered in the big stone central chamber of the Eldest's House. But there were back ways into the humbler portions of that House. Lark showed Foxbrush and helped him smuggle Daylily in and hide her in his chambers.

"Out," Lark had said then.

Foxbrush had started to protest. Then he saw Lark begin to peel back the last shreds of Daylily's ruined underdress and made a swift exit. He stood outside the door (or crouched, rather, for the ceiling was very low) and waited, counting the seconds that felt like years.

But at last Lark called him back in, and he found Daylily clad in the Eldest's old clothes, lying facedown with her shoulder exposed but dressed and well tended by Lark's expert hands.

"It wasn't deep," Lark said to Foxbrush's great relief. "Just a scratch. But I think she might be in shock. And she won't let go of that." She pointed to Daylily's fist, which clutched the bronze stone.

Lark looked up at Foxbrush with sharp, questioning eyes. "She's the lady they're talking about, isn't she. The one who killed Mama Greenteeth."

Foxbrush shook his head. "Daylily couldn't kill anyone." As soon as the words left his mouth, he knew them for the lie they were. Still, he refused to admit it. For a moment he closed his eyes and tried, however desperately, to reclaim a fair image of her, an image he could bear: such as the time she visited his mother's estate at Hill House for the summer, the first time he had seen her since they were children. She'd been a lovely girl of sixteen then, her hair piled high in shining curls tucked under a wide-brimmed hat to shade her fair complexion. Her hands had been gloved when she shook his in greeting, soft gloves of deerskin with jeweled bracelets at the wrists.

She'd scarcely looked at him then. She'd fixed her attention solely upon Leo. But it didn't matter. Not then. Not ever.

Foxbrush drew a long breath. When he opened his eyes again, he found Lark studying him, her little mouth pressed into a line as stern as any scolding mother's. "She's from your time, isn't she," she said. "Is she your woman?"

"Not really," Foxbrush admitted.

"But you'd like her to be?"

He shrugged, embarrassed at this bluntness from the child. "She'll never be anybody's."

Lark nodded at this and looked down at the young woman under her care. In that moment, despite the childish roundness of her face and the older bitterness of Daylily's, they looked very alike. Perhaps Lark felt some kindred link across the centuries. Perhaps she was simply too much a child to care about rumors. However it was, she bent suddenly, compulsively, and kissed Daylily's cheek.

Then she faced Foxbrush. "I won't tell my da. But if something bad comes of this, be it on your head."

Foxbrush nodded solemnly and stepped back to let Lark exit. "She'll not wake for an hour or so," the girl said over her shoulder. "When she does, she'll be in pain, so find me." With that, she was gone.

Foxbrush sat beside Daylily, pulled his knees up to his chest, and waited. As he waited, he frowned and pulled the scroll Leo had given him out of his shirtfront. By this time, it should have been mashed and unreadable. But as though by magic, it remained whole and legible. Foxbrush unrolled it and read:

> *Oh, Shadow Hand of Here and There,*
> *Heal now the ills*
> *Of your weak and weary Fair,*
> *Lost among the hills.*
>
> *You would give your own two hands*
> *To save your ancient, sorrowing lands.*

"Ancient, sorrowing lands," Foxbrush murmured, not realizing that he had begun to read the poem out loud or for how long. He stopped when he heard the sound of his own voice, embarrassed but thoughtful.

He put a hand to his shirt where the tears of the Everblooming had dampened it. And he shuddered suddenly at the closeness of everything, the nearness of the strange and fantastical pressing in upon his life.

When he looked up, he found Daylily watching him.

"Dragon's teeth!" he exclaimed, dropping the scroll in his surprise. "You're awake! She said . . . she told me you would sleep for an hour or more."

"I never sleep long, no matter the drugs."

Her voice was dark and low, quite unlike the bright, crisp voice Foxbrush had only ever heard her use before. He wondered if this was her real voice and the other was fake, another mask.

Daylily tried to turn and groaned, her brow wrinkling at the pain in her shoulder. But she ground her teeth and drew a long breath, then made her face go smooth.

"Shall I get help?" Foxbrush asked, half rising.

"No," she said quickly. "No one. I—" She compressed her pale lips. Then she whispered, "I must go."

"You can't. You were . . . well, you were mauled by a lion."

Her eyes flicked up to meet his again, and her eyebrows lowered, then rose. "What are you *doing* here, Foxbrush? What are you doing in this place?" Her hands gripped the animal skins beneath her, and she glanced about at the small, dark room lit by a tiny fire in the corner, smoky and dank and smelling of mold and animal droppings. It was the most unlikely setting in which to find the fastidious crown prince. And he the most unlikely figure of all! He wore skins like a native, and his skinny arms were bare and darker than she remembered. His hair, which she'd only ever seen flattened down with oil, stood up in wild, wooly tufts and sported more than a few leaves and sticks.

Most altered was his face. A growth of scraggly beard outlined his jaw and chin, making him look older than he was. Lines deepened around his eyes and mouth in the firelight, lines of worry and of fear, but also lines of—what was it? She could not say and did not like to guess.

"You are," said Daylily, pushing her hair back from her face, "possibly the last person I expected to meet in this place."

"I followed you."

It was like an admission of guilt. He bowed his head and could not look her in the eye. A long silence stretched between, each considering the words that hung still in the air.

Then Daylily said, "That was foolish. I did not wish to be followed."

She sat up then, wincing at the pain, and tried to move her left arm. Her shoulder protested, but she could feel for herself that the wound was not deep. She slipped the shoulder of the old, brown-woven shirt into place, and it scratched the wound and stuck to the dressing. "Now," she said, "I will be going." She looked down at the Bronze, still fast in her fist. "I . . . I must . . ."

We must find him.

"What was that?" Foxbrush asked, looking around, startled. He could have sworn he'd heard a whisper of many voices shivering about the room, darting round the walls and vanishing into the fire.

"I heard nothing," said Daylily. She started to rise, but Foxbrush reached out and caught her wrist. She frowned but did not struggle. There was no need. One glance and he would wither and back down.

But this time he didn't. He met her gaze, and though sweat beaded his forehead, he did not break it. "Daylily," he said, "I came to . . . to tell you something. I had to follow because you must hear this. I . . . I won't marry you."

She blinked slowly and said nothing.

"Yes," Foxbrush continued, still holding her arm. She felt his thumb moving nervously up and down over her skin. "Yes, I thought perhaps . . . They found my letter to you, you see, and I thought—"

"Oh," said Daylily, shaking her head and nearly laughing. "Is that all? Did you think it was *you* who drove me to the Wilderlands?"

Foxbrush opened his mouth but settled for a swift nod.

Daylily laughed again, and it was very like the cold, bright laughs he'd known back when she was the darling of the Eldest's court. Foxbrush, flushing so hot he thought his face would melt, hurried on.

"I won't marry you, Daylily. I've made up my mind, and nothing can change it."

"Is that so?"

"Not even your father. I don't want you for my wife. So, you see, you're free now. You can come home and . . . and . . ." He almost could not speak the words but forced them out. "And Lionheart has returned. If you want to, you can marry him instead, and I'll see that it's all right. I'll still be Eldest, I suppose, and I'll have some power." The look on her face frightened him, so he rushed on at full speed. "And I've found a way to save Southlands! They grow elder figs here, and they showed me how to pollinate them, and there's no other market in the Continent that can offer them. Our trade will reestablish, and everything will return to the way it was. We've . . . we've only got to find our way back to our own time."

Daylily, smiling softly, listened to this speech, saying nothing but shaking her head so that her hair fell over her pale face. Only when his words finally trailed into nothing did she pat his hand and firmly remove it from her arm. Then she drew herself up.

"I do not wish to return to Southlands. And I'll not marry anyone."

Foxbrush felt his stomach drop. He saw the truth in her face.

"You go home, if you can find the way," she said. "You go home, and you save Southlands, and you do what you like with your kingdom. But I have a place here now. You see, I too intend to save Southlands."

She rose, clutching the Bronze to her stomach with both hands, and stood over Foxbrush, looking down on him. "I have no use for the poisoned country of our time. But *this* Southlands, *this* Land is rich, and thriving, and full of life. It's—"

Mine!

"—where I'm meant to be. I came here to escape, but I know now that it was for a much greater purpose. Powers beyond our knowledge drive us, Foxbrush. They always have. First the Wolf Lord, then the Dragon, and now, here, beyond the Wilderlands, greater powers still! We cannot always fight them. We must join them and be—"

Mine!

"—made whole."

With that, she lifted her hand and, to Foxbrush's unending surprise, caressed his cheek. "I wish you well, crown prince, and I hope you'll find your way home. But this is my home now, and I'll not return with you to poison."

He tried to swallow, but his mouth was too dry. When he spoke, his voice came in a sad crackle. But the words themselves surprised him as much, perhaps more, than they surprised Daylily. "What do you know of the missing firstborn?" he asked. "Of the missing children?"

Her hand still resting on his cheek went suddenly cold. Behind her eyes something moved, something desperate and struggling. But her face was an unyielding prison.

"I don't know what you're talking about," she whispered.

Even as she spoke, a shudder passed through her body. Her face, already pale, whitened as a new wave of pain washed over her. Foxbrush scrambled to his feet in time to catch her before she fell, and he eased her back down onto the skins, clumsy but careful of her shoulder. She did not resist but drew many shallow breaths, closing her eyes as a sheen of sweat dampened her body.

"We'll discuss this later," Foxbrush said, gently touching the back of her head as though it might catch his hand on fire. "You're sick now, and you must rest. I'll . . . I'll get help."

He stood up and left the room in a hurried, shuffling gait. He thought he heard something whispering behind him:

We must find him. We must go. . . .

He shook off the chill that reached after him with those words and made his way through the dark passages of the Eldest's House. He could still hear the murmur of voices in the great stone room of the Eldest's council, and again shivered at the thought of what those people might do if they knew one of those they so feared even now dwelt under the same roof.

He found Lark in the children's room, sitting upright on her pallet though her siblings were all fast asleep. She saw him and got up without a word, leading the way back to his room. When they neared the door, she whispered, "I did not think she'd wake so soon. I thought I'd given her stronger medicine."

Foxbrush shook his head and held back the curtain for Lark to pass through. The girl stopped in her tracks in the doorway. Slowly she turned to Foxbrush, her dark eyes wide and stricken.

"I was right," she said. "Da's going to kill me."

Foxbrush bent his head to look through the low doorway. "Dragons eat it all!" he cursed.

There was a gaping hole in the mud-and-wattle wall, and not a sign of Daylily, save for a few strands of her red-gold hair.

3

I TOLD YOU, I FELL," Prince Felix explained for what felt like the hundredth time. "I was trying to get a better look at the commotion, and I tripped."

"Over a chest-high railing?" The apothecary binding Felix's wrist in tough bandages with herbs to keep the swelling down gave the prince what could only be described as "a look." It wasn't a questioning look or even a disbelieving look. It was more of a "I've bandaged up too many idiot young men to be surprised at anything by now" sort of look.

"Well, maybe I didn't *trip* so much as *slip*," Felix muttered, avoiding the apothecary's eye.

Following his mad pounce upon the guardsman below, Felix had lain for what felt like hours upon the floor, his hands over his head, as guardsmen trooped over the top of him and hurled themselves against the tower door. He'd not managed to get to his feet by the time the dignitaries of Parumvir reached him. But they'd quickly swept him up and hustled him back to his chambers in the midst of the uproar in the Eldest's Great Hall, fearing more kidnappers might burst from the wings to snatch other future kings for hostage or ransom. No such kidnappers emerged, however, and still Felix was stuffed away in his chambers, guards mounted at the doors, separate from all that was interesting and happening in the outer world.

In the heat of coursing adrenaline, Felix had not immediately noticed the damage he'd done to his wrist. It had taken him even longer to admit that his injury might need medical attention, longer still to convince one of his guards to fetch the apothecary. By the time the apothecary arrived, his wrist was swollen to a good three times its normal size and very painful to the touch.

Felix drank a disgusting brew that was supposed to relieve swelling, all the while grimacing and muttering curses that the apothecary ignored. Then, wiping his mouth, Felix asked eagerly, "Have you heard any news?"

"I try not to," said the apothecary, packing his various supplies into a neat little black bag.

"Are they still holed up in the tower?" Felix persisted. "Has anyone gotten through to the baron? Will they hang Prince Lionheart?"

The apothecary shook his head. "My concern is more with the binding of wounds than the making of them, Your Highness," he said, which struck Felix as rather stuffy. "Don't use that arm any more than you must, no heavy lifting, and—"

"Yes, I know, I know," Felix said impatiently. "I've sprained and broken my share of limbs." *And I've killed a dragon, so put that on your plate and eat it!* "Surely you've heard something. It's been hours now, and no one has bothered to tell me a thing."

"I fear I have been too busy to attend to rumor or gossip," said the apothecary with something of a disparaging lift to his left nostril. "The baroness was taken with the fits in the wake of her husband's abduction and required my utmost attention and skill to bring her delicate mind to a state of equilibrium. . . ."

Felix heard no more. He remained unusually quiet as the apothecary gave a few more instructions and took his leave. His eyes were a little unfocused as he studied his bandage.

The baroness had winked.

He might have imagined it. But he didn't think so. After all, a wink on the face of that plump and powdered woman was not an image Felix's mind was ready to conjure. No, she had winked directly at her page boy.

"She was in on it," Felix whispered.

Of course, none of this was his business. He was here as his father's representative, a courteous gesture from Parumvir acknowledging the shifting power of Southlands and extending goodwill in this time of upheaval. A symbol; that's what he was and nothing more.

But . . .

"Lionheart isn't a murderer."

He was a liar. He was a cheat. He was a scoundrel who'd brought down destruction and danger on Parumvir. He'd betrayed Felix's own sister and caused her pain. Felix's good hand clenched into a fist and he grimaced. Let the blackguard suffer! He certainly deserved it after everything he'd done.

But . . .

"Lionheart isn't a murderer."

The sun was setting, and night looked down upon the stricken capital of Southlands. But somewhere beyond the Eldest's House, in the gardens extending to the distant gorge, a bird, which should have long since gone to roost, sang. The song brought to mind the strange image Felix had glimpsed in the Great Hall, the image of Prince Aethelbald of Farthestshore standing before him (right in midair!) and pointing at the guard below.

Felix scratched the back of his neck and paced to the window, looking out upon the deepening evening. He listened but heard no more of the birdsong, couldn't even be certain now if he'd heard anything to begin with.

Then he crossed to his bedroom door and flung it open, stepping out under the watchful gaze of his guards.

"Your Highness, Sir Palinurus gave us orders not to—"

"See here, am I your prince, or is Palinurus?" Felix snapped. "Last I checked, I outrank all of you, Palinurus included! If you want to take issue, send a note to my father, why don't you?"

"Please, Your Highness, it's for your own safety," the poor guard pleaded.

"Well, come along if you feel the need to protect me," Felix said with a shrug. With that, he marched down the hall, trailing guardsmen behind him. He didn't know where he was going, so he grabbed the first footman he came across and, speaking loudly (because Southlanders always had trouble understanding his accent and he figured louder meant clearer), demanded to know where Middlecrescent's wife was roosting these days. The poor footman, believing he had somehow offended this foreign prince, hastily bowed after Southlander fashion and pointed the way.

"Thanks, my good fellow!" Felix shouted and the poor man cringed and ducked as the prince and his entourage of guards trooped on.

The hall leading to the baroness's chambers was crowded with an assortment of guards and ladies-in-waiting, and Felix would have been hard-pressed to say which he found more intimidating. Indeed, he very nearly gave up hope of seeing the baroness and turned back right there, save that one of the ladies caught his eye and instantly hurried over to him.

"You came!" she said, catching Felix's good hand and squeezing it. She was a lovely young woman with paper flowers in her hair, and Felix blushed, surprised.

"Um, yes . . ."

"The baroness said you'd come," the lady continued. "She said to send you in to her when you did. I was beginning to fear you wouldn't show!"

"Wait." Felix frowned then, his blushes forgotten. "The baroness is expecting me?"

But the lady-in-waiting merely took Felix more firmly by the hand and dragged him back through the crush of people in the hall. His own guards put up feeble protests, but they were obstructed by petticoats and lances and were unable to keep up, while the lady leading Felix dodged all with graceful ease and, at last, hastened Felix through a doorway.

Felix found himself standing alone in a dim chamber dominated by an enormous writing desk. It was to other writing desks what a stone fortress is to a sandcastle. From a desk such as this, a monarch might rule an empire. It was covered in perfume bottles and smelling salts.

"Hullo?" Felix called a little tentatively. The pretty lady-in-waiting had shut the door behind him, but he could still hear the bustle of people in the hall without, the sounds of his guardsmen begging (and being refused) entrance. In this room, however, all was quiet. "I . . . I was told you were expecting me?"

A door opened on the far side of the room. The baroness emerged from some inner chamber, a finger to her lips. "Shhh!" she said. "He's got a headache, the poor lamb."

With this enigmatic statement, she drew the door behind her gently shut and crossed the room, smiling sweetly at Felix as she came. She was a plump and rosy woman when her skin wasn't powdered to look porcelain frail. She had changed from the sumptuous coronation garb into a frilly dressing gown buttoned to the throat, and her hair, unadorned by hairpieces and fake swatches, was thick, graying, and a little frizzy.

She was the sort of person from whom one would expect to receive warm cookies, not plots.

"He got quite a nasty knock on the head yesterday, and I've had to keep him trussed up in my wardrobe for fear he might let something slip," the baroness said, just as though Felix understood a word of what she was saying. She sat down at the mighty desk and selected a perfume, which she proceeded to dab behind her ears. She did not look like a woman recently recovered from hysterics, no matter what the apothecary said.

"Excuse me," Felix said, bowing. "The lady outside said you were waiting for me?"

"Why, yes," said the baroness with another sweet, motherly smile. "I wanted to thank you for jumping on that guard before he could rescue my husband. I thought for a moment all was lost, but your quick thinking quite saved the day!"

Felix stared into that open, round, comfortable sort of face. "I knew it," he said. "I *knew* you were in on it!"

"In on it?" said the baroness innocently. Then she laughed. "Oh, you mean the abduction! Why, of course. It was really mostly my doing, actually, since Prince Lionheart is rather uninformed these days; but I couldn't very well kidnap the dear baron *myself*, so I'm just as happy Lionheart showed up when he did. He's a good boy at heart. As are you, I'm sure. Oh!" She put a hand to her mouth, her eyes rounding with concern. Then she reached out and gently touched Felix's bandaged wrist. "Did you hurt yourself, my dear? What a brave little duck you are!"

Brave little ducks don't kill dragons, Felix thought, though he had the grace not to say it out loud. Instead, he said, "Why would you plot against your own husband? Don't you want him to be king?"

"Oh no, certainly not," said the baroness quickly. "Why would I want such a thing? Foxbrush is supposed to be king; he was dear Eldest Hawk-eye's choice. No one should gainsay the wishes of a dead man—even I know that—but people have a way of getting a little silly where crowns and kingdoms are concerned. But there," she shrugged prettily and smiled again. "A spell up in the North Tower will set my dear baron right. Always does me a world of good when he sends me there during one of my little fits. Such a restful place, high above the noise of the rest of the house. It'll clear his head, and when Prince Foxbrush returns, my dear baron will be the first to welcome him home. Him and my darling Daylily, of course."

"I thought they were both murdered," Felix said, somewhat tactlessly as the baroness's sudden burst into tears proved. He stood by awkwardly as the poor baroness wept stormily into a perfume-scented handkerchief, wondering if he should summon one of her ladies. He'd even made two steps toward the door when the baroness caught his coattail.

"Wait," she said. "I'm sorry. I have these moments now and then. I'm just a wee bit worried about my dear child, you see, and when people start saying dreadful things about murder and whatnot, it just . . . just . . . just . . ."

She was about to go off again. So Felix hastily knelt and took both her hands. Women were not within his realm of understanding or comfort. He'd been close with his sister, Una, but sisters are a different breed altogether and scarcely count as *women.* And of course, he was mad about Dame Imraldera, but that wasn't the same at all.

Here was a woman, a real, strange, weepy woman in distress, and he, as the only man present, should do something about it, he knew. He simply didn't know what.

"Please, baroness," he said. "Why did you really want to see me?"

Tears still dampening her cheeks, the baroness smiled again. "Because you helped us earlier. You leapt like a tiger on that poor guardsman; gave him quite a shock, I'm sure. And as dear Sir Youngwood was giving me my restorative, I thought to myself, '*That* handsome young fellow would help us again.' And we do need help, my dear prince Felix. We do need help."

Felix nodded. Then he shook his head. "I don't see how I can help. Lionheart has your husband trapped up in that tower where no one can get at either of them. How long is he planning to keep him up there?"

"That's just it," said the baroness. "We don't know. We don't know when Prince Foxbrush will return, and I don't think anyone can be persuaded not to start killing anyone else until the Eldest's chosen heir is present and no one can argue his right to the crown. So they need to stay up there indefinitely. I provided everything they could want . . . rope to tie up my husband, a chamber pot for . . . well, you know . . . a good sturdy bolt on the door, firewood in the grate, since the nights are turning chilly. I even put a set of playing cards on the bedside bureau in case they grew bored."

"They're ready for a long siege, then, aren't they?" Felix said.

But the baroness's eyes brimmed with tears yet again. "I just knew I'd forgotten something. I was thinking it even as the coronation began, even as I marched down the Great Hall. I couldn't think what it was, though, until this evening, when I asked my goodwoman to bring me a snack." She bit her lip and squeezed Felix's hand ruefully.

"Dragon's teeth," Felix whispered. "You forgot to give them any food, didn't you?"

The baroness nodded and sniffed loudly, pressing a hand to her quivering chin. But she composed herself with an effort and smiled again. "Now you see, my dear boy, *that* is where *you* come in!"

4

THE HAVEN WAS LARGE, with many lovely, comfortable chambers meant for hospitable refuge in the treacherous Wood. Into one of these—both a sylvan glade of green and a bedchamber with a large, sumptuous bed, depending on how one looked at it—Eanrin half carried the stranger, Imraldera hastening behind.

"Careful. Careful!" she pleaded.

Eanrin dumped the stranger on the bed, where he sank deeply into the blankets and cushions, his blood spilling over all. Eanrin stepped back quickly as Imraldera pushed past to bend over the wounded man. Her brow was stern as she inspected the wound in his leg and the scratches beneath his animal-hide shirt. Eanrin thought he glimpsed a bright gleam from the pouch at the stranger's side, but his attention was diverted when the young man, his face gray and his eyes wide, suddenly clutched Imraldera's hand.

"Starflower! You are alive!"

"Yes, yes, but you won't be for long if I don't see to this," she said sharply.

She shook her hand free, but Eanrin saw that it trembled as she returned to her examination of the wounds.

"Your voice," said the stranger. "I always wondered . . . it is so . . ."

"Hush!" said Imraldera. She turned to Eanrin and barked, "Make yourself useful. Fetch me water and bandages."

The cat-man did not think to argue but dashed from the room with all speed, casting only one last glance over his shoulder. He glimpsed her kneeling down beside the bed, her hands pressed into the gaping leg wound, and heard her sing in her low, throaty voice:

> *"Beyond the Final Water falling,*
> *The Songs of Spheres recalling.*
> *Won't you return to me?"*

This was all he observed. But he muttered under his breath as he rushed to do her bidding.

As the song flowed over him, Sun Eagle relaxed, closed his eyes, and breathed deeply. He then gazed at the young woman beside him, wondering if he beheld a dream brought on by the pain. He had never before heard her sing; could he truly dream that?

"I thought you were dead," he said when the song ended. She remained kneeling, her hands pressed against his leg to stop the bleeding, though blood oozed between her fingers. He reached out and touched her face, but she drew back quickly and stood, her head bowed, her hands still holding the wound. "I never thought I'd see you again. Not after the cord broke."

"Nor I you," she replied, her voice near a whisper. "I believed you lost forever."

"I was," he replied. Then he laughed a mirthless sort of laugh. "I have slain a Faerie beast. More than one!"

"Hush, please," she begged.

"That was the rite, was it not? A boy enters the Gray Wood, kills a beast, and returns a man? A man fit to take his bride."

She shook her head, refusing to look at him, but remained where she stood. "Where is that cat?" she growled.

Sun Eagle turned his face away, grimacing at the pain. Then both of them startled and stopped breathing as a horrible roar erupted in the Wood beyond the walls of the Haven. Lioness had followed the trail of blood this far and found she could go no farther, but there was no sign of her prey. Furious, she roared again and again.

Joining that sound came the high, childish, merciless voice of Nidawi.

"Knights! Knights of Farthestshore! Give back what you took from me!"

Eanrin appeared in the doorway, bringing bandages, a large bowl, and a carafe of water. Imraldera took them and set to work cleaning the wound, even as the lion and the child continued shouting and circling the whole of the Haven, their voices fading and returning with each round. Eanrin stood back and maintained an aloof silence, his head tilted to catch the threats and roars without. But as soon as Imraldera tied the last bandage and stepped back to drop blood-soaked rags into the bowl, Eanrin leaned over their guest and said:

"All right, my friend, time to own up. How came you to irk the lion so?"

"Eanrin!" Imraldera protested and grabbed his shoulder. Sun Eagle looked away, his warrior's face a stoic mask.

"Don't try to be coy," Eanrin persisted, shaking the young man none too gently. "Those are both Faeries out there, if I'm not mistaken, and I smell mortality on you, however long gone it might be. My first instinct is to trust them and not you. Don't take it personally; it's just my way. But if you want me on your side, best to tell all now, or I'm half inclined to give them what they want."

"Eanrin!" Imraldera pulled her comrade back, dragging him across the room, where she glared up at him furiously. Her hair escaped from under her scarf, falling in black coils over each cheek, but she pushed them back with hands that still trembled. "How dare you? Is this not a house of succor? Of sanctuary?"

Even as she spoke, her voice was nearly drowned out by Nidawi's screech of, "GIVE HIM TO ME, OR I WILL REND YOU!"

"Here's the thing, Imraldera, old girl." Eanrin shrugged as casually as though he remarked on the fineness of the weather. "I'm a Faerie man, born and bred, so to speak, and I'll trust a Faerie's word sooner than a mortal's most any day. That's a Faerie out there, and an angry one if I'm not mistaken—"

"REND YOU, I SAY!"

"Granted, we're a temperamental lot as a rule," Eanrin added. "But we don't usually offer rendings unless provoked. So I suggest, before this Faerie lass and her toothy companion begin an assault on our doorstep, we'd best find out what they want him for."

"It doesn't matter," said Imraldera, her face and voice tense. "He is our guest, and he is wounded. Wait at least until he heals—Eanrin! Where are you going?"

For the cat-man had turned on heel and now strode from the room, his red cloak flapping behind him. Cursing under her breath, Imraldera hurried after and caught up just as he opened the front entrance of the Haven and looked out into the Wood.

"Very well, renders all!" he called in his merriest voice. "Come plead your case, and we'll see who is rending whom tonight."

Immediately the great white lioness leapt into the space before the door, her whole face and body twisted with a terrible roar. Eanrin watched through half-closed eyes, his arms folded even as Imraldera startled and ducked behind him, trembling, though she was no coward.

When Lioness had finished her piece, Nidawi appeared. She was a child still, wild and sexless, flashing teeth as vicious as the lion's, if not more so. "Exactly!" she cried. "Everything she said and more!"

"Well, that's not very friendly, tearing limbs asunder and so forth," the poet-cat replied blandly. "And I'm certainly not going to stand by and watch you do it—"

"Thank you," Imraldera whispered.

"—unless, of course, you have good reason, in which case all options will be considered."

Imraldera smacked his shoulder, which served only to broaden his grin.

Nidawi stared up at him, her eyes as wide and feral as Lioness's, panting fast in her ire. Then she drew herself up and became a tall queen, beautiful and severe, strong and sorrowful. Both Eanrin and Imraldera were surprised by this, and even Eanrin took a step back. He felt Imraldera grab hold of his arm, her fingers warm, her body near and trembling with something other than fright.

"I am Nidawi the Everblooming, Queen of Tadew-That-Was," said the Faerie woman. Her hair grew thick about her face, moving as though with its own life as flowers twined green shoots through the tangles, blooming and fading in moments. "That creature you harbor within your walls murdered my people."

"What? All of them?" Eanrin said, his eyebrows up.

"All of them," said she. She extended a long arm, strangely muscular for her femininity, and her fingernails were long like claws and tipped with Sun Eagle's blood. "Murdered my people and razed my demesne until nothing is left that is green or growing, and I am alone." Her hand was palm up, as though expecting a gift or an offering. "His blood is mine. Send him out to me."

"No," said Imraldera fiercely. "You'll not touch him!"

"Easy now, old girl," Eanrin said, putting out a restraining hand even as Imraldera pushed past him and stood, shoulders squared and feet braced, small before the might of that terrible queen. Nidawi took a threatening step forward, and with that step her face aged, her black hair streaked with white, her eyes sank into hollows, and deep pits formed in her cheeks. But she was more terrible still, and her eyes were orange-gold in their hollows, all trace of demure shadows fled.

"I demand in the name of the Lumil Eliasul that you give him up!" she cried.

"No!" said Imraldera again. "Such is not our way or the way of our Lord. Don't use his name lightly and expect us to concede."

"Are you not Knights of Farthestshore?" Nidawi said. "Are you not sworn to defend the weak against the predators of the Wood?"

"Well, my dear lady," said Eanrin, stepping forward to take hold of Imraldera's shoulder and draw her back, for she looked as though she might fly at the powerful queen, "you certainly don't make a great case for yourself, demanding blood vengeance one moment and protection the next. You've said your piece, however, and we will consider it—"

"Consider it?" The Faerie queen shrieked and tore at her own hair, her fingers ripping away the vines and flowers and leaving cuts in her scalp. "I want rest for my people! He must die, I say! Murderer! Parasite! Life-sucking leech! *Send him out to me!*"

With that, she flung herself at them, her mouth gaping wide and black, her eyes too round and too huge to be human. Arms raised above her head as though she would snatch them all and tear them apart, she flew at the door, her hair streaming like white smoke behind her. Eanrin hauled Imraldera back and slammed the door in the wild woman's face; just in time, it would seem, for she struck with such force that the whole of the Haven echoed with it. But the Haven was built for protection, and none could breach its defenses (save perhaps dragons, though that had yet to be tested).

Nevertheless, Nidawi hurled herself at the door again and again, scrabbling and tearing and pulling at the locks, her voice shifting from a crone's to a woman's to a child's and back, each more chilling than the last. And over all this cacophony, Lioness roared.

Eanrin and Imraldera stood in the passage, clutching each other and staring at the door. Then Eanrin, still grasping Imraldera's upper arms, turned her to him and said in a low voice:

"Well, we've heard her side of the story. Best to get his now, so we can decide what to do."

"It does not matter," Imraldera said. "He is our guest."

"According to our *other* guest,"—with a nod to the door—"he's a murderer."

"It's not true."

"He's a savage enough chap, you must admit."

"He's a warrior. But he would not murder."

Eanrin studied the face of the young woman before him. She would not meet his gaze. He drew back, letting her go, and crossed his arms, still watching her intently.

"All right, out with it, my girl. Who is this fellow we've got bleeding on our furniture even as we speak? This man who calls you *Starflower.*"

Nidawi screamed fit to shatter glass, and Imraldera jumped and shifted on her feet nervously. She pressed her lips together as though wanting to refuse to speak. Then reluctantly, she said, "His . . . his name is Sun Eagle. He was my . . ." She cast about for something on which to fix her gaze, anything but the cat-man's face. "He was my intended husband."

"What? You were *married*?"

"No!" Imraldera shook her head. "No, you idiot, we were betrothed."

"You never told me!"

"You never asked."

Eanrin threw up his hands. "Right! Because I should have out and said one day, 'By the by, Imraldera, have you ever promised to marry some fool chap?' Why would I ask such a thing?"

"I don't know why you would." She glared at him. "And I don't know why I would tell you." Then she drew a long breath, and her face relaxed into a gentler, tired expression. "It was a different life, Eanrin. And it was so long ago, before my voice, before my knighthood. . . ."

Her voice trailed off, vanishing behind Nidawi's screams of, "REND! TEAR! BLOOD! FIRE! KILL!" each word punctuated by the thump of her shoulder hitting the door.

Eanrin's head tipped to one side, his eyes golden slits on his face. "So that savage in there . . . he means nothing to you?"

"You are *not* giving him to Nidawi."

"Who said I was?"

Imraldera marched back to the sick chamber, where Sun Eagle lay. The cat-man followed, but she turned in the doorway and raised a warning hand. "Stay out," she said. With that and nothing more, she shut the door in his face. Not one given naturally to following orders, Eanrin put a hand to the latch. But he thought better of it and stepped back, staring at the door as though it would open by magic. Then, with a curse, he stalked down the hall.

Imraldera waited until she heard his footsteps retreating. She turned and found Sun Eagle watching her.

"What's to be my fate, Starflower?" he asked. "Am I to be given over to monsters?"

She shook her head and moved quietly to the bedside. He reached out to her, but she pretended not to see and sat instead on a nearby stool. For a little while, she studied her own hands folded in her lap. Then she said, "She claims you murdered her people."

Sun Eagle shook his head. "I never saw her. Not until some few months past, by mortal count, when she and her lion set upon me in the Wood."

Imraldera looked up and found that Sun Eagle was no longer watching her but had turned his gaze to the ceiling. It was an unusual enough ceiling, for in the shifting of moments it could seem to be made of molded plaster painted in a mural of leaves and sky; then, without altering, it was leaves and sky in truth, gently blowing in a breeze. Such was the way of the Haven, built in the Between but linking the Far World and the Near, existing both in and out of Time.

Sun Eagle's eyes were bright with tears.

"Do you remember that day?" he said softly.

She did not need to ask which day he meant. Across her mind flashed vividly the memory of a fog-shrouded morning when a young man armed with a stone knife descended the deep gorge and, secured to his own world by only a cord, passed into the Gray Wood.

The cord had broken. And she had known he would never return.

"I was frightened at first," he said. "When I realized what had happened, I thought my heart would burst with terror. But then I heard Bear—my red dog, you recall—baying in the shadows behind me."

Imraldera nodded. She remembered the warriors trying to hold back the shaggy hound, which had broken from their grasp and pursued his master even unto certain death.

"He found me and stayed by my side as we wandered forever in this interminable Wood . . . even as we discovered the secrets of fey folk and Faerie beasts, and the dreadful truths of immortality. Always beside me, my comfort and friend."

"Where is he now?" Imraldera asked, afraid of the answer she knew must come.

Sun Eagle's mouth twisted bitterly as he continued to stare up above. "Ask Nidawi the Everblooming. Ask her cursed lion." He drew a shuddering breath, closing his eyes but unable to force back the tear that fell over his dark and hardened face. "They came upon me by surprise. I had never seen her before, never met her or that white devil companion of hers. But they fell upon me when I was vulnerable, and if not for Bear, I should have perished by their bloodthirsty claws."

Imraldera wiped away the tears that were streaming down her cheeks. Sun Eagle, realizing suddenly that she wept, turned to her, struggling up on one elbow. "Please tell me," he said, "that you cried such tears for me when you thought me dead."

"It was a long time ago, Sun Eagle," she whispered.

He nodded. Then he touched the cord around his neck from which hung two beads, the red one marked with a panther and the blue one marked with a white starflower. He hesitated a moment, then tore the cord from his neck and offered it to Imraldera. She looked up, startled.

"You gave me this. Do you recall?" said he. "You gave me your name mark to carry with me into the Gray Wood. Your father gave me his as well, and it was a mark of honor. But when you gave me yours, Starflower, what did it signify?"

Imraldera shook her head.

"Tell me. Please."

"That I would wait for your return," she whispered.

"But you did not wait." Despite the bitterness, his voice was gentle. "You are here, far from our homeland. And you speak with a voice now, like a man."

"The curse of the old god is lifted," she replied, her eyes flashing. "The women of the Land are free, and we speak with strength equal to any man's."

"So I have seen," he said. "So I have heard. But I did not hope to find you alive and liberated. And certainly not so far from hearth and home!"

She told him her story then, her long, difficult tale, even as he lay back upon the pillows and fingered the cord and the two beads in his hand. As she talked, the light deepened and stars appeared on the ceiling. But a fire came to life of its own magic in a fireplace that looked like the bole of a tree, and Imraldera continued her tale. Even the noise of Nidawi and Lioness faded at last until only Imraldera's voice and the crackling of the fire could be heard in that room.

When she finished, Sun Eagle, who had not once interrupted, nodded quietly. Then he again held out the cord and the beads. "You are right," he said. "It was long ago. It was a different life. And you are not bound to wait."

But Imraldera took his hand in both of hers and closed his fingers back around the two beads. "Keep them," she said.

His eyes shone bright in the fire and starlight. With renewed strength, he caught Imraldera by the arm. "I must return," he said. "I have found a way back to the Land. It's not the Land of our time, but it is our home. And it is full of Faerie beasts who mean it harm. Beasts like Nidawi and her lion, and many worse!"

"I know," said Imraldera. "I have seen it."

"Then you know what our people face there. You know the work that must be done to protect them." He tried to pull her closer, but she resisted. "Please, Starflower," he said, "come back with me. Come back to our country and work with me to free our people once and for all. You saved them from the Wolf Lord; you saved them from the Dragonwitch. Can you leave them now to suffer under multiplied terrors?"

"I . . . have a duty," she said, though her voice wavered uncertainly. "I am guardian of this Haven, and I must keep my watch on the gates assigned me."

"So you'll pursue these tasks given you by someone not of our kin? You will labor to protect people not your own and leave the Land to bleed out upon the stones of fey totems? What kind of master would ask this of you?"

Here, Imraldera rose and pulled her arm from Sun Eagle's grasp, for he was weak still from loss of blood. "Starflower?" he said.

"My Lord is good and kind, and whatever task he sets before me is the task I will pursue," said she, then hurried across the room. But she stopped at the door and looked back. "I will help you, Sun Eagle. I will see that you have safe passage back to the South Land."

"And will you stay with me?" he asked.

She did not answer. Perhaps she did not know what answer to give. She stepped from the room, shut the door, and stood a moment in the hall. Candles in their sconces shone a warm glow around her, illuminating the orange fur of a big cat who sat a few paces down the passage, his back to her, grooming his white paws without a care in the world.

He looked around, blinking as though surprised. "Oh, so you emerge at last?" His tail flicked once across the floor. "Have a nice chat?"

"I am escorting Sun Eagle back to the South Land," Imraldera said coldly before turning the other way down the hall, hastening from the cat and his questioning gaze. "Just as soon as he's well enough."

"Is that so?" Eanrin stepped up into his man's form and hurried after, his long strides soon catching up. "And what of Nidawi the Everblooming?"

"If she wants him, she'll have to kill me first."

The bite of those words was enough to stop Eanrin in his tracks. He stood in the passage and watched Imraldera disappear into her library.

"Well, dragons eat our eyes," he growled. "So that's how it is, eh?"

5

D<small>UST BECAME MUD</small> when mixed with the blood seeping through the dressing and rough fabric on her shoulder. But Daylily passed through the jungle, led by the light of the Bronze, which gleamed like a beacon and warned away all those who watched her from tree and bush. She walked with a swiftness that belied her pain and the dizziness in her head, driven by a strength not her own.

Find him. Find him.

She came to the gorge and slid down, unable to see the dirt trail, careless of her safety. And when she reached the bottom she did not stop for rest but staggered into the Wood.

Night gave way at once. She stood in the shadows of the trees, but these shadows danced with dappling sunlight at her feet, and all was cast in green and gold around her. The Bronze, still bright, no longer seemed to glow in her hand. But it pulsed in a driving rhythm that matched the throb in her wound, and she walked as it led her.

A bird sang to her from nearby, and she recognized his song.

"Let it go. Let it go, Daylily!"

The throb in her head was too great for her to stop and listen, or to comprehend anything but the drive.

Find him. Find him.

Shadows quickened. From various reaches of the endless Between, they flowed, stalked, marched, and even danced. Then, before she realized what was happening, Daylily stood surrounded by her brethren, Advocates and Initiates alike.

They carried children in their arms, and more children stood behind them, heads bowed as though weighted by heavy chains.

Daylily felt the beat of her heart speed up to match the rhythmic heartbeats of her brethren. A furious pace that would have burst her open had she belonged to herself anymore. The Bronze in her hand surged with power, reaching out to the Bronze they wore.

The horned giantess, Kasa, stepped forward, her great hooves shaking the earth. She carried a newborn baby in one hand.

"Initiate," she said. "Where is your Advocate?"

"I don't know!" Daylily replied, her voice small before the terror of this creature. Her eyes fixed upon the newborn, which lay quietly, eyes full of Bronze light. "He was attacked by a white lion and chased into the Wood. I could not follow him!"

The giantess studied her as a cat might study the bird upon the lawn. But she said only, "You must find him. Thirteenth Dawn approaches. The twelve must be one on Twelfth Night, and the final blood must be given."

The final blood must be given.

"Of course!" said Daylily, desperate and breathless, for she understood nothing yet simultaneously felt that it all made complete sense, and this frightened her far more than the looming presence of Kasa or the lurking shadows of her brethren or even the silent children. "The final blood must be given! But how do I find him? Where has he gone?"

The shadows began moving on the fringes of her vision. One by one, Advocates and Initiates alike passed on through the Wood and disappeared, dragging the children behind them. Only Kasa remained, and she only for a moment. "Time draws nigh," she said in her voice as deep as a bull's. "Find your Advocate. We will complete the securing of the tithe. But find your Advocate."

Desperately, Daylily reached out. Her hand, by some power not her own, stretched toward the baby in Kasa's arms. For a moment, it wasn't her hand at all.

You can't let this happen! said the wolf inside her.

Then Kasa was gone, taking the baby with her. Daylily stood alone in the green Between, clutching the Bronze until it cut her flesh. Her shoulder throbbed and her face was gray with pain.

But she took a step. Then another.

And across the vast, unknowable reaches of the Wood, Bronze called to Bronze. Daylily walked on fevered footsteps, and the trees made way before her.

It certainly wasn't the most reliable of calendars. But it was all Foxbrush had in this world where hours were told only by the lengthening of shadows, and months by the ripening of fruit in the trees.

Or by the growth of a man's beard.

Foxbrush lifted a hand to inspect the bush that his face had become. Places on his cheeks utterly refused to grow more than the thinnest layer of fluff, giving him a lopsided and patchy appearance. But eventually the rest had grown so thick and soft that most of the thin patches were disguised.

The hated thing. Too hot for the weather, inconvenient for the unsanitary conditions, and far too hospitable to strange crawling beasties. There was no shaving it, however. Redman had shown Foxbrush how to keep it somewhat trimmed with a stone knife, which was an agony. For the most part, he was obliged to let it have its way with his face.

He touched it now as he walked down the path from the Eldest's House, following in Lark's wake. None of his old friends or acquaintances would recognize him now, four months into this unnatural exile. At least he hoped they wouldn't! He doubted very much he would recognize himself were someone to hold a mirror up to him. He'd probably scream at what he saw reflected there.

Foxbrush grinned ruefully at this thought and left the beard alone. Lark had suggested several times that he let her and her sisters braid it as they braided their father's beard. "Keeps it out of your mouth," she insisted. But that was a line Foxbrush the dandy could not quite bear to cross, even now.

The morning was cooler than previous mornings, still warm but hinting at the relief of rainy seasons to come. Autumn swiftly approached, and the elder figs in the orchard were already producing their third crop. Foxbrush had been delighted to learn that these resilient trees could produce four rich harvests in a single year, so swiftly did the fruit ripen. And what a bounty each time! He had never before tasted elder figs, but he knew with the first bite—after Lark showed him how to peel away the skin, which split at the stem and came off like a bandage—that he did indeed taste the near-mythic edible gold about which he'd read so much.

Of course, the folk of the village were not the only ones to appreciate this bounty. Thus, every morning, Foxbrush followed Lark and a cluster of children down to the orchard. (He was still not considered strong enough to participate in men's work but was shuffled off with the young folk every day.) Armed with tiny blowguns and darts dipped in a stinging, itch-inducing poison, they established themselves at intervals throughout the orchard, prepared to fend off any birds, monkeys, lemurs, or other determined connoisseurs of the elder fig's riches.

On this particular day, Foxbrush and Lark took up their regular position on the southeastern fringe of the orchard, lounging in the shade beneath a large tree. Lark enjoyed this task above all others. As important as it was, it also gave her rare opportunity to sit back and rest her tough little feet. She was quite the imperious mistress upon occasion as well, sending Foxbrush running at her command if she felt disinclined to rise and chase off animal thieves herself.

Contrary to her prediction, Redman had not killed his daughter for the aid she'd lent the Red Lady of the Bronze. Indeed, he'd not so much as raised his voice either to her or to Foxbrush when they'd confessed their deeds and shown him the hole in the side of the house. He'd merely sighed and said, "Well, I've had good practice repairing that wall by now, haven't I?"

With those gentle words, shame had heaped upon the heads of the two culprits. And not a sign had been found of Lady Daylily in all the surrounding countryside, nor a rumor of the Red Lady come whispering to the Eldest's village. Other rumors came instead; tales of Faerie warriors, also wearing bronze stones, slaughtering fey beasts and declaring their blood price to the mortals of the Land.

More and more firstborn children disappeared every day.

Foxbrush sat beneath the tree, twiddling the blowgun in his fingers, seeing neither it nor the trees he was supposed to be guarding. Rather his mind's eye saw the girl who was his intended bride.

"Powers beyond our knowledge drive us, Foxbrush," she'd said.

What power drove Lady Daylily; Daylily with her commanding voice and breathtaking strength? She was the one who drove! Had she not commanded him from the moment he first met her?

Yet not even she was strong in the end.

He frowned, his gaze shifting from the blowgun to his feet, skin clad and covered in dirt. What path did he walk that had led him here and left him? Left him with knowledge he could not use and a heart bruised and sore with sorrow.

But that wasn't the whole of it. He frowned even as the thought passed through his head. Yes, he was heartsick, no denying it. But he was also strangely . . . glad. Here he was, smelling like a pig—with an awful growth of brush on his chin, little crawly things residing on his person, and a belly full of equal parts dirt and spicy foods—seated beside a child who stank as much or more than he did.

And he was, in that moment, glad to be alive. Glad to be in this place. Glad for the man he felt he was becoming; a man who would never have existed otherwise. It was an odd sensation, not one he quite understood. But even this pleased him somehow.

"What are you smiling at?" Lark demanded. She'd been weaving grasses into a cord on which she intended to string her blowgun.

Foxbrush, brought back to himself, glanced at her and shook his head. "I don't know," he said.

"You look addled." Lark tested her cord, which broke under pressure. Disappointed, she tossed the bits of grass aside, then shaded her eyes and looked up into the trees. "Monkey," she said, pointing. "You try."

Making a face but game nonetheless, Foxbrush moved into a crouch, slid the dart into his instrument, and raised it to his lips. He stood slowly, so as not to startle the brown monkey, which was daintily selecting a fruit from a near-ripe cluster. After several weeks of practice, he'd yet to hit a target. But he'd come close. And this time, if he took careful aim and breathed as Lark had shown him a dozen times, then maybe . . .

The dart flew through the air. It struck the haunch of the thieving culprit.

And Crookjaw the Faerie beast turned upon Foxbrush a face of such wrath and vengeance, Foxbrush dropped his instrument in surprise.

"Flame at Night!" Lark yelped, leaping to her feet. She put a hand to her pouch, but she had not thought to bring totem tributes that morning and had nothing with which to appease the furious Faerie.

Crookjaw leapt for a near branch but missed and fell to the ground, where he paused to scratch his haunch furiously. Then he was up on his ungainly limbs, his teeth yellow in his sagging jaw as he screeched and hurled himself at Foxbrush.

"Run!" Lark yelled, and if Foxbrush had not been so terrified, he might have noticed a trace of laughter in her voice. As it was, he found possession of his limbs and turned to flee but tripped over a fig tree root and landed hard facedown. Crookjaw paused to scratch once more, then jumped and landed heavily on Foxbrush's back, grabbing him by the hair with one hand, by the ear with the other, and pulling. Foxbrush screamed and tried to twist around to fight. He heard an inhuman voice screeching:

"Evil! Evil mortal! Yeeeeeeee! Stick me with needles? Stick me with itchy sticks? Yeeeeeeee!"

"Crookjaw! Crookjaw! Take your tribute, Crookjaw!" Lark cried out in chant, flinging fallen figs at the monkey and laughing still. Crookjaw, surprised, hopped off of his victim, stuffed a fig into his mouth, screamed again, and once more fell to scratching.

Foxbrush took the opportunity to scramble to his feet. Crookjaw bared his ugly teeth and crouched to spring at him once more. Foxbrush raised his hands to defend himself against the onslaught.

But it never came.

The orchard shook under the beat of enormous hoofs. The three of them, Lark, Foxbrush, and the Faerie, turned as a great giant burst through the fig trees, breaking branches. She was twice as tall as a man, muscular and fur-covered, with wild hair and great elk's antlers springing from her head. Her cloven feet struck the ground in thudding assault, breaking roots and stones as she went.

Crookjaw screamed and scrambled for the safety of a tree. But he never reached its boughs. Kasa's great arm shot out and caught him in mid leap. The Faerie monkey screeched and bit at her hand.

She broke him like a doll made of rushes. Then she turned and fixed her yellow eyes upon Lark.

Yelling inarticulately, Foxbrush flung himself between the giantess and the girl. He stood in Kasa's shadow, and the sunlight shot into his eyes between her branching antlers. He put up both hands in defense, clenching and unclenching his fists. Her cleft lip twisted in a smile at the sight, and she advanced, the dead body of Crookjaw dangling in her grasp.

"Will you stand up to me, mortal, and deprive me of my due?" she asked, and the rumble of her voice and the scent of wildness on her breath could have knocked him over. Foxbrush staggered but did not fall.

She took another step. One of her great feet could crush the life out of him. Nothing could stand in her way. Still he stood with the child clinging to him from behind, and though he could not speak or even move for terror, he did not back down.

Kasa looked into his eyes. And she saw something that made her stop.

The King of Here.

The King of There.

A shudder passed through her, an understanding she could not fully understand. But she stood where she was and advanced no more. Then she said:

"The tithe is due."

It was then that Foxbrush saw the Bronze about her neck. "The first-born!" he breathed and he felt Lark tighten her grip on his shirt from behind. She had seen it too.

"Where is the mistress of this land?" Kasa demanded. "I will speak to her alone."

Neither Foxbrush nor Lark could answer. Kasa looked at them, avoiding Foxbrush's eyes. Then she swung the body of Crookjaw up over her shoulder, turned, and marched off through the orchard toward the village.

Foxbrush collapsed. His knees simply gave out, and he could not have supported himself a moment longer if he'd wanted to.

"Hurry! Hurry!" Lark cried, grabbing his shirt and pulling. "We've got to get to the village! That Bronze Warrior is looking for my ma!"

"Ughh uh," said Foxbrush, which wasn't as articulate as he'd hoped. He was fairly certain his heart had stopped and he was probably dead.

"Get up!" Lark cried, kicking him in her urgency. "We've got to find my ma!"

The reverberations of Kasa's footsteps quaked the ground as Foxbrush and Lark, hand in hand, hastened through the orchard in her wake. Within a few paces, they heard the village warning drums beating, but the sound could scarcely carry above the thunder of Kasa's approach.

She strode through the center of the village, and all fled her path. Up the hill to the Eldest's House she went, and from that vantage point she was visible throughout the village, her great antlers tearing at the sky, the body of Crookjaw swinging limply. She bellowed for all to hear:

"Where is the mistress of this land?"

No one spoke. No one answered. All gathered together at the base of the hill, armed but afraid to make a move. They stared up at the giantess and believed they looked upon their doom.

"Where is the mistress of this land?"

Then one voice called out in answer: "The Eldest will not be summoned like a slave."

The crowd made way as Redman stepped through. He walked from their midst and up the hill toward Kasa, his ugly face full of threats, his red hair shining in the sun. "She is not to be bullied or intimidated," said he. "You will deal with me!"

Kasa looked down upon his approach and sniffed. Her nose was flat and slitted, yet her face was still beautiful after the beauty of Faeries. Her golden eyes narrowed. "You are not king. You are not bound to this country by the beat of your heart and the pulse of your blood."

Redman stood just below her now, caught in the depths of her shadow so that his hair no longer shone. Other shadows gathered in the sky as thick black clouds rushed in to shroud the sun. And yet Redman's one good eye gleamed with fierce fire.

"My heart beats for the Eldest, and my blood flows in the veins of the children she has borne by me," he said. "I am fit to speak for the South Land."

But Kasa stamped impatiently, and she frothed at the mouth like a massive horse champing at the bit. Her mighty hooves tore turf and stone.

"Where is your queen?" she demanded. And again, "Where is your queen?"

Redman, armed with a stone-headed hand plow, took another threatening step forward. He would have fought, and he would have died. Kasa's eyes promised as much.

But in that moment, the Eldest appeared in the doorway of her house. Her youngest child toddled in her shadow, weeping, and she carried a spear in her hand. She strode forward, clad all in white, and she was a tiny, childlike figure herself before the might of Kasa and the Bronze. But she called out a warrior's challenge in a fierce voice:

"I am Eldest of the South Land."

Even Redman backed down as she spoke, and Kasa turned in surprise and perhaps even an instant of fear.

"I am Eldest of the South Land," said Sight-of-Day, brandishing her weapon. "Who are you, woman of the Bronze, that you should approach my door and threaten my own?"

Kasa heaved the body of Crookjaw. It flew in an arc and thudded at the Eldest's feet.

"That is what we've come for," Kasa said. "You owe in tithe for the blood of this Faerie beast."

Blood. New life . . .

The air trembled with words not spoken but felt by all those present. Foxbrush, who had joined the crowd below, felt Lark squeeze his hand and press against him.

The Eldest, however, cast but a brief glance down at the broken body of the monkey. "We owe nothing. Crookjaw lived in harmony with my people. You have murdered him, and we owe you nothing."

"Harmony?" said Kasa with a sound that might have been a laugh among her own kind. "The beast attacked one of your own. I saw how it happened. The beast tore at the face of your own village man and would have slain him had I not interceded. And now you owe the tithe for the blood I spared and the blood I spilled."

The Eldest stepped over the body of Crookjaw, advancing on the giantess. "We owe nothing!" she said. "Crookjaw would never attack one of my people! He had his tribute!"

Kasa turned then. Her gaze swept down from above and fixed upon Foxbrush in the crowd. She raised one muscular arm and pointed directly at him. "Ask the one I saved."

Blood. Saved. Blood . . .

Redman, the Eldest, and all the village turned to Foxbrush then. Even Lark, clinging to his hand, turned her too-old eyes up to his face. Though he did not move a step, Foxbrush felt as though he was dragged suddenly forward and flung into the midst of an accusing throng. He could read the question in every gaze: *Is it true? Are we lost?*

"Tell them," said Kasa. "Tell them the truth of my words."

"Um." Foxbrush stared around, finally looking down at Lark. Her face was stricken with hopelessness. "I . . . I ran afoul of Crookjaw," he whispered, but his voice was caught in the listening silence and seemed to roar in every ear. Then he shook his head, closing his eyes and willing himself to speak despite the pressure of the village stare. "But I don't think he would have hurt me. Not really."

He looked up then and met Kasa's gaze. And she, even from that distance, saw again what she had seen before and felt a waft of coldness pass over her heart.

Then she spoke. When she did, other voices spoke as well, nine other voices from nine other warriors who stood ringing the village, the Bronze shining upon each breast. Their voices rose as one, and they cried out:

The bond is made! The tie cannot be broken! Send us your firstborn!

The sky overhead turned black as night and thunder growled dark threats. In the darkness, the lights of the Bronze shone, beckoning, irresistible.

Lark let go of Foxbrush's hand. He saw her turn her face to the nearest of the lights, which shone so bright it obscured the one who wore it. She started toward it.

"No!" Foxbrush shouted. He heard other voices, the whole of the village shouting, screaming names and threats and protests. Everywhere around him, children of all ages left the shelter of their parents' arms and moved toward the gleaming lights. Foxbrush leapt forward and caught at Lark, struggling to grab her shoulder, her arm. But though he felt the warmth of her skin, he could not take hold. She slipped through his grasp like mist and moved on.

More dark figures, shrouded by the storm gloom, moved into the crowd. Young mothers clutching newborns to their breasts found their arms were empty. Fathers catching up little ones found they caught at airy nothing.

And still the voices called:

Send us your firstborn! Send us your firstborn!

Suddenly the bronze lights went out.

The world plunged into crippling blindness. Foxbrush fell to his knees and pressed his hands over his face, trying to hide himself from the dark.

The storm rolled by overhead. The sun dared shine once more. It looked down from the sky upon the desolate village, where fathers and mothers wept and called their children's names.

6

Nidawi prowled the shadows, moving slowly on her hands and feet like some long-limbed lion herself, placing each foot and hand silently before its mate. Shadows danced across her face, but fire danced in her eyes as she watched the Haven door. The Haven itself was not constant before her vision. Sometimes she saw a great and beautiful house; sometimes it was only a thick grove of trees. Either way it was unassailable, at least in her current strength.

But the door she could watch. She and Lioness.

Days and nights both passed and did not pass in this realm without time, for nothing was stable and nothing changed. Around the Haven itself—perhaps due to the occupant, who was herself once mortal—time seemed to linger, counting out hours and moments alike. But a few paces beyond, there was only the Wood and immortality. Nidawi cared nothing for time, and in this at least she had the patience of mountains. She watched the gloom of night fall and retreat into the gleam of morning more often than she bothered to count. And still she waited.

She could hear voices now and then. Just now, for instance, on the other side of a hawthorn tangle that was also a hard stone wall, she heard the Faerie man and the mortal woman who had turned her away from their door (the *beasts!*), arguing. She crouched beneath the branches, listening and sniffing and watering at the mouth in the eagerness of her desire.

"You brought him here yourself!" the woman said, her voice tense with anger. "You told me you heard the song of the Lumil Eliasul, and you followed it to him. Is that not sign enough for you? Does that not tell you of our Lord's will?"

"I hardly need remind you," the Faerie man replied, his voice too light and cheerful to be sincere, "that the will of the Lumil Eliasul is not always so easy to interpret as all that. To be sure, I believe I was led to this Sun Eagle of yours. However, I don't believe that means we should swallow his every word like rich cream and do anything he asks of us."

"What then? Do you think the Prince would bid us toss him to the lion?"

"I'm not saying it hasn't crossed my mind—"

"Don't play the fool, Eanrin. Not now. That is never the way of our Lord, and you know it. We are here for the protection of mortals and immortals alike."

"Yes, but protecting this fellow doesn't necessarily include traipsing off back to the South Land again, leaving our watch unguarded."

The woman heaved an exasperated sigh. "That's not what I'm proposing, and you know it. I will take him myself to the South Land and learn if what he says is true. If it is, and my people are in more danger than when I last left them, I will remain and help."

The Faerie man did not respond. Nidawi strained her ears for some moments but caught only the sound of his breathing. Then he said, "Remain and help, eh?"

"Yes."

"And you'll return when?"

"I don't know when." She snapped this last, sharp as an iron snare. Even

Nidawi blinked and drew back a little from the bush before pressing her ear to it once more.

The Faerie man, still bright as a morning song, said, "And that's exactly why, if you insist upon this mad little scheme—rushing off without a word from the Prince and so forth—I intend to go along." His voice hardened a little then. "Someone needs to make sure that spinning head of yours stays attached at the neck."

"And leave our watch unguarded?" she replied.

"I've checked the gate locks. They'll hold well for a spell or two. And if I have my way, we'll be gone no longer than a lick of my whiskers, which isn't time enough for anything too dreadful to happen, even in the Between."

"I don't need you along, Eanrin."

"I say that you do."

Nidawi waited for more, but no indication of plans or pursuits came. At last she crept back and found Lioness waiting nearby, growling softly, her tail flicking across the forest floor.

"They're leaving soon," Nidawi whispered. She wore the form of a woman, not yet old but lined about the face with sorrow and rage. Her wild hair was tied back from her face and held in place by sticks and bits of bone, as if she were dressed for battle, though she was armed only with her four strong limbs and her long, curved fingernails. "When they do, they'll take one of their dragon-cursed Paths, and we shan't be able to see them. But you'll smell them, Lioness, and we'll follow. They shan't be able to stay on the Path forever!"

Lioness nodded solemnly, her growl never letting up.

They watched again, two predators crouched at the door. At length that door opened, and out stepped first the woman, her head covered with her long scarf, then— Then! Then! Oh, then came *him*! That *hated* one! Nidawi and Lioness bared their teeth, and only with difficulty did they not leap forth and give themselves away.

Last of all came the golden Faerie man, and he shut and secured the door behind them. With the woman leading the way, the *hated* one limping from his wounds (Nidawi and Lioness smiled at this and tasted again his blood in their mouths), and the Faerie taking up the rear, they stepped onto their fey Path and vanished from the view of their stalkers.

Lioness was up in a second, her nose to the pursuit, and Nidawi raced along behind, suddenly a child, clapping her hands and urging terrible, eager things. They took a Faerie Path of their own, one that ran parallel to that of their prey, carrying them leagues with each stride. And the Wood parted and fell away on either side of them, watching their progress with grudging interest to which Nidawi paid no heed. Her attention was on the hunted.

Until she caught another scent.

"Lioness!" she gasped, reaching out and clutching her companion's tail. "Lioness, do you smell that?"

Lioness's great head came up, and her round, black-tipped ears pricked as she swung her heavy gaze a little to one side of their Path. The trees came into focus around them, tall and threatening, but this bothered neither the lion nor the Faerie. They sniffed and they stared and they listened.

"Cren Cru!" said Nidawi, her grip on the lion's tail tightening. "Cren Cru! He comes after his own in another body! A small, weak one!"

Lioness's lips curled back in a red snarl. Then she bounded forward, and Nidawi, still holding on to her tail, bounded after. Hers was not a mind for plotting or plans, but she had a certain spontaneous cunning about her that could be, and often was, deadly.

A gleam of light ahead; the glow of the Bronze. They pursued it, away from their previous prey, but only for the moment. Then they saw them— it—*her*! They saw their enemy, clad in that strange, frail body bleeding from claw wounds at the shoulder, skin flushed with fever.

A roar shattered the stillness of the Wood, echoing on into worlds and demesnes beyond. And Daylily, clutching the stone that dragged her forward against all her will or strength, looked up into the descending doom of the lion and screeching Faerie queen.

"What was that?"

Imraldera paused midstride and turned to the sound of that echoing rumble. The blur of trees sliding past hardened into the solid growth of the Wood around them as she and her companions stopped.

"The white lion," Sun Eagle said. His voice was thin, for though he had recovered much from his wounds under Imraldera's care and the influence of the Haven, he was still weak from blood loss. But his head came up and his eyes were bright as he stared off in the direction from which the roar had come. "She is near. But not so near as I thought."

"No, indeed. I thought she was right on our tail a moment ago," Eanrin agreed, craning his neck as though to somehow see through the trees themselves. "Sounds like she's on the hunt, all right. But if we're not her prey, than who is?"

"We should go after. We should find out," said Imraldera, but there was a question in her voice. After all, Sun Eagle was not strong, and the idea of walking into the waiting jaws of the lioness and her wild companion was unappealing from any perspective.

"I think . . . not," Eanrin said, though he hesitated. "We'd do best to put some distance between ourselves and those two mad girls, if you know what I mean."

Imraldera agreed but Sun Eagle said nothing. He continued looking after the sound, which by now had died away into nothing. He sniffed the air and bowed his head. Then without a word, he continued on his way, passing up even Imraldera and storming on at a tremendous speed despite the pain that must even now be shooting through his leg. It was as though some force other than himself moved his body and his limbs.

Where he walked, a Path opened up. But it was not the Path they had been following a moment before.

Imraldera saw this and frowned. It seemed a safe enough way, however, and it led the direction they had been following all along. With a whispered curse, she took a step after.

Eanrin caught her arm.

"Oh, is that how we do things now?" he said. "Our Lord's Path disappears, and we just pick up the next one that comes along?"

"Don't lecture me, Eanrin," she said without a great deal of vim. She was tired, and she hated to admit that she was beginning to think the cat-man might be right. It irritated her, and she tried to shrug his hand off but failed. "You know as well as I that there are many safe Paths in the Wood. It doesn't have to be one we know to be good."

"And you're just going to assume that any Path this Sun Eagle of yours follows is good, is that right?"

"Stop calling him 'mine,'" she growled. "It's beneath you to be so spiteful."

"Spiteful? When was I ever spiteful?" said he. But his voice was no longer the cheerful tease Imraldera had come to know so well. It was more like a cat's than ever, but like a wild cat's, full of suspicion. "Look, I haven't felt right about this all along. Not since I first found him and carried him back. I don't deny that part was right, but the rest of this? Tell me, have you heard even a whisper of leading from the Lumil Eliasul?"

Imraldera stared hard at his hand holding her arm, as though to burn his fingers with her gaze. She drew a deep breath and scowled up at him. "No. I haven't. But that does not mean we are doing wrong. We've been given our mission: to protect, to guard. And we've our own good sense and experience from which to draw, as well as what we know of our Lord's will. I believe this is the right course."

He let her go and she turned to face him, crossing her arms over her chest in a mirror image of the stance he also assumed. Sun Eagle marched on ahead as they glared at each other, and the Wood watched, both frightened and amused.

"Do you want to know what I think?" Eanrin said.

"Not especially, no."

"Isn't that a shame, then? Because I'm going to tell you what I think, and you're going to listen, and if you can't give me a fair answer, it'll be dragon fire to pay, you mark my words."

"We don't have time for this."

"We *always* have time. We're in the Between. And it's about *time* someone took *time* to stop and think before rushing off into the unknown at a word from some savage mortal!"

"Savage?" Imraldera snarled out the word. Her face was flushed and she felt the heat of mounting battle inside her. Reasonably, she knew she should back down and step away from this fight that could accomplish nothing.

Yet there she stood, rising to the bait, her mouth filling with words like weapons to hurl at her companion's head. "You keep saying *savage*, Eanrin. Is this what you think of me, then? Am I nothing more than a *savage* to you? Because I am what he is."

"No, you're not."

"I am! I am of the Hidden Land Behind the Mountains! I was born of mortal earth and mortal blood! I was raised by mortal hands the same as he, breathing the air he breathed, living the life he lived."

"The life he lived, eh?" The cat-man's voice was smooth as butter. "If my memory serves, you were poisoned and cursed to lose your voice, while he and all the menfolk of your precious Hidden Land beat you down at their convenience—when they could be bothered to acknowledge your existence at all."

"They are my people!"

"Your people? Your enslavers, rather!" He took another step forward, towering over her. For the first time in all the long ages she had known him, Imraldera saw Eanrin for the dangerous creature he was; a creature older than she could imagine, a creature as much animal as he was man, and all otherness and wild fey menace. His golden eyes snapped with anger, and his teeth looked sharp as a cat's in that near darkness under the trees.

"This is what I think, Imraldera," he said. "I think you've lost your head over this man who once had a hold on your affection. Don't deny it, and don't tell me it was too long ago! I think you've forgotten all that good sense you claim. I think a few pretty words from him, and you'd drop everything you've worked for since you saw to the Wolf Lord's death, everything you've striven for since you accepted the knighthood. You—"

"Stop now, Eanrin," she said, and the muscles in her cheeks tensed with the grinding of her teeth.

But Eanrin rushed on, his words an angry torrent now. "You think you can't put a foot wrong? You think because the Prince has seen fit to use you for his good purpose that you can now start deciding what that good purpose is? Look at this Path we walk! It's not one of our own, and you don't know where it will lead, yet because *he* walks it, you're willing to go tripping along, sweet as you please!"

"You don't even know Sun Eagle, and yet you distrust him. You've given him no opportunity to prove himself."

"You don't know him either! You know only what you've stored up in that mortal memory of yours, and I'm here to tell you it's not so trustworthy as you seem to think."

Her eyes blazed. She would have struck him in that moment had she not caught at the last shreds of her self-control. Instead, she said coldly, "I see no reason for you to continue with us, then. I am perfectly capable of making my own decisions and walking what Paths I choose. I will do as I have purposed, and I'll do it alone."

"Alone? Ha!" The cat-man tossed back his head in a mirthless laugh. "That's a fine joke, that is! So you really believe I'm going to just let you go marching off to certain doom and folly?"

"If you're so certain it's doom and folly, you can turn around and wash your hands of it!"

"That I won't."

"And why not?"

"Because I love you."

The Wood held its breath. A hundred invisible creatures watched from hidden places, biting nails, eyes bulging. Their ears rang with the shouts, the accusations, but all these faded away into this one final, quiet declaration. They watched and they did not move, even as Imraldera stood like stone, unable to breathe or speak or even think.

The poet took a step, closing the distance between them. "Don't pretend you didn't know," he snarled. Then, because he could not bear the look in her eyes, he caught her face between his hands and kissed her; kissed her hard, for he had already seen what her answer would be when she found the ability to speak, but he could fool himself still, in this small moment before the answer came.

Imraldera wrenched away, stepping back so suddenly that she would have fallen had he not deftly caught her upper arm. "No," she gasped, frightened out of her anger. "No, no, no. This is all wrong."

"Wrong?" Eanrin whispered, unable to look at her now.

She put a hand to her heart, uncertain that it still beat, and was surprised to feel it pounding a thunderous pace beneath her palm. She drew a tremulous breath and closed her eyes. "Eanrin, I didn't think . . . I'm sorry, I never even . . . I don't know what to . . ."

She stopped and let that horrible silence linger again, for horrible as it was, it was better than anything she tried to say.

Eanrin spoke softly. "I know. You don't love me."

"No, no please. I do care about you! But we are knights; we serve together." She took hold of his hand and removed it from her arm. His fingers were icy cold. "We can't . . . there could never be . . . Dragon's teeth, Eanrin, *what about Lady Gleamdren?*"

"Who?"

Now Imraldera felt the anger returning, heightened by embarrassment and an odd sensation of shame and even fear. She stepped away from him, shaking her head and glaring furiously. "That woman to whom you've dedicated *centuries'* worth of romantic poetry! Poetry *I've* been copying for more than a hundred years myself! How . . . how could you?"

Afraid she would disgrace herself with tears and render this whole unbearable scene beyond unbearable, Imraldera turned her back on the poet, pressing her hands to her heated face. He growled behind her, "You know Gleamdren means nothing to me. You're making excuses. You love this Sun Eagle."

"No," she said quickly, without looking round. "No, you don't understand."

"But you'll throw away everything for him. This man you were to marry."

"I was pledged to him. It wasn't my decision." She lowered her hands and raised her head, putting her shoulders back like a soldier ready for battle. "But *this* is my decision. And I will do as I have purposed. And I hope—" Her voice faltered but she struggled on. "I hope that we can somehow—"

A hideous shriek shattered the air, and both knights startled and turned to see the figures moving through the shadows of the trees. The first was a great white lion; the second was Nidawi, and she clutched a young redheaded maiden before her, her long claw-like nails held threateningly at the girl's throat.

"Cren Cru!" Nidawi cried. She was old as a hag, but muscled and lithe, and her wild white hair was held back with equally white bones. "Look what I have, Cren Cru! I've got you, and I'll hurt you if you don't show your wicked face!"

Eanrin and Imraldera stared at the horrible figure. They did not know the girl captive in Nidawi's clutches, her arm twisted behind her to the point of breaking, blood running down her neck from five thin nail cuts. They saw only that she was mortal and in great pain.

And she wore a bronze stone about her neck.

"What is this? Are you preying on mortal maidens now?" Eanrin cried, his wrath more potent than he had ever known it to be. Quite exhilarating, in fact, ready to carry him off on a tidal wave of destruction. He drew a knife from his belt and leapt forward.

Lioness moved into his way, roaring, the hair on her back bristling. Eanrin, without changing pace, sank down into cat's form, dwarfed by the massive bulk of the lion but equally vicious. He threw himself at her head, and she was too slow to evade the slash of his claws, which left red lines down her white face. But she caught him with her second swing, the thunk of her paw sending him flying. He struck a tree and landed in the form of a man, groaning.

"Eanrin!" Imraldera cried, then turned on the Lioness and Nidawi. She strode forward shouting furiously, "Drop that girl at once!"

"Girl?" said Nidawi, gnashing her white teeth. "Is that what you think this thing is? A girl? Don't you see the Bronze? Don't you know it?"

But Imraldera saw only the poor mortal, sick and near to fainting, blood running down her pale white skin. Imraldera had no weapon, but she flung out her hands and spoke a sharp word like a command.

And the tree behind Nidawi rose up as though from a long sleep and swung a branch at the Faerie queen's head. It struck her, and she dropped the girl, who fell to the ground, landing on all fours.

For a moment, Imraldera glimpsed a red, bloodstained wolf.

Mine!

A sensation of pure instinct—driven, hungry, desperate instinct—filled the Wood with a potency as hot as fire, as cold as ice, as sure as the oncoming storm. Daylily rose and looked beyond Nidawi, who was grappling with the tree, to a place in the shadows where Sun Eagle suddenly stood.

Mine!

Nidawi, pulling away from the tree—which sank back into itself and its quiet watchfulness—saw Sun Eagle as well. She sprang for him, and he, though his leg must have wrung with pain at every step, dodged her assault and swung out his stone knife, slashing one of her long, muscular arms.

Lioness screamed her fury at the scent of Nidawi's blood. Sun Eagle turned as she sprang, and braced himself, his knife in both hands. Lioness, her eyes red, descended like lightning, her claws tearing, her mouth open and hungry for vengeance.

She fell upon his blade, which plunged deep into her huge, ancient heart.

They landed in a heap, and silence followed the thud of their bodies. Eanrin, picking himself up, and Imraldera, hastening toward Daylily, stared at that mass of white stillness. Then it moved, heaved, and the carcass of the lion fell to one side as Sun Eagle emerged from beneath.

"NO!"

Nidawi, suddenly no longer the powerful hag but a tiny child, screeching with a heartbreak that children should never know, rushed upon the body of Lioness, even her enemy forgotten as the shattering of unbearable grief broke her into sobs. "No! No, get up, Lioness!" She pulled and tore at the fallen beast's body, screaming and gasping between screams.

Sun Eagle, moving swiftly but with a jerking and unnatural pace that betrayed the pain of his wounds, stepped to Imraldera's side. "Come with me, Starflower?" he asked.

She stared at him, unable to speak. Then she took a step back.

His face was a mask. He reached out and took hold of Daylily's hand. "Please," Daylily whispered, "please, we must—"

The brightness of the Bronze flared up and hid them, and when it faded, they were gone. Nidawi cast herself upon the body of the fallen lion, still screaming, no longer able to hold herself upright.

"Go to her." Eanrin's voice was low in Imraldera's ear. She turned to him, stricken, and he would not meet her gaze. "Go to her. Offer her comfort if you can. I'll follow the other two."

"She . . . she would have killed them . . ." Imraldera whispered as though making an excuse. But she could not go on.

Eanrin touched her face. "Go to her," he said again. Then he too was gone, leaving Imraldera in the Wood with the inconsolable Faerie queen.

Afraid her legs would betray her, Imraldera moved to the side of the broken beast and knelt. She gently stroked Nidawi's hair. The ancient child did not seem to notice but went on weeping noisily, casting her voice to the heavens one moment, burying her mouth deeply in the fur of her friend the next.

Then, as sudden as the fall of night, Nidawi sat up. "This is *your* fault!" she shouted at Imraldera, her voice trembling as though the sorrow were both terribly new and terribly old. "You should have given him to me! Now he's killed her too! Cren Cru has taken *everything*!"

She stood up. Though she did not change size but remained the tiny child, she put out her arms and gathered up the enormous bulk of the white lion. Then she too vanished.

Imraldera sat alone beneath the spreading trees. And she bowed her head with deeper shame than she had ever before experienced.

"My Lord," she whispered. "What have I done?"

Deep in the forest, a wood thrush sang, and his voice carried over the vast distance to touch her ear, saying, "Won't you return to me?"

Imraldera wept.

7

LIONHEART'S HEAD came up with a start. He hadn't been asleep, had he? No, he knew better than to sleep again. He groaned a soft curse and twisted his neck, which crackled disconcertingly. All right, maybe he had nodded off. But really, who could blame him?

Though the baroness had seen to it that kindling was provided, Lionheart had not bothered to light a fire in the grate, preferring the tower—and his troubles—sunk into the oblivion brought by night. Now, as he returned wearily to consciousness, he began to think differently. Up here in the tower, where the wind whistled in the eaves and all the world was far below, he was so isolated.

But then, he'd been cut off since his father spoke that final word when the Council declared its decision:

"I hereby strip my son, Lionheart, of all right of rule, both now and evermore. Leave my presence, my son."

Lionheart got to his feet. He could hear by the baron's breathing that

Middlecrescent was not asleep. He could almost feel the baron's enormous eyes watching him. Surely not even an old bloodsucker like Middlecrescent could see in the dark. Could he?

Pretending to be unaware of the baron's gaze, Lionheart crossed to the tower window. It was little more than a lighter patch of darkness, for the sky was not only heavy in the small hours after midnight, it was also cloud covered, making it darker still. Not even the relief of the moon's silver eye could be had on a night such as this. But the Eldest's City was alight with fear and uncertainty, lanterns burning like the fallen children of Hymlumé. And directly below in the courtyard, torches were lit, and Lionheart could see the shadows of angry men going to and fro.

"You know the truth."

Lionheart stiffened at the sound of the baron's voice but hoped he did not betray the icy chill down his spine. He refused to turn but continued looking down into the courtyard.

"The crown should be mine."

Lionheart heard the baron shifting in his bindings behind him.

"Your cousin is a fool at best. A weak man. Not the leader Southlands needs in this time of crisis. It was a blessing, not a curse, when he disappeared those months ago. Indeed," and the baron's voice shifted to a smooth, softer lilt, "I was tempted to bring it about myself."

"Tempted to murder?" Lionheart said, making no attempt to disguise the disgust in his voice.

"Tempted to make the hard decision for the good of the nation. As every true king must." The baron rose heavily to his feet. Lionheart had given his captive enough rope to allow him to stand, but not enough that he could take so much as a step away from the iron ring in the wall. Middlecrescent drew himself up to his full height and breadth and spoke with an earnestness Lionheart had never before heard from him.

"You know the truth, deep in your heart. You've known it for years now. When the Dragon fell from the sky, who kept Southlands strong? When your father, your mother, and your fool cousin Foxbrush were imprisoned in this very house at the Dragon's mercy, who maintained unity among the barons? Who dealt with shortened resources, with isolation, with panic and gradually spreading anarchy as poison filled every beating heart? Who was it, Lionheart? Tell me, who?"

Lionheart did not answer. He put out a hand to support himself against the wall, glad once more for the darkness. A burden of fear and guilt weighed him down, and though he listened, he could hear no song or leading. Only the baron's words like daggers in his back.

"Your mother would have known. Had she been alive when the Council made its decision, she would have backed me. She would never have let Hawkeye name such an imbecile his heir. The hope of Southlands? Bah!"

"That's . . . not true," Lionheart said slowly. "Mother always liked Foxbrush." Actually, his mother had always seemed to prefer her nephew to her son, which had done nothing to foster good feeling between the cousins. Somehow, Queen Starflower, stern and masterful as she was, had seen something in Foxbrush that she believed her son lacked. Had she survived the Occupation, Lionheart did not doubt she would have supported her husband's decision to instate Foxbrush as heir.

The thought was a bitter one. Lionheart bowed his head.

"Then she was a greater fool than I've always believed," said the baron. "She knew what Southlands needs. A strong Eldest. A ruthless Eldest, even. A man who can bring it back from the brink of collapse and see it thrive once more!"

Lionheart did not answer, and silence fell for a little while. Even beyond the door, all was quiet. Were guards still stationed there, they might have fallen asleep for all the sound they made.

"You know this is true, Lionheart. You know it as well as I." The baron shifted, tugging uselessly against his bindings. "So why are you giving up your life for the sake of a cousin you know will never be fit to sit on your father's throne?"

It was a fair question. As much as Lionheart would have liked to ignore it, he knew it was fair. He didn't want to see Foxbrush in his father's—in *his*—place. Could there be a greater disaster for Southlands? Could there be a worse fate?

And could there be a keener shame than watching his cousin and rival take everything that had ever been meant to be Lionheart's? Foxbrush deserved none of it!

Lionheart leaned his head against the window frame. The window itself was open, but though the high winds blew cold around the tower, they offered no relief. "My Path led me here," he whispered.

"What?" the baron demanded, tilting his head.

"My Path led me here." Feeling as though he might collapse under the weight of words he did not wish to speak, Lionheart turned. As he turned, the moon emerged from behind a cloud and lit him from behind while simultaneously falling into the baron's enormous eyes. "It led me here, and here I'll stay until it leads me on."

"Your path has led you to your death," said the baron. But his voice was less confident now. For in that moment, he could see what Lionheart could not. He saw the moon shining, and it looked to him like a gentle eye, watchful and concerned. He saw how its light fell upon Lionheart's hair and seemed to shine there as a crown. And he saw the thin wisp of cloud that drifted across the moon and took the shape of some enormous bird, wings spread in gathering protection, a creature of monstrous and mythic proportions, a creature of power and benevolence and wrath.

The baron quaked. Slowly he sank back down upon the floor.

The vision passed and clouds swallowed up the moon, leaving the high tower in darkness again. Lionheart, exhausted, returned to his post by the door. How tempting it was, for a moment so brief it might not have existed at all, to open it and give way. To let the course of history progress as it wished, with strong men in power and a hope for a brutal revival. To let himself be carried off, a traitor to be tried by the Council and hanged. To give up. To give in.

But he stood with his back to the door and crossed his arms. "My Path led me here," he whispered. "And here I'll stay."

They were silent for so long, they might each have drifted off in the darkness to realms of far dreams.

Suddenly the baron said, "Who helped you?"

"What?" Lionheart frowned and peered through the gloom at the prisoner he could not see. "What did you say?"

"I know you could not have done this alone. You could not have secreted away these ropes of mine, or the kindling, for you would have been recognized. You had help from the inside. Who was it, Lionheart? Was it Blackrock? Or Evenwell? Disloyal dogs at heart, I know, for all their protestations of friendship."

"No," Lionheart said and hastily added, "There was no one, baron. I acted alone."

"Liar."

"Well, yes. But I'll say no more."

"You don't need to. I'll get it out of you. Before you hang."

Lionheart made a face. His throat was parched for want of water, and his stomach was empty. The threat of death made none of this more bearable, and he growled, "Do what you like, baron. You'll not get a word from me. Despite what you might think, I do still possess some shreds of honor."

"Honor?" said the baron, musing over the word. He was quiet again for some time. Then he said, "So it *was* a woman."

How anyone could come to that conclusion based off Lionheart's words was testimony to a keen, near-animalistic cunning. Like a scent hound following the culprit across marshy ground, so the baron pursued a line of reason, however faint and untraceable it might be to another.

"Think as you will," Lionheart said, perhaps too quickly.

"A woman," said the baron again, musingly. "How intriguing this game becomes. Now, I wonder what—"

He broke off with a gasp. Lionheart, glad for the reprieve, took a seat on the floor and rested his tired head in his hands. He began to wonder if the night would never end.

The baron spoke with gentle venom: "I'll have her hanged as well."

Lionheart looked up sharply, and his heart began to pound. He must be mistaken. He must have fallen asleep, into some dreadful nightmare. He must have invented that sound from the shards of a tired mind pushed over the brink. He *must* have.

Because he couldn't bear to believe he'd truly heard tears in the baron's voice.

8

From the base of the hill, Foxbrush watched the enormous bonfire built near the Eldest's House, a beacon into the night. Many men and women worked to gather fuel, driving the flames higher and hotter, a defense against the darkness and a light to those who had ventured into that darkness.

The warriors had gone. Led by Redman and Sight-of-Day, men and women alike, they had marched from the village and into the jungle, spreading out in all directions, searching. Surely the Bronze Warriors would have left some sign. Surely they could not have gone far.

"Please!" Foxbrush had begged, catching Redman by the arm. "Please let me come with you!"

"No," Redman had replied, shaking him off. "You must follow your Path, and it does not lead with me."

"I can help!" Foxbrush had tried to insist, catching up a weapon and holding it awkwardly. "I know I can!"

But Redman had been adamant. "You must remain here, Foxbrush. Follow your Path."

Then he had gone, leading the village warriors in desperate hunt, calling Lark's name as he went. And Foxbrush remained, watching the jungles into which everyone disappeared.

Useless. Shrugged off. Despised.

The story of his life.

The sun traveled swiftly across the sky and plummeted beyond the horizon. Those who'd stayed behind built up the fire, glad for some task at which to busy themselves. But they shook their heads and motioned Foxbrush away when he offered to help. So he stood now alone, his arms crossed against a cold that seeped from the inside out.

It was his fault. But how could he have helped it? He should never have shot the monkey. But how could he have known it was Crookjaw?

It didn't matter. Lark would suffer for his mistake.

To Foxbrush's horror, he found tears on his face, running through his beard. He cursed and dashed them away, turning from the bonfire back to the jungle. Hours ago he'd ceased to watch for any sign of return. The warriors would stay out searching for days. Then, like all those who had lost their firstborn over the last many months, they would return, heart-broken, spirit broken.

"Your red lady is stealing the blood of the South Land."

He started walking. He hardly knew why or where he thought to go. He merely started walking, away from the light, into the darkness. Perhaps some path opened at his feet and compelled him to follow. He could not say and really didn't care. That was Redman's way of thinking, not his own. So he simply walked, and as he walked, he whispered:

> *"Just at the mirk and midnight hour*
> *Of thirteen nights but one,*
> *The warriors bear their bronzen stones*
> *Where crooked stands the Mound alone.*
> *There you must win your Fiery One*
> *Or see her then devoured."*

Since coming to this place, his eyes had grown more used to seeing in the dark, and he was familiar enough with the trail he now sought to follow even in the night. He walked close to the jungle but did not enter, making for the orchard. Things shifted in the heavy foliage. He turned and thought he glimpsed eyes . . . many eyes, red and gold and silver and green, that gleamed in the blackness, then flickered out, only to gleam again briefly, like fireflies.

He knew them for what they were. But for some reason he did not fear them. "Have you come for tribute?" he asked.

One pair of eyes blinked. Then, for a moment, he thought he saw a face that was nearly human, save for the long, sharp beak. It vanished after only a brief glimpse, but then a voice came.

"We will fight."

It was not a human voice, nor did it speak in any language Foxbrush knew. But he understood it deep in his mind.

"We will fight. We will help."

"Who?" Foxbrush asked. "Whom will you fight? Who is our enemy?"

The response came in another voice, hoarse and rasping as a water bird's. It said, "The Mound! The evil Mound."

More creatures, Faerie beasts all, gathered in the shadows beyond his vision; small and unthreatening, large and intimidating, and everything in between. They gathered, and their eyes blinked and stared at Foxbrush. He knew he should be frightened. Somehow, he couldn't work up the energy for it.

"Well, good," he said, shrugging at the jungle and moving on his way toward the orchard. "I'm glad to hear it. Fight away, and let us know how it goes, won't you?"

"*You must lead us.*"

Foxbrush snorted and did not deign to answer. The skittering, flapping, shuffling, stomping, slithering of many unseen creatures followed him, and the jungle on his right writhed with the movements. But they did not step beyond its fringes, and he did not go near enough to see or touch.

"*You must lead us!*" they all called in their bizarre tongues. "*Lead us into battle!*"

But he stopped up his ears to their pleas. In the orchard, their voices died away into whispers and then to nothing. Real fireflies glinted now, like small pixies themselves. Night birds and nimble-fingered lemurs had their way with the fig trees' bounty, for no one had been posted to chase them away.

And somewhere among the trees, someone was crying.

Foxbrush made his way through the orchard, slipping between twisted trunks and stepping over gnarled, grasping roots. He parted the curtains of heavy leaves until at last he found the one who wept.

"Nidawi?"

He had not seen her in months, not since that dreadful night when Daylily had come upon them in this very orchard, before the elder figs ripened. But here sat the Everblooming, surrounded by fireflies whose gentle glow illuminated her tear-stained face and the white body of Lioness cradled in her arms. She wore the form of an old woman, a woman who is the last of all her friends, alone in a strange world where people no longer recall the life she knew, the family she loved, the places she held dear. Her tears were the awful tears of memories slowly slipping, and they gleamed as they fell like little fireflies themselves and caught and sparkled in Lioness's fur.

She did not look up as Foxbrush approached, but cried on. All wild sobbing had faded, withering her into the form she now wore. Her wrinkled hands clung to the mighty carcass, however, as though they would never let go.

Foxbrush knelt, gazing upon the dead Lioness, the red wound in her breast. Once more he felt tears on his face. He put out a hand and smoothed the noble muzzle of the great cat. Then he let his hand trail down and rest upon Nidawi's.

She looked up then, transforming in an instant to the form of a tiny child, bewildered with loss, looking for comfort, for understanding.

"She's dead!" she said.

"Yes," said Foxbrush. He took hold of her hand and she, reluctantly, let go of Lioness enough to let him wrap his fingers about hers. "What happened, Nidawi?"

"Cren Cru," she said, gnashing the name through her teeth. "Cren Cru killed her. The Parasite! As he kills all of mine. He wore a body armed with stone, and he drove it into her heart!"

She let Lioness slip from her arms then and flung herself suddenly at Foxbrush, wrapping her scrawny limbs about his neck and weeping into his shoulder. He held her, frightened but making soothing noises and murmuring things he could not later recall. When at last her quivering body began to still, he said, "Who is Cren Cru, Nidawi?"

She straightened into the form of a woman again. A mature, hardened woman with the face of a bereft mother. "Come," she said, taking Foxbrush's hand and pulling him to his feet. "Come and I will show you."

She stepped onto a Faerie Path as lightly as though stepping through an open door, and led Foxbrush onto it as well. The night was already so strange, what with the beasts in the jungle, the warriors with their bronze stones, and the hollow-eyed faces he'd witnessed around the bonfire, that Foxbrush had not the strength to be surprised at this. Indeed, he felt he would never be surprised again! So he followed Nidawi, and his peripheral vision caught brief glimpses of wood and tree and rock and hill sliding past him, all within a few strides. And he realized, without knowing what it was he realized, that Southlands was riddled with Faerie Paths lingering just beyond the range of his senses and understanding, but as real as the air he breathed.

They passed gorges and villages and great stretches of jungle. Within a minute, or possibly two (though even so brief a time meant nothing), they came to the center of the Land Behind the Mountains.

Nidawi stepped off the Path, pulling Foxbrush behind her. "Look," she said, pointing.

There it stood. Somehow, Foxbrush felt he'd already known, though he never could have said as much if asked. It was like the knowledge of a sickness deep inside, as yet showing no symptoms but already working terrible carnage upon the body and the spirit.

The Mound of Cren Cru grew up from the soil of Southlands like a tumor grown on a heart. It was a mound of black earth, three times the height of a man but no taller; and sprouting from that earth, so thick as to be a sort of coat, were twisted branches, sharp, thorn-covered, bristling, and dead. They looked like antlers or horns, a thousand horns jutting up from the dirt, which was like a bulbous head.

Foxbrush, from where he stood holding Nidawi's hand, saw with a clarity he could not have known had he looked through his unaided mortal eyes. By Nidawi's power he saw all the Faerie Paths of Southlands crisscrossing the land, rising up from the gorges, and flowing down from the mountains. All of them streamed to this one central point like the veins of a body, pulsing.

There fell upon Foxbrush's heart a shadow of horror such as he had never known, not even when the Dragon dropped in fire from the sky and covered his world in smoke and poison. That, at least, was a dread he understood, a dread of teeth and scales and flames and fumes.

This was something he could not understand, and in his ignorance he trembled and despaired even at that one swift glance.

He turned away, looking at Nidawi instead, who stood facing the Mound with an expression of intense hatred, hatred that could not be bound into one age, so she was all ages in that moment: old, young, beautiful, childish, frail, strong, awful.

"What is it, Nidawi? What is that thing?" Foxbrush asked.

"Once upon a time," she said, and her voice was that of a little girl speaking from the thin, lined mouth of a crone, "there was a Faerie queen, Meadhbh by name, who ruled the land of Cren Cru. She wore a bronze crown set with twelve bright prongs, and she drank a wine as red as blood, which some said was blood indeed. She fed it to her consorts, and when they died, one by one, it was said she killed them. For she did not desire consorts. She was queen, and she was beautiful, and she was a great power. She needed only her demesne, the Faerie realm Cren Cru.

"But rumor of her murderous games did fly across the Between and fall upon the ears of that queen my people called Bebo Moonsong. Bebo left her own demesne and traveled to Cren Cru, to find Meadhbh and question her as to her doings. But Meadhbh took offense and thought to prove her innocence in a battle. She fought to kill Queen Bebo Moonsong, and when she could not, she took her own life.

"She was a Faerie queen, however, so she had two more lives to live. But she had taken one of her lives of her own free will, and this was a sin, a curse, a blight upon existence such as none but a Faerie lord or lady may understand! The remaining two lives were too evil to her, too unbearable. Thus she took them as well, denying the gift of Faerie queenship and severing the ties with her demesne. She left no heir, for she had loved no man, be he Faerie or mortal.

"And so the demesne of Cren Cru fell silent as death. But a demesne cannot die, not with the blood of its Faerie queen spilled upon its ground. It drank up the blood, and it felt something like life, the lives Queen Meadhbh had forgone.

"So Cren Cru rose up, alive and not alive, disembodied and wandering. It had no queen and it had no bindings, for the land itself was devastated by Meadhbh's evil. And it traveled, a being without spirit, without heart, without blood, without knowing of itself or understanding. Only a shadow of awareness. Neither alive nor unalive, but a force of instinct driven to find . . . to find a . . ."

Here Nidawi stopped and wrapped her arms about herself, unable to continue for a long while. Her teeth tore at her lips as she struggled to get the words out. Then she said:

"A home."

Foxbrush tried once more to look at the Mound. But he could not bear it and hid his face in his hands.

"It took bodies," Nidawi said. "Lost folk wandering the Between, immortals and mortals. It found them and it took them, and so it became aware of being, of life, of the need to belong. Twelve in all it took, and it melted down Meadhbh's twelve-pronged crown to give each of them a piece, a binding. Twelve made one by the strength that was Cren Cru. Then it set about to lay claim to a world."

Her voice became a whispering shudder, little more than a breath. "Many worlds it took. Each time, it latched hold and the Mound appeared out of nowhere. And the twelve warriors moved at the will of Cren Cru, believing still that they were their own. Every time it took hold, the warriors passed through the land demanding the firstborn children. They formed blood debts and demanded tithes, and if any refused to give of their firstborn, the warriors took what they wanted by force. Twelve days and twelve nights they would gather the tribute and pay it, driving the children, one by one, into the door of the Mound."

Nidawi looked up at Foxbrush, and though he still hid his face, he could feel her gaze.

"The blood of the firstborn was not enough. So the remaining warriors would go out again. They would make more of their kind, and spread through the land, taking the second born, and after that, the third. And eventually, whole worlds were eaten up. Mighty kings and queens fell as the Parasite drank up their lives, ate up their people! And when it was through, and even the warriors themselves had killed one another, spilling their own blood in tribute, there would be nothing left. And Cren Cru would wander on. And he would gather new warriors and start all over.

"He cannot learn! He has no mind! He has no real being save that which he steals! So every time he destroys a world and still can make no place for himself, he moves on, and he does it again. And again. And again and again! And the spilled blood never brings new life, and the decimated lands never revive under him: He can only destroy, never create; even as Meadhbh only killed herself and never brought forth life."

She stopped speaking. Foxbrush began to believe she was through. But at last she said, "I never thought to see him in Tadew. Then one morning, I woke. And there he was. And the Twelve moved through my kingdom, and they demanded tithe. I resisted and expected to die even as all the other Faerie kings and queens who resisted the Mound did die!"

Here she sighed, such a sad, such a lonely sigh that Foxbrush lowered his hands and gazed upon her with great compassion, wishing he had the strength to ease her sorrow.

"I am Nidawi the Everblooming," she said. "Though he sucked out my strength, it only bloomed again, always new. Always bright. He could not kill me." She bowed her head, a wrinkled, haggard shell of a woman. "So he took all my people, and he left me alone. Without a demesne. As homeless, as empty, as lost as he. I had only Lioness . . . and now, he has taken even her from me."

"What," Foxbrush whispered, "can be done? Can anything be done?"

"So I asked," said she. "So I demanded! I journeyed far, I journeyed wide, I journeyed deep and deeper still. I passed through the Netherworld itself, across the Dark Water and on to the Realm Unseen where the Final Water flows into the Vast. I stood upon that shore, and I shouted beyond the Highlands, demanding justice! And if justice could not be had, then mercy, mercy, mercy." Her hands clenched at the memory, as though even now she made her plea.

"The Lumil Eliasul came. The Prince of the Farthest Shore beyond the Final Water. He came to me and held me there, beside that darkened flow. And he told me of mercy, and he told me of justice. And he told me of the King of Here and There."

"The what?" said Foxbrush. "You mean . . . you mean Shadow Hand of Here and There?"

She gave him a puzzled look then. "I don't know this Shadow Hand," she said. "I know only of the King of Here and There. And it is he, the Lumil Eliasul told me, who will enter the Mound and see my people put at last to rest."

With this, she took Foxbrush's hand and turned him away from the clutching Mound of Cren Cru. It had no eyes and it had no life, and yet Foxbrush could not escape the feeling that it watched them as they took a Faerie Path and returned the way they had come. Even when at last they stepped into the familiar orchard and he smelled the ripeness of figs around him, Foxbrush could not shake the feeling that Cren Cru watched and Cren Cru waited.

Lioness's body lay where they had left it. Nidawi, seeing it, began to weep once more. She let go of Foxbrush's hand and gathered up her dead friend, holding her tight. Then she turned and looked at Foxbrush over the white fur, her face framed by death and sorrow.

"I've killed my share of his warriors. As many of them as I could find. But he takes more. You cannot kill his warriors and hope to kill him too. You must enter the Mound itself."

"What?" said Foxbrush, sudden realization hitting him like a club. "You mean . . . you mean *me*? Personally?"

"Yes," said she. "I vowed that I should wed the King of Here and There for the service he would render me. And you are he, for you are king of this land where Cren Cru has once more latched hold."

"No!" said Foxbrush, raising both his hands. "No, I'm not king of anywhere. They've not crowned me Eldest in my own time, and—"

"They will. And you will feel then the tie to your kingdom that binds you throughout all ages. You are King of Now and Then. You are King of Here and There. And you will destroy Cren Cru."

She blinked and then she was gone, taking Lioness with her. Foxbrush stood in firefly light beneath the spreading fig trees. But he did not feel alone, despite the loneliness pressing in on all sides, hungry and tearing and lost. He backed away, disoriented, uncertain where to turn even to find his way back to the Eldest's House.

A voice on the wind in the far, far distance called mournfully, *Foxbrush? Where are you, Foxbrush?*

He spun toward the sound. And found Daylily standing behind him.

9

The moment Sun Eagle took Daylily's hand and pulled her onto the Faerie Path, she felt the wolf attacking her from the inside. She could feel the physical rip of the great stakes to which the wolf was chained pulling up from the soil of her mind, twisting and tearing as they went. The chains themselves strained to the point of breaking. Then one of them broke.

Daylily screamed and with surprising strength pulled herself free of Sun Eagle's hand and collapsed there in the Wood. The trees backed far away, afraid of her and of what the stone around her neck represented. But they cast their shadows long, and it was black as night, save for the gleam of the Bronze.

Sun Eagle stood over her. He said, "Get up."

"I can't," she gasped, and her voice was that of the wolf. "I can't get up! I'm still caught in these dragon-cursed chains!"

"Not you. Her!"

"No!" snarled the wolf through Daylily's mouth. "You've done enough to her! It is *my* turn now!"

But Sun Eagle knelt and took hold of Daylily by the hair on top of her head. He yanked her face back and smacked her across the jaw, drawing blood where her teeth cut into her lip. Then he dropped her, stood, and stepped back.

Daylily slowly pushed herself upright and gazed at Sun Eagle through the tangles of her hair. "What are we?" she asked, and it was neither the wolf who spoke nor the voice of the master inside her. It was her own voice, soft and tremulous. "What have we become?"

"Strong," said Sun Eagle. "We have become strong."

"You killed . . . I . . . killed . . ." She ground her teeth, unable to breathe. Sun Eagle stepped to her side once more and put his hands around her, helping her to her feet. Her body shuddered through a breath, and she leaned heavily against him.

"Twelfth Night is near," said he. "It is time you learned, Initiate. It is time you knew."

They progressed in silence through the Wood, following the Bronze. Their wounds pained them, but they moved as though they felt nothing. The dominant force inside them did not heed pain.

They crossed into the Near World, back into Southlands, and still their Path led them on. The bronze stone around Daylily's neck heated until it scalded the skin over her heart, but she did not try to move it. She followed her Advocate until at last, even as Foxbrush had stood with Nidawi, she stood before the Mound of her master. The Mound she had seen in nightmarish visions and hoped, upon waking, had been nothing more than a nightmare.

The Mound into which she had sent children.

Cren Cru sucked at the life of the land. And though he had no face, it seemed to Daylily as though he smiled upon her a hungry smile. And he said, using her own mouth: *Mine.*

"I was lost in the Wood Between," said Sun Eagle, standing stern beside her. "I was young, and I knew nothing of immortality or the Far World. I was ignorant and weak and small. I should have died. But Dinhrod the

Stone found me, and he became my Advocate. I was brought into the Circle of Twelve and given the Bronze. And now, all those who dwell in the Far World fear me."

Fear us.

"But," said Daylily, struggling to find words of her own, for she felt as if her mouth no longer belonged to her, nor her voice nor her heart nor the blood in her veins. "But you told me Dinhrod the Stone is dead. You were stained with his blood."

"He died on Thirteenth Dawn," said Sun Eagle. "Twelve days and twelve nights, we gather the firstborn and present them as tithe. On Thirteenth Dawn, the Advocates themselves contend for the right to enter the Mound and become one with the master. Dinhrod was not victorious. He was slain by his brethren, and he died in my arms. Another won the honor to enter the Mound."

Mine.

Daylily stared across the way at the great, thorn-clad growth of Cren Cru. She saw a little door, scarcely more than a hole in the side of the hill. Through it poured an awful stench. She remembered then with dreadful clarity all those nightmares she had tried to forget, all those children whom she had helped to carry, helped to lead.

The tithe of firstborn. The spilling of blood to make new life. A home. A stronghold among the worlds. We must, we will, we need to possess!

"Twelfth Night is near, when we will make the final offering," said Sun Eagle. "Then, come Thirteenth Dawn, I too will fight. I will battle my brother and sister Advocates for the right to pass through Cren Cru's door."

There was deadness in his voice. Daylily looked up at him, and in his eyes, however briefly, she thought she glimpsed . . . what was it? Desperation? Fear?

But when he turned to her, all such traces were gone. "It is the best end. It is the only end. Should I be victorious, I will enter the Mound, and you will become Advocate in my place. And you will take an Initiate, and the circle will be complete, never again to be broken. All this Land will be your home. No more Twelfth Night. No more Thirteenth Dawn."

No more failure. No more searching, searching, searching. No more desolation. We will be home. They will be home.

I will be Home.

"And we will rule," said Sun Eagle. Daylily realized that her mouth had also moved in time with his, had spoken words that were not her own.

The wolf inside her snarled and tore at her with a fury she had not yet known, and she screamed at the pain of it. Even as she screamed, however, she turned and fled. The wolf drove her, and the Bronze did not burn or try to fight. She fled to the sound of frantic, haunted howling, away from the Mound, away from her Advocate, away from herself. But the wolf pursued, and the wolf would catch and devour her if she did not give in to the call of the Bronze. What escape was there? Death on every side, as sure as when she'd walked the paths of the Netherworld!

As sure as when she'd betrayed Rose Red.

There was no hope. No light burning in this darkness. Even the glow of the Bronze itself was as black as pitch, as empty as a bottomless chasm.

She collapsed. She did not know if she lay in the Wood Between or the Near World or the Far. It did not matter to her then. The wolf worried at her, but she could feel the wolf even now being dragged back in chains. Cren Cru, who had taken her, who had become her, who was more Daylily than she was herself now, would overpower all and drive her to whatever end it saw fit. And she would convince herself that it was her own choice and her own doing. But for this little slice of existence, she knew the truth.

"You'll have to let it go."

She shuddered at the voice of the songbird that alighted on the ground before her. In this dark place, his white, speckled breast seemed to glow with his own light.

"What are you doing here?" she gasped, the words scarcely audible.

The bird turned his head to one side, gazing at her out of one bright eye. "I am always near," he sang.

"You're following me?" She bared her teeth. "Go away. I don't want you."

"You want me more than you know," said the bird. "But you must let the wolf go."

"I can't," said Daylily. "Not anymore." She felt the Bronze weighing her down, and for a moment she was the wolf tied to the stakes, brought low by chains and bindings. "It's too late."

"It's never too late," said the bird. "Not while I lead you."

"You don't lead me!" Daylily said. "No one leads me!" And she lunged at the bird, her fingers snatching, but he flew from her grasp, light as drifting smoke, up into the branches of a tree she had not seen standing near.

She stood and realized that what she had thought was the blackness of despair was in fact the deepness of night surrounding her. She even saw a glimmer of fireflies and, up above, between the branches of the tree, stars gleamed in the sky. The bird had disappeared, but she felt somehow that he was near. She smelled sweet things on the wind, the scents of fruits and nectars, contrasting with the smells of rot and spoil.

She turned. And found herself facing Foxbrush.

"Daylily!" he gasped, his voice as frightened as though he saw a ghost.

She could scarcely discern his face in the gloom. But she recognized him at once by some sixth sense she did not know she possessed. She stood a moment beneath the spreading fig tree and the starlight, and she stared at him. He was all the things she had fled; but where had her flight led her?

"Daylily!" he spoke her name again as though he wanted to say something more but could not find the words. He took a step toward her.

Then she fell into his arms.

This could not be Daylily. It must be some phantom or some dream, come to walk the waking world. It *could not* be Lady Daylily of Middlecrescent! For Daylily never wept as this girl wept, her face buried in Foxbrush's chest, embracing him in trembling desperation. Foxbrush stood as still as a totem stone, his arms at his sides, and she clung to him and dampened his shirt with her tears. Slowly he lifted his arms and wrapped them around her, holding her close to his thudding heart. All thoughts of what he had just seen and heard—the stone, the broken Lioness, Nidawi and her strange declarations—fled his mind. Everything about him was caught up in this one dreadful, horrible, wonderful moment. He held on to Daylily and he loved her more now than he had ever before loved anything or anyone. He felt strong and he felt weak; he could both move great mountains and be knocked down with a feather.

They stood thus for some time, and time meant nothing to either of them. Many eyes watched: eyes of the bird in the branches of the tree above, and the fireflies darting to and fro, and the fey beasts in the jungle shadows. And yet they were completely alone in that piece of eternity.

At last Daylily stepped back, though she still held Foxbrush by the arms. She could not meet his gaze but stood with her head bowed, weighted down by the enormous pull of the Bronze around her neck. Foxbrush saw it, and he recalled with sudden, gut-wrenching pain what Nidawi had told him about Cren Cru.

"Twelve in all it took, and it melted down Meadhbh's twelve-pronged crown to give each of them a piece, a binding."

He put out his hand and took hold of the Bronze. But it burned him, and he dropped it quickly, drawing a sharp breath of pain. Daylily let go of him then and placed both her hands over the stone, hiding it against her bosom.

"Twelfth Night is coming," she said. "Eleven nights have I been bound by the Bronze."

Her voice was strange and thin. Foxbrush frowned without understanding and wondered if she would let him hold her again. Somehow, he didn't think it would be a good idea to try. "It's been months, Daylily," he said. "Months since I saw you."

She shook her head. "It has been eleven nights. And Twelfth Night is coming. The final tithe is demanded."

Foxbrush licked his cracking lips. "You are not one of them," he said, though he knew he deceived no one, not even himself.

"I am not one," Daylily whispered. Her shoulder was stained with fresh, oozing blood from the wound Foxbrush had watched Lark dress. Her body trembled with the pain of it, but she could scarcely feel a thing through the Bronze she wore. "I am not one. I am many. And I am gone."

"No!" said Foxbrush, and his voice was more fierce than she had ever heard it. He reached out to her, grasping her arms. "No, you are not one of them! You are yourself and . . . and you don't have to go back!"

She looked up at him, and for the first time, Foxbrush saw Daylily. Not the Lady of Middlecrescent, cold and calculating, nor even the lovely girl who had flirted with Leo all those long summers ago. She was Daylily herself, and she was frail and frightened. But there was a wolf in her eyes.

"I love you," he said. He didn't know why he said it then. He knew only that he could not have helped himself, not though his life depended on it.

She blinked and for a terrible instant he believed she would vanish in that flash of her eyelashes. But when she looked at him again, she was still, however briefly, herself. "I know," she said, reaching up to touch his face. "But I am gone."

He felt the tips of her fingers brush like cold fire against his skin. And then, Daylily's mouth moved, but a voice that was not hers spoke.

Twelfth Night is near. Come away....

Though she stood before him, Foxbrush felt her dissolving in his grasp. "No!" he shouted. "You don't have to go back! Stay with me, Daylily! Stay!"

Then she was gone. Foxbrush stood in the orchard, his hands grasping empty air.

In the branches above his head, a bird trilled a silver melody, a stream of music flowing into the night. And Foxbrush believed he heard words in the song.

> *Oh, Shadow Hand of Here and There,*
> *Heal now the ills*
> *Of your weak and weary Fair,*
> *Lost among the hills.*
>
> *You would give your own two hands*
> *To save your ancient, sorrowing lands.*

"Well, isn't this a pretty dish of fish?"

Foxbrush started and looked down at his feet. To his surprise, he found a pair of golden eyes shining up at him, made luminous by the glow of firefly light.

"I followed my quarry this far," said the cat, speaking in the voice of a man, "only to find the trail cold here. Tell me, mortal, have you seen a girl with reddish hair pass this way? I think I should like to scratch her eyes out. If it's all the same to you, of course."

10

O R PERHAPS I WON'T SCRATCH HER. Perhaps I will merely give
her a disapproving stare. I haven't quite decided."

"Who are you?" Foxbrush stumbled back from the cat, which he could
barely see in the night, other than those luminous eyes. In the past many
months he had seen more than his fair share of Faerie beasts and had
become uncomfortably comfortable with their strangeness. But, while this
cat was far from the largest or most threatening encountered, he somehow
frightened Foxbrush more than even the giant Kasa.

For Foxbrush felt, though he could not say why, that he *knew* this cat
somehow.

"I'm far too busy to deal with stupid questions," the cat replied, turning
his head this way and that, delicately sniffing the air. "I pursued the mortals
deep into the Wood only to lose their trail entirely. But I picked up hers
again eventually, and she led me here, of all places. The South Land. Yet
again. I can never seem to be rid of this place."

The cat's voice was surprisingly bitter. He stood and padded around beneath the fig trees, sniffing some more. He came to the place where Nidawi had sat with the dead body of Lioness, and his lips curled back in a hiss. Then he fixed his gaze upon Foxbrush.

"What do you know of Nidawi and her murdered companion? I can smell that you were here at the same time as Nidawi and the red warrior. Are you harboring a murderer, mortal?"

"Daylily is no murderer," Foxbrush said with more courage than he felt.

"Daylily, eh?" said the cat. "So you know the warrior girl."

The cat stood up then and disappeared into the form of a tall man with a golden, shining face that was visible despite the darkness. It was an angry face, its anger carefully masked in disdain. He looked Foxbrush up and down and, like a cat posturing for battle, began to circle him. "And who are you to be mixed up in the affairs of Faerie queens and murderers? You don't seem either important or threatening. Why should they both come here to you and not trouble to kill you? They both are so dragon-kissed keen on killing things, each other included. Why not you?"

That was when Foxbrush knew. He didn't know by virtue of any logic or reason. One cannot stand in the presence of immortals and expect reason to be of any use. He knew in a place far deeper, a place of childhood memory that understands the strange orders of worlds more completely and more simply than reason ever will.

"You're Bard Eanrin," Foxbrush said.

"Got it in one," said the cat-man dryly. "But that's not the question, is it?"

"I . . . you . . . You're not blind. You have both your eyes," Foxbrush said. A little stupidly, he thought afterward with some embarrassment. One can't hope to simply strike up conversations with legends and come across as remotely intelligent, however.

"That I do," said the cat-man, his teeth flashing what might have been a smile but was probably a snarl. "And a nose. And a mouth. And an irritable humor this evening, a humor that is urging a certain amount of biting, scratching, and . . . and, yes, I'll say it. *Rending*. Rending is the order of the evening, in fact. So if you would prefer not to be rent, answer my question and . . ."

Eanrin stopped. He had drawn closer to Foxbrush by now, swelling up with anger threatening to burst. But his nose was still at work, and he smelled something he was not expecting, something that made him step back, his brow sinking into a frown. His voice altered to a softer tone, a little frightened even, when he asked, "Why are you on that Path?"

Foxbrush looked down at his feet. Once more he saw nothing. And yet Nidawi, Lioness, and Redman had all remarked upon the same thing. So Foxbrush shrugged. "I don't know," he answered. "I can't see it. I wish I could but I can't."

"You can't see *that*?" Eanrin's frown deepened still more, dominating his shining face. "And you thought *I* was blind?" He crossed his arms. "I'll not ask you your name again, so I suggest you confess it now and we'll move on from there."

Foxbrush fumbled in his shirt and removed the scroll Lionheart had given him. "If you please, Bard Eanrin," he said, "I am the one to whom you sent this message."

The poet-cat was not one to be easily startled or put from his ease. Thus the expression of surprise and then incredulity that filled his face was even more disharmonious with his golden face than the scowls he wore. "I've sent you no message," he said.

Foxbrush nodded, changed his mind, and shook his head. "Um. Actually, I think you did. Through my cousin. Leo. Prince Lionheart, that is, of Southlands. Except he's not really prince anymore; I am. But still he, well, um, he—"

"Please!" said Eanrin, and if he had been a cat, his ears would have gone back. "I can't bear drivel at the best of times, and I'll not hesitate to say that tonight is *not* the best of times. So choose your words with care, mortal." His mouth flashed a smile that did not touch his eyes. "I don't know this Prince Lionheart of whom you speak, nor this Southlands, unless you mean this dragon-kissed—oh, pardon, I do mean *Lumé-blessed*—South Land in which we now stand."

"I do. I'm . . . I'm out of my time."

"Sylphs?"

It never ceased to amaze Foxbrush how easily the people of this era accepted the idea of time wandering. "Yes. Sylphs."

The poet-cat sniffed, his lip curling a little. "Fancy that." His face was now all smiles, but they were smiles of extreme dislike, for cats are quick to form impressions and not so quick to change them. "Either way, I don't know you, and you don't look the sort I would ever bother knowing. So speak up and explain."

"Um," Foxbrush said, and when Eanrin's hand twitched, he blurted out hastily, "Please, you wrote this a long time ago, or . . . or . . . or perhaps you will write it very soon now, since I don't suppose it's happened yet, and you had it sent to me, and I'd like to know, um, if you please—"

Cursing various bits of dragon anatomy (including but not limited to teeth, tails, wings, and spines), Eanrin snatched the scroll from Foxbrush's trembling hand and pulled it open with enough vim that, hearty though the parchment had proven over time, it tore on the edges. His eyes darted back and forth, up and down, seeming to read the verses in no particular order, and rather faster than an ordinary man might. In mere seconds, he grinned over the edge of it at Foxbrush and said, "I never wrote this." Then he looked at it again, and the grin slid away, leaving in its place a puzzled frown. "But . . ." He scratched an ear thoughtfully, closing one eye as he did so. "But this *is* Imraldera's hand."

Foxbrush, who did not understand the significance of this statement, stood silently and waited. The cat-man read the scroll a third time.

"It's not my usual style." Eanrin's face became a degree more thoughtful. "Though I have been experimenting with ballad stanzas recently, so it's not beyond the realm of possibility or chance that I *might* turn my hand to a piece of this type. Given the right inspiration." His voice became very bitter as it fell from behind his smile. "I don't see a word about my lady Gleamdren, however, so there's really no telling."

"Please," said Foxbrush humbly. "I just want to know what it . . . what it means."

"How should I know?" the cat-man snapped. Then, after a brief battle with himself, he shook his head and spoke in a kindlier and almost melancholy tone, if a being such as he could know melancholy. And his smile softened into something more sincere, if sadder than he had yet worn. "It's addressed to this Shadow Hand of Here and There, so I would imagine, if I did—or do, in the future—send this to you, you must be he. Is your name, perchance, Shadow Hand?"

"No," said Foxbrush.

"Pity. But that is the way of poetry. Poetic names are not always what you might expect. They are often titles as much as anything. And from the sound of it, this Shadow Hand will, as it says, *'give his own two hands'* to some Faerie queen and thus acquire his name—"

He broke off suddenly and stood with his mouth open, staring at Foxbrush without seeing him. Then he said, "By my king's black beard!" and held the scroll up close to his face, murmuring in his silken voice:

> *"The wolf will howl, the eagle scream.*
> *The wild white lies dead.*
> *Tears of Everblooming stream*
> *As she bows her mourning head."*

The poet's head came up, and for the first time he fixed Foxbrush with a gaze of real, earnest interest. "This has come about," he said. "I saw these events. I saw the wild white killed and the tears of the Everblooming."

Foxbrush felt his heart shiver. "It's . . . it's all coming true, then."

An eager light sprang to Eanrin's eye. "My dear fellow, you have brought us a foretelling of the future! Written in Imraldera's own hand! She must have known you would see me, and she sent this back to me. I wonder why she . . . but no. It doesn't bear considering." He let the scroll roll up with a snap and squeezed it in his fist. "She—or I—or someone, anyway, has sent us a foretelling. Tell me, if you are from the future, do you know how this will play out? Do you know what this means?"

Foxbrush tried to swallow, but his throat was too dry. "I was hoping you could tell me."

"Useless mortal," said the poet, though without malice. "We've got to find this King of Here and There, that's certain. And he, from the look of it, will defeat this Mound and the warriors in some epic and appropriately poetic manner."

Suddenly the night all around them exploded in a cacophony of voices.

Strange, inhuman, cawing, rasping, braying, thumping voices, all speaking the same words in their variety of languages.

"*We will help! We will fight! We will drive the Mound away!*"

Even Eanrin started at this, and he and Foxbrush both turned in place as the darkness came alive with dozens of shining fey eyes. The Faerie beasts, the surviving totems, drew in upon them in the orchard. They swung in the boughs of trees; they crawled upon their bellies; they flew upon dark breezes; they trod the grass in solemn prance. Animals and yet not animals, with eyes more alive, more alert than any mortal's could ever be. They drew in and they glowed with their own immortality so that the darkened orchard became nearly as bright as day.

And out from their midst stepped Nidawi in her fiercest aspect, beautiful and vicious with teeth bared.

"Lumé," muttered Eanrin. "This is highly unexpected."

"King of Here and There," said Nidawi, stepping forward and making a reverent sign with her hand before Foxbrush. "I have gathered the totems of this land. They do not wish to perish by the hand of Cren Cru's warriors. They do not wish to see another kingdom fall to the Parasite. They will help you. Lead them!"

"What? Him?" said Eanrin, turning to Foxbrush, his eyebrows shooting up his forehead in surprise. "This squinty-eyed mortal?" Then he glanced down at the Path beneath Foxbrush's feet. "Well," he said, then, "Well, well."

Foxbrush faced Nidawi and looked upon his future in her eyes. He whispered the words from the poem he had by now committed to memory.

> "*Bargain now with Faerie queen,*
> *The Everblooming child,*
> *If safe you would your kingdom glean*
> *From out the feral wild.*"

He said in a voice that he wished to be strong but which quavered a little despite his best efforts, "Nidawi, I do not know that I can do as you ask. But I will try."

"If you try, you will do," said Nidawi. She stood alone even in that crowd, walled in by her ancient sorrow. But deliverance stood before her in the form of this mortal. Had not the time of fulfillment come? Had it not been spoken to her on the shores of the Final Water? "I have been promised."

She stepped out through the veils of her own small world of grief, and she took Foxbrush's hands in hers.

"King of Here and There," she said, "Twelfth Night is upon us. Lead the beasts to Cren Cru's Mound by the Path I showed you. Kill my enemy as you must."

Foxbrush had aged since looking upon the Mound, since holding Daylily in his arms. He had aged by many years in one night, and though his face was still young, his eyes were much older. He looked by that light of Faerie eyes very like his uncle Eldest Hawkeye before the dragon poison corroded away his might.

"I will do what I must," Foxbrush said, and he did not resist when Nidawi, still holding his hands, drew him toward her. But when she leaned in to kiss him, he turned his head to one side and said, "No. Please. I have to ask you—I must *bargain* with you."

"Bargain?" said the Everblooming, her lovely head tilted to one side.

He nodded. "What will you do should I succeed? Should I destroy your enemy and put your people to rest once and for all . . . will you do something for me?"

"Of course," said she. "I will marry you."

"I . . . I would rather you protected Southlands."

The Faerie beasts watching whispered together, a rumble of growls and caws and hisses. And they and Eanrin all watched Nidawi to see what she would say in response.

Nidawi studied Foxbrush's face. Thinking did not come easily to her ever-shifting mind. She was much better at spontaneous feeling and overwhelming emotion. But she liked this mortal, for all his faults, and for his sake she made the effort and thought about his request, however briefly. Then she replied:

"If you destroy my enemy, King of Here and There, I will see to it that no Faerie beasts will enter your kingdom unbidden again. All these you see gathered, they and I will build gates such as you have never before seen. Beautiful gates."

"Can you do that?" Foxbrush asked, his eyes suddenly lit with hope. "I mean to say, have you built such things before?"

"No. Why would I?" She laughed then, a faint echo of the merry, manic laughter in which she had gloried before the death of the white lion. "But I can do anything I set my mind to! You kill the Parasite, little king. Let me handle my side of the bargain!"

She squeezed his hands then, and Foxbrush shuddered. His face was pale and gray in the growing light of day. "I will give you both my hands, Nidawi," he whispered. "To seal the bargain."

"What?" She made a face, sticking out her tongue and wrinkling her exquisite little nose. "What would I want with your hands? I'm not one to collect such gruesome trophies! Keep them, mortal. Use them well and kill my enemy!"

"But . . . but the story. I've read the story. I'm to give you my hands to save—"

"I don't want them." Nidawi dropped her hold on him and stepped away, older and fiercer than she had been a moment before. "I want Cren Cru dead!"

"*Dead! Dead! Dead!*" said all the Faerie beasts together.

"Lead us, king!" cried Nidawi. "Lead us to our vengeance! Lead us to our victory!"

And all the immortals raised their voices in such a shout that those in the village heard and fled to their homes in terror at the sound. The orchard itself shook with the thunder of it, and even Eanrin, caught up as he was in his anger and disappointment, found his heart beginning to race, thrilling at the power of those eager voices pledging faith and fight to this one humble mortal.

But Foxbrush, when the noise at last subsided, responded quietly, "Um. Can someone please point the way?"

11

Felix had known a number of interesting experiences in his young life. He had survived more than one dragon attack (a feat few could boast); his body had been taken over by a goblin enchanter while he suffered under the influence of dragon poison; he had lost his mind and many times nearly lost his life, only to be healed at the last. He had held the sword of swords, the mighty Halisa, in his own two hands and with it brought low the Bane of Corrilond herself (though, granted, he hadn't known it was the Bane of Corrilond at the time . . . or Halisa either, for that matter).

All this to say, Felix was a lad with adventures aplenty under his belt. But that did not make this current adventure any more palatable.

For one thing, it didn't seem sporting to hide behind a door while the baroness summoned one of her guards inside, then to hit the guard on the back of the head with a decorative urn the moment the door shut behind him.

The guard fell like a toppled oak and lay inert amid shards of urn.

A knock at the door, and the pretty lady-in-waiting called from without, "Is everything all right, my lady?"

The baroness stepped swiftly forward and used her voluminous skirts to hide the fallen guard just as the door opened and the lady peered in. Felix, holding bits of broken pottery in his good hand, his sprained wrist pressed to his chest, ducked out of sight. The baroness said lightly, "Oh, everything is fine, Dovetree, my pet! I dropped an urn, that is all."

"Over Sergeant Fleet-Arrow's head?" asked Lady Dovetree, who was no fool. She looked pointedly at the booted feet sticking out from under the baroness's skirts.

"How clumsy of me, yes?" said the baroness with a laugh. "Now do run along, dear, and let no one disturb us."

Lady Dovetree raised an eyebrow but curtsied and departed, shutting the door with a firm click. Felix sprang out of hiding and turned the key in the lock. He then remembered how to breathe and stood gasping, pressing a piece of pottery to his heaving chest.

The baroness began undoing the buckles on the unfortunate Fleet-Arrow's boots. "Come help me, lovey," she said with a smile at Felix that was simultaneously winsome and commanding, a formidable combination. "You look as though you've seen a fright! Have you never hit a man before?"

"Not with an urn," Felix admitted. "Won't she tell someone we're assaulting guardsmen in here?"

"Who, Dovetree?" The baroness giggled and, with a surprisingly vicious tug, pulled the first of the guardsman's boots free. "No, she is loyalty herself. Absolutely devoted to me. Do hurry, sweetness!"

Felix, in a bit of a fog, obeyed, kneeling and working at the armor buckles and straps with the trembling fingers of his good hand. Between the two of them, they stripped the man to his linens. Then, at the baroness's direction, they rolled their victim onto a rug and dragged him to the adjacent dressing room beyond the study. This was made difficult by Felix's wounded wrist, but the baroness proved stronger than she looked.

"Lionheart was a bit squeamish himself about hitting the page boy," she said conversationally as they went. "What little mouses young men are these days! My dear baron wouldn't think twice about clunking another fellow over the head if it served his purpose. But then, I suppose there aren't many men like my dear baron!"

Her dear baron against whom she was actively plotting. Felix rolled his eyes heavenward and began to think longingly of his nice quiet home up north, that which so recently had seemed dull. He thought he maybe could do with a little dullness just about then.

The baroness flung open a wardrobe, and a page boy tied up in curtain cords blinked out at them. Felix nearly dropped his hold on the guardsman.

"There's someone in your wardrobe, my lady!" he gasped.

"Of course," said she with a disarming smile. "How are you, Cubtail? Head feeling better?" she asked the boy, who was gagged but who shrugged agreeably enough. He even slid over obligingly as Felix and the baroness hefted the guardsman into the wardrobe. The baroness then hurried to grab a number of belts and the sash off a dressing gown, with which she trussed up the unconscious guardsman with shocking expertise.

"Now, sit tight and don't make a peep," said the baroness, patting the page boy on the head before she shut the wardrobe door once more. She turned to Felix. "Let's see about getting you into that uniform!"

"It'll never work, you know," Felix said as he followed her back to the study and the pile of discarded armor and leathers. "I'm too pale, for one thing. And they'll spot me by my accent, for another!"

"Oh, it'll be too dark up in the tower for them to see you, and you won't need to talk," said the baroness, holding the breastplate to Felix's chest. "This doesn't fit right."

"It's upside-down," said Felix, taking it from her. "Why won't I have to talk?"

"I'm sending Dovetree up with you. She'll say the wine is from me, in thanks to those noble souls willing to risk life and limb for the sake of my dear baron, and so on. They'll sip the wine, they'll fall over unconscious, and you'll get Lionheart to let you in."

"I still don't understand," said Felix in last feeble protest as he pulled the guardsman's jerkin over his head and the heavy boots on his feet, "why you need *me* for all this. I'm not even a Southlander!"

"But you jumped to save Lionheart."

"Yes, but that was . . . different." He didn't think it worth trying to explain the vision of Prince Aethelbald standing in midair. It didn't make sense in his own mind anyway; he might just choose to forget it.

"Besides," the baroness continued in what was probably intended to be a comforting tone, "if they catch you, they probably won't execute you, you being the crown prince of our strongest ally. They wouldn't think twice about hanging Dovetree, or me, for that matter! But you might just pass it off as a lark and be no worse for wear."

Somehow, this wasn't the reassurance Felix might have wished.

"I only wish she'd seen fit to tell me of this mad scheme of hers a few minutes *before* expecting me to carry it out."

Lady Dovetree led the armored guard with the shuffling gait through the corridors of the Eldest's House, muttering angrily as she went. He dared not respond for fear of having his accent overheard. He wasn't certain he could speak above his thudding heart in any case.

"I mean, she's a dear old thing," said the lady-in-waiting. She carried a bottle in the crook of one arm and a couple of flagons emblazoned with rampant panthers in the opposite hand. "But she is *so* forgetful! Imagine concocting an elaborate plot like this and forgetting to inform the chief participants?"

It was about four o'clock in the morning, and the House had quieted down since the explosive events of the previous day. Nevertheless, Felix couldn't help looking over his shoulder, terrified that someone would overhear Lady Dovetree's complaints (justified as they might be). They progressed on their way unimpeded, however. Felix, the bandages on his wrist hidden beneath a flowing guardsman's sleeve, bore with him a sack full of what he assumed were supplies for Lionheart and the imprisoned baron. Knowing the baroness, she'd probably stuffed it full of pastries and confections and neglected to add little extras like water.

But it wasn't his plan. And it wasn't his rebellion. In fact, it wasn't his business at all, and Felix was dragon-eaten if he could figure out how he'd ended up stuffed into an ill-fitting Southlander uniform and following this strange girl (who was very pretty, if rather ill-tempered) through these silent halls.

"Aethelbald wants me to help," he muttered, quietly enough that Lady Dovetree couldn't hear above her grumbling. It wasn't a reason that made a great deal of sense. But somehow, Felix knew that he would keep on this strange course until the end. He would do anything for the Prince of Farthestshore.

They met almost no one until they reached the Great Hall. Here, at the heart of all the dire doings, the House was alive and throbbing with fear. Barons whom Felix did not know whispered together, exhausted from many hours of hopelessness but unable to retire to their beds for rest. Guardsmen stood along the fringes, their commanding officers conferring with the barons, all equally at a loss.

When one of the guardsmen stopped Dovetree and questioned her, she said brusquely, "A message from the baroness to the duty guard of North Tower. She sends succor to them in thanks for their efforts."

The guardsman looked rather longingly at the wine in Dovetree's arm but let her pass, never so much as glancing at the sweating Felix, who kept his head down, hiding beneath his spiked helmet. They proceeded with a few more similar pauses across the Great Hall and at last to North Tower itself. Dovetree, her peevish mutterings now suppressed, moved with an assured stride that impressed Felix. One would never guess she was about treasonous doings that could easily get her hanged were she caught.

They climbed the stairs, which were dark and difficult to navigate, for none of the kings of the last many generations had thought to install lamp sconces in this particular stairwell. When they wound at last to the top, however, they found three guardsmen sitting in a pool of lamplight. Three chamber doors stood behind them, but it wasn't difficult to pick out behind which Lionheart and his prisoner were ensconced. That door, the one on the far right, was battered and dented from all the attempts to break through.

"Greetings from Baroness Middlecrescent," said Dovetree crisply as they stepped into the guardsmen's vision. At the sight of an elegantly dressed lady-in-waiting, the guards quickly pulled themselves to their feet, standing at attention and surreptitiously tugging their armor straight. "My lady wishes to express her thanks for noble duty in the face of need."

The guards exchanged looks at this. After all, sitting outside a locked door didn't strike any of them as a particularly noble duty. But they had been up here in the silent dark, ineffective and frustrated, for several hours now while great men below plotted (equally ineffective and doubly frustrated). As Dovetree poured out and passed the wine their way, they took it gratefully enough and drank deeply.

"Keep up the fighting spirit, men," said Dovetree, reclaiming the flagons. "Silent Lady grant you strength, and all that."

"Silent Lady shield us," they muttered in halfhearted response.

Dovetree turned and started back down the tower stairs. Felix, surprised, hurried after. He waited a few turns before reaching out in the dark and catching what he hoped was her shoulder.

"Where are you going?" he whispered. "They didn't fall asleep! What are we supposed to do?"

"*We* aren't doing anything," Dovetree replied, shaking him off. "I have fulfilled my part of the plan. Now you will fulfill yours. Don't worry," she added in a kindlier voice, "they'll nod off any moment now. You'll have your chance. Wait here."

With this, she left, and Felix stood alone in the darkness, clutching the sack of supplies. His mouth was very dry, and sweat soaked his stolen garments, though it was not hot up here in the tower.

But he had only to wait a few moments before he heard a heavy *thunk* overhead, followed soon after by a thickened voice saying, "Lumé, mate, what are you . . ." This trailed off into another *thunk* swiftly followed by a third. Soon after, snoring.

Perhaps the baroness would prove a cunning conspirator after all.

Lionheart guessed that he had probably been *more* tired than this upon occasion. During that long voyage to Noorhitam in the Far East, Captain

Sunan of the good ship *Kulap Kanya* had made Lionheart work for his passage. Those were some long days followed by sea-sickening nights . . . and sometimes even the nights were spent freezing up in the lookout, too high above the deck for anyone's comfort as the ocean rolled and murmured secretive threats beneath him.

Certainly those had been far more exhausting times, the threat of death by falling or drowning as present as the current threat of hanging.

But somehow, this was no comfort.

Lionheart stood and stretched again, pacing the narrow space between the heavy door and the window. He would have to sleep eventually. He glanced at the baron. He could feel his prisoner's gaze, though shadows hid his face. Even bound hand and foot, the baron was too dangerous to leave unwatched. And he showed no signs of sleep himself.

I'll die of pure exhaustion, Lionheart thought as he looked out the window at the sky. *Stabbed by a unicorn, assaulted by dragons, threatened by kings and emperors alike. But I'll die for lack of sleep at the end.*

It seemed comically appropriate. But he couldn't manage a laugh.

By now the clouds had rolled on, and the stars were making the final turns of their nightly dance. In another hour, the inky blackness would give way to blue, and another hour after that the sun would rise.

What sort of world would it shine down upon? What sort of future?

The sound of armored bodies collapsing beyond the door brought Lionheart whirling about. He didn't know what had caused those sounds and wondered if the desperate barons below had thought of a new instrument with which to assault his barricade. He strode quickly back to his post and placed his ear to the door but heard nothing more than the pound of his heart in his throat.

Then at long last, he heard a voice. It was too low to understand, but Lionheart guessed it was male. He made no response and, after a tense half minute, the voice repeated, louder:

"Leonard? Leonard the Lightning Tongue?"

Lionheart recoiled from the door as though bitten. As far as he knew, no one in all the Eldest's court knew of his jester name and the identity he'd assumed during his five-year exile while Southlands was dragon occupied.

"Leonard, are you there?" The voice sounded as though it was trying desperately not to be overheard. "Please answer!"

"Who is that?" Lionheart demanded.

"It's Felix. Prince Felix of Parumvir. We met in Oriana two years ago, if you remember. You performed for my family." A pause, then, "And I saw you again in the Village of Dragons."

Lionheart stared at the door, and if he were a dragon himself, his gaze would have burned it to cinders in a moment. But had he not seen the royal insignia of Parumvir? And now that he thought of it, he had glimpsed Felix in the Great Hall during the mad abduction. In the frantic terror of enacting the baroness's plot, he'd seen without recognizing the lad who had brought down a guard and quite possibly saved Lionheart's neck. Felix . . . Una's brother . . .

"That's not my name," Lionheart said. He could feel the baron's gaze upon his shoulders, but he refused to look around.

"I know," said the voice beyond. "I know all about what happened. Una told me later, you know, after the Dragon was killed. She's . . . she's married now, had you heard? To Prince Aethelbald?"

Lionheart nodded, which was foolish, but he couldn't quite find words to respond. A silence followed during which he knew the baron was putting together pieces of a story Lionheart did not wish him to know. He demanded, "What are you doing up here, Prince Felix? It's not safe."

"The baroness sent me with supplies for you."

A hissing curse from behind told Lionheart that the baron had overheard. Now whatever suspicions had been brewing in his mind were confirmed. Lionheart's neck wouldn't be the only one forfeit at the end of this foolish adventure.

"I've drugged the guards," Felix persisted. "Or, well, *I* didn't personally. But they're drugged, and you can open the door and take these supplies. I can't guarantee they'll help much, but better than nothing, right?"

Better than nothing. They might be just enough to give Lionheart time for that fool sylph to catch his fool cousin, to send Prince Foxbrush, Hawkeye's legitimate heir, reeling back into the court of the Eldest, fey addled but alive.

"How do I know you are who you say you are?" Lionheart demanded. "How do I know this isn't a trap?"

Another pause, during which Lionheart felt his rising hopes slowly crumbling away.

Then Felix said: "I know the name of the Queen of Arpiar, Ruler of the Unveiled People, Mistress of the lands between the Karayan Plains and the Sevoug Mountains beyond Goldstone Wood. She is Varvare, daughter of Vahe and Anahid, servant of the Prince of Farthestshore."

"Rosie," Lionheart whispered.

And with the name came a sudden wash of peace over his soul. Whatever happened now, she was safe. She sat upon her throne, come into her rightful inheritance. He could not hurt her anymore.

"Rosie . . ."

He heaved the heavy bolt out of its brackets and undid the iron locks and bracings. With a groan of relief, the door inched open, and Lionheart saw Felix's pale face in the lantern light beyond, wearing a spiked Southlander helmet.

"Take it, quick!" Felix said, pushing the sack through the doorway into Lionheart's arms. "I don't know how long the drugs will—"

"Not long enough for you, wolf-bit pup!"

A gauntleted hand fell upon Felix's shoulder and hauled him back. Lionheart cursed and put his shoulder to the door, trying to slam it closed, to drop the bolt again. But strong men on the other side pushed against him, and their combined strength was more than his. The guardsmen broke through, and Lionheart hadn't time to so much as go for his knife. Two of them fell upon him, pinning his arms and bringing him to his knees. The third struck him three times across his face. Still he struggled against them and might have freed himself.

But more guards poured through the door then, guards who had been waiting in the darkened stairway. Outmatched by far, Lionheart fell on his face, his arms twisted behind him.

"Did you think we were fools to fall for such a trick?" said the guardsman who had struck Lionheart, flexing his fist. He turned to Prince Felix, who stood in the grasp of more strong men who had stripped the helmet and breastplate from him.

"But you drank the wine!" Felix protested, furiously.

"That wine wasn't drugged," said the leader of the three. "We were told to play along and let you get the door opened for us. Worked like a charm."

"Who told you?" Felix turned as a movement in the stairway caught his eye, and he saw Lady Dovetree appear at the top of the stairs, very pretty with her arms crossed over her chest. "You?" he cried.

"Don't be angry, Prince Felix," said she. "They'll probably not hang you, and now I can be certain they won't hang me either. I love the dear baroness, of course, but not enough to *die* for her!" And she laughed at this, a cruel sort of laugh that belied any declarations of love.

The Baron of Middlecrescent rose then, cut free from his bindings. He rubbed his wrists thoughtfully, and a guardsman offered him a cloak to cover his naked torso. He drew it about himself with kingly dignity and strode to the doorway without a glance to his right at Lionheart upon the floor, or to his left at Prince Felix. Nor did he look at his wife's traitorous servant but fixed his gaze straight ahead, moving as though none of them mattered or existed.

But at the top of the stairway, he said over his shoulder, "Bring them."

12

*T*WELFTH NIGHT. *Twelfth Tithe.*

    Is this fear? Is this desperation? Is this . . . is this hope?

    So many strange sensations, all of them an agony. Oh, to be free of these bodies! Oh, to be made whole once more, to be established, to be strong! To rule and be ruled.

    The beating of these many hearts, large and small, all beat as one, joined in purpose.

    Our purpose.

    My purpose.

    She bled out upon her kingdom. She took her own life, and she bled, and she died.

    New blood must flow for life to renew. So eat them, devour them, take them deep inside and drink of their lives.

    Twelfth Night. Twelfth Tithe.

    Then, come Thirteenth Dawn . . . renew!

They traveled the fey Paths of the land as naturally as Foxbrush might have strolled the halls of his mother's house, and they carried him unprotesting along with them. It was like being swept out with the tide, though his feet trod on uncertain soil beneath. All around him the surviving Faerie beasts of the land were silent with the focused intensity of the hunt. Their desire to drive Cren Cru from this land that had been their home was stronger than their desire for life. Even though, if they succeeded, they themselves would have to leave the land forever.

Foxbrush wondered how many of them, like Nidawi, had lost their former nations to the ravages of Cren Cru and his warriors?

Eanrin, once more a cat, paced sedately at Foxbrush's side, his eyes half closed and his tail up, but his ears a little back with tension. He indicated by the very lie of his whiskers that he didn't deem Foxbrush worth bothering with and refused to initiate any talk. Foxbrush, however, was unschooled in the language of cats.

"You know, you don't have to come along with us," he said to the cat. "I mean, this isn't your fight, and . . . well, the poem is a bit vague on the details, so I can't promise anything. I—"

"So are you saying you'd prefer I did *not* come along and therefore remained ignorant of the events as they unfold tonight?" said the cat icily. "Would make for a poor bit of poetry later, if you ask me."

"I hadn't thought of it that way," Foxbrush admitted. "You're right. I suppose you should be there. It's for the best."

"The *best*? Hardly," said Eanrin, his ears lowering still farther with ire. Had it been possible, he would have ignored the young man beside him entirely. The lad was a weakling, and a mortal weakling at that, and Eanrin wasn't feeling too keen on mortals at the moment. But he could not deny the clarity of the Lumil Eliasul's Path opening at Foxbrush's feet. It was an enigma to be sure. One he would sleuth out if he possibly could.

He muttered in a low growl that Foxbrush could not understand,

"Besides, I have unfinished business of my own to attend to this night." The face of Sun Eagle was all too present in his mind; Sun Eagle, stained in the white lion's blood.

Sun Eagle, looking into Imraldera's eyes and calling her *"Starflower."*

The cat began to growl.

"You know," said Foxbrush, unaware how close he came in that moment to having his ankle scratched, "it would have made everything much easier if you'd just written it out in plain speaking."

"What?" said Eanrin, twitching an ear Foxbrush's way.

"Your message," Foxbrush continued. "It's daft to send something that important in poetry. I don't even *read* poetry, not by preference. If, in the future, you'd just write it out plainly, everything that happens tonight, I mean, I'd be much obliged. That is, the future me will be obliged. Or the past me." He frowned. "Actually, I'm not sure which of me it would matter to. Either way, do you think you could work it out?"

Both Eanrin's ears flattened to his skull. "I'll keep it in mind."

Foxbrush glanced down at the cat. Bard Eanrin of Rudiobus was proving far more foul tempered than generations of childhood rhymes would suggest. But then, whoever said those rhymes were reliable sources of information?

Foxbrush squeezed Leo's scroll tightly in one fist and tried to focus on the strange, otherworldly shapes surrounding him. Like the cat-man, none of the beasts on this death march were bound to a single shape but constantly shifted into other shapes as well: some human, some reminiscent of human, some not human at all.

But they all trusted him. They all expected him to fulfill the promise given to Nidawi beside the Final Water.

They were all fools.

At Foxbrush's feet, though he could not see it, a Path opened up, leading straight ahead. He pursued it unknowing, whispering as he went: *"There you will win your Fiery One, or see her then devoured."*

Ahead, a light glowed brighter and brighter on the horizon. Not the glow of the rising sun.

This was a bronze light.

Had she governed her own body, she would have collapsed in weakness and despair. Her shoulder throbbed, her wound torn open with exertion, its soothing dressing long since vanished. But that which dwelled inside Daylily did not understand her pain, so it drove her, and she moved as she was driven. Through the darkness, through the Wood, through the Faerie Paths stretching across the land. She knew where she went with a knowing that was not her own.

The center of the land. The heart where the tumor festered.

Twelfth Night. Twelfth Tithe.

The wolf inside her, weakened to the point of death but struggling still, growled. *You say I made you cruel. But at least I never made you false!*

"You made me betray Rose Red," Daylily whispered as she stumbled on, her head heavy with the presence of both Cren Cru and the wolf.

I never made you anything. I am *you. I am the true you! The one you hide from the world; the one you can't bear to admit exists. But I am true.*

As true as knives to the heart. As true as poison in the blood. As true as love or hatred living buried in a wounded heart.

How long had she known it, this secret truth? Since that summer, long ago, when she had traveled to the mountains to spend her holidays in countrified isolation with Lionheart and Foxbrush. That summer when she had first heard the cry of a wolf, lonely and forlorn in the forests of night. How her heart had responded to that sound!

And in that response, the truth that was the she-wolf inside Daylily had sprung to vicious life. A life that must always be suppressed, always be secreted away to those dark corners of her mind that no one could find. Bound down with chains, deprived of freedom . . . yet it dominated her existence still more in captivity.

"I don't want any part of you," Daylily said. "Not anymore."

Then let me go!

A trill of notes. "Then let it go."

Daylily closed her eyes, recognizing the voice of the songbird. She should have known he would follow her even here, on this dark Path to her master's door.

"Let it go, Daylily," the bird sang in gentle, compelling melody.

But the thunder of Cren Cru's driving pulse called to her, and she surrendered to it and allowed it to pull her deeper still. Deeper into places of her mind where the wolf could not come.

She came at last to the center where the Mound latched hold and sucked at the lifeblood of the Land. Around the thorn-raised Mound stood the warriors, her brethren. They had all arrived before her, but this did not matter. She felt her heart beating in time with theirs, and she was one of them, and she was one with them. They stood in a great circle, Advocate and Initiate, surrounding the Mound. Their bronze stones glowed brighter and brighter, filling their faces with light even in this dark place. And between each warrior stood the firstborn children brought for the final sacrifice.

Daylily saw Sun Eagle and she took her place on his right. Briefly he looked at her, and she thought perhaps she saw him and not his master looking out of his eyes. What did that expression say?

Forgive me! Forgive me! Forgive—

Then his mouth moved, even as hers did, and they spoke in their unified voice:

Twelfth Night. Twelfth Tithe.

Daylily looked down then at the children standing between her and her Advocate. They were all so young, not yet in adolescence, their bodies unformed, their faces round, and their eyes, which should have been full of life, were full only of the Bronze. They stood unbound, for they needed no bindings, caught as they were in Cren Cru's spell.

The child beside Daylily had red hair. Daylily gasped and craned her neck to look more closely. She thought she looked upon her own face, empty and horrible, filled with Cren Cru. The child stood like one dead, her lips gently parted, her head a little to one side. She was empty other than that which filled her.

Better to be devoured by wolves than to become one such as that!

Daylily reached up and took hold of the Bronze about her neck. What she intended to do, she could not say. Perhaps drive that sharp end into her own heart. Perhaps drive it into the child. She took hold and pulled it from her neck.

All her brethren did the same. They cried out together, they and Daylily, saying to the night:

"From blood springs life! From life springs blood!"

Then each of the warriors plunged his or her medallion into the turf. And the stones suddenly grew twice—three times—ten times what they had been, great boulders of shining bronze, and the light they reflected off one another made the surrounding area bright as day.

Save for the yawning mouth of Cren Cru's Mound. No light could penetrate there.

One by one, the warriors stepped forward, leading children behind them. Daylily fell into step behind Sun Eagle, leading the redheaded girl and others as well. She smelled the reeking death in the hole, smelled the breath of her master. The wolf inside her bellowed its revulsion at the stench, but Daylily herself could not resist it.

She watched her Advocate lift the children who followed him. He took them, one at a time, and threw them into that gaping void. And when he had finished and his unresisting captives were sent to their doom and immediately forgotten, he backed away, returned to his stone, and stood with his eyes fixed upon the Mound. And always his mouth moved in chant:

"From blood springs life! From life springs blood!"

Now Daylily herself approached the doorway, and the children paced quietly behind her. Her mouth spoke in chorus with her brethren even as she reached out and chose the nearest child.

Twelfth Night! Twelfth Tithe! her master urged her with frantic eagerness.

But the wolf inside her said, *Look at her! Look at what you do!*

And Daylily paused. She looked into the face of the child who wore her own features, but younger, unspoiled, and true. For an instant, the bronze light cleared from the girl's eyes, and they were dark eyes that gazed up at Daylily with momentary recognition.

"Red Lady—" Lark gasped.

Daylily, with a strength beyond mortality, threw the girl into the darkness and reached for the next child.

The wolf in her mind screamed.

Only it wasn't the wolf. It was a sound outside, beyond the Bronze, a scream rising in violence and intensity. The screams of many, many animal voices, and in those screams were words of bloodshed and vengeance.

Daylily, the child in her arms clutched tight to her breast, turned in place and looked out to the dark landscape beyond Cren Cru's lit circle. She and the other warriors paused in their chant and saw the gathering of dark shadows, rising up, ready to overwhelm all the bronze light. And these shadows shrieked their fury. Their fury, and the name of their champion:

"Here and There! Here and There! Tremble before the King of Here and There!"

Faerie beasts, displaced and dispossessed from all corners of the Between, flashed their teeth and their claws and their weapons. But they were afraid to draw any nearer to the Mound. Then one stepped out from amid their number, and the thing within Daylily recognized him as a figment from her dreams, and Daylily herself, what was left of her, desperately fighting for use of her own eyes, recognized him, and her heart leapt, then sank at the sight.

Foxbrush, on trembling feet, strode out from that shadowy throng and stood just within the light of the Bronze. It cast upon his face weird highlights that could not warm his pallor. He awkwardly held a lance of crude make in both hands, as though he wasn't quite certain whether the pointed end should be up or down. So rather than make a decision, he raised it above his head, and with that motion silenced his fey army.

"Warriors of Cren Cru!" he shouted, though his voice cracked and he was obliged to clear his throat. "Give back what you have stolen and leave this land forever."

"No!" shouted one voice from among the Faerie beasts. Nidawi stepped forward then, a rabid child frothing at the mouth. "No, kill him! Kill them all!"

Foxbrush bowed his head and whispered nervously, "I've got to at least make the offer. It's traditional."

"Burn tradition! Kill my enemy!" Nidawi shrieked. And the other Faerie beasts shrieked in a building, roaring echo. Then, before Foxbrush could recover himself enough to speak a word, his army broke from his command and flowed down into the valley of Cren Cru. They threw themselves at the wall of bronze light and the warriors ringing there.

The warriors waited by their stones. And as the Faerie beasts set upon them, the warriors slew them. Agonized screams of death replaced the screams of battle and bloodlust as the Faerie beasts fell before that unbreachable wall.

Foxbrush, however, remained at the top of the incline, lying facedown where he had been knocked in the rush, both arms stretched out before him, still grasping the lance. He pulled his head up, spitting out dirt and turf, and saw the bloodshed below. They were dying in droves, and the warriors remained unharmed beside their stones.

"This won't do."

The voice was Eanrin's, speaking near Foxbrush's ear. Foxbrush felt two strong, long-fingered hands grab him by the shoulders and pull him to his feet. He stood gasping for the remnants of air that had been knocked from his lungs. Eanrin studied the carnage below, and his lip lifted in a snarl. "This won't do," he repeated. Then, "I've got an idea. Follow me, little king!"

With that, he gave Foxbrush a push to start him moving before darting on ahead so quickly that Foxbrush, staggering, very nearly lost him. But for the first time, something glimmered beneath Foxbrush's feet, and he thought he saw, however briefly, the Path of which everyone had spoken. However it was, he stumbled down the incline, following the trail of the crimson-clad poet, who darted between the Faerie beasts into the space between two great bronze stones. The light from the stones had dimmed in the onslaught, and now their individual glows did not reach so far as to touch one another, leaving small gaps of darkness. Into this darkness, Eanrin plunged, and Foxbrush, gripping his lance, his shoulders hunched and his head low, prepared to follow.

But then one of the warriors turned from his fight and, seeing the flash of Eanrin's cloak, sprang after him. This was a savage warrior with a long black braid whipping behind him, his skin shiny with sweat, his clothing splashed with browning blood.

And Foxbrush hesitated for one moment as the words flashed through his brain:

First let pass the man in red,
Then let pass the brown . . .

How he hated poetry!

Something struck him from behind. Whether foe or friend, it did not matter, for the blow caught him hard between the shoulders, once more knocking all the breath from his body. He staggered under the impact and fell headlong through the dark shadow, landing within the inner circle.

Someone grabbed him by the back of his head, yanking his chin back. He felt the sharpness of a stone cut him behind the ear. A half second more and his throat might well have been slit.

But Eanrin leapt at Sun Eagle and knocked him to the ground, and the stone dagger flew wide. Foxbrush, gasping and clutching the wound at his neck, twisted around to see the cat-man and the dark-skinned warrior grappling upon the ground. Sun Eagle got the upper hand, kneeling on Eanrin's chest, grasping his throat in a choke hold. But Eanrin, who was stronger than he looked, brought his knee up sharply into Sun Eagle's back, dislodging his hold.

Foxbrush, using his lance for support, got to his feet and prepared to join the fray, uncertain if his help would be welcome. But something caught the tail of his eye, and he turned.

Daylily, still wearing the bloodstained gown of Eldest Sight-of-Day, stood at the door of Cren Cru's Mound, surrounded by empty-eyed children, one of them caught in her arms.

But it wasn't Daylily who looked out of her eyes. Her mouth opened, and words poured forth:

King of Here and There! We have heard rumor of you ere now, the promise spoken on the shores of the Final Water. So the time of our meeting is come. And yet, we do not fear you as we believed we would.

"Please," Foxbrush said, his knuckles whitening as he clutched his lance tighter. "Let her go. Return the children you stole."

That does not suit our purpose.

"I'll . . . I'll kill you," Foxbrush said, taking a trembling step forward.

Kill us? You'll have to catch us first!

"No, wait!" Foxbrush shouted, dropping his weapon as he put out both hands. But it was too late.

The creature that was Daylily hurled itself and the child it held into the mouth of the Mound.

Foxbrush, without stopping to think, ran. The distance to the door stretched on for a small forever, like an impassable dreamscape. Then the doorway seemed suddenly to reach out, to grab him, and he plunged into the darkness within.

13

H E STOOD IN THE GREAT HALL of the Eldest.
Considering he'd been expecting sudden and searing death, this wasn't all that bad. Surprising, to be sure. But not bad, exactly.

Great pillars rose up from the floor to support the high roof, and elegant railings framed the galleries above. Enormous windows, open to the darkness outside, lined the walls from floor to gallery, from gallery to ceiling. Through these poured a light colder than moonlight, and it shone upon long, filmy curtains embroidered with starflowers and panthers, which fluttered without the aid of a breeze, like so many writhing, elongated phantoms.

Odd, Foxbrush thought, frowning where he stood. He wondered if this strange, cold light was playing tricks on his eyes. *This looks like the old Great Hall. From before the Dragon.*

He began to tremble, and the fear he'd expected from the moment he stepped through that black doorway finally caught up with him. For the old hall had been decimated by dragon fire, torn down by dragon claws. Yet it was that hall he saw before him, not the new, unfinished one of his day.

Have I stepped back in time again? Foxbrush wondered. *Or rather, forward in time? Or . . . or . . .*

And then he saw a sight that told him he was nowhere in time, nowhere in reality, or at least, no reality that he knew.

High above the galleries, in the empty space between the supporting pillars and the arched roof, ghostly figures floated. Like dust motes drifting in directionless patterns, so these figures floated, arms and legs out like the points of a star, heads bowed over chests, hair floating like that of drowned men underwater. Weightless they wafted, never touching one another, as though each was a world apart. Hundreds of them filled the space above Foxbrush's head.

The lost firstborn.

Foxbrush craned his neck back to stare up at them, those wraithlike children. The cold light washed their dark skin pale and their dark hair silvery, and they seemed to glow faintly with a pulsing luminosity. Were they dead? Were they beyond dead? Some of them looked *thinned*, as though their very existence was being drained away, leaving behind a flickering residue of reality. Some of them possessed scarcely any remaining form but drifted in and out of visibility like curls of white smoke.

But some were still solid. And among these Foxbrush spotted a shock of red hair, vibrant hued even in that eerie light.

"Lark!" he cried. His voice echoed through the cavernous hall. Everything was bigger, he now realized, than the hall of his memory. He and the floating figures above him were no more than mice compared with the vastness of this place. He ran across tiles that were each half a field in length, and the pillars were like tall mountains around him. Above his head, the drifting form of Lark vanished in the swirling bodies of the children, only to reappear farther away. Foxbrush chased her, uncertain what he hoped to do but unwilling, even so, to let the girl out of his sight.

It's useless to run, you know.

Foxbrush staggered to a halt and whirled around to face the voice that had spoken behind him. There was no one there. Only darkness at the end of the hall where everything vanished beyond all hope of light. His heart thudding in his breast, he searched the deeper shadows behind the pillars and beneath the windows.

Are you looking for us? You are more foolish than we thought.

"Where are you?" Foxbrush cried.

Not here. This is your memory. You'll not find us.

"Are . . . are you in my mind?"

No. You came to us. You are inside us. But we must use other minds to take shape, for we have no shape of our own. This is your memory within us.

Foxbrush cursed. He turned again to search for Lark up among the children above. He'd lost her. Frantic, he ran, his eyes upturned.

He nearly collided into Daylily.

She stood before him, no longer wearing the Eldest's garment but adorned in the wafting rags of her wedding gown, as ghostly pale as the children above, her red hair, bereft of its life and curl, falling in straight sheets on either side of her face, over her shoulders.

"He is drinking," Daylily said.

Foxbrush yelped and nearly fell over backward. She looked like something from a dream or a nightmare, beautiful and awful at once.

"He is drinking," she repeated, her breath so cold it steamed in the air. Her eyes stared straight ahead, not at Foxbrush, not at anything, wide open and unseeing. She lifted her hand and pointed to the children up above. "He is sucking the life of Southlands through the lives of Southlands' firstborn. He is drinking their memories. He is drinking them."

Foxbrush looked again at the children. Many of them were so far gone! What would happen when they faded away entirely?

"We must stop him, Daylily," he said, turning urgently to her. He wanted to reach out and touch her but somehow didn't dare. "You must help me."

She cannot help you. She is ours. She is—

"Mine," Daylily whispered.

Mine!

Daylily took a step toward Foxbrush, still without seeing him. Her upraised arm reached out, stretching toward his face. He knew he could not let her touch him, and he stumbled back. Then he turned and ran.

You have so many fears. So many wonderful, fascinating, mortal fears! And we know what to do with those.

The enormous tiles beneath Foxbrush's feet shifted, then rippled like water. His feet sank into them as though he had tried to run over the surface of a bog, and he was dragged down to his knees. He struggled to pull himself free, but it was useless.

"Useless."

There are some voices that sound far worse in memory than they ever were in reality. So it was with this voice. The very sound of it was dread and rejection, all things most shameful falling upon Foxbrush's ears. He turned, his eyes widening with terror, to what he knew he must see.

Lionheart stood above him. But he was taller here in this place of Foxbrush's memory than he ever would be in the real world; Foxbrush always thought of Lionheart as much bigger than he was.

"Useless," said the figure of Lionheart, and he laughed at Foxbrush's plight. "That's what you always were. From the time we were children, what have you ever been but a useless tag-on? And you think *you* can be Eldest?"

You? Eldest?

The words poured from Lionheart's mouth and rushed together around the pillars, across the windows, through the galleries, among the drifting bodies of the children. The floor beneath Foxbrush churned at the sound, sucking him farther down. He gasped and put his hands out to try to pull himself up. But his hands caught too and sank to his elbows. He glared furiously at Lionheart, who was laughing now.

"A king, Foxbrush? You weren't even a good damsel in distress. Didn't you cry when she pulled the button off your shirt? I think you did. I remember!"

We see it in your mind!

"And that mother of yours . . . do you know why she never wanted to see you? Why she hid herself away in her rooms, a half-crazy recluse? Do you know why?"

We see it in your mind!

"Because you look like your father. Oh, not everyone can see it! But she can. Every time she looks at you. He was a weak man too, and he knew it.

So he set out to prove his strength, and he subdued her, and he beat her, and she could only pray that he would leave again on one of his long trips to the lowlands. And you . . . *you*, Foxbrush . . . crying at the window as you watched his carriage roll away. *'Where is Papa going?'* you'd ask, and what did she say to you, Foxbrush? What did she say?"

Tears streamed down Foxbrush's face, and each one that fell seemed to drag his head after it. He sagged, his arms and legs caught in the floor, almost willing now for it to swallow him up.

"You know what she said." The figure of Lionheart crouched before Foxbrush, caught his chin in one hand and forced him to look up, to meet those hateful, laughing eyes. "Tell me, Foxy! Tell me what it was!"

"She said . . ." Foxbrush choked on his own tears. They sat as bile in his throat. "She said, *'He's gone to the Dragon's own house, and may he never return!'*"

"Well done." The figure of Lionheart grinned. He let go of Foxbrush's chin and patted his head like a good dog. Then he sat back on his heels, and his grin grew lopsided, turning into a leer. "Then one time he left, and he never did return. One day, in another vain proof of strength, he ran afoul of a duelist's blade, never to rise again. Another failure.

"But your mother looks at you, and she still sees him in your eyes. You are so like him, Foxbrush! Useless. Worthless. Will you be Eldest?"

You?

"Will that somehow prove your strength? Will you take a girl like *her*"—with a sweep of his arm to where Daylily stood staring down on the two of them, unseeing—"for your bride? You, of all people?"

You?

Foxbrush raised his haggard face. It was a titanic effort, for he felt his weakness pressing him down into the sucking floor. But he raised his face and looked across the gloomy hall to Daylily. Beautiful Daylily, powerful Daylily. Strong, unbending, unmoving Daylily.

She met his gaze. For a flash as bright as the Bronze—brighter even— she saw him and knew him. She could not see the figure crouched before him, for her memories of Lionheart were not the same as Foxbrush's. She could not see the Great Hall of the Eldest, for all around her was nothing but barren wasteland under a starless sky. And in that sky, the forms of the stolen children floated and gave of their memories, gave of their essence, feeding into the greedy will of Cren Cru as it sought to latch hold of that which it could never have. Cren Cru was all that was left now in this place of her mind. Cren Cru was . . .

But then she saw Foxbrush sinking into the dry, dusty ground, brought low with shame. She saw him and drew a surprised breath, for she knew it was him, truly *him*. Not a mere memory, but Foxbrush himself, clad in those ugly, stinking garments, his face half hidden behind a ragged beard.

She opened her mouth to speak his name. But to her horror, she realized he was looking at her.

Just as she saw him in his true form here, so he saw her. Not the self she always presented, not the beautiful girl, the ruthless conspirator, the cold, unreachable beauty. He saw *her*.

He saw the wolf.

"Daylily!" Foxbrush cried, all thoughts of the near-Lionheart forgotten as he stared at the red she-wolf bound with bloodied chains to the great stakes. How he knew that foam-mouthed beast for the girl he loved, he could not say, for reasonable thought had long since fled. He knew in the depths of his frantically beating heart, and he surged toward that knowledge, pulling against the will that sought to swallow him.

"Foxbrush," said the wolf.

And at the sound of his name falling from that mouth, Foxbrush felt his strength reviving. He fought the hold Cren Cru had upon him, heaving himself up and onto his feet. The floor remained unstable, but the tiles had shrunk now, and he stood up to a full man's height. On unsteady but determined feet, he started toward her, toward the wolf. "Daylily," he said again, his hands reaching out to her chains, eager to free her.

The figure of Lionheart lunged at him from behind, wrapping powerful arms about him and hurling him from his feet. Foxbrush fell upon the tiles, which shattered like shards of glass into blackness. He put up both hands to protect his face, but now the figure of Lionheart was gone and, in its place, a shadowy form swooped down upon him and struck him again, on the face, on the chest. He tried to hit it, but something bit his hand with razor teeth and worried it like a dog pulling flesh from a bone. Foxbrush screamed and pummeled at nothing, for there was nothing to strike: no body, no form, only teeth and biting pain.

Daylily watched, and the wolf surged against her chains, ravening. "Let me loose! Let me loose!" she roared. "Let me kill it!"

"No!" Daylily cried, lost in her mind, uncertain of her own body and form now. Was she herself? Was she the wolf?

Was she Cren Cru?

"Let it go."

From somewhere up above, the song of the wood thrush fell down upon Daylily. The next moment, she felt the bird himself alight upon her shoulder, though she wasn't even certain she had a body anymore. She turned to the bird, and he looked at her with his bright eye. How could he follow her, even here, even into the heart of the Mound and her own blighted mind?

"Let it go. The time is now."

"If I let it go, it will kill us all," Daylily whispered.

"No, Daylily," sang the bird. And suddenly he wasn't a bird anymore. She found herself standing beside the form of a man, but not exactly a man. More like what man was intended to be at the beginning of Time and the Near World, before the ravages of mortality took hold and corrupted what should have been most fair. This Man was the realized ideal, the realized potential, and more besides—so much more! This form he wore could only just contain the glory of his majesty and the Song that burst from the inner depths of his being.

She knew him at once. She had seen him before, in the House of the Eldest. She had seen him enter the gate and then, two hours later, walk away again, and she'd never spoken to him. But she had known, even in that distant glimpse she'd had, that this person, this Man, was someone she must either love or hate. There could be no other response to him.

He looked at her now with his ageless eyes: deep, bottomless wells of kindness and strength. The Prince of Farthestshore, Lord of all the Faerie, son of the King Across the Final Water.

"No, Daylily," he said to her. "It will kill you only if you cling to it. But if it dies, others will die as well. For they need you, Daylily. They need you as you truly are. Not this thing you pretend to be, this mimic of the real woman.

"Let it go. Release the wolf into my care and keeping, and I will show you how the worst in you, all that you most fear, may be transformed. Let the worst be made the strongest, the truest, the best!"

He put his hands on her shoulders. And suddenly she was the wolf herself, crouched in her chains, slavering at the mouth.

"Please!" she said, and her voice was the wolf's, and the wolf's voice was hers. "Set me free!"

The Prince smiled. Then he reached out and broke the chains.

The red wolf jumped forward and shook, and the shackles fell away, ringing as they struck the hardened ground. Her great claws tore at the soil, and she felt strength returning to her, beyond any strength she had ever known.

Then she leapt into a run across that barren landscape, chasing the dark shade that attacked Foxbrush. Running beside her, shoulder to shoulder, was a great golden Hound, and she matched her stride to his, pace for pace, and her heart thrilled in rhythm to his; as unlike the driving rhythm of Cren Cru's shared purpose as a brilliant spring dawn is unlike the vacuum of deep space.

That which she had feared most in herself—that which she had struggled most to hide—the strongest, deepest part of her soul—flew now with every stride. Her eyes fixed intently upon the shadowy nothing that struck and bit and clawed at Foxbrush as he struggled with it on the ground, helpless before its wrath. He could not see it; neither could Daylily.

But she could smell it. The stench of greedy, desperate searching for something that could never exist. The slayer of worlds, the stinking Parasite.

"You are the Protector!" the Hound declared, and she knew he had called her by her true name, the name she had never known existed. "Now strike!"

She was not the Betrayer.

She was not the Manipulator.

She was not the Destroyer.

"You are the Protector!" bayed the Hound. "Mighty Protector! Courageous Protector! Beloved Daylily, strike!"

The she-wolf sprang at the shadow. Foxbrush looked up in time to see the red fury falling, the flash of white teeth, the burn of intense blue eyes, and he thought he saw his own death. But her jaws clamped down upon the shadow itself, upon the being of Cren Cru that hid inside this Mound and stole the minds of those it wished to possess. But *it* was nothing. It was no more than a bloodied, suicidal dream.

She took that dream between her teeth, and she tore it into pieces.

———

Reeeeaaaaarraaa!

The high, piercing screech shot across the empty wasteland, tore through the sky, cutting it so that raging red light shone through. To Foxbrush, it seemed as though the rest of the floor beneath him shattered and pillars crumbled and the ceiling overhead broke to reveal fire. A wind rose up, howling in agony, and it whirled through the children gathered above, tossing them like so many leaves in a storm. The walls gave way, collapsing in silence, for they were unreal, and nothing could be heard anyway over the continuous ravaging shriek of Cren Cru.

Foxbrush stared at the destruction, at the children falling down and down, for there was nowhere for them to land now. And he realized that he too was falling, and all the world was made up of that single, ongoing scream.

14

THE STONE KNIFE LAY just beyond reach.

Eanrin saw Sun Eagle's hand reaching for it across the blackened grass, and he brought both fists down hard between the warrior's shoulder blades, knocking him flat, then reached out and snatched for the knife himself. It was like a dead thing, and Eanrin shuddered and hurled it far into the darkness beyond the bronze light, where the frantic voices of the Faerie beasts rose like a wall all around.

Sun Eagle spat dirt from his mouth and sprang to his feet, standing opposite Eanrin. The two circled each other before the mouth of the Mound, alone within the surrounding Bronze other than the remaining children, who stood silent and unmoving before the doorway to their doom.

Eanrin glanced at them, cursed, then turned a flashing smile at Sun Eagle. "Did we interrupt some charming little ritual? How inconvenient for you. But you know, child sacrifice isn't the thing these days, not since Meadhbh played out her hand all those ages ago." He spoke lightly, but fury laced each word.

Sun Eagle's face remained as stone. When he spoke, he said only, "You've lost her."

"Yes, she ran where I'd prefer not to follow," Eanrin agreed, placing his feet carefully as he eyed his enemy. He saw that Sun Eagle was slowly approaching one of the bronze stones, but he could not guess why. He prepared to spring before Sun Eagle could reach it. "Our little mortal king has gone in after her, and he's the hero of this tale, or so the future me implies, so we'll just—"

"She never loved you."

The smile fell from Eanrin's face.

"She would never love one such as you. Her heart is always with her people. Her heart is always with me." Sun Eagle's face was hidden from the bronze light, darkened by shadows cast from the Mound itself. But his eyes glowed with a spirit that had nothing to do with Cren Cru, a spirit that remained vital and resisting, deep in the center of his being. "Even as I wandered the Wood alone—even as I prepare to enter the darkness of my master—even in that darkness, her heart will always be mine."

"Dragons eat you," Eanrin whispered.

It was then that the Mound collapsed.

It fell away like a melting candle but left nothing behind as it went, disappearing into a swallowing emptiness, silently at first. Then the scream caught up—reaching out from the depths of Cren Cru's pain into this world—and shot through those gathered, through the bloodied brawl beyond the bronze light, knocking warriors and beasts off their feet, leaving them curled up in sympathetic agony, clutching their ears.

Eanrin, his mouth twisted with pain, forced his eyes open. He saw the warriors, eleven of them now, none wounded from their fight so much as brought low by this shrieking that filled the worlds within their minds. They crawled in shuddering anguish toward their stones.

Something landed beside Eanrin. He turned, and to his great surprise, he saw Foxbrush lying as though he'd landed from a ten-foot drop, the breath knocked out of him but alive. Foxbrush also put up his hands to cover his ears, his mouth opening in a scream that could not be heard above the shrieking of Cren Cru.

Then, quite suddenly, the shrieking stopped, replaced by the roar of a great wind. It was enough to set the smaller of the Faerie beasts flying, caught up and hurled like dandelion fluff into the night sky away from the breaking center. The wind rose up from the black hole where the Mound had stood, swirling in a twisted rush.

Eanrin reached out and grabbed Foxbrush's arm, and the two of them, straining against the wind, supported each other to their feet. They heard then a new set of screams.

Turning, they saw the warriors beside their bronze stones. The stones, larger than life, fixed into the turf, were melting. Runnels of liquid bronze ran down into a pool on the ground, steaming there before sinking into the dirt and vanishing.

And as the stones melted, the warriors themselves faded to wisps of nothing.

The giantess Kasa howled. Her stone broke at the sound and vanished in an instant. She herself, caught in the twisting wind, dissipated and was gone, never to be seen again. Her brethren, watching her fate, screamed with redoubled terror.

Foxbrush stared at them. Then he pushed himself from Eanrin's grasp and turned to the one bronze stone that stood without its warrior.

"Daylily!" he gasped. Though the wind threatened to fling him off his feet as it had the Faerie beasts, he put his head down and started toward the stone.

"What are you doing?" Eanrin cried, his voice barely audible.

"I've got to reach her! I've got to find her!" Foxbrush replied, but since his face was turned away from the poet-cat, his voice could not be heard. But Eanrin read his purpose in the set of his head and shoulders, and the words of the ballad sprang to his mind.

> *No lance, no spear will save the night,*
> *Nor bloodshed on the ground.*
> *This alone will be your fight:*
> *To hold your lady, hold her tight*
> *When once again she's found.*

Eanrin leapt forward and caught Foxbrush's arm. He put his mouth to the mortal's ear and shouted to be heard.

"Grab the stone! Hold on to it and don't let go!"

Foxbrush nodded and Eanrin released him. Another wail broke suddenly into nothing, and Eanrin turned to see that a second bronze stone had disappeared, taking its warrior with it. Then he saw Sun Eagle standing in stoic silence, staring at his own stone as it melted away. There was little of it left now.

"Lord, grant me strength," Eanrin muttered between bared teeth. Then, the wind propelling him from behind, he ran to Sun Eagle and threw himself at the stone. He took it in both hands.

It burned.

"Dragon's teeth!" Eanrin shouted and yanked his hands away.

Sun Eagle looked down. The wind should have knocked him over, but he braced himself against it, his shoulders back, his chest bare and covered in old bloodstains and scars. He was fading around the edges, losing his form and substance as the Bronze melted away. His long black braid whipped behind him, melting into the night, and his eyes were mere dark slits as he gazed at Eanrin.

Eanrin reached out to grab the stone again, cursing at the pain but determined. "Hold on!" he shouted, looking up at Sun Eagle. "Help me!"

Sun Eagle bent down, his face level with Eanrin's. And the cord around his neck dangled, the bead with the white starflower flashing bright for an instant.

"Tell her she is always with me," Sun Eagle said.

Then he brought his fist down, striking Eanrin in the jaw and knocking him over. Eanrin let go of the stone, and when he did so, it burst.

With a cry, Sun Eagle vanished, carried away like smoke in the wind.

Foxbrush was thrown from his feet several times as he struggled toward the stone, his mind a cacophony of sounds and sights he could not understand. But the Bronze gleamed in its melting. And there came to his mind suddenly the woodcut image in *Eanrin's Illustrated Rhymes*, the one he had seen long ago as a child.

King Shadow Hand, bearded and fierce, holding the Fiery Fair as she melted.

He could not see Daylily, had caught no sight of her after the wolf tore into the shadow of Cren Cru. The ceiling and floor had broken, and she had vanished, lost in the storm of pain and the whirling fall of the stolen children.

And now here he was, somehow back in this world. The phantom children were nowhere to be seen, not Lark, not any of them. All he saw was the stone.

He reached it at last and stood over it, watching helpless as it collapsed on itself. What had Eanrin said? Hold it?

"This alone will be your fight," he whispered.

He put out both hands, one bleeding from bite wounds, the index finger partially torn away. They shuddered with redoubled agony as they neared the stone, which radiated a dreadful heat.

Then, with a cry, Foxbrush grabbed it.

Pain coursed through every nerve of his body, up his arms, his shoulders, into his brain, down into his very core. He screamed and wanted to let go, but some drive beyond self-preservation made him tighten his hold instead, even as the Bronze dripped over his fingers, melting his skin and bones along with itself.

Suddenly Daylily stood beyond him. Daylily, wolf or maid, he could not say. It did not matter; it was she in truth.

She stared at the Bronze, at his hands. Then she looked at Foxbrush, her eyes, always unnaturally large, enormous in her face.

"Foxbrush!" she cried. "Let it go!"

He screamed still, unable to stop for the pain. But he shook his head.

"Please!" she cried. "You have to let it go!"

She grabbed his shoulders, forcing him to look into her face.

The wind and the pain and the howls of the dying warriors.

The burning, burning, searing heat.

All of this vanished in the depths of her gaze.

"It'll destroy you, Foxbrush," said Daylily. "Don't love me. Let me go."

Foxbrush shut his mouth against his own cries, closing his eyes. Tears of utmost pain streamed down his face, and he thought his head would explode.

Then he looked up again. He poured all his soul into Daylily's eyes, all his heart into his words.

"I'd give my life for you."

Another shriek, and another warrior vanished into the rushing wind. Daylily stood, her bloodstained dress caught up in a cloud, her red hair streaming, her being much faded. She stared down at the young man clutching the Bronze and his own destruction.

And she saw there the painful truth of his words, and it smote her to the core. He would die for her. This man she'd despised. He would die for her, and he would deem it a worthy death.

"Foxbrush." She whispered his name.

He tried to respond, but the pain was too much and he screamed again, his body convulsing. But his hands never let go.

Daylily reached out. She put her hands around his.

She could not feel the burn that he felt, but she could feel the strength of his grasp.

"Hold on, then," she said. "Hold on to me."

The stone continued to melt. Bronze sizzled and bubbled and pooled away at their feet. One by one, the Twelve Bronze disappeared, and the warriors followed their master into oblivion.

But when the last stone joined its brethren and became nothing but a sodden mass and then not even that, soaking into the ground . . . when the wind streaked up into the night sky and vanished, leaving behind a breathless hush and many Faerie beasts lying low, their hands over their heads . . .

When Lumé crested the horizon and gazed into the place of darkness where for so long he had not dared to shine, his great golden eye fell upon two figures kneeling together in the dust. The one strong, clad in rags, held the other, who fell against her in shuddering weakness, his head upon her shoulder, his face buried in her neck as he wept. Her hair cascaded over him in a comforting shield against everything he must soon face.

And she held his ruined, melted hands in hers.

15

L ARK HAD NEVER WALKED on clouds before.

She decided these probably weren't *real* clouds. Real clouds held the rain, and that meant they had to be wet, or at least a little soggy. These, however, were more like what storytellers and poets *want* clouds to be: indescribably soft and springy yet solid enough that a little girl might walk upon them.

Or perhaps she was simply not solid enough herself anymore to fall through.

Either way, she didn't mind. After all the horror of recent memory—horror that her conscious mind had been too numbed to recognize, but that her raging subconscious had experienced in all the vibrancy of dreams-come-true—a stroll in the heavens was quite pleasant.

How she had come here, she couldn't decide. She had vague recollections of the shadow's scream, followed by a long, long fall. Then she'd opened her eyes and found herself lying upon this cloud that was softer than lamb's wool. All was gray-blue around her with the promise of dawn nearing. She got to her feet, unsteady at first, then started walking, stepping from cloud to cloud.

There were other children. None of them were near enough to call out to, but she could see hundreds of them all round her. Dark children of the South Land, clad in garments very like her own. Her brothers and her sisters through the binding of the nation.

They had all passed through the black door of the Mound.

Lark shivered at this almost memory. It couldn't be a real memory since she had been unconscious, lost at the time in the light of the Bronze. But somewhere deep inside, she came so close to remembering, it was frightening. She would spend the rest of her life trying to forget what she had never truly known.

Lumé began to rise. The clouds, dark purple beneath her feet, came alive with red, with saffron, with gold, rippling like swiftly moving water as the light spread farther and farther. Lark heard gasps of delight from the great crowd of children surrounding her, but then those gasps were swallowed up in the sound that followed.

The sound of Lumé's Song.

He appeared on the edge of the horizon, lordly and powerful, a vision-filling giant even at this vast distance. He was young and he was old, and his hair streamed like flames, and his body flamed as well, a vibrant flame full of life. From his mouth poured the Melody, and it was the Melody itself that exploded with light, and shot the colors across the clouds, across the waking world.

As Lumé rose, he danced, and Lark found she longed to dance as well. She raised her hands above her head, and her feet moved in a rhythm hitherto unknown. All the children danced, each a different dance, unique in its pattern, hundreds of inimitable patterns that moved together with the Song of Lord Lumé and scattered tufts of light-infused clouds beneath their feet.

They raised their sweet, childish voices and sang. Theirs was not the language of the Sun, but language did not matter here, high above the worlds.

> *"I bless your name, oh you who sit*
> *Enthroned beyond the Highlands!*

I bless your name and sing in answer
To the Song you give!

"My words in boundless gladness overflow,
In song, more than words.
Joy and fear and hope and trembling,
Bursting all restraint!

"Who can help but sing?"

So the sun rose and danced across the sky. And his Song became milder, more distant as he climbed those high blue vaults, and the clouds gave up their brilliant colors to become a softer, gentler white. Lark, exhausted and happy, sat down suddenly, closing her eyes, feeling the warmth of Lumé's blaze upon her skin. The darkness of Cren Cru's Mound was all but forgotten now.

When she opened her eyes, she found herself gazing into the face of a friend she had not known she knew.

"Hullo," she said.

"Hullo," said the Prince of Farthestshore. He crouched down before her, and his smile was more beautiful than Lumé himself. He wasn't a man, exactly, but he wasn't a Faerie either. Lark didn't know what he was, but she didn't think such questions mattered now.

"Thank you for the Song," she said.

"Thank you for the singing," he replied, and this she thought strange. With Lumé, Hymlumé, and all the hosts of gleaming stars to sing for him, why should he care about her one, feeble voice? Yet the delight was evident in his eyes.

Lark blushed, so pleased at the Prince's pleasure, she hardly knew which way to look.

The Prince said, "Are you ready to go home now?"

"Go home with you?" she asked hopefully.

But the Prince of Farthestshore shook his head. "Not yet, Meadowlark," he said, and she liked how her full name sounded when he spoke it. "I need you to sing in your own world a little longer. Are you ready to do that for me?"

She sighed and shrugged. "I'd rather go with you."

"What about your ma and da? Your sisters and your brother? Don't you think they need you?"

The words weren't spoken as a reprimand, but Lark felt shamed even so. She'd forgotten about her family. "Ma needs me to watch Wolfsbane," she said. "My sisters aren't big enough yet."

"Your ma needs you to love and to hold, and your da needs your singing," said the Prince of Farthestshore. He stood then and put out a hand to her. She took it eagerly and let him help her to her feet. Somehow she knew that all the children walked with the Prince of Farthestshore, that he led them each by the hand. But she was alone with him still. How this could be was too much to ponder, so she didn't. She merely enjoyed herself and the walk across the sky, and the now-distant Song of Lumé falling down from above. They passed through unknown portals, across clouds, across starscapes, across distant oceans and green sweeps of valleys, and it took her breath away. She pointed and exclaimed, and the Prince of Farthestshore joined in her merriment, laughing delightedly at her enthusiasm, and answered questions as she asked them, though she'd not be able to remember what he'd said later on, down in the thin air of the Near World.

But she would never forget the sound of his voice, nor the joy she experienced during that walk. She never told anyone—mere words failed to describe something so sweet, so dear, so magnificent—but she thought of it often, even to her dying day.

Suddenly she saw her home, the Eldest's House upon the hill above the jungle village. She stopped then, tugging on the Prince's hand. "Wait," she said.

"What is it, Meadowlark?" he asked her gently.

"Foxbrush." She frowned and one of those dark recollections she wished to ignore came back to mind. She saw Foxbrush down in the darkness, battling the shadow that had imprisoned her. Battling to save her and all the children of the South Land. A fight he could not hope to win. "What about Foxbrush?"

"I will take care of him," said the Prince. "You may trust me."

"I know." But Lark's frown did not dissipate. "I would like to go to him first, if I may. I'd like to find him and see for myself. Please."

The Prince smiled yet again. "Gentle child, brave child," he said. "Yes, you may see your friend and thank him for what he sacrificed. He has bravely fought the fight I placed before him, and he has earned your gratitude and love."

With that, the Prince turned and led Lark in a new direction. She saw trees, forests, gorges pass beneath her feet in a few strides. Then she saw the center of the Land, the deep valley where the Mound had latched hold and the starflower trees were uprooted. Now there was nothing but a blackened hole in that place, a scar to mark Cren Cru's coming and passing. Lark shivered at the sight.

But she saw too that starflower vines already crept across the ground, covering the scar with their soft leaves and bright faces. "All will be well again," Lark whispered.

"All will be well," the Prince of Farthestshore assured her.

Deep in the jungle, Redman and Eldest Sight-of-Day, leading the warriors of their village, felt a tremor through the ground at their feet. A shadow that had kept their hearts captive for long months lifted suddenly, leaving all of them breathless. They did not understand why. But the Eldest turned to her husband, her dark eyes seeking his.

"Lark?" she said.

But he shook his head. "We should return to the village," he said. So they turned and hastened back through the winding jungle trails. As they went, they heard the voices of hundreds of Faerie beasts singing out in all their chattering, braying, cawing, roaring tongues:

"He's dead! He's dead! The Mound is brought low! The Parasite is plucked from its hold! Cren Cru is dead!"

Then, as though in answer, other voices sang back:

"All hail the King of Here and There! All hail the Fiery Fair!"

The villagers understood nothing of this, and many were afraid. But

Redman took his wife's hand, and he found strength there to hurry on and discover what they might.

When they reached the village, it was alive with shouts and joyful cries. The warriors around the Eldest dropped their weapons and ran, arms extended. For the firstborn were come home. Mothers pressed children to their breasts, and fathers wrapped strong arms around families once more made whole. And all wept and talked and trembled with gladness in the growing light of that morning sun.

The Eldest and Redman, however, stood quietly looking on. For they saw no sign of Lark.

The orange cat sat a little to one side, grooming his paws, but his ears were back, listening. He didn't feel up to joining the mayhem but maintained a rhythmic and focused lick-lick-lick, concentrating on one sorely blistered toe at a time.

Nidawi, however, was dancing.

"He's dead! He's dead! Cren Cru is dead! My enemy! At last he's dead!"

She whirled about the whole of the circle where the Bronze had so recently stood, leaping and cavorting, first in the form of a child, then that of a maid, a woman, a crone, all dancing to a wild music ringing in her head.

Then suddenly she found herself before the crumpled form of Foxbrush held in the arms of a mortal woman.

Nidawi stopped and looked at him, her champion. Did champions weep as this one wept? It was so strange!

She knelt beside him, ignoring Daylily and making quite certain that her own immortal beauty far eclipsed anything the mortal could offer. But when she reached to take Foxbrush in her arms, Daylily growled in her throat. Nidawi, startled, pulled her hands back and gave Daylily a quick once-over. Then the Faerie nodded with grudging respect and said:

"He is my hero."

"As he is mine," said Daylily, her arms tightening protectively. "The hero of all Southlands."

"And Tadew-That-Was. And Etalpalli and Uleonore and Waclawa-so-Lid . . . all those who are avenged this Thirteenth Dawn." Nidawi's body trembled with the passion of her words, and her gorgeous eyes brimmed, then overflowed with tears. "They are free! They are *free!*"

"We are free," Daylily whispered, gazing down at the one who lay inert in her arms. She could not say if he was conscious. He lay with his head in her lap, eyes open, tears streaming. He breathed very lightly and gazed up at the dawn-streaked sky. She thought he had a look about him as though he heard beautiful music that she herself could not quite catch.

His hands were burned into a mere abstract remnant of what they had once been. Hideous to look upon and unimaginably painful. One could no longer even see where the teeth of the shadow spirit in the Mound had torn and broken them; those wounds were nothing compared to the ruin inflicted by the melting Bronze.

But he lay as though the pain were far from him, as far away as that Song to which he listened.

Nidawi followed Daylily's gaze and saw Foxbrush's hands for herself. She sniffed, recoiling a little at the stench of burned flesh. Then she looked at Daylily again and tilted her head of black, leaf-strewn hair to one side. "Do I know you?"

"No," said Daylily.

"You look familiar," the Faerie protested. "All you mortals look so alike, but there's something about you . . . Have I threatened your life at one time?"

"It was not my life you threatened," Daylily replied.

Nidawi looked at the lion-claw wound in Daylily's shoulder, still bright red with blood. She looked, and her eyes narrowed, and she almost spoke. At the last, however, she shook herself and turned once more to Foxbrush. His eyes were closed now, and perhaps he slept. "Did you see?" Nidawi asked. "Did you see how he did it? How he killed Cren Cru?"

"He did not kill Cren Cru," Daylily replied. "I did."

"What? *You?*" This was enough to startle Nidawi right out of her beautiful form into that of an astounded child. Her mouth and her eyes opened wide, and she laughed wildly at the idea. "*You* killed Cren Cru? But you are not the King of Here and There!"

"Am I not?" said Daylily. Then she shook her head, gazing down into the still face of Foxbrush in her lap. "No, I am no king and no hero."

But across the vast distances of time, of memory—of echoing dreams and hidden wishes—across the many voices singing songs in the faraway heavens from places neither mortal nor immortal have seen—came a voice. The voice of a girl child, fierce and brave and strong. And it said, so distantly it might perhaps have never spoken at all:

"I am King Shadow Hand of Here and There! And I will slay you, fiend of darkness!"

The voice passed over both Nidawi and Daylily, and they shivered and did not look at each other for a long, trembling moment.

Then Daylily said, "I could have done nothing had he not come for me. Had I not seen him there, in the darkness."

She said it to herself, but Nidawi heard and nodded solemnly, her youthful face very old. Then she stood up and shook out her bounty of hair, raining leaves and flowers upon both Daylily and Foxbrush.

"I suppose I won't marry him after all," she said, crossing her skinny arms across her equally skinny chest. "I was going to, you know, after he killed my enemy. But if he didn't . . ." She snorted and shrugged. "No matter! I'll still see to it that the gates are built and this land of yours is protected."

With that, she turned and cupped her hands around her mouth, prepared to give a great shout. Instead, however, her voice came out in a tiny gasp. She could not breathe for a spell, and her face turned blue. Then she let out all her air in a great, gusting shout.

"Children!"

Daylily looked up, hoping—desperately hoping—to see the children of the South Land, well and whole. Instead, she saw so many tiny, falling stars, flickering lights descending from the sky. Hundreds upon hundreds of them, of every color known to mortals and more colors besides that Daylily could not see and, therefore, perceived only as brilliant white. They fell from the heavens, streaking toward Nidawi, who put out her hands to them. And the Faerie queen herself grew up into the tall, stately, enormously comforting form of the most beautiful mother in the world. Tears streamed down her face as she reached for the lights, which whirled around her in such a glitter and swirl that she was all but obscured from Daylily's vision.

And Nidawi called out names through her tears: *"Wema! Taigu! Minjae! Erila!"*

Many more names fell from her lips, as though each one of the thousands of lights was known to her and beloved by her. And though they made no sound, their flickering beauty seemed to speak back to her, saying over and over, *Mother! Mother! Mother!*

Daylily watched this reunion silently, her breath coming slow and steady.

"Touching scene, yes? Nothing quite like a mother reunited with her little ones. Even if those little ones are scarcely better than ghosts."

Daylily looked at the cat by her elbow and was not surprised to hear a man's voice fall from his lips.

"I always like this bit at the end of an adventure," said Eanrin, giving one of his blistered paws another lick. "There'll be broken shards aplenty to pick up soon enough. But for the moment, all is hugs and kisses and happy reunions." He looked down at Foxbrush, and his whiskers drooped. All brightness fled his voice when he asked, "Is he . . . alive?"

Daylily nodded. She realized there were tears on her cheeks. "Only just, I think," she said. "Only just."

"Well, we'll see about that!" Suddenly the cat was gone, and in his place sat a man clad in red. Eanrin took Foxbrush's ruined hands from Daylily, tugging a little when she proved reluctant to relinquish them. "I can help. I can't fix it, but I can help," he said.

Daylily looked at him, then nodded and released her hold. Eanrin, wincing at the pain in his own hands, pulled Foxbrush from her lap and laid him out flat upon the ground. Starflowers, clustering fast, put out eager vines to touch Foxbrush's face, but Eanrin impatiently shooed them away. He took Foxbrush's hands in his and, closing his eyes, sang in a rich, mellifluous voice.

> *"Beyond the Final Water falling,*
> *The Songs of Spheres recalling,*
> *A promise given of a hero and a crown,*
> *Won't you return to me?"*

Daylily watched, her arms wrapped around her middle as though to somehow hold her spirit at bay. For she could feel the wolf straining, struggling . . . weeping.

What was this frightening feeling she had so long suppressed? In the time since she'd allowed herself to care for Lionheart and watched her heart break into a thousand pieces, she'd nearly forgotten this sensation.

But it wasn't the same. Not really. What she had felt for Lionheart had been fiery, desperate, dangerous, and even—she knew this to the very depths of her soul—destructive. It had left her ravening inside, ready to tear apart even her loved ones for the pain of it.

This was different. This was quieter, gentler—easy to mistake for something else, even. And yet, as she looked at those mangled hands—so twisted and raw, the blackened flesh creeping away from bare bones—she knew in her heart. She didn't know what to call it exactly, or perhaps she was simply afraid to name it.

One thing alone she knew for utter truth. This feeling was similar to her feelings for Lionheart in one aspect only: hopelessness.

Eanrin, his eyes still closed, his brow puckered with concentration, continued to sing. A faint wish that the power of that song might possibly mend all that was broken passed fleetingly through Daylily's mind. But it was not to be. Wounds closed up, skin knitted at tremendous speed as only magic can cause. But it knitted over two hands distorted beyond all use.

At last, Eanrin sat back with a sigh. He wiped his brow and looked up at Daylily, and there was no trace of merriment in his face. *"You gave your own two hands and saved your ancient lands,"* he said.

Daylily blinked. "Pardon?"

"Nothing." Eanrin shook his head. "I've done all I can. He's fallen into a deep trance, and I cannot wake him."

"Will he live?"

Eanrin managed a smile. It wasn't an especially cheerful smile, but it was sincere, and it made his face more beautiful than all immortality could offer. "Aye, he'll live, girl. Are you his Fiery Fair, then?"

Daylily did not breathe. If she breathed, she'd disgrace herself with weeping. A few tears escaping was one thing, but if she gave way to sobs, she did not know if she could recover herself. She reached out and took one of Foxbrush's crippled hands in her own, her thumb tracing up and down over the magically renewed flesh, feeling all the twists and unnatural breaks that would never truly heal.

At last, believing she had mastered herself, she said, "Actually, he was mine."

Then she laughed, a gulping, hiccupping sort of laugh, and there was no stopping the weeping then.

Eanrin, a little embarrassed at such a display, got to his feet and turned his back on the two of them, allowing Daylily some dignity. He stood with his hands clasped behind his back and looked out upon the world in this deepening dawn.

Nidawi was dancing once more, dancing with a trail of sparkling lights following her wherever she went, and Eanrin's immortal ears could just discern faint traces of laughter. The children of Nidawi had been lost in the Mound too long to retain their bodily form. But their spirits, their essences, the individuality of each and every one remained alive and thriving and full of bright light. Eanrin smiled a little despite the heaviness in his heart and the smarting of his blistered fingers and palms. Ultimately, what did physical bodies matter? It was the truth of the thing that counted.

There flashed through his mind the image of Sun Eagle disintegrating, turning to smoke. He cursed and clenched his fists, bowing his head.

When he looked up, he saw the Prince of Farthestshore approaching.

"My Lord!" he exclaimed, and his exclamation brought Nidawi to a pause in the midst of her dance. She turned about, saw the Prince, and cried, *"Lumil Eliasul!"* Then she ran to him, trailing the flickering lights of her people behind her and shedding her motherly form, becoming the child yet again as she fell at his feet. The Prince picked her up, and she wriggled in his arms like a puppy. "It came true! Your promise! My children are rescued!" she exclaimed and kept lunging at his face, trying to kiss him.

He laughed and restrained her gently, his wild, fey child. "Of course it came true. When will you learn to trust me as you should, Nidawi Everblooming?" His words were a chastisement, but his voice was kind, and she squirmed with pleasure at his attention.

Another child, a mortal with a crop of red hair, watched Nidawi from behind the Prince's back, her expression both a little jealous and a little frightened. She turned large black eyes up to Eanrin and offered him a shy smile.

Then she saw Foxbrush lying behind him, and a small "Oh!" escaped her lips. She let go her hold on the Prince's coattails and ran through the spreading starflowers, past Eanrin, and fell on her knees beside him, across from Daylily. "What's happened to him?" she demanded. In this magical place, her rough and ancient tongue shifted so that Daylily could understand it.

And Daylily, her face quite red, her eyes swollen, shook her head, allowing her thick hair to cover her for a moment. Then she said from behind this veil, "He saved me. He saved us all."

"Will he wake up?" Lark asked, her gaze fixing on Foxbrush's destroyed hands, unable to look away.

"I hope so," Daylily replied softly.

"You *hope* so?" Lark sat up straight, pushing the tangles of hair out of her face. "Why don't you stop hoping and *do* something? Don't you know anything?"

"Know what, child?" Daylily asked, confused and a little intimidated in the face of such passion. "What do you mean?"

"I'll show you!"

With that, Lark put out her small hands and grabbed Foxbrush by the ears, lifting his head off the ground. She planted a kiss right on his mouth—a childish, sweet, innocent kiss, but no less full of love for that.

Foxbrush blinked, once, twice, unseeing. The third blink, and his vision cleared. He looked up into Lark's small face so close to his own. She smiled and let go of his ears so that he hit his head hard on the ground. "Ouch!" he said even as Lark turned to Daylily.

"Kisses work every time," said the girl triumphantly. "And I *am* the Eldest's daughter."

16

ELDEST SIGHT-OF-DAY and her husband stood with their younger children around them at the top of the hill. From this vantage, they saw their daughter approaching from a great way off, and it took Redman's restraining hand on Sight-of-Day's arm to keep the Eldest from running to her. "No, no," he said gently. "Let her return to us."

So Lark raced up the hill, and Foxbrush followed more slowly behind. The child flung herself into her parents' arms, and her sisters and brother pulled at her clothes and hair, asking many questions, while Redman and the Eldest were silent in their joy.

Foxbrush hung back, hiding his hands behind his back, trying not to stare at that scene of happy reunion. But at length, Lark turned and pointed to him, saying, "Ma! Da! Foxbrush came to save me! He entered the darkness, and he found me!"

"Don't speak of that darkness, child," Sight-of-Day said quickly. Then she turned to Foxbrush, and her face, lined with many cares, was as lovely then as it must have been when she was a young and fresh maiden. "We owe you a great debt," she said.

Foxbrush shook his head. "No, I did nothing. Lark is more the hero than I."

"That isn't so," Lark protested, leaving the shelter of her mother's embrace and hurrying to Foxbrush's side. She reached out and took one of his hands, and the Eldest and Redman saw for the first time the ugly crippling. "He rescued me," Lark said, holding that hand in both of hers, her eyes shining up at his face. "He entered the darkness, and he saved me."

Redman looked down at Foxbrush's feet. And he saw the Path as he had always seen it. And he saw, if only briefly, where it had led.

He met Foxbrush's gaze and saw there suffering, but also hope and a budding, growing courage. Foxbrush, looking into that twisted, disfigured face, raised one of his twisted, disfigured hands in salute. He even smiled, though there was pain in the smile as he said, "It's all about blood and love, Redman."

"In the end," Redman agreed. "In the end. And it is good."

"It is good."

Lark looked from her father to her friend. Suddenly her glad smile fell and tears sprang to her eyes. "You are leaving?" she asked.

Foxbrush, startled, looked down at her. He realized, though he had not known it himself, that she was right. "I . . . I am," he said quietly. "I must."

"But—" Lark broke off, bowing her head and fighting back the tears. "I thought you'd stay with us awhile. I thought I'd grow up, and then we would marry, and I'd teach you how to use the blow darts, and . . ." She stopped and quickly rubbed her eyes. "No. You must go. I understand."

Then Foxbrush knelt and held her tight, long enough to seal the memory of that embrace in both their hearts. He stood at last, bowed to the Eldest, clasped hands with her husband, and gave each of the little redheaded children a solemn kiss upon the brow.

"Follow your Path with courage, Prince Foxbrush," said Redman.

Foxbrush turned and started down the hill, his feet for the last time treading that dirt roadway as the eastern sunlight cast his shadow long.

"Don't forget the wasps!" Lark called behind him.

"I won't," he assured her.

Another few paces, then:

"Clusters of six figs at least, and you need to replenish them!"

"I'll remember," said Foxbrush over his shoulder.

"Peel them at the stem, or you'll get juice on your fingers!"

Foxbrush stopped and looked one last time at the family above, the Eldest and her husband standing with their arms around the daughter who was crying silently.

"Don't worry, Lark," Foxbrush said, feeling tears of his own on his cheeks. "I'll never forget you."

Daylily could not decide whether she stood in the Wood Between or the Near World. The sheltering trees overhung her head, and they were so thick that even the morning sunlight could not pierce through. She looked out from them to the village and the hill, and she watched Foxbrush as he made his good-byes.

Behind her, she felt the presence of the Prince of Farthestshore. But she dared not turn to face him.

"I never forget a promise!" Nidawi was saying, perhaps a little defensively. She stood with her arms crossed, the lights of her children hovering around her head. "But . . . but I don't see why I have to do anything just *now*. A century or two won't hurt anything."

"You forget the effects of time on mortals, Nidawi," said the Prince, his voice stern. "You must honor your promise to the King of Here and There."

"Yes, but," Nidawi whined, her pretty eyes lavender with pleading, "I'm not even certain *who* the King of Here and There *is*! He"—with a thumb jerk toward Foxbrush, approaching from a distance—"is the one who'll wear the crown and all, but *that one*"—with another jerk at Daylily, standing quietly to one side—"claims to have actually killed my enemy. It's all most perplexing!"

The Prince of Farthestshore smiled, but his voice was no less stern when he said, "Yours is not to reason the wherefores and hithertos. Yours is to honor your promise. Your enemy is dead. Now protect this nation from further Faerie invasion."

Nidawi looked for a moment as though she would like to protest. Then, with a sigh, she sank into the form of a child and dashed off, disappearing into the jungle. But her voice carried back for some time, calling, *"Beasts! Beasts! Faeries of the Far! To me, to me, to me!"*

"Well, that should keep her occupied and, I do hope, out of trouble," said Poet Eanrin, who stood with his back against a tree, watching all with a bored expression that belied the beating of his heart.

The Prince of Farthestshore turned to him then. "My brother," he said, "it has been some time since last we spoke. Will you walk with me?"

If Eanrin had been in his cat's form, his ears would have flattened. But he shrugged coolly enough and fell into pace beside his Lord. They walked together into the shadows, disappearing behind green leaves and vines. Daylily found herself alone. She wondered what the Prince might say to the cat-man. She wondered if he would speak to her. She could not say whether she desired or dreaded such an exchange.

Foxbrush drew nearer, and Daylily pulled herself upright and began, out of habit, to school her face into the cold, calm mask she had worn for so long. But the wolf inside her shook her head, and she thought, *Whom do I deceive but myself?*

She would not play the fool to her own games. Not anymore.

So when Foxbrush approached the welcoming shade of the jungle, his ruined hands hidden behind his back, she smiled. The sight of her smile took him aback, and he stopped dead in his tracks, staring. His face, behind the beard, twisted into a variety of expressions, none of which Daylily could read, none of them an answering smile.

Suddenly the Prince of Farthestshore stood before them, and they forgot each other and their fears in the far greater fear of his presence. For he was unlike anything they knew, and they could not, with mortal eyes, quite perceive him, not in a bodily form. But he stood there, more real than real, and they felt the brightness of his gaze upon them.

"Come," he said, and where he went, they followed.

They walked through Southlands.

They skimmed over jungles, lakes, rivers.

They passed over fields and towns and villages.

They flew like birds. They swam like fish. They ran like deer through the meadows.

And still they walked behind the Lumil Eliasul, not daring to look at each other for fear of losing sight of him.

And then he stopped, and they stopped as well. They saw him extend his arm, pointing, and they could not have resisted turning their gazes where he indicated even had they wished to.

"See now, King of Here and There," said the Lumil Eliasul, and he spoke to both of them in that moment. "See now what I have purposed for you."

They saw orchards. Vast, sprawling, ripening orchards, heavy with golden fruit, alive with birds and bees and . . . and yes, with wasps. These grew in a thriving land, a land that was not Southlands as either of them knew it, but which was Southlands at its heart, at the core of the nation's spirit. And both of them, man and woman, felt in their own hearts the lurch of love, of kingship.

"Do you see it?" asked the Prince.

They nodded, unable to speak.

"Will you remember it?"

Daylily nodded. Foxbrush said, "I hope so."

The Lumil Eliasul turned to Foxbrush then and took his ruined hands. He held them tight, and Foxbrush felt strength entering his body, a strength beyond any he had known.

"Now and Then. Here and There," said the Prince of Farthestshore, and he spoke the words like a name. "This is the truth, and you will hear it, and I will cause you to remember. If you were always to see before you the future I have shown you here, the way would be too easy . . . too easy to ignore, to forego, for why would you need to follow it? And that would be the greatest disaster ever to befall Southlands.

"Instead, I will send you back to that place and time where the air is too thin for you to see my distant purpose. And you will have to walk the Path a single step at a time, trusting that it will lead you safe at last. But

I will send you the memory of my promise, and when the road becomes too difficult, you will think on it and you will keep walking, even as I have called you.

"This is the truth, Foxbrush Fourclaw-son: The strength of your hands is the strength of mine."

Then the Lumil Eliasul let go of Foxbrush and stepped back. Daylily, watching all with hungry eyes, saw that the twisted fingers and roughly healed flesh were unaltered. But she saw something else as well.

Where Foxbrush's shadow fell, cast by the light shining from those vast, unending orchards, his hands were whole. Though mere shadows, they spoke the truth in strong fingers and sinews, well-knit muscles over delicate bones. And Daylily knew that this was the secret of this man she had known most of her life, but never truly known: He was made of more than her eyes could see. He was made of stronger, firmer stuff.

"Shadow Hand of Here and There," she whispered.

Somewhere, from a great distance, a voice called. It was a lonely voice, completely lonely as only the wind can be, but without sorrow. It called with a dogged stubbornness that both Daylily and Foxbrush had heard before.

Foxbrush! Where are you, Foxbrush? I am coming for you!

The Prince of Farthestshore smiled. Then he called in answer: "This way!"

The sylph, who had so long searched (without knowing how long, for time did not matter to its breezy consciousness), heard the voice of the Lumil Eliasul and let out a gleeful screech. Then it whipped and blew to this place that was neither in the Near World nor in the Far, nor even in the Wood Between. Summoned by its Lord, it skirted all boundaries of all worlds and came to this place of vision.

"Aad-o Ilmun!"

"And I thank you for it," the Prince replied with a smile as the sylph, its form only just discernible to Daylily and Foxbrush, cavorted before him. "Are you ready to fulfill your promise to Lionheart?"

"I am," the sylph replied, eagerly dashing to blow amongst the treetops of the orchard, only to gust back in an instant to where the two mortals stood waiting. "I am ready! Are you Foxbrush?" it asked, turning to Daylily.

"No!" said she hastily, and the sylph addressed itself to Foxbrush then, reaching out to snatch him up.

"Come!" it cried. "Back to your own land! Back to your own time-bound world!"

"Wait!" Foxbrush cried, for the sylph would have carried him off at once if it could. He turned to Daylily, and he found it suddenly difficult to breathe. She was so wild, so disheveled, and so strong, stronger than he had ever seen her. But she was weak as well, he thought, and there was a vulnerability in her eyes that he had not seen— No! This was not true. He had seen something like it once before.

In the look she had given Lionheart the night he left her standing on the dance floor.

"Daylily," he said, "I won't marry you."

She closed her eyes, though only for a moment. Then she looked at him and said, "I know."

"That is," he hastened on, "I won't marry you unless . . . unless it is what *you* want. Not what your father wants, or the barons or Southlands or politics or . . . or any of those fine excuses they've fed you all these years. I won't marry you for those reasons, because I love you too well."

He put out his hand, and in that light she saw it as whole, just as the shadow it cast. "Come back with me. Help me save Southlands in whatever capacity you see fit. As my queen or as my friend. Either way I . . . I don't think I can do it without you."

She caught his hand in both of hers. She said only, "Foxbrush!"

Sometimes there is no need to say more. Especially when sylphs are catching you up and hurtling you across time and space and worlds. Sometimes the clasp of hands—the one strong, the other weak—is more than enough. For through the clasping of hands, the pulse of blood may be felt; and the equal pulse of love and the understanding of love without words.

17

Meanwhile, Lionheart faced his imminent hanging.

Twelve hours or so of living under the looming threat of death made the certainty of death no more palatable now. His heart beat a frantic pace in his throat as guardsmen hauled him roughly down the stone stairs of North Tower. He could hear shouts going up throughout the House as word of the baron's rescue traveled.

"Lionheart! Lionheart, I'm sorry!" Felix gasped from behind. Lionheart tried to look around, to catch the young prince's eye. But he was struck in the jaw and told to face forward, and he did not have the strength to disobey.

So, in the wake of the baron's wrath, they marched at double-time down the stairs and through the Great Hall. The baron did not pause and waved away all those who flocked to him full of questions and concerns. He led them all out to the courtyard alight with torches that cast an eerie glow in that predawn gloom. A glow that made the scaffold standing in the middle of the yard—right where the old Starflower fountain had been before the Dragon destroyed it—look like some sort of otherworldly creature. Perhaps a dragon itself.

"Iubdan's beard!" Felix exclaimed when he saw it, yanking against the strong arms of the guards who held him. "Are you all out of your minds?"

Sir Palinurus and other lords of Parumvir staggered down from their chambers and, nearly as frantic as the prince himself at the sight of Felix so near the scaffold, fell upon the baron like so many vultures, pecking him with protests. But guards with fierce and frightened faces pushed them back, using the butt end of their lances roughly enough to show willingness for more violence if necessary.

The baron stood ringed in torchlight, surrounded by his guards, and his face was unreadable. It was not difficult to believe that he could and would order the death of his strongest ally's crown prince.

Instead, however, he turned to Baron Blackrock, who stood near him. "Have the Baroness of Middlecrescent brought to me," he said softly. Baron Blackrock, trembling, hastened to obey, only to be caught by Middlecrescent's restraining hand. "In chains," Middlecrescent added, more softly still.

"Yes, my liege," Blackrock gasped, though Middlecrescent was not yet his sovereign by law. He hastened away, summoning his men to follow.

The baron turned to Lionheart and Felix, surveying them with his cold eyes. Then he said, "Where is the girl? My wife's lady who aided in this little venture?"

"Here, my lord!" cried Dovetree, hastening forward and curtsying deeply before the baron. She smiled most winningly and was very pretty in that place of execution. "At your service."

"My service?" echoed the baron, eyeing her. His thin lids closed partially over the dark bulbs of his eyes but could not hide the light reflected there. "I do not keep traitors in my service."

"What?" Dovetree gasped but had no time to say more before guards, at a motion from the baron, fell upon her and bound her, screaming, alongside Lionheart and Felix. "But, my lord! I saw to your rescue! If not for me, you'd still be—"

"Traitors will be granted no voice," said the baron, adjusting the cloak he wore over his naked torso, fastening the buckles at the shoulder. "Gag her."

Felix felt sick as he watched rough-handed men stuff rags into the girl's mouth and tie a gag in place, muting Dovetree's continued screams. Her eyes kept rolling toward the scaffold, and suddenly her knees buckled and she lay all but fainted upon the courtyard stones. Felix wished he could comfort her and had to remind himself that she had tricked them, had certainly brought about Lionheart's death and, quite possibly, his own (given the look in the baron's eye).

Lionheart stood with his head down, staring at the stones beneath his feet. Looking at him, Felix thought how strange it was to be here in this faraway foreign court beside the jester-prince, waiting to be hanged. It was perhaps stranger than their meeting in the Village of Dragons.

"Leonard," Felix whispered, and Lionheart glanced at him through the thick tangle of hair falling over his forehead. "Leonard, forgive me. I didn't know."

"Of course you didn't, Prince Felix," said Lionheart. But he couldn't find more words to say, so he stared again at his feet.

Where was the Path? He had been promised a Path! But he saw only shadows and torchlight and the ominous scaffold, so near. Was this it, then? Was this the one and only quest that he, Childe Lionheart of Farthestshore, would face? *Make peace with your father and . . . die.*

But if so, what then? Had he a right to complain? He, who had plunged into the darkness of the Final Water and stared down the flaming throat of the Dragon . . . he who had been renewed, restored, forgiven.

"Very well," he whispered to the one he hoped was listening, though he saw no sign of his presence. "Very well, my Lord. If this is what you would have of me, let me die with honor."

Let me die for the sake of the cousin I have hated. And in my death, let me show love.

And that was the moment—with the pound of his blood in his temples and the rush of terror he could not suppress roiling in his gut—the moment he knew the impossible had happened. He loved Foxbrush. He loved his cousin, and he would die for him. Foolish Foxbrush. Weak Foxbrush. Chosen heir of the Eldest, baffled fool.

But none of that mattered, not now. Lionheart would die for him, and it would be a good death.

So Childe Lionheart stood straighter, throwing his head back and unbowing his shoulders. The guards restraining him shifted their grips and watched him uneasily, but he took no notice of them. He looked at Felix, and his eye was bright and his voice did not tremble when he said, "All will be well. Wait. Just wait . . ."

At that moment, the voice of the baroness was heard ringing across the courtyard. "I do not see why you should handle me so roughly! I can walk quite well on my own— *Darling!*"

The baroness wafted across the courtyard in a flutter of butterfly frills. She flew to her husband, her face full of smiles, exclaiming, "Darling, how glad I am to see you well and whole! Have you quite changed your mind, then?"

Her guards caught her; otherwise she might have thrown her arms around the baron's neck. He looked as though he had swallowed snake spit, his eyes bugging out from his face. But he spoke as quietly as ever, more quietly perhaps.

"How dare you speak to me thusly, woman?"

"But, darling," said the baroness, as yet unaware of her peril, looking perplexed at the shackles on her wrists and the hands clamped like more shackles on her arms, "what do you mean?"

"You betrayed me," said he. The gray of dawn streaking the sky fell upon the baron's face and made him look so very old. Beneath the shielding cloak, he was a withered, wrinkled, gray man. And his voice was so low that only the baroness and those two who held her heard what he said (and those two turned their faces away and hoped to forget, as they valued their lives!).

"You betrayed me. The one person in all this world whom I have trusted completely."

At those words, the baroness lost all trace of the silliness that so regularly painted her face more thickly than cosmetics. With deep sincerity she gazed up at her husband and tried to put out a hand to him, forgetting that she was restrained.

"My love," she said, "I could never betray you. You betray yourself, but I will only ever bring you back."

But the baron could not bear her words or her face. He turned away, and those standing nearest caught a glimpse of agony such as they had never seen in the eyes of any lord of Middlecrescent. When he spoke again, however, his voice was firm enough to say:

"Hang the traitors."

Dovetree tried to scream, nearly choking on the rags in her mouth. The baroness turned and saw her lady-in-waiting being carried up the scaffold steps. "Oh!" she cried, struggling against her guards. "Let poor Dovetree go! She's done nothing to merit this!"

"She betrayed you, my dear," said the baron with deep bitterness. "Let traitors hang with traitors."

Sir Palinurus shouted, and all the men of Parumvir raised an angry, threatening cry. The guards holding Prince Felix dared not move, for they saw the promise of war on those northern faces, a war they knew Southlands could not hope to win. But the dread of their master was great, and they stood frozen, unwilling to free the prince without the baron's word, unwilling to drag him up that rickety stair and, with every step, drag their nation closer to destruction.

Felix watched Lionheart being pulled away, behind the collapsing Dovetree and before the confused baroness, who kept saying, "My dear girl, it will be all right! Lumé, child, don't carry on so! You'll be all out of breath!"

The baroness had strength in her. Just when one might most expect her to give way to hysterics, she seemed calm and motherly, smiling even at Lionheart as they were arranged beneath the nooses. Perhaps this was but the form of her hysterics.

Lionheart closed his eyes. As his hands were bound before him and he breathed the stench of the guardsman's breath upon his face and heard the creaking of the scaffold floorboards, he pictured in his mind, as he had promised himself he would, a face. A sweet face with enormous silver eyes, otherworldly, strange, and lovely, crowned in roses.

"Beyond the Final Water falling," he whispered as the noose was placed around his neck.

And Felix, standing below, watching all, wished desperately that he could look away. But he couldn't. He stood staring, and he found himself saying, though he couldn't hear his own voice in the din of the crowd, "Aethelbald, please . . ."

A wolfish snarl exploded over the heads of all those gathered.

An immediate hush fell upon the courtyard as everyone gasped and whirled in place, seeking the source of that horrible sound.

Another snarl, and now Felix saw the crowd parting, men and women falling back upon one another, dropping torches that sputtered out on the stones. This did not matter, for daylight grew keener by the moment. Indeed, it seemed as though the sun burst over the edge of the world quite suddenly, striking the eyes of all those present so that they believed they saw an enormous red wolf in their midst.

Then Daylily's voice rang out against the stone.

"Unhand my mother at once, you dogs!"

No one moved to stop the wild, red-haired maid who sprang across the courtyard, past the guards, and up the scaffold stairs. She took a knife from the hand of the guard standing beside her mother, and in a single stroke (though the fibers were thick and tough with age), she cut through the rope. It fell like a dead snake upon the floor.

Then she turned and did the same to Lionheart's and Dovetree's nooses. And no one moved or spoke, for they all believed they must be dreaming. This wild creature in savage garments made of skins standing protectively before the three prisoners, her face so beautiful and so fierce, could not possibly be Lady Daylily! They must all be dreaming.

Even the baron, standing with his mouth agape, could not find the will to speak a command. His daughter turned on him with the ferocity of a she-wolf, and for the first time in his life, the baron was truly afraid.

Another voice, much gentler than hers, spoke then. Though it was mild, it drew every eye away from the wild apparition of Daylily on the scaffold.

"I have returned."

Shadow Hand of Here and There. They all knew him at a glance. His untamed black beard, his strange, ancient clothes; the sight, the smell, the sound of old, old days that emanated from his face and every movement of his body as he made his way to the center of the courtyard, walking in a path of new sunlight. His frame was perhaps narrower than they might have expected, but his bearing was upright and his stride commanding, as befit any hero of old.

And while his hands hung at his sides in crippled ruin, the shadow cast by the sun showed strong hands clenched into fists.

He walked up onto the scaffold as a king might ascend the dais of his throne, and he took his place beside Daylily, with Lionheart at his back. He looked out upon those gathered, upon bound Prince Felix, the gathered barons. Last of all, he fixed his gaze upon the Baron of Middlecrescent.

Middlecrescent began to tremble.

"Do you know who I am?" the figure of legends asked.

The baron nodded.

"Speak it, then."

But Middlecrescent could not find his tongue. So the bearded man raised one of his ruined hands and declared to all assembed there, "I am Foxbrush, chosen heir of my uncle Hawkeye, and rightful ruler of Southlands. Is there any who would contest me?"

Many eyes turned to Middlecrescent, many jaws clenched, many breaths caught. All waited for what they knew must come.

But the baron bowed his head. And he said nothing.

Suddenly Baron Blackrock, who had long resented and hated Middlecrescent for reasons best left unearthed, stepped forward and cried, "Middlecrescent tried to seize the throne before the Council had even declared you dead!"

With that cry, the other barons joined in, and soon the courtyard was a storm of noise. Felix, standing with the Southlander guards, felt the tension go through them; yet another fear of impending war, this time of a more insidious nature: civil war.

But a second wolfish snarl cut through the chaos and brought all the barons to silence, looking over their shoulders for an enemy they could not see. Daylily stepped back again and nodded to Foxbrush.

Foxbrush said, "Bring Middlecrescent before me."

The guards holding Felix—who were no fools and could sense which way the wind was blowing—left him standing as they joined their brothers surrounding the unresisting baron. They did not need to force him, for he went before their prodding as quietly as a panther, his eyes smoldering but hooded. He looked up at Foxbrush and then went down on one knee before him.

The act was as contemptuous as though he'd spat in the prince's face. Even backed by Daylily, Foxbrush flinched at the sight and for a moment forgot who he was. Then Daylily touched his arm, and he pulled himself together.

"What defense do you make before these accusations?" he asked.

"None," said the baron.

"Do you deny that you attempted through trickery and force to take the throne before the due course of law could be decided?"

"I do not deny it."

"Do you deny that you attempted to execute my cousin Prince Lionheart"—here again the crowd gasped, for Lionheart had not been named 'prince' in public for many a long month—"without fair trial?"

"I deny nothing," said the baron.

"And this good woman, the baroness, your wife. And . . . and . . ." Foxbrush blinked and looked around at Dovetree, who was biting down so hard on the cotton in her mouth that her jaw might actually break. "I'm sorry," he said, "I have no idea who you are."

"Leave her for now," said Daylily.

Foxbrush shrugged and addressed the baron once more. "Your sins are many, and your guilt is great. By your own admission, you condemn yourself before the barons of Southlands, all my gathered court, and the ambassadors of our allies."

The baron looked up into the face of a king. He hated it. Oh, how he hated to admit it, even in the very depths of his heart. But it was a king he faced, not Foxbrush, the malleable boy he had intended for his daughter's husband. A king in power, and a king with the support of the nation behind him.

"What do you suggest I do with you, baron?" Foxbrush asked.

"I suggest you hang me," said the baron.

"*No!*"

Everyone started at the suddenness of the cry. The baroness, liberated from the noose but still chained at the wrists, scrambled down the scaffold stairs, nearly tripping over her frilly skirts. "No, no, no, don't say such a thing!" she scolded her husband, wringing her hands in his face. "No one should hang; you know that, my love! Daylily is back, and dear, dear Foxbrush, just as I always told you! And he will be Eldest as is right, and no one—*no one*—should hang!"

With those words, she flung her still-bound arms around the neck of the man who would, but a few minutes before, have seen her dead, and she clung there like a limpet.

For a moment Foxbrush stood baffled by this turn of events. Recovering himself, he said, "You have a single advocate, then, Baron Middlecrescent. Is there another who would speak for you?"

Daylily felt the words reach out and touch her like the coldness of a knife. She was aware of Lionheart's gaze upon the side of her face, and she knew that he too was transported suddenly back to a cold winter's day, when an innocent girl with the face of a goblin was brought to trial before an angry mob. *"Is there no one who can speak for you?"* Lionheart had asked her then.

The girl had looked right into Daylily's eyes. Daylily had seen the pleading, the desperate hope. And yet she had said nothing.

All of this washed over her, and she reached out to support herself on the scaffolding. Then, as the echoes of Foxbrush's question faded into silence, she said, "I will speak for my father."

All eyes fixed upon her, including the baron's. He watched this unknown creature with fearful eyes. For this was not the girl he had crafted and formed so carefully over the years to fulfill his intended purpose. This wild thing, this wolfish beauty, was something he dared not name. She could not be his daughter. But she looked down upon him, and in those wolf's eyes he saw, of all strange and horrible things, kindness.

"I will speak for him, my lord," she said to Foxbrush. "I plead for his life not on his own merit, for indeed, he deserves nothing from you. But I ask you for undeserved grace in light of the grace you have so recently shown me."

Lionheart thought he must have died in truth, hanged some moments ago by the neck. For only in some other world beyond the veil of mortal life would he ever have expected to hear such compassion from the mouth of Lady Daylily!

But Foxbrush nodded solemnly. "Very well," he said. "I will spare his life. But I hereby strip him of all his property and riches, bestowing them upon his rightful heir, Lady Daylily of Middlecrescent. And the former baron will be escorted to the borders of Southlands within a month's time, never to return. Should he ever be discovered within my realm again, he will be thrown once more upon the mercy of my court."

So the baron was hauled to his feet, still with the baroness clinging to him, weeping gently in relief for his life. He was escorted out of the yard, with all the eyes of his friends-turned-enemies watching. He cast a last glance back over his shoulder at his daughter and the man who would be her husband.

And he thought, *It was a good plan. It might have worked.*

Then he was hurried into the House under armed guard, and the door shut behind him so that he did not hear the murmur that erupted in the crowd at his going. The murmur soon turned to something like a cheer. Then someone shouted out in a clear, golden voice:

"All hail Eldest Foxbrush!"

"Hail!" responded the crowd in spontaneous agreement. Hands rose in high salute, and the cheer burst out in good earnest now, as though a coronation had just been held, not a sentencing. Foxbrush, standing on the scaffold with Daylily on one hand and Lionheart on the other (poor Dovetree collapsed to her knees and shivering behind), gazed out into the throng of those who were now his people. And he thought he saw the whole of Southlands, both ancient and future: the wild jungles of yesterday, the shining cities and ripening orchards of tomorrow. He loved it with the love of pounding blood. For he was king, both now and then. He was the King of Here and There.

A bright face caught his eye. A face he almost recognized but couldn't quite see behind the double eye patches it wore. A brilliant smile and a wave, and the face disappeared into the throng before Foxbrush could even say for certain that he had seen it.

None of this mattered, though. For suddenly Daylily took him by his ruined hands, turned him to her, and pierced him to the quick with the intensity of her eyes. To his relief, she closed them and leaned in to kiss him. He'd never kissed anyone before. But then, he'd never saved lives or passed sentences or ruled nations before either. He could learn as he went, and somehow he didn't think the learning would be all that bad.

The cheers of the crowd grew, and Felix whooped and hollered as loudly as the rest of them, raising his sprained wrist above his head. For this is how heroic tales should end. Everyone knows it, poets and soldiers, peasants and nobles, ladies and gentlemen and children and grandparents. Everyone knows this: The end of all stories of love and blood should be a kiss. The kiss of true love found and finally recognized.

Lionheart, standing by, grinned at the dazed expression on his cousin's face and even clapped Foxbrush on the shoulder. He could not quite bring himself to look at Daylily, but that didn't matter, for neither did she look at him. She smiled as she had never smiled before, and the smile itself turned into a laugh.

She reached up and patted Foxbrush's cheek. "You're going to have to shave this beard," she said.

"Iubdan's razor, yes!" Foxbrush replied.

EPILOGUE

IMRALDERA STOOD in the doorway of the Haven. Around this space of existence, twilight was falling, turning the brown and green shadows of the trees to violet and dark blue. She gazed far into the surrounding forest, into the deeper reaches of her watch. Searching the Paths for any sign of . . .

"Ouch."

She looked down, frowning at the white lion cub that had wrapped itself around her ankle and begun to chew. "Stop it now," she said firmly, sliding her foot up from between its grasping paws. It blinked cross-eyed up at her, unable to understand why anyone wouldn't want to be nibbled on. It opened its mouth and offered a roar that was perhaps less impressive than it imagined.

Imraldera shook her head but bent and picked it up, allowing it to gnaw on the end of her head scarf as she turned her attention once more to the forest. Deep amid its shadows she could see lights approaching: faint, many-colored lights like fireflies but constant in their glow. She believed they were coming to the Haven.

"Raaaaawr," said the lion cub, putting a velveted paw on her nose. A subtle threat, implying, *I could use my claws if I wanted to.* Imraldera pushed the paw away and shifted the cub so that it lay like a baby in her arms, its little paws curled over its chest. It blinked sweetly and fell asleep with a suddenness that might as well be magic.

The lights drew nearer in such number that, small though they were, they set the Wood to glowing as they neared. Soon Imraldera's ear caught the faint sound of a song being sung by a pair of merry voices. One voice she did not recognize, though she thought it belonged to a child.

The other she knew as well as her own.

> *"For she is a darling, dreadful gel,*
> *Her face so fierce, your heart will quell!*
> *I'll have no other, have no other*
> *To dance with me but her!*
>
> *"Oh, she is a darling, dreadful gel,*
> *If you can't love her, run pell-mell!*
> *She glanced my way, and hard I fell.*
> *I'll dance with none but her!"*

Soon, lit by the fey glow of Nidawi's rescued people, Nidawi herself came into view of the Haven, a dancing, laughing Faerie child, her elbow linked with Eanrin's as they sang at the tops of their voices.

Despite the merriment of their song, Imraldera felt her heart lurch at the sight, and she hugged the lion cub more tightly to her. It awoke and shook its head, then turned, ears pricked toward the sound of those approaching. When it scrambled, Imraldera put it down and watched it bound into the clearing beyond the Haven door. There it sat, tail twitching, as Nidawi and Eanrin stepped through the greenery.

Nidawi stopped her singing at once, her eyes fixing upon the cub with a concentration that bordered on ferocious. Her nose twitched, and the vines twining her hair twisted suddenly with alertness.

The cub gazed up at her, its head a little to one side. "Raawwr," it said, which was probably meant to be intimidating.

"Raawwr!" Nidawi replied, dropping to all fours. She crawled to the cub, and the two of them touched noses, and all the Faerie lights brightened and whispered together, pointing at the scene below.

Imraldera stepped over the threshold, her arms crossed defensively. But her voice was sweet and perhaps a little humble when she said, "I thought you two might like each other." She avoided Eanrin's eye but was all too aware when he drew nearer to her. She smiled at Nidawi, who tentatively touched the top of the cub's head with one finger. "You seem as though . . . as though you might find much in common."

Nidawi sat up. She did not smile or laugh or show any signs of pleasure. Her face, though clothed in a child's features, was solemn and quiet, and her eyes looked dark for a moment. Indeed, Imraldera felt her heart stop, and she braced herself for she knew not what.

Then Nidawi said, "I shall call him Lion."

Imraldera nodded and found she was able to breathe again. "It is an apt name," she said.

"Rawwr," said the cub before pouncing on Nidawi's foot. Nidawi cuffed him and sent him rolling, which pleased him mightily, for he pounced on her hand next and bit it, hard. Anyone other than the Everblooming would have screamed, but Nidawi giggled and picked up the cub. While he dangled in her arms, chewing affectionately on anything he could reach, she turned to Imraldera.

"Tadew is gone," she said. As she spoke, she lengthened, transforming into a strong woman with a beautiful, sad face. "My demesne was destroyed by the Parasite."

"I am sorry," said Imraldera, her heart in her words. "I am so sorry for your loss."

"Loss?" Nidawi shrugged, then looked up at the lights surrounding her. They, as though beckoned, flooded down and lit upon her and on the lion cub, who tried to eat them but could catch none. Their colors turned the whole of the evening into a bath of rainbow light, and Nidawi was more beautiful than ever in that glow.

"My children are safe," she said. "They have lost their bodies, but they have not lost themselves!"

The lights, unable to find places to settle upon Nidawi, turned then to Imraldera. They rushed to her, and she felt the beat of wings, the touch of many tiny hands. And she could hear voices now as they drew closer.

We live! We live! The Lights Above sing of our lives, and we live!

"Cren Cru is dead," said Nidawi. "And I, in gratitude to the King of Here and There, have seen to it that no more Faerie beasts will enter the South Land from the gorges below. I and my people have built great, strong bridges as locks, and I have placed wards upon them that will prevent all . . . save perhaps dragons." She shrugged. "But what can be done about dragons?"

"You are very kind to my people," said Imraldera. "I thank you for this service on their behalf."

"Will you then be kind to mine?" Nidawi, shifting the cub into one arm, reached out the other, cupping her hand so that more of her children could sit upon her palm. Then she extended it and all those little lights to Imraldera, as though offering a gift. "Tadew is gone. They have nowhere to go. I cannot take them with me through the Wood, for they will not be safe. I would lose some, and others would die, and others would fall sick, and . . ." Her brow puckered with worry, which did nothing to mar her beauty.

Imraldera put out both her hands. "I will keep your children here," she said. "They will be safe in the Haven with me, and they may help me in my work if they wish."

Nidawi smiled and poured the lights from her hand into Imraldera's. As she did so, the other lights around her rushed to Imraldera as well, whirling around her, pulling her hair and her garments teasingly, laughing and kissing her with the tiniest of kisses all over her face and neck. Then they streamed past her through the door, into the Haven. And soon all the windows were bright with colored glows as they explored up and down this enormous new home that was as a kingdom to them.

The Haven would be a lonely spot no more.

A few lights remained hovering around Imraldera's shoulders and the top of her head. Nidawi, pleased, smiled at them and melted into the form of a girl just on the brink of womanhood, neither child nor adult but something in between. The cub climbed up onto her shoulder and chewed on her ear.

"I will leave you, then," Nidawi said. "I have many Paths to explore, and Lion here will keep me company. When I have found a home for my children, I will return."

"We will wait for you," said Imraldera. Then, though she hesitated, she reached out and stroked the lion cub's ears, which were so soft as to be irresistible, even though he always tried to bite in response. A fitting companion for the Everblooming, Imraldera thought, backing away again.

So Nidawi left, the cub gamboling at her heels. And when she went, the colored glows of her people winked out, one by one. But Imraldera could still feel them and hear them around her, as bright and lively as ever. They simply could not shine as they might wish to without their mother's presence.

Imraldera stood awhile watching the place where Nidawi had disappeared into the Wood. She tried to think of something to say, and she could feel Eanrin watching her, could sense him also trying and failing to come up with a fitting word.

"That was kind of you," she said at last.

He didn't respond. When she dared glance his way, she found him idly pushing at the cuticles of his nails, like a cat grooming his paws. His face was as placid as a calm sea and equally unfathomable.

"To bring Nidawi here, I mean," Imraldera continued. "I am sure she was grateful in her own way. And I was glad for the opportunity to introduce her to the cub."

Eanrin nodded and, without looking at her, said, "Once in a while a kindlier instinct takes over and, despite all my best efforts, has its way with me."

"Oh, come!" said Imraldera, trying to laugh, to make things natural. But a laugh wasn't natural, and she knew it. Rather, she should have a curt reprimand for him, some sarcastic remark and a scowl.

But nothing was natural now. She wondered if anything ever would be again.

"You're kinder than you like to let on, Eanrin. Why don't you come inside and tell me what has happened, for I—"

"I couldn't save him, Imraldera."

She felt her heart sinking down to her stomach, to her feet. "I . . . I did not expect you to," she whispered. Then she watched as Eanrin turned his hands over, and she saw the blisters lining each finger, ringing his palms. Faeries heal far more quickly than mortals can dream, and Imraldera knew that these wounds should long since have vanished. Yet Eanrin held on to them and allowed them to continue giving him pain.

She reached out and tried to take his hands, but he drew them back, tucking them under his arms, his shoulders hunched and his head down.

"I tried to save him," he said. "I held on to that dragon-eaten stone of his, and I think I might have done it in the end. But . . . but I let go, Imraldera, and Sun Eagle is gone. Vanished in smoke, I don't know if ever to return."

How long ago was it now since she'd first wept for the loss of Sun Eagle? It was so difficult to keep track of time. Imraldera put a hand to her heart and felt the swell of sorrow there, and she knew she would weep again. But not now. Not here.

"Eanrin," she said gently, and there were no tears in her voice, "you did what you could for him. For all of them. Please come inside. Rest awhile, and then tell me what you must."

"What I must tell you," said Eanrin, lifting his head but still refusing to meet her gaze, looking instead out to the Wood in the direction Nidawi had gone, "are his final words. He asked me to tell you that you are always with him." He drew a deep breath and let it out slowly. "Now that is done."

"Thank you," Imraldera said. Once more she reached out to him, touching his arm. But her touch seemed to shoot fire through him, and he stepped away, out of her reach, into the growing darkness in the clearing.

"I am leaving," he said.

"What?"

"Yes. I spoke to the Lumil Eliasul, and he told me that I should go, even as I asked. I am leaving the Haven at once. But don't worry," he hurried on before she could make a protest. "You won't be alone here. The Prince has promised to send more knights, and others as well, squires in need of training. You won't be alone to keep this watch. Indeed, you'll have more help than ever, and better help than I can give."

Imraldera stared at him, and the sorrow in her heart flared up into something else. Frustration, perhaps. Or anger. Something she could not quite name, but it was enough to bring the blood boiling in her ears and her voice snapping a little harshly from her mouth.

"And does my opinion mean nothing in all this? What if I don't want you to go? What if I don't want other comrades in this watch? What if—"

She stopped then, for he had given her a look, and in that look she saw a painful hope. One she could not answer. So she stopped and closed her mouth, turning away.

"No, you are right," she said at last. "It is probably for the best."

The silence grew so deep around them that she could even hear the voices of Nidawi's children calling to one another inside, though they could make a sound no louder than a mosquito's hum. She began to wonder if perhaps the cat-man had slinked away into the shadows without another word, and she could not bear to look and see.

Then he stepped up beside her and took her hand. He pressed something into it, a little scrap of a parchment, and closed her fingers around it. He held on a moment longer than necessary.

"That's for you to copy," he said. "Just a little rhyme or two. Copy it out and hold on to it for a while. If you should meet a fellow named Lionheart—a mortal man, a prince—give it to him and tell him it's for his cousin, Foxbrush."

She felt then the brush of his lips on her forehead.

"Good-bye, Imraldera," said Eanrin.

For some long minutes, Imraldera did not enter the Haven but stood in the surrounding evening, holding herself and thinking nothing, for her head and her heart were too tired for thought. Some of Nidawi's children came to find her and tugged at her hair and clothes, urging her to come inside. She allowed herself to be led down the passage to the library and, at last, to her desk. It sat piled high with neglected work, and someone—one of her new, eager helpers—had lit a candle and trimmed her quill.

For a moment, she hesitated. Then she opened up the page Eanrin had given her and read the badly scribbled lines. She frowned and read them again, then a third time. "What dragon-eaten nonsense," she muttered at last and felt better for it.

Taking up her quill and drawing an empty page before her, she began to write, copying in her neat script of Faerie letters these lines:

Oh, Shadow Hand of Here and There,
Follow where you will
Your fickle, fleeing, Fiery Fair
O'er woodlands, under hill.

She'll not be found, save by the stone,
The stern and shining Bronze,
Where crooked stands the Mound alone,
Thorn clad and sharp with awns.

How pleasant are the Faerie folk
Who dwell beyond your time.
How pleasant are your aged kinfolk
Of olden, swelt'ry clime.

But dark the tithe they pay, my son,
To safely dwell beneath that sun!

Oh, Shadow Hand of Here and There,
Hardened ground you till,
And still your fickle, Fiery Fair
Flees o'er woodland hill.

The wolf will howl, the eagle scream.
The wild white lies dead.
Tears of Everblooming stream
As she bows her mourning head.

Bargain now with Faerie queen,
The Everblooming child,
If safe you would your kingdom glean
From out the feral wild.

Oh, Shadow Hand of Here and There,
Heal now the ills
Of your weak and weary Fair,
Lost among the hills.

You would give your own two hands
To save your ancient, sorrowing lands.

Summon now the Faerie beasts
Beneath the spreading tree
Lead them where the darkness feasts,
And this is what you'll see:

Just at the mirk and midnight hour
Of thirteen nights but one,
The warriors bear their bronzen stones
Where crooked stands the Mound alone.
There you will win your Fiery One
Or see her then devoured.

First let pass the warrior red,
Then let pass the brown.
But when you see her flaming head,
Then throw your weapon down.

No lance, no spear will save the night,
Nor bloodshed on the ground.
This alone will be your fight:
To hold your lady, hold her tight
When once again she's found.

You would give your heart and life
For she who'll be your wife.

Her heart will turn within your hold
To a red-hot brand of iron,
To melting, molten, lava gold,
And how your hands will burn!

But hold her fast and hold her tight
And yet you'll win this terror night.

In broken sleep upon the ground
The dear one lost now lies.
Yet a kiss in faithful friendship found,
And love opens wide eyes.

Oh, Shadow Hand of Here and There,
Crippled now you bide.
But free and fierce is Fiery Fair
Your own, your hard-won bride!

You gave your own two hands
And saved your ancient lands.

The king returns to home and hall,
To throne and crown and glory.
And ever stands he proud and tall,
The crippled Shadow Hand. Recall
You now my ancient story!

ABOUT THE AUTHOR

Anne Elisabeth Stengl makes her home in Raleigh, North Carolina, where she lives with her husband, Rohan, a passel of cats, and one long-suffering dog. When she's not writing, she enjoys Shakespeare, opera, and tea, and studies piano, painting, and pastry baking. She studied illustration at Grace College and English literature at Campbell University. She is the author of *Heartless, Veiled Rose, Moonblood*, and *Starflower*. *Heartless* and *Veiled Rose* have each been honored with a Christy Award, and *Starflower* was voted winner of the 2013 Clive Staples Award.

Learn more at *anneelisabethstengl.blogspot.com*.

COMING SOON

THE NEWEST
TALE OF GOLDSTONE WOOD

Golden Daughter

Timeless fantasy that will keep you spellbound.

More Adventures to Enjoy

Journey to an Old Testament–Style Fantasy World

To learn more about R. J. Larson and her books, visit rjlarsonbooks.com.

No girl has ever become a prophet of the Infinite. Even though the elders warn that she will die young, Ela of Parne heeds the call of her Creator and is sent to bring His word to a nation torn asunder by war. But can she balance the leading of her heart with the leading of the Infinite?

Prophet by R. J. Larson
BOOKS OF THE INFINITE #1

Kien Lantec is not a prophet. But when this military judge-in-training receives marching orders from his Creator, he can hardly refuse. With his new role as the Infinite's messenger leading him in unexpected directions—and away from the woman he loves—it won't be easy to follow His path.

Judge by R. J. Larson
BOOKS OF THE INFINITE #2

As questions of love and faith become tangled with ancient feuds and treacherous plots, can the warrior king Akabe, his mysterious queen, and his trusted friends Ela and Kien Lantec find the Infinite's path... or will they fail as so many others have before them?

King by R. J. Larson
BOOKS OF THE INFINITE #3